# PRECIOUS
# BLOOD

# PRECIOUS BLOOD

## JONATHAN HAYES

HARPER

*An Imprint of* HarperCollins*Publishers*
www.harpercollins.com

This book is completely fictional: the individuals and forensic cases contained herein are an invention, and any resemblance to individuals or forensic cases living, dead, current, or in the past is purely coincidental. That said, the story takes place in the real New York City, as it existed on the cusp of the twenty-first century. As a matter of pride in my work, my workmates, and my workplace, I would like to make particularly clear that, while my description of the facility and staff of the Office of the Chief Medical Examiner involves a real building at a real location, my portrayal of the interior of that building and the people inside it is pure fiction: I've worked at the OCME for seventeen years, and want to work there seventeen more. . . .

Designed by Leah Carlson-Stanisic

ISBN: 978-0-06-073666-8
ISBN-10: 0-06-073666-6

*To Cricket Coleman*

No matter whether I'm getting it right or screwing things up,

she's always an unstoppable force of love

Violence and the sacred are inseparable.

—RENÉ GIRARD (FROM *La Violence et le Sacré*, 1972)

# PRECIOUS
# BLOOD

SUNDAY,
DECEMBER 1

Steve Whittaker, MD, deputy chief medical examiner for the City of New York, finished his crime scene notes and signed his name with a flourish. Pushing back from his desk, he saw that the mosaic of diplomas that covered his office wall was out of kilter. He stood, frowning. Harry must have knocked his med school diploma, the largest of them, as he was emptying the bins. Squinting, arm stretched, Whittaker tipped the frame until it was even, the HARVARD UNIVERSITY neatly aligned with the JOHNS HOPKINS on his pathology diploma. On the lower row, his New York license, the testimonial from his forensic fellowship, and his board qualifications were more modestly framed, but one glance at the wall was enough for anyone to see they were dealing with a world-class forensic pathologist.

He hadn't earned his position by good academic credentials alone: Whittaker was a political animal, and proud of it. He'd risen to the top of both national forensic pathology associations, been treasurer of the National Association of Medical Examiners, and run the Path-Bio section of the American Academy of Forensic Sciences. It was widely thought he'd be AAFS president within the next couple of years.

At meetings, after any cocktail party or plenary session, he'd slip back to his hotel room and write down anything useful he'd gleaned. Not about residue patterns for new gunpowders or techniques for developing friction ridge imprints from well-preserved bodies, but rather the little details that could lubricate his further ascent: whose drinking problem had taken a turn for the worse, whose wife had just been diagnosed with leukemia. He saw his talent for recognizing and exploiting the weaknesses of others as a necessary evil, a Darwinian trait that let him prosper as weaker men failed. He knew that it irked people; it still stung that when Julie left him, she'd sent him Machiavelli's *Prince*. It was a petty gesture, and betrayed her lack of understanding of how life was played, a fact underscored by her having left him for Jenner.

The thought of Jenner irritated him, and he was still scowling when the phone rang. District Attorney Klein. It was their second conversation in less than three hours, and Whittaker tried to strike a tone somewhere between professional and collegial. He started to detail his observations from the scene, but Klein cut him off, wanting only the gist—typical Klein.

Whittaker reluctantly summarized his findings, smoothly assuring Klein that he would conduct the autopsy personally.

"Actually, you won't be performing the autopsy yourself: you'll have company. Girl's father has hired some local forensic pathologist, guy named Jennings. I tell you, Whittier, I'm sick of every asshole with a law degree calling in favors and making demands. I feel sorry for the guy, really I do, but would it have killed him to call at a decent hour?"

Whittaker pressed the phone against his ear, struggling for words. "Jennings? Do you mean *Jenner*, Mr. Klein? Dr. Edward Jenner?"

"Jennings, Jenner, something like that. Is he any good?"

"He was formerly with this office. I fired him last year."

"Jesus. Incompetence?"

Whittaker was silent for a second. "He's not so much incompetent as . . . emotionally ill-equipped for the work. The post–9/11 recovery work was a bit too much for him."

Klein snorted. "Then you're probably better off without him. Either way, he's their pathologist, he's probably at the scene right now, and he'll be joining you for the autopsy. Give him any help he needs, and leave me the hell out of it. Understood, Whittier?"

Whittaker felt it best not to correct him. "Understood, sir."

They had found her in the East Village, nailed to the wall of a railroad flat in a town house on Tompkins Square Park.

Jenner waited on a bench in the park, a six-block expanse of grass, trees, walkways, and basketball courts. Despite the cold, a few Brazilians were kicking a soccer ball around on the paved area in front of him.

The park was much better kept than it used to be. Although his loft was barely fifteen minutes' walk away, he hadn't been here in ages, and he was surprised by how polished the neighborhood had become since he'd been out of circulation. Back when he'd first started at the medical examiner's office, another murder in the Ninth Precinct would have raised few eyebrows, but everything was changing so quickly.

The punks and neo-hippies had been shoehorned out of their squats, replaced by a cheery wave of young families, students, models, and trendy Japanese kids who, like everyone else in the East Village, had escaped to New York to reinvent themselves. The punks and neo-hippies now panhandled sullenly on the edges of the park, usually with a bandanna'd half-pit-bull puppy at their feet to amp up compassion. Occasionally a grimy anarchist, unable to accept that his territory had long since been overrun by McLaren strollers and yoga mats, would provoke a "confrontation" with a patrol cop, and a mini-demonstration would erupt among the street kids, only to fall casualty to sunshine, talls of St. Ides malt liquor, and general ambivalence.

Across the street, a young officer, beefy in Kevlar vest and winter coat, stood by the yellow crime scene tape in front of the town house, talking with a woman holding a laundry bag. Lieutenant Rad Garcia of the Manhattan South Homicide squad stuck his head out of the front door, spoke to the officer, then motioned Jenner over.

Jenner stood and stretched stiffly. The ball bounced toward him; he trapped it neatly, then kicked it to one of the Brazilians—rudimentary soccer skills, one of the vestiges of a junior year at the University of London. He crossed Seventh to the town house. The officer nodded at him, lifting the tape to let him in.

Three seventy-seven East Seventh Street was one of the nicer buildings, a two-family brick town house with blue window boxes and a low front wall separating the small concrete front yard from the sidewalk.

Andrea Delore lived—had lived—in the top floor-through. Walking up the steps, Jenner noticed a dark brown smear just below the knob of the front door; he was struck by how blood always stood out. Above the buzzer was a small rectangular frame, with the words DELORE/JONG written in neat capitals. Broad smudges of black fingerprint powder bloomed around the buzzer and door frame; pushing the door open, Jenner saw that the smudging carried over onto the inside frame.

The hallway air was stiflingly hot and thick, almost sticky with the smell of death. He paused in the open doorway and looked back down the front steps. Behind him, the cop was waving back the first of the sightseers. Jenner watched him return to chatting up the woman with the laundry, and then realized he was stalling, avoiding going in.

The stairwell was long and narrow, the yellowing floor a honeycomb mosaic of small cream and black tiles, black wainscoting on the walls. The stairwell had been decorated with arty, black-framed photographs, black and white, some close-ups of tribal-style tattoos, some female nudes, and some female nudes with tribal-style tattoos. On the first landing he saw a Russian-looking religious triptych in a gilt frame that looked as if it had been stolen from a church.

Lieutenant Garcia was waiting for him, leaning on the balustrade on the third-floor landing. Black hair slicked back, mustache neatly trimmed, the smell of Aramis rising off him in waves, Garcia looked sleeker and better groomed than Jenner remembered; the homicide squad was suiting him nicely. Garcia had always been a popular cop, a man who could drink with the uniforms, flirt with the support staff, and joke with the bosses. He'd quickly risen from detective to sergeant and now lieutenant, borne aloft on the post–9/11 retirements.

He straightened, and they shook hands warmly. "Hey, Jenner. Good to see you." He gestured behind him. "Joey Roggetti from the Ninth is the lead—bit of a hotshot, but he's basically an okay guy. Crime Scene's nearly finished. Whittaker left the body up."

He paused for a second, then put a hand on Jenner's shoulder and looked him in the eye. "Listen: it's pretty ugly in there. You don't need to go in—I can just bring the scene photos by. You sure you want to do this?"

Jenner flushed. "Her family isn't paying me to sit around looking at pictures. Besides, it's not like I haven't done this before—I'm fine, Rad."

He looked down the hall, past Garcia. Two crime scene detectives were dusting for latent prints. The older one, Mike Seeley, saw Jenner's reflection in the oval stand mirror he was processing, turned, and gestured with a nod of his head.

"Hey, Doc. She's in there."

The directions were unnecessary; dazzling white light flooded the hall from the room just ahead to his right, and Jenner could hear the repeated click of a camera shutter.

The room was large, enormous for the neighborhood, with high ceilings. The broad archway of the entrance reminded Jenner of a music-hall stage, the theatrical feel enhanced by two high-wattage stand lamps set up by Crime Scene.

At first, he couldn't see her body through all the cops. A meaty guy in his thirties in a dark olive suit, tie limp around his thick neck, was talking with two criminalists and a uniformed cop. Joey Roggetti, Jenner assumed. They were standing in an arc in front of the body, intensely lit by the Crime Scene lamps; it reminded Jenner a bit of one of those life-size nativity scenes. They parted as he walked toward them, and Jenner saw the girl's body.

He could feel Garcia watching him as he walked toward her, the tension filling his chest with every step, the smell of her blood thickening in his nostrils. It had been a long time.

But as he drew close, he felt no difference, no dramatic change. There was no blood rushing in his ears, his heart didn't shudder in his chest the way it did in a panic attack.

Did this mean he was finally all right? He'd been gone almost a year, months on the couch, waiting to feel normal again, watching Jerry Springer as his cat nudged at the ice cream container on his chest. And now he was right back there, and he hadn't changed at all. The smell of blood, the smoke of burning dust rising from the lamps, Christ, even the way he'd just walked up and been ushered into the fucking building, it was all the same.

And when he saw the body, the little wash of revulsion that passed through him wasn't about the girl at all: it was about him. He felt himself encysting, like some kind of parasite secreting a protective shell around itself as it burrowed deep into the flesh. The girl didn't make him feel anything; it was just another body, not a girl anymore. A case.

The man had nailed her to the wall, and then rearranged the lamps in the room to illuminate her as she hung there. A white couch had been dragged opposite her, a comfortable place for him to sit and admire his handiwork; the fabric had smeared blood from where he'd sat.

And there was something odd, too: in front of her pinned, out-stretched left arm, a muted TV set pumped a barrage of fast-cut images, the MTV logo floating in the corner. Had he put her up and then just sat down and watched TV?

Jenner looked at her, hanging like a horror-show waxwork, naked, spread-eagled, upside down, her body a pale X caked with blood. Hardware-store-shiny bolts nailed her feet to the wall. Red wheals crisscrossed her body, the skin broken along curving lines.

He needed to take her down, get her down fast. She'd hung there long enough, stared at, exposed, vulnerable. Dead.

He turned to Detective Roggetti, muttered an introduction, and asked for gloves.

"Sorry, Doc. I could ask the uniforms outside, they probably do."

Detective Seeley called, "We got some, Doc. Large do you?"

Jenner nodded, then caught the packet Seeley tossed his way. He looked for somewhere to put his overcoat; Roggetti said, "Just give it here, I'll hold it for you."

Jenner, now in shirtsleeves, tore open the packet and put on the gloves: thick rubber gloves, size nine and a half, textured fingers, kitchen-bright sink'n'dishes yellow. No matter how many times he'd gone through this ritual, the gloves always seemed out of place, a jolt of cheery normality inside the charnel house.

He looked at her again, unaware that the detectives were watching him. She'd bled heavily from her nose and mouth, but there was no obvious lethal injury. The body was threatening to slide from the wall, the head and neck kinked against the floor. Flicked across the white wall by her legs and trunk were twisting and curving spatters of drying blood, spatter cast off from whatever he'd used to whip her.

Two bolts pinned her left foot to the wall, and another pierced the right, just by a small ankh tattoo.

Jenner turned. "Hey, Mikey—any trash bags over there?"

Seeley rummaged under the kitchen sink, pulled out a large black leaf bag, and handed it to him. Jenner briefly scanned the floor, trying to catch patterns in the bloodstaining. He could make out nothing but pooling, fluid purge from her nose and mouth, worse because he'd nailed her up upside down.

"You guys finished processing here?"

Seeley nodded. "Photographed, swabbed, a once-over for trace—the white-glove treatment, Doc. Whittaker was bitching because we weren't done by the time he got here. He didn't want to wait for us to take her down. She's all yours."

Jenner nodded, then unfolded the plastic bag and laid it on the floor in front of the girl to protect himself from any invisible blood soaked into the carpet. He knelt on the bag and began. He worked without effort, almost without thought, experienced hands moving fluidly, sliding methodically over her trunk, feeling for broken ribs, carefully moving the breasts to rule out hidden wounds.

He found a row of three identical oblongs of adhesive residue on one arm, each about the size of a poker chip; he waited while Seeley photographed them. He was calm. He was okay. He could do this.

He gently tilted her head to expose her neck. He rolled her lip down; the inner surface was split and bruised, the teeth intact. He looked at her eyes, the bright blue-green irises vivid against the hemorrhage in the whites. Her face was purple and congested, with countless tiny red dots in the skin; strangulation could cause blood vessels to pop like this, but so could the body position after death. Since there were no neck marks, and she was upside down, positional asphyxia was a real possibility.

He lifted her hair, draped wetly over the back of his hand, like a curtain on each side, and saw that her left earlobe was bloody and split, probably from a ripped-out earring. The right was torn, too: probably deliberate.

He'd driven two bolts into each wrist, crushing through the small bones. Her yellow plastic Magilla Gorilla watch was still working.

"Anyone got a flashlight?"

He took Garcia's Maglite, leaned forward again, and shone the beam over her mouth and cheeks. There was a faint tracery of whitish gray particles on the cheeks, probably from a duct-tape gag. What did he do with her hands? Was she conscious when he nailed her up?

He stood. "I need to get her down. Can I get a hand?"

Rad Garcia stepped up. "Let's do it."

The two knelt in front of her, awkwardly supporting her shoulders and head as Seeley tugged at the loosened bolts at her ankles. They went slowly, lifting her away from the wall so she didn't fall; in the heat of the lights, Jenner could feel the sweat plastering his shirt against his skin. As the ankle bolts came out, her body lurched forward, and Jenner braced her bare hip against the wall with his shoulder as Seeley struggled to control her calves.

"Gently . . ."

Seeley guided her legs as they moved her carefully out onto the carpet and laid her out. Garcia and Seeley stood, slightly out of breath; Jenner squatted by her body, rolling her onto her side; he could see no wounds on her back.

He stood, still looking at the girl on the floor, then at the wall where she'd hung. He turned to Seeley. "Mike, you through with the other rooms?"

"We took a quick look around, didn't see anything out of place. This seems to be where the action is, Doc. But go ahead and look if you want to."

Jenner walked down the narrow, dark hall toward the bathroom. He poked his head into the first door, opposite the kitchen. A student's bedroom with an unmade bed, white walls decorated with unframed pencil sketches. A half-unpacked suitcase lay on top of the small desk, the chair behind it pushed back against the radiator near the window. Next to the suitcase, an iPod and tangled headphones, a ring of keys, some rolling papers, and a scatter of brown seeds.

He went on down the hall to the second bedroom, the door wide open. The hallway light was off and didn't respond to the switch, so Jenner opened the bathroom door and turned the light on.

He bent for a second, then gently pulled the bedroom door toward him.

"Found something?"

Jenner turned to Garcia and muttered, "You might want to tell Crime Scene that you always see more with the lights on, okay? Tell them it's not an episode of *CSI*, it's a goddamn murder scene."

He pointed at the frame. "The strike plate has been torn off. Look at the door near the lock; this thing has been kicked in."

He knelt, then turned. "Rad, ask Mike to come here with a camera, a forceps, and an evidence envelope."

"What have you got?"

Jenner turned on the Maglite. "There's a clump of hair here. It's blond and long—not the victim's."

"What do you think, the killer's or the roommate's?"

"Well, it still has hair bulbs at one end, so it was torn out. I guess it could be the killer's, but judging from the living room, he seemed to be really in control." He squinted. "And this hair is bleached—the roots are much darker."

He turned to Rad. "I think we're looking at a second victim."

Seeley's assistant appeared at the end of the hall. "Lieutenant, the DA is here."

Jenner followed Garcia back to the living room. Assistant District Attorney Madeleine Silver stood between the light stands, staring down at the body.

She shook her head and said, "Wow. That piece of shit really did a number on her . . ." She turned, nodded grimly at Garcia, then saw Jenner. She gave a soft smile and said, "Hey, Dr. Jenner!"

"Ms. Silver."

She was of average height, early forties, curvy with feathered hair and the warmth of someone who hugged a lot, like a kindergarten teacher or elementary school counselor. Meeting her for the first time, junior defense attorneys took one look at the pearls and tennis bracelet, then dismissed her as some soccer mom treading water until her husband made partner and they moved to Scarsdale. But in the courtroom, the pearls and the gloves came off, and if the defense was foolish enough to expose their neck, she'd rip out their throat and spit it onto their cap-toed Oxfords. After her first trial, when, legend had it, she'd made a rapist cry on the stand, Mike Merino from the DA's squad had called her Mad Dog, and it had stuck; she drove a Honda minivan with a MADDOG license plate.

She put a hand on his arm tenderly, looked into his face with soft brown eyes, and said, "How are you doing?"

Jesus, did *everyone* know? Jenner stepped away, muttering he was fine, thanks.

She let him go and said, "You're working for her family?"

He nodded—good, change the subject. "Yes. The roommate's uncle is a good friend."

Her eyes narrowed. "Y'know, I've never been at a death scene with a private forensic pathologist before."

He shrugged. "Yeah. It's a first for me, too. Her dad is a pretty well-connected lawyer in Boston, and he's been pulling strings."

She snorted. "Not just any lawyer, Jenner—corporate counsel for Massachusetts. DA Klein called me himself to invite me here. On a Sunday, no less!"

She smoothed her hair. "So, what do you make of the scene?"

He looked at the body. "I really don't have any background story. Can you fill me in?"

The solicitousness vanished. "Well, Doc, what we have is this: victim is a law student over at Hutchins, lives here with your friend's niece. They *may* be lovers, the two women who live downstairs don't know for sure. They *think* so, but they're not sure. But *they're* lovers, okay?"

"The women downstairs?"

"Yeah, they own the building." She continued. "Anyway, they're at their house upstate in Woodstock, and they have a fight. Sandy drives back into the city around four a.m., drops her car at the garage, then walks home. She's really tired, but she can't sleep because the TV's on really loud upstairs. So she calls up to the dead girl, Andrea, no answer.

"She tries to sleep, but it's not happening, TV's still blaring away. She calls them on the phone again, again no reply. Now she's really pissed, so she goes up and knocks on the door. Still no answer. She's starting to freak out, so she gets her passkey and goes in.

"She says she immediately knows something's really wrong because of the smell—apparently she's got this thing about smell, makes scented candles and such—so she runs downstairs and calls 911."

Jenner nodded. "What do you have on time of death?"

She gestured toward the kitchen. "Empty mailbox, open letters on the kitchen table, no messages on the answering machine. Oh, and the phone's dead—the line's cut in the kitchen. Her body's pretty fresh, and the lights were on. She's in full rigor, so we're thinking last night, early this morning at the latest."

She paused, waiting for a reaction. Jenner had none.

"We didn't find a weapon." She hesitated a second. "And I don't know what to make of your friend's niece—" She glanced at her notebook. "Ana de Jong. We don't know if she was here, if she's a victim, a witness, an accomplice, whatever. No one knows where she is."

Jenner shook his head. "There's a good chance she's a second victim. The bathroom door's been kicked in, and I found a clump of long, bleached-blond hair."

"Shit! I was hoping she wasn't there." Her eyes went to the wounds on the body at her feet. "God. If he's got her, I almost hope she's already dead—God knows what he could do with her, tucked away somewhere private."

They walked down the hall toward the bathroom, where Seeley was processing the door frame. She asked, "What can you tell me about Ana?"

"Nothing—I'd never heard of her before this morning. The victim's father woke me six thirty a.m. Douggie Pyke—my friend—had given him my name. And now I can't reach Douggie—he's working somewhere in Africa, and his satellite phone number isn't working."

She shook her head. "That must have been a hard conversation, the one with the dad."

"He seemed pretty tough. He told me his daughter had been murdered, that Douggie said I was good, said he knew my fees, and could I start right away. And that was it—the whole conversation lasted five minutes, tops."

Mike Seeley, standing by the door with a hand lens, interrupted. "Jenner, what do you think? There's some blood spatter on the door here, really fine. It's weird, like contact transfer with half-dried blood."

Jenner squinted and peered at the bloodstains. "Yeah, I can see what you mean. You think maybe the blood was already half dry before he kicked the door?"

He looked at the door. There were small stove-in depressions near the handle, but the damage was limited. "And why isn't it more battered, Mike?"

Seeley shrugged. "It's pretty shitty quality, Doc. Maybe it just buckled rather than really falling apart . . ."

"Do you think he could have done it barefoot? Usually there's a shoe imprint or two near where the outer surface breaks, and I can't see anything here."

Seeley tipped his head, studying the door thoughtfully. "Yeah, I was wondering about that. Tell you what, we'll print the whole outer surface, see if we can get a footprint."

Madeleine Silver said, "Would a footprint be any use? I mean, I know they print babies' feet in the hospital, but . . ."

Jenner shook his head. "Probably not. But sometimes you can get a match—for instance, pilots and flight crews have their feet printed for possible identification after a crash. At the least we'll get his foot size, and that may give us an idea of whether he's unusually big or small."

"I see." She scribbled in her notebook, then tucked the pad into her purse. They walked back toward the living room. She was quiet for a second; Jenner could almost feel it coming.

"So . . . I thought you quit forensics."

"Pretty much. Mostly I've been reviewing medical records for asbestos litigation cases, not glamorous, but at least the cat and I get to eat. And I don't want to do fieldwork anymore."

She smiled at him and pressed his arm. "And yet, here you are . . ."

"If it weren't Douggie's niece, I'd have said no." He asked her if she'd spoken with Whittaker.

"He figures she was likely strangled, given the eyeball hemorrhages. No obvious sign of sexual assault, but she is naked, so . . ."

Jenner agreed it looked like an asphyxial death, but said he didn't think it was a strangulation; either way, the autopsy would resolve the issue. She hesitated, then asked if he thought there was any chance the roommate could have killed her, either alone or with an accomplice.

"That was her in the hall photos?" he asked. "Ana? The blond girl?"

Silver nodded. "The woman downstairs ID'd her. She looks pretty athletic to me."

"Well, she may be strong, but I doubt anyone her height and build could get that body up onto the wall like that, certainly not by herself." He shook his head. "But look at the victim—the way the body is shown, spread out naked like that? A man did this."

"Yeah, I agree," she said, nodding firmly. "I just want to keep an open mind."

"Well, there's the hair, too. I think she's the second victim. I think he's got her."

"Christ, I don't want to even think about it." She looked around the apartment. "Where's Garcia?"

Jenner said, "I think he was calling the chief of detectives, let him know you're looking at a probable abduction."

She cursed, turned away to call her boss.

His back was cramping up; he stretched and straightened. He realized how tired he was. He'd gone to bed after 3:00 a.m., and had been woken before dawn. It was almost 10:00 a.m. now, and he needed a shower and some sleep.

He'd had enough. He'd call Garcia and Seeley later for an update, maybe come back for a look at the rest of the apartment once they'd finished processing it. And, he figured, if the DA was already asking questions, Whittaker would do the autopsy that afternoon.

*Jesus! Whittaker* . . .

He patted Silver's shoulder, and she nodded at him as he made his way toward the door. He formally introduced himself to Roggetti, and took his card before leaving the apartment. It was just politeness—Roggetti was officially the lead investigator, but Garcia would call the shots.

On the landing, he glanced down, then called to Seeley. "Mike—you got this pink mud here?"

"Thanks, Doc. We got it already; I couldn't make a shoe imprint out of it."

Rad Garcia stepped past Jenner, hand covering the mouthpiece of his cell.

"I've got to talk to Madeleine."

Jenner nodded. "She's briefing DA Klein, I think."

They shook hands, and Jenner headed for the staircase.

"Yo, Jenner."

He turned back to the detective.

"Nice to have you back."

Outside, a small crowd had gathered at the perimeter, and he saw the antenna of the Channel 7 Mobile News van poking up into the bare branches halfway down the block. He slipped under the tape and nodded to the perimeter cop as he made his way through the spectators. The morgue wagon was turning onto Seventh as he flagged a cab on Avenue A. He was home less than ten minutes later.

Jenner lived on the top floor of a converted lightbulb factory on Crosby Street, between SoHo proper and Little Italy. He'd bought the loft several years back with inheritance money from his grandfather. He had enough left over for interest to cover his maintenance costs; now that he wasn't working so much, his taxes had dropped, and he'd found that life was quite manageable on his sporadic income, so long as he was careful. And it wasn't like he was going out much or anything.

The loft had been a good investment: the area had become fashion-
able, and its value had soared. They'd cleaned the facade that summer,
and on sunny days the brick glowed a deep golden red.

He paid and climbed out of the cab, shoving his change into his coat
pocket. Unlocking the entryway door, he saw Julie's name still next to
his on the buzzer; he kept forgetting to remind Pete to take it off.

Takeout menus and car service flyers were plastered down with shoe
prints on the lobby floor. He pushed the elevator button and heard the
answering grind of machinery.

He rode up, blearily staring at the eddies in the worn gray linoleum
floor. There was a bump as the elevator settled on the sixth floor.

Dove gray light filtered through the hall skylight. Across the hall, Jun
Saito's doorway was open. Jun was standing in the doorway, swaying to
Santo and Johnny's "Sleep Walk," holding a bottle of beer. Seeing Jenner,
he tipped his gray Kangol cap from his eyes and straightened.

"Jenner? I thought I heard you come in a half hour ago."

Jenner shook his head. "Too many Red Stripes, my friend."

Jun's girlfriend Kimi appeared in the doorway behind him and said
something in Japanese to him, then saw Jenner. "Hi, Jenner. Tell Jun it's
time for bed."

"Jun, go to bed."

Giggling, she pulled Jun inside; as Jenner closed his door, he heard her
call out, "'Night, Jenner."

Inside his loft, all the curtains were drawn, and the heated air made
the large room seem coddled and close. At the other end of the room,
a small Noguchi lamp on his bedside table made a warm hollow of
golden light. His robe was on the floor by the bed, and his notepad
lay open by the phone, Andrea Delore's address scrawled on the top
page.

He tossed his coat over the ladder-back chair by his desk, and undressed in the bathroom. Taking off his watch, he saw it was already 10:15 a.m. Cursing the loss of sleep, he stepped into the shower.

He dried and put on a T-shirt and pajama bottoms, then brushed his teeth. He turned out the bathroom light and walked toward his bed. He was exhausted, but he didn't know if he could sleep—the room was dark, but he was awake, wired. He should call Douggie, tell him what was going on. *Fuck.* He sat on the bed.

And then stood quickly: in the corner of the room, half hidden by the tall curtains, stood Ana de Jong.


She was holding a grubby pink raincoat closed over her sweatshirt. Jeans, white sneakers. She was tan and blond, slightly snub-nosed, eyes pale blue; she looked like she'd just stepped off a farm in Iowa, except for the bloodstains on her pant leg and tops of her shoes.

She said, "Dr. Jenner. My name is Ana de Jong . . ."

He'd recognized her from the hallway photos. Apparently, he'd been wrong about the second victim.

"How did you get in?"

She started to shake. "Please . . . My uncle . . . He said I should come . . . He had keys to your loft in his studio downstairs."

He, Douggie, and Jun all kept keys for one another's apartments. "He told you to just come into my loft? When was that?"

She began to cry, slow, coarse sobs racking her body, and as she bent, she let the raincoat fall open, and he saw the blood smeared on her sweatshirt.

"You're hurt—"

"I . . . I cut myself . . . Climbing over a wall."

She dropped to her knees, her face in her hands; there was blood on her fingers, too.

He said, "I'm going to call 911—I want you to go to a hospital, and I have to tell the police you're alive."

She shook her head urgently. "*No! No police!*" She was biting her lip, eyes filling with tears. "Please . . . you can't call the police." She laid her arm across her belly. "It's just cuts—really, just cuts . . . It's not as bad as it looks."

The blood on her clothes seemed mostly dry. He stood, waiting for her to stop sobbing.

When she didn't stop, he said, "I'm sorry. Please don't cry."

She straightened, sniffling.

He was silent a second, then asked if she needed a lawyer.

She looked at him, eyes wide, and said, "A lawyer? Why would I need a lawyer?"

"I know about your roommate. And now you're here, covered in blood, and you won't let me call the police." He sat on the edge of the bed. "I think perhaps you should speak with a lawyer—"

"No, no, you've got it all wrong! You know about Andie? Is she . . ." Her voice trailed off as she mouthed the word.

She was lying to him now—how could she have got out of the apartment and not known her friend was dead? She was manipulating him—enough. He stood, picked up the phone, and dialed Garcia.

"*Who are you calling?*"

"The detective leading the investigation into your friend's death."

"Please don't . . ." She grabbed his arm. "Please, Dr. Jenner. My uncle said you're his friend, and that you'd help me."

Voice mail. Jenner left a message, asking Garcia to call.

"Listen, this is your business, not mine: you can leave if you want. But if you're going to stay, you've got to talk with Lieutenant Garcia."

She stood in front of him, trembling, twisting the bloody cuff of her sweatshirt sleeve. Looking down, he saw her jeans were covered with doodles, little hearts and random figures in ballpoint pen. When she looked at him, her gaze reminded Jenner of an automatic camera trying to focus when its batteries were too weak.

He shook his head.

"Come into the kitchen and sit down—you look exhausted."

She asked if she could use his bathroom. He waited for her at the kitchen table. When he heard her in the bathroom, crying hard, he got up, turned the taps on, and noisily banged pans and plates around in the sink.

After a quarter of an hour, the bathroom door slid open, and she came over to the kitchen area. He motioned to a chair, and she sat, holding her stomach a little gingerly.

"It hurts?"

She nodded.

"I should look at it. You want some water?"

She shook her head, then jumped up as the entry phone buzzer rang. Jenner picked up to see Rad's face on the monitor. "Hey, Jenner, let me up—I've got follow-up."

Jenner buzzed him in.

He turned to her.

"Miss de Jong, Lieutenant Garcia's a good cop. He'll be straight with you. If you haven't done anything wrong, tell him what happened, and I promise he'll help you."

She rubbed her eyes wearily. "You know him?"

"Maybe ten years now."

"What does he look like?"

"Look like?" Jenner blinked.

She was serious.

"Hispanic, early forties. Average height, a little thick in the middle. Black hair, mustache. Why?"

"And you trust him?"

"With my life." It was true.

She stood in front of him, hugging her shoulders, and said, "I don't have much choice."

"I also know some good defense attorneys."

"I don't need a lawyer. I just need someone I can trust."

She slipped back into the bathroom. Jenner shrugged, and opened the door to wait for Rad.

\*   \*   \*

Garcia walked in, coat over one arm, paper coffee cup in the other hand.

"So, there's been a development: apparently there was a 911 call early this morning. The patrol responded to 311B, found nothing, and called it in as a false alarm. The original call came from a phone box over on Avenue B, so they couldn't do anything else."

Garcia was nosing around by the counter. "You got decent coffee, Jenner?"

Jenner shook his head. "Actually, I was just about to go back to bed."

"So why did you call . . ."

He trailed off, staring over Jenner's shoulder, seeing Ana de Jong in the bathroom doorway.

Jenner made the introductions. Garcia nodded warily. "You okay? You know, we're looking for you . . ." He sat down.

"I was hiding."

"Why?"

"Because I didn't want to die."

Rad shook his head and sat heavily in Jenner's armchair. "What's that supposed to mean? Where were you?"

"In a Laundromat over on Avenue B, then in my uncle's loft downstairs."

He was watching her closely. "Were you in the apartment when your roommate . . ."

She nodded, her eyes filling with tears.

"Why didn't you call the police?"

"I did. That was me calling from the pay phone near the Laundromat."

Garcia motioned for Jenner to join him away from the kitchen area. He spoke quietly. "I'm thinking this might be a better place to talk to her than over at the precinct."

He glanced at her, then turned back to Jenner again. "Whatever happened, the kid looks like she's had a rough night."

She sat down opposite them. She made a little grimace and said, "It's like a job interview."

Garcia made a show of opening his notebook, taking out his pen. "Okay, Ana. I want you to tell us exactly what happened."

She hesitated; the uncertainty made her seem terribly, terribly young.

He pressed her, his voice soft. "Ana, listen: I'm trying to help you. If I was doing this by the book, I'd bring you in right now." He paused. "Basically, you tell your story here, or you tell it at the precinct. Your call."

"No." She shook her head. "Here."

She sat. She clasped her hands, working her thumbs together, looking down at the floor. But when she tried to start, the tears returned; Garcia got up and sat next to her, draping his big arm over her shoulder as she wept.

She looked up at Jenner, face flushed and wet. "I think I need a drink."

Garcia looked to Jenner and nodded.

Jenner poured her a large scotch and set the tumbler in front of her. She took the glass and took a big gulp, then made a face. She sniffled a little and looked down at her hands.

Garcia looked at her in mock suspicion and jostled her shoulder. "Hey! Are you even old enough to be drinking this?"

She wiped her eyes and said with a weak smile, "I'm twenty-one." She took a sip of whisky, coughed, then said, "I'm sorry—I'm not used to this stuff."

Jenner sat at the table. "Can you tell us what happened now, Ana?"

She nodded. And then she began, her speech quiet and halting.

"Andie and I were in Cancun for Thanksgiving. We just got back this afternoon—we hadn't even finished unpacking. We got pizza, and then Andie had to work on her law school Web page, so I went into my room and lit up a blunt. It was like, maybe, ten p.m.? I heard the buzzer, and a minute later Andie came running in and told me to put out the joint because there's a cop outside. I was freaking out, but Andie said just stay in my room because he was just there about something for school."

Realizing what she'd just admitted, she turned to Garcia; he was scratching away in his notepad, not reacting. Reassured, she went on.

"So I closed the door and opened my window to air the room out. I heard Andie say she was alone, but then they went into the living room, and I couldn't hear them so well.

"I was pretty high, so I just lay there and waited. After a while I realized that Andie wasn't talking anymore, just the guy. Then I heard her kind of . . . screech.

"I didn't know what to do. I picked up the phone, but it was dead, and my cell was in the kitchen. I got up to see what was going on, but before I opened the door, I heard him hit her, hard, and I heard her fall, and then I got really scared."

Her shoulders were shuddering. "And then I didn't do *anything* . . ."

Jenner said, "If you'd tried to do something, he'd have killed you. There was nothing you could have done—you have to understand that."

A tear was trickling down her cheek. "You weren't there."

"No. But I saw what he did."

She gave a dismissive half shrug, then sharply pulled the glass toward her and took a good belt of scotch; this time, there was no grimace.

She wiped her mouth, then continued, her jaw set.

"First thing he did was turn on the TV, really loud. Then he started moving all around the apartment, searching. I heard him go into the kitchen, then the telephone suddenly jerked and started sliding toward the door—he was following the cord to my bedroom. I got under my desk just as he came in.

"He yanked the bed away from the wall like it weighed nothing, then went through the closet, and then he came over behind the desk. I thought he'd found me, but he just opened up the wardrobe. His feet were right next to my head; he was wearing army boots and they had pink mud on them, and I could smell blood. But he didn't look under the desk."

She took another gulp of whisky.

"Then he went to the bathroom, and then Andie's room. When I heard him start to go in her room, I went into the kitchen, but I couldn't find my cell. I could hear her moaning. I heard him coming back, and I hid under the counter until he went back to the living room.

"There are window guards in the kitchen, but I figured if I made it to the bathroom at the end of the hall, I could try to climb down the trellis into the garden.

"That's when she started to scream. He must have stuck something in her mouth, because she suddenly stopped. It was like I was paralyzed—I knew he was hurting her, and I wanted to help, but I just couldn't move."

Seeing her start to shake, Jenner said, "About what time was that?" Keep her focused on the details.

She shook her head. "Maybe eleven p.m.? A little later, maybe."

He nodded. "Then what happened?"

"I was too scared to move. I just lay there under the kitchen counter, trying not to breathe. Smelling the linoleum and just . . . *listening* to him doing stuff to her. I kept telling myself, he's going to rape her and then he'll leave, and then it will be over, and we'll be okay in the end. But then I heard the drill."

She picked up the tumbler and drained it, then put it back on the table. She looked at Jenner, then slid the glass to him. He poured and set the tumbler in front of her.

"He turned up the TV real loud, but I could hear him using the drill, like . . ." She breathed slowly, concentrating, then continued, stronger now. "It didn't sound like when you drill wood.

"That went on for a while. And he was talking to her, but she wasn't saying anything. Then I heard the whipping sound, over and over, and she wasn't making any noise. And he kept talking to her, but I just knew she was dead. I could feel it. And I think he was taking pictures, too; I think I heard a Polaroid camera—I recognized that sound when the print comes out."

"And you were in the kitchen? Did you see a flash or anything?"

She closed her eyes, trying to remember. She shook her head.

"No, I didn't see a flash. But I was tucked all the way under the counter, and I wasn't looking out. I knew if he came back to the kitchen to get his stuff, he'd find me—he'd left his badge on the table, and his jacket was on a chair, with his walkie-talkie."

Garcia asked if she'd got a good look at the badge; she hadn't. It looked like a typical white metal police badge.

Jenner asked if Andie made any noise after she'd first heard the camera.

"No, I don't think so. But the TV was really loud. And there was some kind of burning smell—I don't know what that was."

Garcia said, "Did you see or smell smoke?"

"No." She shook her head. "It wasn't like a smoky smell, more chemical, like metal or something. I didn't recognize it.

"I was trying not to hear what he was doing to her. It took him a long time, and then he stopped moving around, but he didn't leave. I was lying there waiting for him to come in and find me and hurt me, but he stayed in the living room. And then I realized he was just watching TV. And that was when I decided I was going to get out of there alive."

She looked up at them, her words now fast.

"I checked his jacket for his gun, but it wasn't there. So I took a kitchen knife and started to crawl down the hallway to the bathroom, trying to stay in the shadows. I'd only made it halfway to her door when he said,

*"Ana?"*

*She lunged to her feet and ran, but he was incredibly fast. His fist grabbed her hair, jerking her backward, the knife flying out of her hands, her hair ripping out of her scalp as she spun around the corner.*

*She stumbled to the door handle, slammed the door hard on his reaching hand. He gasped and pulled back. She closed the door and slid the bolt, and he was instantly pounding at the door, trying to kick it in. She ran to the window, threw it open, and screamed as she tried to squeeze through the bars, the whole room booming as his foot smashed against the door.*

*She could hear the door splintering as she breathed in and out, trying to wedge*

*herself through the gap. There was a shattering noise as he burst through, and she pushed hard, and finally swung out onto the trellis, but immediately lost her grip and fell onto the trash barrels fifteen feet below.*

*Half-conscious on the wet flagstones of the yard, unable to breathe, she looked up; he was standing there in the window, looking down at her in the rain. His face and chest were covered in blood—he was naked.*

*He was smiling through lips smeared with Andie's blood, smiling at her as he said, "Ouch! That had to hurt!"*

*He watched her struggling to catch her breath, struggling to crawl.*

*"Run along. I'll come for you so we can play later . . ."*

*Then she was crawling, moving across the rotting leaves and glistening flagstones toward the back wall.*

*"But where will you go? No more Mommy. No more Daddy. Poor little Ana! All alone . . ."*

*He heard her sob, and his tone changed abruptly.*

*"I hope you're not crying for that bitch! You know, she wasn't really your friend. I'd barely started on her when she gave you up: she told me you were there, tried to get me to play with you instead!" He laughed sharply. "I didn't believe her, but I guess the little whore was telling the truth . . . So, where were you hiding?"*

*She'd reached the sundial now, and managed to pull herself to standing.*

*He started to clap slowly, the sounds echoing in the wet garden. Then he stopped and said, "You do know there's nowhere you can go, don't you? Wherever you go, I'll come for you. And I'll take you away, and make you special, too."*

"Then I climbed up onto the sundial and pulled myself over the wall; I cut myself on the bottle glass in the concrete on top. I went through the yard, out the gate onto Sixth, yelling the whole time, but it was cold and pouring, and there was no one on the street. No one to help . . ."

She breathed out. Jenner could smell the alcohol on her breath; when she spoke, he realized she was starting to slur her words. "I called 911 from the pay phone on B, but then I thought, what if they send *him*? So I ran to the all-night Laundromat and called my uncle's satellite number, but couldn't get through. Someone must have called 911 for me, because the cops came to the Laundromat pretty quick."

She gave a little smile. "But I was already moving by that time—they drove straight past me. I stole the raincoat from the Laundromat and ran to your building. It took forever to get through to Uncle Douggie from his apartment; he told me to call 911, but when you dial 911, they know where you're calling from, so I wouldn't. He couldn't dial 911, so I gave him Andie's home number in Boston to tell her dad.

"He called later, and said he couldn't reach you, but I should just go on up to your loft. And that you were one of his best friends, and you were going to help Andie's dad, and you would help me. And I said I would, but I was scared, I guess. When I finally went up, you were gone."

She looked at Jenner and flushed slightly. "I didn't mean to just, like, break in like that. I knocked, but there wasn't any answer, and I couldn't stay in the hall, so I went in."

Jenner said, "Why didn't you say anything when I got home?"

"I didn't hear you come in—I think I fell asleep for a little. I was in your TV room. I heard you in the shower; I waited a bit until you were, like, decent."

Garcia said, "And the rest, we know."


They were all quiet for a while. Garcia had her describe the man—white, mid-thirties, average height, muscular build. Shortish hair, she thought. Clean-shaven. American accent, nothing special. That was about it; she'd only seen him briefly, through the rain, a silhouette in the dark window. She didn't recognize him, had no idea how he knew all about her.

The detective stood, cell phone in hand. "You're going to have to make a formal statement at the precinct. And we're going to need you to look at mug shots."

She looked to Jenner, pleading. Jenner said, "Rad, do you think—"

Rad shook his head. "Jenner, this has to be by the book."

Jenner steered him to the door.

"Sure, she has to make a statement, but does it have to be *now*? This thing about the shield and the police radio . . . Can you keep her out of it for now, at least until you know what's going on? Maybe take her statement here?"

Garcia gave a slow shrug. "I don't know what to do. I feel for the kid, but we both know this piece of garbage is probably faking it, tinning his way in with a fake shield. He's probably some kind of rent-a-cop or something, some scumbag with a fake badge, a burglary kit, and a Radio Shack walkie-talkie. She's a witness, she's seen him, she's got to help us."

He looked back at her, sitting at the table, watching him decide her fate; his face softened.

He breathed out wearily. "Okay, I'll tell you what: when I know what's going on, I'll get together with Silver and the bosses, and we'll have a nice sit-down and decide what to do. I'll get Internal Affairs on board. She can rest up here for now, but make sure she understands that sooner or later she's coming in."

Rad slipped on his coat, walking toward the door. He turned. "And Jenner? She's your responsibility now. She doesn't leave this apartment without me knowing about it. Okay?"

Jenner nodded, and let Garcia out.

And then he was alone in his apartment with Ana.


They looked at each other for a second. He saw the shiver of her thin shoulders in the gray hooded sweatshirt, and then she lifted a hand to her brow in exhaustion, and he saw all the blood again.

He shook his head. "C'mon. I better have a look at those wounds."

She swayed as she stood; he couldn't tell if it was fatigue or because she was pretty drunk.

In the light of the bathroom, standing in front of him as he sat on the edge of the tub, she stripped off her sweatshirt and stepped out of her jeans, hiking up her tank top with her good right hand so Jenner could examine her wounds. She looked straight ahead, stiffening as he swabbed her belly with peroxide, clenching her teeth but making no sound. The wounds were ragged, but the glass hadn't gone deep. He cleaned her palm, then did his best to close the injuries with Steri-Strips, wrapping her hand in layers of gauze.

"Finished," Jenner said. "I don't have anything your size, but there's pajamas in the closet behind you. Just leave your clothes in the tub— later, I can get you something to wear." There was a muffled "Thank you" as he closed the door behind him.

When she hadn't come out after fifteen minutes, he tapped on the door and let himself in. She was sitting on the floor in his pajamas, crying. She'd been sick, and Jenner wiped her face with a damp washcloth, and then led her to the bed.

He sat beside the bed for an hour; she would quiet and then start to cry again as the grief and fear carved through the exhaustion. He finally gave her half an Ativan, and she was asleep before she'd finished her water, slumped against him.

He let her head down onto the pillow and tugged the sheet up over her chest.

He went back to the bathroom. He wiped several coat hangers down with rubbing alcohol, then carefully hung her clothes to dry. He took three clean paper shopping bags from the kitchen; when the clothing was dry, he'd use them to package it for the crime lab.

He quickly examined the clothes for hairs or fibers or secretions, but there was so much blood he couldn't see anything, particularly under the soft glow of his bathroom lighting. The blood on the uppers of her white K-Swiss sneakers looked dry, so he dropped them into a paper bag, crumpled it shut, and put it by the front door.

Lips drawn tight, Whittaker took the front stairs down into the morgue. The day's autopsy list had been short, and the techs, having put away the bodies and wiped down the tables, were watching videos in the lounge or smoking in the loading bay. The corridors were deserted save for a couple of empty gurneys, the dull gray metal of one tarnished by broad smears of drying blood.

He looked down the dingy hallway and sighed. It certainly was a grim place. The pale blue tiling on the walls was dirty and battered, and the linoleum flooring had been patched so many times that it kept catching the brake guards on the gurney wheels, and tearing up even more. The chronic damp had corroded the wiring, and a quarter of the fluorescents along the main corridor were either out or flickering; the only light that worked reliably was the bug zapper.

Morale was low lately—the chief's illness, budget cuts, the general debilitation of the institute, all had taken their toll. But soon it would be his to put right: the chief would sooner or later have to accept that you just can't fight pancreatic cancer, that you have to give in, embrace it, and let the world move on.

The thought soothed him, and he hoisted his shoulders and set off in search of Roundtree, the mortuary director. Roundtree could deal with Jenner.

Jenner tried Pyke yet again. There were some tinny clicks and a burst of digital static, then the furred buzz of a ring tone. Pyke picked up on the second ring.

"Jenner?"

"Yes. I wanted to let you know Ana's with me."

"Thank God. How's she doing?"

"Physically, she's okay. Otherwise, pretty much what you'd expect. I gave her something to help her sleep."

"Thanks for looking after her." Pyke paused, then said, "I'm sorry I had to get you involved—I know this is probably the last thing you want. But you're the only person I know who knows about this stuff."

"It's okay."

"Jenner, she needs someone with her now, and I'm in Cameroon. It'll take me at least a week to get back to Yaoundé. I had to ask."

"Douggie, it's okay," Jenner said again. Sitting at the table, he finished off Ana's scotch. "You never mentioned her."

"Tell you the truth, I hadn't thought about her much. Her parents made me her guardian back when we were close. When she was about seventeen, I got a call that they'd been killed in a car crash. I went down to Orlando, signed some papers, but since then, pretty much the only contact I've had with her has been to okay her expenses. She started college in Florida, then transferred up to New York last year. She's a sweet kid, but she's never depended on me."

The static burst back in for a second, and when the signal came back, Pyke was saying, "I spoke with Andie Delore's parents. Her father will be calling you—he's an attorney in Boston, and he wants an independent expert to keep an eye on the investigation. You're still doing private forensic work, right?"

The signal faded out for a second, then swept back in with a roar of distortion.

"Jenner?"

"I'm here."

"Tony Delore is going to call the Manhattan DA and set things up with him."

"We spoke this morning, it's all set."

"God, that was fast—when I talked to him, he'd only just found out about his daughter."

Jenner said, "He seems the kind of guy who gets what he wants, and fast."

The receiver began to buzz; the signal went dead, replaced by a high-pitched electronic chatter. Jenner hung up.

He checked his watch. Whittaker always hurried his autopsies, dissecting, weighing, and measuring, and closing as quickly as he could; Jenner needed to examine Andie Delore's body before Whittaker rushed it out.

He dialed the number almost without thinking.

"Mortuary."

Lester Roundtree, the mortuary director, was, as always, pissed off about being called in to work on a Sunday. He was being his usual passive-aggressive self, sitting in the lime green mortuary office, watching the

Giants on a portable TV. He only picked up the phone because the ring-ing was ruining the color commentary.

"Hey, Tree. It's Edward Jenner."

"Hey, Doc! How you doing?" He sounded genuinely pleased.

"Pretty good. You? Dr. Vargas says you're running all five boroughs."

"Yeah, yeah. It's all bullshit, but at least now it's *my* bullshit, know what I'm saying?" He let out a rolling guffaw.

Jenner grinned. "I'm actually calling about business. Whittaker has a case today, homicide, white girl, mid-twenties, from the East Village. Has he done it yet?"

"Shit, Doc! Who knows what's up with that! I thought you were the police calling. The morgue truck went out on the pickup this morning, but Crime Scene sent them away. Cops called back round eleven a.m., but the wagon was stuck way uptown. Figure the body won't even get here until two p.m. Whittaker's been cursing the DA up and down for making him do the case today. You coming down?"

"Yes. I'm working for her family."

"Yeah, I know. Whittaker came by a while ago, said I was in charge of you. Didn't look none too happy either."

The two laughed, and Tree added, "Just don't be getting me in trou-ble, okay?"

"Don't worry. I'll be a complete professional." He paused, then added, "Good talking to you."

Jenner hung up the phone. He never missed the place, but he some-times missed the people. Bad pay, terrible hours, even worse conditions, but a great crew. He couldn't have survived the World Trade Center disaster without them.

Thinking about 9/11, he felt his mood grow dark again. How quickly everything had changed, his old life burning away during the months of recovery and identification work. Good-bye contentment, good-bye security.

The phone rang; he let the machine take it. Tony Delore calling on his cell from somewhere on the Merritt Parkway in Connecticut, New York–bound. He was glad Jenner was involved; he'd asked around and had heard good things about Jenner. He'd be in New York by 3:00 p.m.;

please could Jenner call him at the Waldorf as soon as he'd finished his examination. Delore left the hotel number, then hung up, a businesslike man handling his daughter's death in a businesslike way.

Jenner showered quickly, then dressed. He needed someone to watch over Ana, and he was leery of approaching the police. Besides, what did he think they would do? A verbal threat wouldn't be enough to get them to assign a detail to guard the girl.

He knocked on Jun's door; Jun was awake—Jun was always awake, writing code, debugging code, watching *Aqua Teen Hunger Force* on his enormous plasma TV. Jenner outlined the situation, and Jun set a chair in his doorway without a single question: from that position, he could see the elevator and the emergency stairs; if anyone tried to use the freight elevator, he'd hear it. The precaution seemed elaborate, but the killer had made an explicit threat, and Jenner was taking it seriously. And Jenner had no idea how Jun, a Japanese national, had gotten hold of it, but Jun owned a gun.

He went back to his loft. In his bed, Ana de Jong lay where he'd left her, golden skin against the navy of his pajama top, hair spilling like corn silk onto the mascara-stained pillow. He wrote her a note and put it on the bedside table where she was sure to see it. Then he headed out, locking his front door behind him. His retirement was officially over.

The Office of the Chief Medical Examiner of New York City is wedged into the unattractive sprawl of medical buildings on the city's eastern hip, a blandly ugly stretch of First Avenue running from the Veterans Administration Medical Center at Twenty-third, up past Bellevue's Victorian brick facades to the glitzy new buildings of the NYU medical complex. The medical examiner's office on the corner of Thirtieth is classic Failed Mid-Century Modern, completely lacking any architectural grace, a blocky pile clad in Pan Am blue tiling with windows in pitted aluminum frames.

On most days, the sidewalk in front of the building was a busy mix of white-coated doctors shuttling between the NYU hospitals to the north and Bellevue to the south, black limousines dropping off Upper East Siders for a tummy tuck, homeless men from the shelter on Thirtieth, and frock-coated Orthodox Jews in wide fur hats. But on that gray Sunday afternoon after Thanksgiving, the street had the chilled emptiness of a desert in winter.

Down the slope in front of him, the East River looked cold and leaden under the dull skies, and across the water, the derelict brick warehouses on the Brooklyn waterfront were sunken in thin gray fog. The breeze rattled the flag rope against the pole in front of the office, a gloomy, discordant clinking.

It was the first time he'd been back. In the days after 9/11, family and friends had crowded the neighborhood, plastering every wall, fence, and tree along the streets near the office with MISSING flyers, hopeful snapshots of people on vacation, dressed up for parties, in graduation gowns—the people they loved but couldn't find. Crowds milled in front of the old Bellevue buildings on First Avenue, clutching toothbrushes or combs—any object with a possible trace of DNA from someone they'd lost, anything to know the truth.

Inside, he waited while his driver's license was photocopied and administrators were informed of his arrival.

The lobby hadn't changed—gray carpet, gray walls, photographs of various New York City street views. It had always bothered Jenner that there were no people visible in any of the photographs.

The door to the mortuary stairs cracked open, and a young black man in green scrubs asked, "Dr. Jenner? Mr. Roundtree asked me to bring you down and get you set up. Dr. Whittaker's still doing the rape kit, so you've got a few minutes."

Jenner followed the technician down into the basement. Bright orange steam pipes kept the stairwell stiflingly hot, but as they entered the mortuary area near the walk-in body coolers, the corridor seemed

to be completely without heat. He'd never seen the halls so dirty. There
was yellow caution tape tacked in an X across the open doorway of the
smaller walk-in body cooler, with a piece of paper on which was written DOESN'T WORK! in red marker, along with a smiley face; someone had
added tears to the face.

His escort stopped at the door to the men's locker room.

"Door combination's seven-five-five—Hank Aaron's home run total.
There's scrubs in there. Shoe covers, gowns, caps, and masks are outside
the autopsy room. I'll be in the morgue office if you need me."

Jenner changed, then walked down the hall to the autopsy room and
stepped into the anteroom.

Andie Delore's body would be the only one up; the rest of the day's
cases had already been finished. Jenner looked at the list. Five bodies
from Manhattan—a prostitute found naked and strangled, floating in
the Harlem Meer in Central Park; the driver and front-seat passenger
in an SUV rollover; a heroin addict who'd OD'd in a McDonald's bathroom, and an eighty-year-old woman found putrefying in her bathtub.
A fairly quiet day.

He put on shoe covers and a flimsy tissue cap, tucked a paper surgical
mask into his pocket, and entered the autopsy suite.

It was a long room, with stained linoleum floors and the same dilapidated blue tile as in the hallways. There were eight autopsy tables, each a
bulky steel platform that was little more than a giant sink covered with
a heavy metal grid to support the body. Next to each table was a hanging
scale and a cutting board for organ dissection. Andie Delore's body was
on the central table, surrounded by a crowd of people.

They were all there, as if he'd just stepped out of the room for a
break a few minutes ago, instead of disappearing for two years. Tommy
Bailey, short in stature, shorter in temper, Motorhead tattoos and
long, Lemmy-style mustache, slouching against a table waiting for
Whittaker to ask to see the girl's back. Antwon Terry, the morgue photographer, muscular and graceful, speaking softly into his cell phone,
trying to talk himself into a gig at a Bed-Stuy social club. There at the
head of the table was the day supervisor, Lyddie Diaz, peach lipstick

carefully lined with brown pencil, gold Fourteenth Street doorknocker earrings, long peach fake nails, standing blithely with her hands on her hips as if she had no idea that the cops were checking out her world-class ass.

And in the middle of the room, lit up by the table lamps, Steve Whittaker. Even though Whittaker was bent over, facing away, Jenner spotted him easily: the deputy chief medical examiner was a notoriously heavy sweater. Even on this cool fall day, before the autopsy had begun, before he'd even put on the waterproof plastic gown, surgical mask, and plastic face shield, Whittaker's scrub top was soaked dark green.

Detective Roggetti stood near the head of the table, hands in pockets, rocking back and forth on the heels of his loafers; Jenner noticed that his mask was upside down. Seeing Jenner, he perked up. "Hey, Doc!" he said brightly.

Jenner nodded to him and saw Whittaker stiffen; the deputy chief did not look up. Lyddie Diaz rolled her eyes.

Whittaker was in the middle of the sexual assault evaluation. He'd examined the body surface for hairs, fibers, and secretions or other trace evidence, and had swabbed and made smears on glass slides of the girl's mouth and genitals; they'd test the swabs for chemicals found in ejaculate, and the slides for the presence of sperm cells. Forehead beading with sweat, Whittaker was now inspecting her pelvis.

Jenner moved deliberately into Whittaker's field of view.

"Dr. Whittaker, I understand the Delore family has informed the office that I'll be attending the autopsy on their behalf."

Whittaker nodded, continuing his exam.

"Steve, I'd like to examine her face, if I may."

Whittaker straightened.

"Dr. Jenner, let me make one thing perfectly clear. You are here because we've agreed to extend this courtesy to the victim's family. You are not here to do the autopsy. You are not here to supervise my performance of the autopsy. You are here to observe my performance of a thorough medicolegal examination. When I've finished—and only when I've finished—you'll get an opportunity to examine her yourself.

In the meantime, if you in any way approach, touch, or interfere with the body, I'll have you removed from the building and banned from this facility for the rest of my tenure here. I have nothing further to say to you: this girl's unfortunate death requires my complete attention."

Jenner stepped back, stung. The onlookers, variously titillated or embarrassed, avoided meeting Jenner's eye. Antwon Terry, oblivious because he'd been on hold, sauntered over to bump elbows with Jenner, a traditional greeting in the morgue, where bloody gloves and gowns made handshakes difficult.

Noticing Tommy Bailey standing next to Jenner, Whittaker snapped, "Bailey, come over here, put away the swabs and slides, and seal the kit for me, right now, please. And don't disappear—I don't want to have to scour the halls looking for a tech."

Jenner sighed. His return to forensic pathology was off to a beautiful start.

Andie Delore's legs were deeply tanned. She'd worn a scoop-neck single-piece bathing suit in Cancun; now, as her body lay on the table, propped by a metal block under her shoulder blades, her wounds seemed to float above the radiant white skin of her torso. Curving lash marks, dried to a dark liver red, crisscrossed her belly, chest, and thighs, but under the bright lights over the autopsy table, Jenner could see there were no penetrating injuries. Her face was discolored, blotchy and purple from her position, but had no wounds. Her neck, lolling backward from the drape of her trunk over the block, was also free of bruises and scrapes.

Whittaker announced that he was going to open the body, and the onlookers put on their masks. He was fast, slick even. He quickly examined the body cavities and removed the organs, passing them to Tommy Bailey to weigh. There were no surprises. There was some bruising in the scalp, but not enough to explain death, particularly since examination inside the head revealed no brain injury.

The neck dissection revealed no bruising in the muscles, no crushing of the windpipe or Adam's apple. There were some small hemorrhages in the tongue, which the girl could have caused herself, biting involuntarily as she was gagged.

"And that, Detective, is that," said Whittaker, stepping back from the table and turning to face Roggetti. He pulled off one bloodied rubber glove, stretched it back, then shot it forward into the trash. Then he tore off the other glove and tossed it, mask and face shield quickly following.

Roggetti said, "So why did she die, Doc?"

"Probably positional asphyxiation. I'm going to pend the cause of death until I know if she had drugs in her system, but I'll certify her death today as a homicide. Call me if anything else turns up that I need to know about."

He turned and walked out of the autopsy room without another word to anyone.

Roggetti turned to Jenner.

"Doc?"

"Detective?"

"I'm pretty sure I got that, but I'm not one hundred percent sure. Would you mind going over it again with me? And maybe could we step outside while the orderly sews her up?"

Jenner turned to Tommy and asked him to leave her up on the table after he'd closed her torso. He and Roggetti walked into the corridor.

"So she was, like, strangled, right?"

"Well, not exactly. The tiny red dots all over her face and eyes are petechiae, little popped blood vessels. In strangulation, the hands trap the blood in the neck and head, and the blood vessels burst because too much blood gets trapped in the face. But that can also happen if you're upside down and the face becomes really congested."

Jenner explained that most strangling victims have at least some external markings on their necks, even if they're subtle, and hers was clean. How long could she have continued to breathe, nailed upside down to the wall? Even if she'd been suspended upright, she could have asphyxiated—crucifixion victims died from suffocation as their breathing muscles became exhausted and failed.

"But I think what pushed her over the edge was that he duct-taped her mouth to keep her quiet—I saw some residue on her face at the scene. Once he shut her up, he immobilized her somehow and hung her on the wall, upside down and with her mouth sealed off. She would have gradually asphyxiated, even if her nostrils weren't covered."

Roggetti, shaking his head, muttered, "Jesus . . ."

Jenner nodded. "I'd like to think it was quick, but she was young and fit. I don't know if she was still alive when he started to whip her. But at the scene I did notice some adhesive marks on her arms—I think he might have sedated her with patches of a transdermal painkiller like Fentanyl."

Roggetti's cell phone rang. He raised his palm to Jenner as he looked at it, then said, "Doc, I gotta take this. I'll see you later, okay?" He headed off toward the loading bay exit.

Jenner was about to open the autopsy room door when a gravelly voice called out, "Well, look what the cat dragged in!"

He turned to see an elegant blonde, fiftyish, in a white cotton shirt and stone gray khakis tucked into scuffed black army boots, a pair of chic black-framed glasses dangling from a cord around her neck.

"Well, if it isn't famous forensic anthropologist Annie Carr! Living proof that all the good women are either married or gay . . ."

"And the best women are both." She hugged him hard and kissed him softly. "Edward Jenner. How the hell are you, handsome? I thought I'd never see you here again." She ruffled his hair, beaming.

He smiled back. "Makes two of us. I'm kind of okay. Happy to see you, not so happy to be here. You? How's Sara?"

"We're good. We just got a golden retriever—a baby can't be far off." She looked over his shoulder into the autopsy room. "Are you here about that girl from the East Village? I heard about it—really nasty."

"Yes on the girl, yes on nasty. What are you doing at work on a Sunday?"

"I'm teaching in Quantico this week, and I wanted to go over my specimens. I should scoot—say good-bye before you leave, okay? I'll be in the Anthro room. Kiss kiss." She loved flirting with Jenner. At first, he used to get an adorable stricken look: he wasn't sure what he could say in return, and what was over the line. It had taken him a while to learn that if Annie liked you, there pretty much *was* no line.

Alone in the autopsy room, Jenner set to work. Tommy had hurried off to smoke in the loading bay; the four-to-midnight shift would put her away. The only sounds were a dripping faucet at the other end of the room, and the hiss of the steam pipe.

He looked at her face again. She'd been washed; the skin was pale now, glinting wet under the bright light, the petechiae now more visible, like a very fine rash. Jenner could still make out traces of whitish gray adhesive around the mouth.

He turned his attention to her chest—there was a possibility that he'd killed her by compressing her thorax, perhaps kneeling on her until she died—but Jenner found no chest wall bruising.

He looked at the hands; he suspected that Whittaker's examination of them had been cursory—it always had been. He peered at the fingernails, clipped by Whittaker during the sexual assault workup. Nothing to see.

He studied the wrists, the ragged purple-black bolt holes. He couldn't tell if it was just a trick of the light, but there seemed to be a blue discoloration of the wrist distinct from the holes. He incised the forearm and inspected the tissue underneath. A film of blood spread in a poorly defined band around the wrist, separate from the bolt injury. A handcuff mark, perhaps?

He incised the other wrist and found a similar subcutaneous film of blood; the wrist hemorrhages weren't like the well-circumscribed patterned skin injuries caused by handcuffs. The bleeding was more marked over the backs of the wrists and, he saw as he extended the incision, continued down over the backs of the forearms: he had bound her wrists together, probably palm to palm.

Moving her wrists, trying to determine the exact position of her hands in the ligature, he noticed a pale area at the base of the left thumb. He squinted—it was pretty faint. He took his right glove off, closed his eyes, and gently stroked the skin.

He felt a slight depression in the surface.

He walked to the doorway and turned out the lights, then took the plastic bag containing his Maglite and his Zeiss hand lens from his pocket. The waning daylight from the clerestory windows was just a mud gray glow, the room otherwise dark.

He pulled over a metal stool and sat next to the girl's body. He shone the flashlight over the right wrist, tilting the beam, tilting his head, turning her wrist. There it was: two, maybe three, shallow depressions at the base of the right thumb, in the fleshy part of the back of the hand.

He went to the other side of the table and examined the other wrist under the light. Again, depressions in the base of the thumb.

He was looking at bite marks. The killer had bitten her, tied her wrists together and bitten her across the bases of her thumbs.

He wanted a second opinion; he needed confirmation. He knew it was petty, but it was important to him that he find something that Whittaker had missed. And that people in the office found out about it.

He strode down the hallway to the Anthro room. Annie was perched on a stool at the steel table, a little frown of concentration on her face as she touched the pincer tips of a head-span calipers to a crumbling brown skull. She peered up at Jenner over half-moon glasses when he came in.

"Annie, sorry to bother you, but can I borrow your eyes? I think I've found something."

"Ooh. Field trip!" She smiled. "Sure, Jenner."

In the autopsy room, he showed her the marks. After a few seconds with the hand lens and flashlight, she gave a low whistle.

"Yeah, dental imprints. Score one for Jenner!" She walked around the table and inspected the left wrist. "On the right, I think you've got a deeper depression from a cuspid, and next to it an overlapped incisor. Left is a bit too faint for me to call."

She smiled at him proudly and tousled his hair again, as if he were an eight-year-old, *her* eight-year-old. "Whittaker missed them?"

Jenner nodded. "Look, do you think you could tell him you found them? That you happened to be walking by, had a quick peek at the body, and noticed them? I really don't want to deal with him." He knew the word would get out that he had found them.

"Edward Jenner, modest to a fault. Sure, I'll take the credit. Want me to call an odontologist? Don't you swab these for saliva and epithelial DNA?"

"Well, that's a problem. Whittaker hosed the body down after he'd finished his external exam, and he rinsed her a few times during the autopsy. Anything that was there is gone now."

"Damn."

Annie looked down at the girl's body.

"Tell you what, Jenner. I have some UV film in the refrigerator. We can photograph the injuries when you're done. The crushed tissue should show up pretty well on UV—we should be able to get a decent sense of the teeth patterning and the shape of his dental arches. Whittaker could have the odontologist excise the skin."

"I doubt the impressions will be good enough to stand up in court. And Whittaker's not going to want to carve up the daughter of a prominent lawyer."

"You're the boss. Or should have been." She winked and left to find the photographer.

Jenner felt a little high from his find. The UV bite mark photos might reveal a full imprint of the dental arches, good enough to ID a suspect. He returned to the body.

At the foot of the autopsy table, he crossed the girl's legs to make her body easier to turn over, then stood on the side of the table and reached across to grasp her right arm. He pulled her toward him, gently supporting and protecting her face as she rolled onto her front.

He examined the areas under the skin of the back and neck, again looking for signs of compression. He was about to cut into the base of the neck when he stopped: there was a curious group of brown marks just below the hairline. At first he thought it was from something she'd been lying on, but the markings were too sharply defined, little dull red-brown curlicues about one-eighth of an inch long.

A necklace imprint, dark from drying? There had been no jewelry, but perhaps it had been torn off, like the earrings. But a necklace torn from her neck would create linear scratches, not a row of neat little marks.

He wiped them with a damp paper towel, to make sure that it wasn't dried blood. It looked like some kind of burn; it had been carefully inflicted.

He took out the plastic Ziploc bag in which he'd brought his flash-light and hand lens. Tearing the bag open, he laid it gently on the marks, smoothing down the surface and pressing the margins with spread fingers to keep the plastic taut. Carefully, with a fine-point Magic Marker, he traced the row of figures onto the plastic. He lifted the plastic sheet from the neck, waved it gently to dry it, and then folded it and tucked it into his pocket.

He had just finished his exploration of the subcutaneous tissues of the back and his posterior neck dissection when Annie Carr returned. Antwon was on his way. Taking off his gown, Jenner showed her the curious pattern just below the hairline.

"Ha! Whittaker's going to just *love* this."

He smiled. "Thanks, Annie. Call me and let me know what you find, eh?"

"Sure thing. Look after yourself. It's good to have you back, Jenner—think about sticking around, okay? It's not the same without you."

They hugged good-bye, then Jenner headed to the loading bay. With a bit of luck, he'd be at the Waldorf by 5:00 p.m. He was already thinking about what he'd say to Tony Delore.

*   *   *

The Delores had a suite on the Astoria Level, the Waldorf's concierge floor. Mrs. Delore, a handsome, graying brunette in a white shirt and tweed jacket, met Jenner in the entryway and led him into the lounge. Mr. Delore was on the phone, laptop open, jotting down addresses and times as he spoke with a funeral home.

She offered him coffee, which he declined, and a drink, which he also refused. Where her husband was crisp and authoritative on the phone, she seemed to fade into the background. She sat opposite Jenner, but didn't make small talk; there seemed to be a tacit agreement that Mr. Delore would run the show.

After Jenner had waited for an appropriate length of time, Delore stood, terminated his conversation, closed his laptop, and joined them. A tall man with gray hair and dark eyebrows, he was wearing a navy suit, a blue shirt with crisp white collar, and a dark tie. Rather than sit next to his wife on the couch, he drew over another chair, positioning himself so that the three of them sat in a triangle.

"Sorry, Dr. Jenner. Just talking with your district attorney, making sure he's keeping some pressure on the police." He leaned over and shook Jenner's hand perfunctorily. "We know each other a little bit from the National Governors Association meetings."

He opened a clipboard and laid it on the table, placed a pen neatly across it, then said, "Now. DA Klein tells me you went to the scene of . . ." He flushed, reached up to tug at his tie. "Yes, that you've been to the scene where . . ."

He closed his eyes, then tilted his head down, his lip working as he began to cry.

His wife stood and put a hand on his shoulder; he tried to wave her away, but she caught his hand and stayed. She pulled him to her and stroked his head as he wept.

Jenner said, "Mr. Delore, I can't imagine how hard this day has been for you. Perhaps it would be better if we spoke a little later."

Delore, sobbing, tried to shake his head, but his wife said, "I think that would be best, Doctor. We have your telephone number. When he's had a chance to get some rest, my husband will call you." She nodded to Jenner, grateful.

Jenner stood as she helped her husband to his feet, then put an arm around him and led him from the room.

Jenner let himself out.


Ana was still in his bed when he got home. She got up quickly and made a feeble show of tidying the bedroom.

He shooed her into the TV room and ordered pizza. They ate at the kitchen table, both too tired to speak. After dinner, she took a long bath. She tried to make him take the bed, arguing that he was much taller than she was, and that she felt really guilty, him being uncomfortable on the couch. But he wouldn't hear of it, and insisted that she keep the bed.

It wasn't a wholly altruistic act, he realized: at some level, he liked her gratitude. Still, at six-foot-two, for him the couch was an uncomfortable prospect; it was just as well he was exhausted.

But he couldn't sleep—the day wouldn't leave him alone. The girl on the wall. Whittaker. Tony Delore weeping in his plush hotel suite. And now Ana, in his space, in his bed.

He was wired; he needed to come down, to feel himself again. He got up and went to his desk. He opened up a mahogany case and took out a double-sealed bottle of tincturing alcohol, a glass laboratory flask, and several dark vials of floral and herbal extracts.

After the whole 9/11 thing, when he finally admitted to himself that he was coping poorly, Julie bullied him into seeing one of the government-funded therapists. Dr. Rother had said it might help him to get the collection of essential oils. Jenner, amused, had bought the set, only to be amazed at how wonderful he found the small library of scents. He later explained slightly sheepishly to Rother that the oils hadn't helped him in an *aromatherapy* way, but had helped him get out of his head and back into his body. Working with the oils was a purely sensual pastime, with no goal beyond experiencing the scents. Learning to spot the different aromas, experimenting with blending extracts, observing how the scent changed as the perfume met the air, provided Jenner with an almost Zen immersion in a natural, *real* thing: a fleeting moment of pure sensation that couldn't be touched by burning fires or collapsing buildings, by radiation or by weaponized bacteria.

At first, he'd struggled to tell ylang-ylang from jasmine, but soon he could easily separate the sweetness of jasmine grandiflorum from the heady, erotic perfume of night-blooming jasmine sambac, and before long he was discriminating between Bulgarian and Turkish extracts of the same rose species. His favorites were the grasses—hay, mellilot, flouve—the thick, coumarin scents, sweet as vanilla, made him feel as if he were lying in a field at sunset in late summer.

He decided to work on saffron. He'd once extracted a saffron essential oil, but beyond the absurd cost, the scent of the oil had been fleeting. He found a four-hundred-year-old tincture recipe in the online archives of a society of French food historians in Beaulieu, and spent the rest of the evening experimenting at his desk. He began by gently heating diluted alcohol, then dropping three thick pinches of brick red saffron threads into the warm glass flask. He swirled the flask, savoring the warm, buttery scent of the stamens as they swelled and turned crimson, watching the alcohol's almost imperceptible change from gin clear to the palest of canary yellows. He dipped a test strip, clipped it to a stand, smelled it, and then methodically sniffed it and made notes during the first hour of the dry-down. After one last sniff, he closed his notebook at 1:00 a.m. and put sheets on the couch.

When he turned out the light, Julie's cat, invisible all day, slipped out from under the club chair. The cat crept warily across the floor, then jumped up onto the couch to lie against him. Jenner was already asleep.

# DECEMBER 2

J enner had had nightmares for months after 9/11, but they had finally gone away, replaced by solid sleep, dreamless and deathlike.

He woke suddenly, disoriented, on the couch. Then he remembered: he was in his living room, in his loft, with Ana de Jong. Awake, eyes still closed, he felt the light through his lids. He remembered traveling with Julie in Spain, driving through Castile–La Mancha in early autumn. The road wound through fields of pale violet crocuses, and as they neared Consuegra, the air filled with the scent of saffron.

He opened his eyes, the saffron still in his nose. He sat up stiffly. It wasn't a dream: Ana was at his desk, wearing his pajama top, perched on his chair, going through his things. She was looking through the mahogany box, examining each vial in turn. He watched her take out the vial of Egyptian jasmine, unscrew the silver cap, and sniff it.

She'd had a bad night. Jenner had woken, then lain awake on the couch, listening to her cry. He wondered if she knew he'd heard.

She put the jasmine back and began sniffing the cabreuva. She tucked one tan leg underneath her and glanced absently in Jenner's direction, eyes widening a little when she saw him watching her.

"Hi," she said. "Sorry! I didn't mean to wake you, Dr. Jenner."

"No, you didn't. Don't worry."

"Dr. Jenner?" She swiveled the chair to face him, leg still tucked under, looking tiny in Jenner's pajama top.

"Please call me Jenner. Edward, if you have to; my friends call me Jenner." She was sitting half naked in his house, wearing his clothes, going through his things: she might as well call him Jenner.

"You don't like your first name?"

"Not much." He hated it. "You had a question?"

"No, I had to tell you I accidentally spilled one of the perfumes. I'm sorry."

The saffron tincture. He told her not to worry. She was probably wondering why a man would have a collection of twenty glass vials of perfume oil in an elegant wooden case; let her draw her own conclusions.

Then he caught sight of her left hand and understood why she'd spilled the oil. He'd never been particularly good at dressing wounds; he'd bandaged her cut hand into a wad of white the size of a boxing glove.

"How does your stomach feel?" he asked.

"A bit sore. Not too bad."

"I should probably have a look at it." She made a little face, and then stood up gingerly, gently pressing one hand to her belly.

"In the bathroom again?"

Jenner nodded and got up, securing his pajama bottoms with his hand as she padded past him. He followed her into the bathroom, then squeezed by her to get the bandages and antiseptic.

He sat on the edge of the tub, and she lifted the pajama top, exposing her thighs and belly. How unself-conscious she was! The easy intimacy, the gesture of trust, it all made him uncomfortable. Her deep tan was accentuated by the contrast with her white panties. They said "Hi, Sugar!" in pink on the front, and there was a kitschy little picture of a waving sugar cube.

"This is going to sting a bit, okay?" She nodded and bit her lower lip.

Jenner slowly stripped off the bandaging he'd used to cover the scrapes on her lower belly. As she'd gone over the wall in the backyard of her building, the bottle-glass spikes embedded along the top had cut her hand badly, and carved three raking slices into her lower abdomen. The wounds were now raised dark seams of flaking clot, the skin around them unevenly bruised. They were clean, though.

"Jenner," she asked as he sprayed antiseptic, then carefully applied fresh gauze and bandages, "will I have a scar?"

"I think you probably will. Yes."

Her expression didn't change, but her eyes brimmed with tears.

He hurriedly said, "Give me your hand now."

As he unwrapped the mitten of gauze and then redressed the cut, the tears came faster and faster, spattering hotly onto Jenner's hands as he pressed the last of the tape into place. He stood, waiting for her to stop crying. When she didn't, he tentatively reached up to pat her head; it was the best he could manage. She threw her arms around him and buried her face in his chest.

He saw himself in the mirror, the girl sobbing against his chest, watched himself put his arms around her, hold her stiffly as she wept.

Christ. Why *him*?

The man ran along the East River in the dawn sleet, his hard paces splashing thin gray mud in all directions. The sodden hood of his sweat-shirt was plastered against his scalp and neck, the cold, clinging garment heavy as the hand of God on his back.

Despite the cold, he ran in shorts. He used to have beautiful New Balance running shoes, but his last pair had finally fallen apart over the summer. He needed his money for his projects, so he ran in work boots laced tightly around his knee socks. His feet had callused hard, and he barely noticed the pain of each foot strike through the uncushioned soles.

His route along the waterfront was more an obstacle course than a path, zigzagging through crumpled piers, fenced lots, collapsing brick walls, and barren fields strewn with junk.

He was thinking about the house on East Seventh Street, what he'd done there.

After he'd finished with Andie Delore, when he calmed down, he'd caught sight of the TV screen; he had sat there transfixed and incredu-lous. MTV's *Spring Break: Daytona Beach*, an actual, real-life orgy, naked men and women, broadcast for all the world to see. He'd lived a life apart, mostly; spring break at his small rural university had been nothing like that. Or maybe he just hadn't known about it; he knew some students went south to Florida and the Carolinas. But he'd never gone, never had any real idea what it was about. Even if he could have afforded it, no one would have invited him.

How *available* they were, those girls! They danced for the camera in tiny bikinis, jiggling and writhing, all golden brown skin and glistening flesh, hot, slippery prizes for the mobs of boys. But it was the boys he really stared at, buff and vigorous in the sunshine, stripped to the waist, their skin smooth and tan. Had they never been adolescent, never had pimples? Where were their scars? he wanted to know.

In the bars at night, half-naked girls lay giggling as boys lapped alcohol from the hollow between their breasts. The drunken girls kissed each other on the mouth as the boys hooted like apes, and the girls cursed as if they were men, and the boys ate it all up like hungry little piggies crowding at the trough. And when they were vomiting drunk, they paired off and staggered away to finish what they'd begun, graceless and bestial.

He shook himself. Where they had chosen debasement, he had stayed pure.

He thought about the day before, coming back to his factory, her dried blood crusted on his white skin like lichen, rust red over gooseflesh. He had smeared her blood right up to his neck, had walked home in the rain, head bowed into the scarf that concealed it, half delirious from the scent. Home and naked, he knelt on his mattress, holding the whip to his nostrils, the blood in the braided leather of the coiled whip clotted, but glossy and still damp.

He had knelt there, swaying slightly as he drew in her scent fully. The cold, the mortification of the cold, made it richer, intensified his sense of smell. The aroma of her suffering rose into his head in a vast crimson wave, filling him, expanding inside him. He was back there in the room, watching her flesh twitch with each stroke, watching her eyelids flutter, remembering how her life had ebbed away with one final convulsive gasp as she'd stopped breathing.

He'd worried he'd given her too much Fentanyl, that she'd be dead before he really got to work. But she'd been alive, and when he drove the first bolt through her feet and her limbs had stirred feebly, he'd rejoiced.

He'd taken the Polaroids from the box and set them neatly before him. Desire grew in him as he remembered the dry smoke of warming metal, the pop of each flash, that instant tungsten glare washing the girl's skin white under the red, freezing her shuddering chest as she was dying. The later photographs were best, the ones after he'd realized that her mouth would look prettier open.

Oh, God—how *right* he had been . . .

As he approached Newtown Creek, fences and factory walls blocked the path along the waterfront. He cut back and forth, running inland in front of the factories, then a few blocks north until he could get back to the water, working toward Pulaski Bridge, a shadow in the mist ahead.

Running helped him focus. While he ran, he made his plans. But today his concentration was poor. Because last night, he had been seen. Ana de Jong had seen him, hard and slick with blood, revealed in his true, exalted state. Had she felt the energy? It burned through him like a glowing halo, an intense white light radiating off his skin. When he'd looked down at her from the window, she'd seen him and gasped! He'd felt his body flooding the night with light.

Ana had seen what no other living soul had witnessed, seen his power manifested in its purest form. By now, she'd know what had happened to her friend, know how he had fed upon her, how he'd transformed her. And she'd seen his own transformation, the majestic spirit that rose inside him when he killed, its mighty arms stretched wide and grasping.

Lost in his thoughts, he'd passed Pulaski Bridge. He had to concentrate; she was disturbing his focus, and he couldn't let that happen. Wednesday night was fast approaching. Ana had interrupted him, stopped the Work before he had done much more than prepare the main elements. On Wednesday, he'd take his time. He was learning, getting better. On Wednesday, there'd be no interruptions, and he'd finish the Work properly. There were a few more elements he needed, a couple of errands to run, but he was almost ready to begin her transformation.

And she would be very beautiful indeed.

★   ★   ★

Roggetti had the radio in the Crown Vic on 1010 WINS; every twenty minutes the station was recycling its coverage of the murder. They were waiting while Rad and Ana met with Internal Affairs—it seemed kind of cloak-and-dagger to Jenner, the anonymous apartment in the non-descript housing projects on the edge of Chinatown, kept by the bureau for meetings with confidential informants.

He wondered how Ana was holding up. She'd been quiet on the ride down, gazing out at life on the lower Bowery—jewelry stores filled with Chinese gold, lighting shops, fruit stalls, all bright and bustling under the winter drizzle. Rad had explained the process to her—IAB would show her mug shots as well as current NYPD ID photos. He told her again he didn't think the guy was a cop.

"He was no cop," Roggetti had declared. "Cop wouldn't have let you get away."

She'd leaned her head against the glass and hadn't seen Garcia jab Roggetti in the ribs.

She'd been in there for three hours now.

The car smelled of beef with broccoli and sweet and sour pork. Jenner gathered the white paper takeout containers, climbed out and dumped them into the trash at the corner, then got back in.

Roggetti was looking dopey and well-fed. He handed Jenner the case file, then folded his jacket into triangles, tucked it against the headrest, and tried to find a comfortable position for a nap.

Jenner looked at the Polaroids again, flipping through the fat stack slowly one by one. He'd never seen anything like it. He'd spent three months on a fellowship at the Behavioral Analysis Unit at the FBI Academy in Quantico, Virginia, endless hours in the serial killer archives, wired on coffee and horror. In all that time, in all those murders, he'd never come across anything so meticulously planned and executed, so *theatrical*, as the Delore killing. And if the killing itself was unprecedented, the body display was extraordinary; the bastard was rewriting the serial killer handbook.

*Serial killer.* No question. He was looking at the girl hung on the wall;

there was no way that a first-timer had created something so sophisticated, so *evolved*. Every element in the killing had profound meaning, from the way he'd killed her through to the way he'd displayed her body. He'd have killed before; maybe not as fully developed, probably not with the same level of content, but there'd be other victims out there.

He looked up to see Roggetti peering over the seat back.

"So, Doc—why do you think he did that? Turn that girl upside down and nail her to a wall?"

"I don't know. Part of the problem is we don't know what else he would have done to her if Ana hadn't interrupted him."

Roggetti looked disappointed, so Jenner said, "But we can speculate a bit, based on what we have here." He held the photo up to show Roggetti. "She was upside down and vulnerable. It's possible that this was a purely sexual display—maybe he was showing off his ownership of the body, his complete power over it. Or maybe he had a particular fantasy image he was trying to create when he was disturbed."

Roggetti muttered, "Well, the whole fucking thing looks pretty disturbed to me."

Jenner nodded. "One thing that's really interesting about this man: he has zero fear of being caught. None. His fingerprints are everywhere, he doesn't run when he sees Ana getting away. Either he doesn't care, or he believes that he won't—or can't—be caught."

"So why did he pick Andie Delore?"

"That's the ten-million-dollar question, Joey. We know that, we have motive, and once we have motive, well, then we're on the first rung of the ladder."

Jenner scooped up the photos. He'd found a headshot of the girl alive, among all of these images of her dead. She was pretty, but not strikingly so. Wealthy background, but money was a completely unlikely motive in a crime like this. Boyfriend? Ana said that Andie hadn't dated for at least six months, maybe more. Revenge—on her, on her lawyer dad? That seemed absurd, given the extreme circumstances.

Yes. The ten-million-dollar question . . .

There was a tap on the window. He slid over, quickly slipping the photographs back into the thick brown folder as Ana squeezed in next to him.

She smiled at him and brushed the hair out of her eyes as she sat back and chatted animatedly about her meeting. She hadn't seen the guy in any of the photos she'd looked at, not felons, not cops. And the IAB detective had made it clear to her just how unlikely it was to be a cop. The computer sketch artist had been to the Rhode Island School of Design, where she wanted to do a master's in photography. Plus he was really cute! She laid her head against the window, still smiling, and tapped the glass with the back of her ring.

Jenner knocked softly on the bathroom door.

"Ana?"

There was a soft slush of water; he heard her sliding up to sit in the big tub. The wet air trickling out into the hall was fragrant with lemongrass and aloe.

"Yes?"

"I have to go out for a little while. Will you be okay?"

She was silent a second, then asked where he was going.

"I just have to take care of a couple of things—I'll be down in your uncle's studio."

"Will you be long?"

"A couple hours. Just call me if you need me—a friend of mine will be in the hall, in case you need anything. His name is Jun."

She said, "Your neighbor, right? My uncle mentioned him."

"Yes."

She slushed back down. "Okay. Thanks."

Across the way, Jun was leaning against the door frame, eating Lucky Charms from the box. He was wearing surfer shorts, his fake dreadlocks gathered under a big green wool tam.

"Need some coffee, Jenner?"

Jenner shook his head.

"How's she doing? It's all over the papers. You see the body?"

Jenner nodded.

"Sounded pretty bad." He took another fistful of cereal.

"Yeah." Jenner pulled the door shut behind him. "I'll be a while. I need to make a few calls, and I don't want Ana to hear."

"Take your time. I have a stack of papers on raster graphics to grade, and they'll all suck. These kids think if you've mastered *Donkey Kong*, you're already nearly a video game designer."

Walking down the stairs, Jenner remembered the first time they'd met. Jun's girlfriend at the time, an exquisite model from Hokkaido with a deep tan and an ocher sunburst tattoo on the small of her back, had overdosed on methamphetamine. Jun had appeared in Jenner's doorway, tapping lightly on the frame, explaining carefully that he'd heard about Jenner's work, and wondered if Jenner would perhaps help him with a problem. The two had worked with the Japanese embassy to repatriate her body, and had been friends ever since.

Jenner knew Jun was involved in video game design, and was doing graduate work at New York University, but it wasn't until Jun invited him to an open house at the school that he'd discovered his friend was a legend: apparently, while still an undergraduate at Keio University in Tokyo, Jun had written some sort of genius video game software—not a complete game, but a software element so brilliant that the code was still in use today. It had made Jun rich enough to buy his loft in the Lightbulb Factory, and then open a Stüssy store in Aoyama, which promptly earned him a second fortune.

The door from the stairwell onto Pyke's floor was in frosted glass, etched PYKE: WORLD IMAGE. Douggie owned the whole fourth floor, and had divided his space into living areas and a studio. The studio was as much an archive as a workspace; white enameled cube shelves covered two walls, packed with magazines and books that Douggie had either been published in or was collecting. There were dozens of photographs, everything from Pyke's own work to photographs by John Wylie and

Dennis Hopper. The single color photo was a twenty-by-twenty that had originally appeared on the cover of *ZOOM*—a self-portrait of Douggie in a bear suit with the Hong Kong supermodel Sarah San.

Jenner sat down at the big steel desk and booted up Pyke's Mac: time to see if Whittaker had killed his data access privileges.

Within minutes, Jenner knew that Whittaker had missed at least one opportunity to humiliate him. A few keystrokes took him onto the Violent Criminal Apprehension Program; his passwords to CODIS and AFIS and even some of the regional databases were still valid. He now had access to investigational records from the country's most violent murders.

He began. For search parameters, he guessed at things about Andie that might have appealed to her killer—her age, her occupation, modality of homicide (here, Jenner went with the generic "asphyxia"), and location.

A three-year record search in VICAP only delivered a handful of consonant cases, homicides that, for all their viciousness, turned out to be disappointingly straightforward. Worse, all seemed to have been closed by capture or death of the perpetrator. He printed out short case abstracts on all six anyway.

Maybe the last killing was too recent to show up in the database? Busy state police officers and detectives pissed and moaned about spending hours inputting data into a federal program they thought of mostly as a research tool for federal showboaters. Despite the Bureau's offer to install a free, dedicated terminal in any office requesting one, compliance with VICAP was lax, and even in departments where the reports were submitted, the program had low priority. Accordingly, many—maybe even most—murders never made it into the database at all, or if they did, it was often after a delay of months.

He would have to do it the old-fashioned way. He opened his small black address book and placed it flat on the desktop. As an ME, he had lectured frequently at regional and national meetings and at the NYPD Death School; he was happy talking casework with the cops, whether from big-city precincts or single-man squads in the ass end of nowhere, many of whom had terrible forensic backup. By the time he resigned, he'd almost filled the address book. Now he combed through it, culling the names and addresses of detectives, state troopers, criminalists, a cadaver dog trainer, even a couple of undertakers—anyone who'd know about any unusually violent deaths in their area.

It was close to 5:00 p.m. when he started calling; he'd missed the eight-to-four shift. Many of his contacts had already left, but Jenner found that introducing himself and the reason for his call was all the entrée he needed. Striking out in the five boroughs of New York City, he began calling farther afield.

By 9:00 p.m. he had burned through his numbers for southern New York and northern New Jersey and had nothing to show for it. He was now on eastern Pennsylvania; he decided he'd give up as soon as he got as far as the midpoint of the Pennsylvania Turnpike.

Danny Barton had retired from the Ninth Precinct a couple of years back and gone over to the Pennsylvania State Police. He was stationed near Romen—halfway to Ohio. This would be his last call for the night.

No answer, no voice mail. Just as Jenner was hanging up, a state trooper picked up. Barton had left for the day, so Jenner left a message.

"Wait—Doc Jenner? From the New York ME's office?"

"Yes?"

"Doc! It's Bobby Dowling! I was in the Ninth with Danny, retired six months ago, Danny brought me on up. You remember me? We had that working girl who went out the window on East Fourth at A, the one who killed the bartender at that bar down the street from Spiral?"

Jenner did remember him—dark hair, average height, thinning hair, a little soft in the middle, a fast talker. They spoke for a few seconds about life in New York versus life in the country, then Jenner, his stomach starting to growl, said, "Bobby, the reason I called, it's a bit of a long shot, but I'm looking to see if you guys have caught any extremely violent murders recently, anything weird."

Dowling paused. "Doc, you didn't know we got the Smith case?"

"The Smith case?"

"You don't watch TV? Couple of weeks ago, in Romen, we had the girl who was decapitated."

Jenner stopped tapping his pen.

"A homicide, Bobby?"

"Worst I ever seen. Girl named Sunday Smith. We're running the investigation—Romen is like a one-stoplight town, maybe three cops in the whole county. Less, even. Good guys, but this is way out of their league. She wasn't just decapitated: she was all hacked up. Happened maybe two weeks ago. I'm kinda surprised you never heard of it—it was on CNN!" He sounded a little aggrieved.

"I haven't been watching the news very much. What did she look like, Bobby? Blond, brunette? How old?"

"Young. Dark hair. Not really from around here—she's in her last year at some college in New York, took the semester off, moved home for a while. A tough break."

Jenner asked which college.

"I wanna say NYU, but I don't think that's it. I can check. But wait, there's more."

He paused, as much to savor the opportunity to tell the story one more time as to gather his thoughts.

"So Jimmy Barrett gets the call from a construction crew working on a barn nearby—door ajar in residence for maybe a couple of days. Not expecting anything, walks through the living room, nothing unusual, through the hall, nothing. He's calling out 'Hello? Anyone home?' Goes upstairs, nothing. Goes back downstairs, walks into the dining room, nothing. Figures he'll close up the house, call it in as nothing disturbed, family away. He's just about to leave when he pushes through the swing door to the butler's pantry, then notices blood on the door to the kitchen. So Jimmy pulls his gun and calls it in. Opens the kitchen door real slowly and *boom!* Blood everywhere—walls, floor, even the ceiling. But y'know what? Jimmy doesn't even notice it. Because he's staring straight into the eyes of the dead girl's head, right there on the countertop . . .

"I tell you, guy was nearly hysterical. Jimmy's so freaked out, what with the blood and the head and all, he doesn't see the weirdest part of all: her head is sitting in a puddle of milk."

"*Milk?*"

"Yeah. The coroner here—he's not like New York, but he seems like an okay guy—he said they kill the girl, cut off her head, and a while later put it in the milk. You could tell he put it there on purpose because of the blood splatter in the milk—he had to lift it over and place it right there in the middle."

Jenner was quiet.

"I tell you, Doc, it was the freakiest fucking thing I've ever seen. You walk into the kitchen, and *bang!* The head's right there, in this puddle of rotting milk. Swear to God. Jimmy's still seriously fucked, nightmares, the works."

"You said she was cut up?"

"Oh, yeah—big-time. Body's lying on the floor nearby, hacked open. It looked like someone tried to do an autopsy on her."

Jenner leaned back in his chair. "Any ideas on the perp?"

"We've got nothing. Zip. They brought in a special blood-splatter guy with the State Police criminalistics crew from near Pittsburgh, but they got nothing usable. I mean, they got some prints, but no matches in regional databases or through AFIS. I said at the time—and you know just how much I like working with the feds—they should call the FBI, but the coroner wasn't having any of that, particularly from a new guy."

"And where's the investigation at now?"

"Nowhere. She was alone in the house, family out of the country, no one saw anything. We think she may have known the killer—there was snow, and it looks like he came right on up the front path and knocked on her front door. No tracks anywhere else, and the doors and locks and windows are fine."

He paused, and in the silence Jenner could hear his grinding frustration.

"We really got nothing. The rest of the family is out of the country, and she had apparently lost touch with her local friends after she went off to college. Nothing looks to be stolen. This close to I-80, it could have been a random thing—y'know, some freakfest looking for kicks just takes a turn off the highway, and it's Sunday Smith's unlucky day. VICAP showed up nothing, whatever that's worth."

"Sexual assault?"

"Don't know. She was starting to go bad. The rape kit showed a questionable on semen, but the lab guys at Lifecodes think the specimen may be too degraded to extract DNA. There's nothing else to suggest rape. Really, we're at a brick wall. And everything got put on the back burner last week after the school shooting. I got a bad feeling that this one is going to get away."

Jenner said, "Bobby, we might be able to help each other." He briefly described the Delore killing, then asked if he could have a look at Dowling's case file.

"Doc, that'd be great. Some of the bosses here are real arrogant pricks, but this one's got to the stage where he'll take all the help he can get, short of the feds. I'll dupe the paperwork, and burn a CD of the crime scene and autopsy photos. Shoot me an e-mail with your address, and if I catch a slow night tonight, I'll be able to get it to you tomorrow. It's only a two-hour drive, plus some of those mopes on the Ninth squad owe me a drink or two."

As Dowling spelled his e-mail address, Jenner felt the hair on his arms prickling.

TUESDAY,
DECEMBER 3

She was making Jenner breakfast. It felt good to do something, anything, rather than just sit around, slowly going insane. She felt guilty, being in his space. He didn't like having her there; he was polite enough, but she clearly made him uncomfortable. He never said much, and she'd noticed that when she came into a room, he'd leave fairly soon afterward. Not immediately, but fairly soon.

Whatever. Even if the breakfast didn't make him like her, it made *her* feel better.

Rad said it was best if she just stayed put until things had sorted themselves out. She agreed—it wasn't as if she had anywhere else to go. And Joey Roggetti had stopped by her apartment and brought a suitcase of her clothes. Spending all her time at Jenner's would be hard enough, even if he weren't so withdrawn around her; she found she couldn't focus enough to read or watch TV.

Jenner said she should call some friends and have them come over and hang out, but it felt too soon for that; she liked not having to *talk*. She'd lost her cell phone, and told herself it would be a pain to get their numbers. Although it wouldn't, really. Anyway, she wasn't sure he really meant it.

Busy work was good, though. She'd done laundry (his as well as hers), folded stuff. Putting it away, she discovered his secret: his apartment might be spare and modern, but behind the sliding slabs of dark wood that hid his closets, Jenner was as messy as any other bachelor. Any *straight* bachelor, at least. And there had been a bonus: when Jenner saw her putting his clean clothes into his closet, he'd blushed. That was kind of cute.

She smiled at the thought, standing at the range in one of his tattered gray sweatshirts. She cracked eggs into the skillet, and stole a glance over at the couch to see if Jenner was still asleep.

He was handsome. Too old for her, sure, but definitely good-looking.

Dark hair, green eyes. When he slept, he relaxed a little, and his face seemed younger. But sad: even in sleep, his face was sad. Rad said he'd had problems after 9/11, and warned her to tread gently around the topic; he hadn't lost anyone or anything, he just had a bad time, apparently, with all the bodies. It was weird she could read it so plainly in him. Or maybe it was just that she knew he was messed up, and was projecting it onto him. But there was something around his eyes, shadowy, and in his look, the way his gaze would settle on her and quickly dart away.

She was still studying his face when his eyes opened.

She quickly looked away. "Hey. Sorry if I woke you. I wanted to have breakfast ready when you got up."

Jenner rubbed his eyes. "Where did you get the bacon?"

"Jun picked it up for me at Dean & Deluca. Look—I made blood orange juice! Just the thing for a coroner, hah hah."

Jenner made a face at the pun, but smiled as he took the glass.

She went back to the range and busied herself with the eggs, then cut thick slabs of bread and put them into the big steel toaster.

She kept her back to him. "Hey, Jenner? You allowed to talk to me about Andie?"

"I don't know if I should. Do you need to talk about it? Rad can get you a grief counselor."

"A grief counselor? No, thanks. I'm okay."

He sat up. "It would really be a good idea if you spoke with someone."

"Okay, I will, I will." She picked up the butter, still turned away. "So you can't talk with me about Andie, I get it. But can you talk with me about me?" She paused. "Do you think I'm in danger?"

He got up and walked over to the table and sat, forcing the lie: "I don't think there's much risk. He's probably long gone. But I think it'd be a good idea to take it easy, hide out here till your uncle gets back. Then maybe you could both go somewhere together."

She turned to face him, eyes now red-rimmed, faking a smile to match his lie.

"Oh, we can talk about it later—I don't want to spoil your breakfast!

Eggs, bacon, toast, OJ. You have jam? I can make more toast if you want."

She put everything onto the tray and carried it to the table, her feet sliding quietly across the dark wood floor.

She slipped the tray in front of him from behind, so he couldn't see her tears.

The man tried again.

The cursor flickered tentatively on the screen, then the university splash page loaded in stuttering blocks.

He moved through the sequence of screens quickly, knowing his stolen phone signal could hang at any second. From the administration page, to admissions, to archived admissions.

He opened a separate Command Line Interface window, rattled off a few keystrokes, and then he was in, all the safeguards and barriers bypassed.

He watched the choppy scroll of surnames, tapping the space bar to halt it when he reached *D*. He overshot and landed on DELORE_ANDREA; he stepped up one line, highlighted DE_JONG_ANA, and pulled up the record.

He remembered Ana's admission photograph from months back, when he was first considering Andrea Delore; she peered into the camera like a little pixie, her hair short and spiky. Since that photo, she'd put on weight—what did they call it, the Freshman Fourteen?—but the curviness suited her; she had been too thin before. Her hair was longer.

The architects of the university's Next Millennium Data Access project had created a system that allowed administrators, depending on their system privileges, access to every scrap of paper associated with a particular student, from first admissions inquiry through to the final alumni donation. The page linked to her active schedule, her grades, everything, even a scanned copy of her personal essay. He skimmed through it—trite crap about what she hoped to contribute to the school, to the world. How her sense of herself had changed after her parents died in a car crash, blah blah blah. That crash had been her lucky day, he figured: her SAT scores were pretty average, and her personal essay had the same crap as all the others he'd read, so it pretty much had to be the crash that had nudged her onto the Accept pile.

He found that her tuition and extracurriculars were guaranteed by a trust fund at a national bank, the trust based in Orlando. He moved on a page.

Now, *this* was more like it. The Contacts page listed two legal guardians; one was in Florida, but the other was right there in New York, on Crosby Street, barely a mile from Ana's apartment.

He wrote down the name and address, then added the phone number, just because it was there—it wasn't as if he was going to call. Then he copied the rest of her files onto his desktop and logged off. He beat a drumroll on the countertop with his hands, ending with an imaginary cymbal crash.

He snorted as he imagined what he and Ana would chat about if he called her up. He giggled, and realized he was aroused.

No, not now, later. "Kittens to drown, cats to skin!" as his father used to say when he had work to do.

True to his word, Bobby Dowling arrived just before noon with a sheaf of photocopied notes and not one but two CD-ROMs.

He wouldn't stay for coffee. "Thanks again, Doc. On my way to see my boys in the Ninth. We got a deal—I give them photos and prints from my scene, they buy me breakfast. It's the least they can do: I don't even work here anymore, and I'm *still* saving their sorry asses."

"Thanks, Bobby. I'll call you. Good seeing you." Jenner walked him to the door. Ana, who'd been in the TV room, slipped behind Jenner into the kitchen, ignoring them.

"Take care, Doc," Dowling said, craning his neck to catch another glimpse; he looked at Jenner with admiration, nodding his head and mouthing the word *Nice!*

"You too, Bobby," Jenner said, closing the door without explanation. He waited to look at the files until Ana said she was going to watch a DVD. She shut herself in the TV room; when he heard the lilting theme of Fellini's *Amarcord*, he got down to work.

He turned on his desk lamp and fanned out the file. Dowling had said that the area canvas was completely negative, so he went straight to the crime scene report, and then the autopsy report.

Jenner always started with the written report and diagrams, then checked the photographs for inconsistencies and omissions. This approach often taught him as much about the quality of the crime scene units handling the case as it did about the case itself; the Pittsburgh crew had clearly been brought in because they were very good indeed.

The kitchen was the large country type—reading the text, Jenner imagined a yellow linoleum floor, pale yellow walls, a cream porcelain sink the size of a New York City park bench, cheery white trim on the windowsills over the sink, which would face out onto the back lawn, or maybe fields. A bird feeder near the window.

The body—the torso—was near the doorway to the hall, the legs in an east/west direction. The criminalist had drawn her as a folded stick figure, knees bent, legs crossed, stick arms akimbo, the squared-off lines of the upper body ending in a truncated uptick representing the neck.

The head, a small open oval, was sketched in on the kitchen counter next to the torso. An amoeba-like pencil line surrounded it, and another fine line led to the word MILK in the margin. Similar fine lines radiated from hatch marks along the walls, and irregular ovals on the floors and countertop, filling the margins, BLOOD, BLOOD, BLOOD, BLOOD. It reminded Jenner of a perspective drawing, the lines converging on a nightmarish vanishing point in the center of the kitchen.

He slipped the CD labeled SCENE into his laptop. The photographer had done a fair job of establishing and orienting shots, but the perspectives seemed arbitrary, and all the body shots were distorted by weird angles. The close-ups were sloppy—the shapes of blood smears on the wall were visible, but the markings on the rulers taped next to it for scale were illegible. Jenner suspected the Pittsburgh team had better images.

He skipped through the opening sequence of front door (no force marks), unremarkable living room perspective, unremarkable stairway perspective, unremarkable dining room perspective, tabbing quickly through the images until he reached the kitchen door.

With the door shut, there was little hint of the carnage within—no wonder that the responding officer had almost called it in as nothing. There was a small spot of blood at knee level on the kitchen door, but there was no blood on the frame, nor on the paneling on the side of the stairway, nor on the wall or the big plate cabinet on either side of the hallway. He flicked back to the shot of the inside of the front door, also clean. Then forward into the kitchen.

Her body was naked, belly down, arms splayed, legs half crossed. There was an arc of blood spatter low on the counter cabinet near the trunk, and the upper torso lay in a large puddle of maroon to brown blood that spread across the floor. There were thinner smears around the floor, ugly little skids in dry brown clot.

In the closer shots, the backs of her legs were clean, with some smeared blood on the posterior torso, probably from when he'd undressed her. It was likely that he'd killed her in that position, been on her back as he cut her throat from behind, like sacrificing an animal, arterial blood spurting sideways from the left carotid, bleeding out forward onto the floor underneath her.

He would have stayed behind her to sever the head, lifting her up and back with his palm under her chin as he worked on separating it.

Jenner could see no ligature marks on legs or arms.

He moved forward in the sequence. There was a surprising amount of blood on the walls, not large droplets but fine spatter, almost mist. Dowling had said he'd cut her up: there must be injuries on the front of the body. A ceiling shot showed some more of the blood mist on the low pendant lampshade, actually inside the shade.

And then the head, on the island in a coagulating lake of yellow/cream milk, with a few small dark clouds of blood. The face was expressionless, eyes half closed, lips berry dark and dry, matted long dark hair settling into the curdled milk. The photos were blurred, as if the photographer was having difficulty focusing on his subject.

The haphazard images made it hard to tell the precise positioning of the head. It took him a couple of minutes to confirm his suspicion: her head faced the hallway entrance, so that the face would be the first thing seen by anyone who walked in.

The photo sequence stopped after the head; Jenner wondered whether the photographer just couldn't take it. Whoever it was hadn't covered the front of the body, at least in this series; of course, the coroner's pathologist and the crime scene unit would have photographs.

He created a folder on his computer desktop, copied the images from the kitchen into it, then set them playing as a slide show, five seconds per image. He watched them cycle in sequence for a few minutes, then turned to the autopsy report.

It was mediocre, the work of a hospital pathologist out of his depth, some part-timer with rudimentary forensic training who pitched in when qualified personnel were unavailable.

He tried to tease out meaning from the poorly organized report; making a quick sketch of the front and back of a woman, he went through the document, isolating injuries and diagramming them on his body chart.

The wound pattern began to emerge. Two major injuries: decapitation, and a complex penetrating injury of the chest. The torso wound was truly bizarre, an X-shaped gash across the trunk, almost like crossed sword slashes, but with some kind of patterned detail. The prosector's description was awful; Jenner needed the autopsy photographs.

He was flicking through the papers, trying to find the pathologist's body diagram, when he heard a soft "Oh."

The image onscreen changed and there was another, even softer, "Oh."

He turned to see Ana standing behind his chair, staring at the computer screen, at that point filled with Sunday Smith's head, mouth slightly open, the background clumping yellow milk fat and brown blood.

He stood, calling after her as she turned and walked quickly to the bathroom, closing the door behind her.

He shut the laptop and followed her. He could hear her sobbing inside.

"Ana."

"Did he do that, too? Did he kill that girl, too?"

"I don't know. It's possible."

"You think he did, don't you?"

"I think maybe he did."

"He cut off her head? Is that what he did to Andie?"

"No!" This was all spinning out of control. "No, it's not. But you know I can't talk about that."

She opened the taps in the tub to full, the water blasting out.

He tried to speak above the roar of the water. "Ana, I'm sorry you saw that, but I can't miss anything that might help us get him."

She shut off the taps. Jenner leaned his head against the bath enclosure.

"When did he do it?"

"About two weeks ago."

"Here? In New York?"

"Pennsylvania."

She was silent for a while.

"How many has he killed?"

"I don't know. But the police have his fingerprints. He'll be caught soon, I promise."

"Don't make promises you can't keep. How can you promise that, Jenner?"

"Look, he may not even be in New York anymore. We know he's moving around."

"Fuck you, Jenner. You don't know anything about him that I haven't told you. Joey said fingerprints are no use until you have a match—do you have a match? No, you don't—you'd have told me if you did. You've got nothing."

He wanted her to stop. She turned the water back on, and again he tried to speak over the sound.

"We're learning more about him. It takes time. And you're safe here."

He waited for a reply, but there was none. She turned the taps down, and then off.

"How's your hand?"

"Leave me alone."

He didn't want to look at the photos anymore; they made him sick. He didn't want to look at the autopsy protocol anymore, didn't want to be part of it anymore.

He went back to the desk, sat down, and began working on it all again.


Happy to be back in Brooklyn for his last run of the day, Meng Shunxi hurried down the street toward the river, the large paper bag of feathers clutched to his chest in an awkward bear hug. Li Ha Wei had taken his MetroCard, so Shunxi had walked up the Bowery and across the Williamsburg Bridge, pocketing the two dollars they gave him for subway fare. His thriftiness had made him a little late, but it was the pre-Christmas rush, and there'd be workers at Fujian Feather and Display of Williamsburg late into the night. Even so, he didn't like being down by the waterfront after dark.

He'd had a busy day, starting with an early delivery of four dozen peacocks to a fussy designer in SoHo, who'd bitched about the lack of ostrich tail feathers. What did he expect Shunxi to say? In recent years, South African ostrich farms had cut their feather shipments by almost 80 percent. It wasn't his fault—the man had been lucky to get even peacock feathers. If there was a problem, take it up with Mr. Tan!

Next he'd taken a case of birds of paradise novelty figures to a florist's on the Upper East Side, then two boxes of pheasant and coque to a Lower East Side milliner before stopping to eat with Wei on Doyers Street in Chinatown. Then back to the factory in Williamsburg, where he'd spent most of the afternoon boxing marabou boas in red and purple-blue for shipment, then packaging smaller red feathers for hat decoration. Fujian Feather was known mostly for their peacock, but this year red feathers of all kinds had been huge; Mr. Tan said this was because of a strange group of older American women who always wore red hats.

Mr. Tan was a good man, and a hero to Shunxi. Like Shunxi, Tan was *ren she*—a "snake person," a Fujianese who'd been smuggled into the country. Mr. Tan had won asylum, and had opened a tiny workshop, making small birds from feathers, which he sold on the street in Chinatown. Little more than a decade later, he owned a factory and warehouse in Williamsburg, and a national business as a wholesale distributor of feathers and feather novelties, everything built on the labor of a constantly changing staff of Fujianese illegals. Mr. Tan had been good to him; Tan was from Fuzhou, and often teased Shunxi, who was born in Xiamen, about his "incomprehensible monkey dialect."

Feeling the cold, Shunxi pulled the feathers tighter to him. It was his last run, carrying overstock—six dozen peacock feathers and a dozen crimson boas—from the Manhattan store back to the warehouse. Since most of the deliveries were small, he could manage them easily and cheaply on the subway, saving Mr. Tan money and solving the problem of Shunxi not having a driver's license.

He looked around him, staring into the empty shadows. This part of Brooklyn was getting better, but nearer the water, away from all the houses and apartment buildings, the streets were still dangerous. The delivery men were prey for youths from the nearby projects; two years earlier, Wei had almost been beaten to death by a group of teenagers not two blocks from where he was now walking. Wei told Shunxi later that while they were hitting him, he didn't cry out: if the police had caught him, he'd have been deported. The project kids hunted them specifically for that reason.

Shunxi walked a little faster.

Ten more minutes, and his day would be done. Tonight he would meet up with Wei and Mr. Zia from down the hall, and they would gamble and drink.

He heard footsteps behind him. He kept walking. Six more blocks.

After passing a streetlamp, he glanced back. The man behind him was a white man in a peacoat and a New York Fire Department baseball cap. A white man: Shunxi breathed a little easier. He crossed the street anyway.

The man stayed on the other side, but soon caught up; he tensed, but the man passed him as they neared the low bridge. Shunxi felt a little sheepish as his anxiety dissolved. Like an old woman, he thought.

A half block before the bridge, the man stopped to tie his shoe. Shunxi's sheepishness was instantly replaced by wariness. Ahead he could see the small floodlights on the factory's sign; just two more blocks.

The man called to him. "Hey."

Staring fixedly forward, Shunxi broke into a slow jog. Nearing the shadow of the bridge, he looked back quickly and saw the man sprinting soundlessly toward him across the street, a clublike object in his fist. Shunxi ran as fast as he could, holding the bag even tighter in his panic.

He got barely ten paces before something slammed his ankle out from underneath him. He crashed forward, sprawling, scarlet feathers spilling onto the dark asphalt.

Stunned for a second, Shunxi regained his focus, and struggled to pull himself to his hands and knees, his ankle tendon cut, his foot flapping obscenely from a pant leg gleaming with dark blood. The man stood in front of him, a small ax in his hand, absently tapping the back of the ax head against his palm as he looked down at the deliveryman, wreathed in fluffy boas.

Shunxi lifted his open palm to the man and stammered out, "Please! No money! No have money!" Ignoring him, the man was examining the feathers.

This wasn't about money.

Weeping and gasping in pain and terror, Shunxi began to crawl, pulling his mangled foot. The man stood, stepped quickly over the feathers, and came up behind Shunxi as he scrambled toward the light of the intersection.

The man had no intention of letting him go. He kicked Shunxi's good leg out from underneath him, sending him facedown into the gutter.

Coming to his senses, Shunxi opened his mouth to scream, but the man stomped one foot down onto his back, then smashed the hatchet blade into the back of Shunxi's head. He held it in place for a short while, riding the rhythmic shudders; when the convulsions slowed, he pressed the head down into the gutter with his foot, stepped back, and gave a quick twist to free the blade from the skull.

He walked back to the bag and squatted. He tore the rest of the scarlet marabou feathers out of the bag, scattering them in the street, then looked through the bagged peacock feathers with care. Some of the feathers had been bloodied, and in others the vanes were clumped together from damp and grime, but the deeper feathers were pristine. He selected two packages, each with a dozen perfect plumes of iridescent emerald green and royal blue, then walked on down toward the East River.

Jenner woke to his name, the blanket tangled around his chest, his legs bare and chilly. She was standing next to the couch, wearing a T-shirt.

"Jenner," she said again.

"Are you okay?"

"Please come and sleep in the bed with me."

His head sank back into the pillow.

"Please, Jenner. For me. I can't sleep."

He stood, and followed her to the bed. She slid over, all the way over to the far edge of the bed, and held the sheets open. When he hesitated, she patted the empty space next to her.

He climbed in; as he reached for the lamp, he saw an almost empty highball glass of whisky on the bedside table. He turned off the light, then turned back to her. He looked at her, lying there looking at him; in the dark, her hair was edged with silver. He turned away, and she pressed up against him, a slender arm over his chest. She fell asleep before him, and as she did, he realized he was stroking her wrist and the back of her hand.

When Jenner woke, the sun was glaring through intermittent drizzle, glinting off the wet streets toward the East River.

He needed to see the crime scene photographs from the Pittsburgh crew. The autopsy photos were sloppy Polaroids shot in some local hospital morgue or funeral parlor, the wider shots showing too little, the close-ups hopelessly out of focus. He waited until 9:00 a.m. to call, which was a mistake—Dowling had already been summoned to a four-car pileup on I-81.

The morning passed quickly. Ana seemed quite cheerful, almost smug. She went through his CDs and pronounced Jenner's taste Not Bad (she means *for my age*, he thought). She settled on Radiohead, and hummed along as she made the bed, badly, and tidied the kitchen, putting the plates and dishes back in the wrong cupboards.

Jun stopped by, clearly wanting to meet Ana. Jenner was in the middle of introducing them when Rad Garcia called: Jenner took the phone into the TV room, leaving the two to get acquainted. The ID section had matched fingerprints from the Romen scene to the partials from East Seventh Street. Andie Delore's preliminary tox screen was negative, the rape kit negative for semen.

Jenner thought for a second, then said, "One thing: there was no sign of forced entry in Romen—it looks like she let him in. I'm thinking that that cop trick may be part of his MO."

Garcia said that he'd get the word out through Public Affairs, and tossed in a couple of "Detective Jenner" cracks before he hung up.

Jenner called Mr. Delore in Boston, already back at the office. The attorney was his blustery self again, brisk and matter-of-fact. He muttered, "Of course!" when told about the negative tox, and "Thank God," to the results of the sexual assault workup; he didn't ask after Ana.

Now that there were known victims in two states, he wanted to know if the feds would get involved in the investigation. Jenner said the local investigators would make the call after reviewing the issue—the cases had only just been linked.

He asked if Jenner thought involving the Bureau was a good idea; Jenner said he wasn't sure that the FBI could add anything to the New York City investigation, and the state police were doing the right things in Pennsylvania—Dowling was good, and the criminalists seemed on top of things. Besides, any involvement by the feds would come at the cost of putting local noses out of joint.

Delore said that he'd think about it, and seek counsel from his colleagues. In the meantime, he thanked Jenner for a job well done, and thanked him for his discretion and sensitivity. He asked for a report in writing and an invoice, then told Jenner he could consider this engagement finished, adding that he'd be recommending him to attorneys in need of a forensic expert.

Outside in the main room, Ana had switched to Outkast, and was singing along to "Ms. Jackson." Jun was sprawled on the couch, this time in brown cords, a long sage green knit sweater vest, and the gray Kangol, grinning.

Jun called out, "Dude! Your houseguest can't sing for shit! I feel sorry for you!"

"Just be glad *I'm* not singing."

Ana said, "Jenner, what's a kogal? Jun says he's dating one, and he won't tell me what that is."

"A very colorful Japanese girl who likes to wear expensive clothes that other people pay for. He's joking—Kimi's great."

Jun snickered. His girlfriend was coming over for lunch, then they were going shopping in NoLIta, where the boutiques were swankier than in the East Village and trendier than in SoHo. Jun ordered scallion pancakes, crabmeat and pork juicy buns, and barbecued pork from Star of the East, which he said was definitely the best Shanghainese restaurant in the city; he was playing the New York Asian card, showing off for Ana.

Jun was at the door paying the deliveryman when Bobby Dowling called. Jenner took the phone back into the quiet of the TV room.

Dowling listened to Jenner's news, congratulated him on nailing the link, and told him to hand the case file off to Garcia. They chatted a bit about the feds, about how they do it in NYC, and how other jurisdictions, even in small towns, sometimes do it better. "But, Doc, for chrissakes, don't tell anyone I said that!"

The sound of laughter rose from the kitchen. Jenner said, "Well, Bobby. It's been good working with you—good luck with this case."

"You're out then, Doc? I know you signed on as a consultant, but I figured you'd want to see it through."

"I kind of do, I kind of don't. The Delores have buried their daughter now. I think my part in this is finished."

"I wish I could say the same thing, but I have a feeling things will pick up for our investigation tomorrow, after the funeral. I thought I'd go, show the family some respect; I think a lot of the guys will."

Jenner wasn't following. "I'm sorry, Bobby—what funeral?"

"Sunday Smith's. Her parents got back into town yesterday, they're burying her tomorrow."

"God! I thought she was buried weeks ago."

"No, sorry, my fault, I should have told you she wasn't buried. Her family's Mormon, and they were in Asia, testifying or whatever they call it. It took forever to even notify them, let alone for them to get back stateside."

Jenner thought for a second.

"Can I have a look at the body? Where is it?"

"Romen Funeral Chapel, just outside of town." He paused. "As far as seeing the body . . . well, what do you mean by 'have a look'? Shouldn't be a problem for you to examine her, but if you're talking about opening her up, that's something else."

Jenner thought about the autopsy report; if the autopsy protocol was so piss-poor, God only knew what they'd missed.

"It kills me to say this, but I think she needs a proper autopsy. No disrespect, but that first pathologist was clearly way out of his depth."

"Well, Doc, that could be a problem. You've got no jurisdiction— heck, you're not even technically an ME anymore. They're good people, the parents, but they've been through a lot. Their daughter had her head cut off, and they just flew ten thousand miles to bury her; I just don't see them going for it."

Jenner could hear the detective clicking on his ballpoint pen.

"Bobby, look: speak to them, see if they'll agree. You know how to talk to people. I wouldn't ask if it wasn't important."

Dowling sighed. "I'll ask. But these are fucking pious people—I think the only thing that matters to them is that their daughter is with God now."

"Tell them this man will continue to kill until he is stopped, that other mothers and fathers will lose their daughters. That this could help stop him."

"I'll try. I'll go over there now and sit down with them. I'll call as soon as I have an answer."

Kimi had arrived, dazzling in her platinum blond wig, frosted peach lipstick, and an electric blue smock tied at the waist with a vibrant orange sash. Her orange go-go boots had at least four inches of platform. Jenner winked at her, then sat. They'd started lunch while Jenner was on the phone, but had set a plate for him.

Jenner announced that he might be going to Pennsylvania; if he went, it would probably be overnight. He casually suggested they keep Ana company. He wouldn't be leaving for a couple of hours, so they had time to go shopping, at least for a while.

After lunch, Jun and Kimi put on their coats and sunglasses and said good-bye. Kimi held the door open, and turned to ask Ana if she was coming. Ana shook her head, suddenly wan. She gave Kimi a little hug, then closed the door behind them. When she turned to Jenner, he thought she might start to cry. He put an arm around her shoulder; as her arms slipped around his neck, it felt almost natural, the press of her body against his, almost as if it belonged there.

\* \* \*

Bobby Dowling called a couple of hours later: the Smiths had agreed to let Jenner do a second autopsy, but had stipulated that he couldn't examine her head internally. Dowling would meet Jenner at the Gas'n'Go just off the Romen exit on I–80 at 8:00 p.m.

He left the city in the mid-afternoon, picking up a rental car at National on East Twelfth Street. Past Wilkes-Barre, the fields were covered with snow and the roads were black and slick, the snow along the berm melting and dirty. Near dark, the sun broke through, and the western sky looked like mercury, bright and dense and heavy in patches.

Dowling was late. The night had brought the cold, and Jenner shivered as he climbed out of the car into the bright light of the overhead lamppost at the Gas'n'Go. He went into the convenience store, newly fitted with acid green siding, a sharp contrast to the semi-derelict gas station. He nuked two frozen burritos and ate them in the car, washing them down with a can of Coke, regretting it immediately afterward.

He found a PBS station broadcasting a concert of Satie piano pieces, and turned up the heater. At around 9:30 p.m., Dowling's cruiser pulled into the station. Dowling was in uniform, a snappy wide-brimmed hat over his hefty winter coat. He walked across the plaza, one gloved hand outstretched in apology, the other holding up a black case to show Jenner the camera they'd given him to document any findings.

After exchanging greetings, they got back in their cars, and Jenner followed Dowling onto country roads. Away from the highway, the light died out rapidly. They passed a few farmhouses, isolated in the night and the snow, but little else until Jenner saw the funeral chapel floodlit in the distance. It was a fairly sizable brick building with a colonial white clapboard front, low columns, and a small steeple-like structure on its roof. It was nondenominational and looked churchlike, but not so much that it would put off the nonbeliever.

The funeral director, an older black man in black slacks and a short-sleeved white dress shirt without tie, opened the door for them. Mr. Divell was polite and helpful but clearly not enthusiastic—Jenner would be creating more work for him, and, as he told them several times, he had elected not to pass the costs of the additional labor on to the family.

"I'll set her up in the embalming room for you, Doctor. I am hoping that you brought your own equipment with you—we are a small facility, and we obviously cannot provide the sort of accoutrements to which you are accustomed in your institute."

He had a grave air and an obvious fondness for language. His voice was surprisingly deep and oaky for a small man, and he pronounced the word *accoutrements* in the French manner.

"Thank you for taking the time, Mr. Divell. All I really need is a disposable apron, a pair of gloves, and a scalpel."

Mr. Divell gave a slight nod of satisfaction.

"These things, we can provide you with."

Barbara Wexler got off the 6 train at Twenty-third Street instead of Union Square. She could pick up *Paris Match* at Dina Magazine Superstore on Twenty-first, and she needed new batteries, and Alkit Camera on lower Park Avenue sold AAs in packs of ten for pretty cheap. She couldn't remember whether they closed at 6:00 p.m. or later: it was already 6:15. Her gamble paid off—Alkit was open until 9:00 p.m.

Leaving the shop, she realized how much colder it had gotten. She walked down Park into Union Square. The north plaza, in summer filled with local farmers selling fresh fruit and flowers, was barren, empty except for a few skateboarders. She turned left on Seventeenth and walked toward her apartment, between Second and Third, opposite Stuyvesant Park.

Even in winter, she liked the park, with its heavy Victorian cast-iron fencing and concentric oval paths. On its west side, it was bordered by the Friends Seminary, a handsome meetinghouse school in red brick and white trim, the wide proportions elegant confirmation of its Quaker origins. The park could be a little bit creepy—a lot of homeless guys hung out there—but it was a pocket of nature in the middle of the city, and if it wasn't Michigan, it was a little breath of fresh air among the relentless press of buildings.

Nearing the park, she narrowed her eyes and scanned the path ahead for weirdos, but couldn't see much in the shadows. Hurrying to the sidewalk across from the park, she didn't notice the man standing by a large suitcase, studying the church service schedule; if she had, she wouldn't have given him more than a second's thought.

While her building, a prewar three-story brownstone, had a nice view over Stuyvesant Park, her apartment was a dingy studio toward the back on the third floor. It was a residential block, but both the ground and second floors were offices, a methadone clinic on the first floor, with two shrinks splitting the second-floor floor-through; she actually wasn't too worried by the clinic, but had made a big deal about it when she was bargaining for her rent.

She collected her mail—junk, mostly—then set off up the stairs. From the second to the third floor there was an abrupt change in the upkeep, the way roads change the moment you cross county lines from an affluent to a poor one. In the gloom of the top landing, the runners were threadbare, and the area behind the balustrade was stacked with broken air conditioners and office chairs. The building was pretty empty at night; sometimes, when the wind picked up, or the old house settled a bit, it could be a little unnerving.

But with fresh paint and Pottery Barn furniture, she'd made her little apartment warm and cheery. She opened the door with a smile; her cat was in the entryway, pacing in front of the little table where she put her keys.

She hung her coat on the rack, the cat pressing against her ankles, purring. She glanced at her answering machine: four messages, all old. She didn't know why she kept Brad's last message—there was nothing romantic in it. He didn't even sound friendly.

She was such a victim! She smiled, and felt good about herself for at least having moved on to the point where she could now smile about her relationship with that asshole. All the same, she thought, it would have been nice to come in out of the cold after a long day to find at least one message waiting.

She put her magazines (she'd splurged and bought a copy of *L'Express* in addition to the *Paris Match*) next to her one chair—another splurge, an oversize, overstuffed armchair. She had almost not bought the *Match*— she could have lived without another tribute to Johnny Hallyday—but there was a good-size piece with lots of photos about Princess Stephanie of Monaco. More than one person had told her she looked a little like Princess Stephanie, and sometimes, after a couple of glasses of chardonnay, she thought so, too. A little.

She pulled out a can of cat food for Milo, then cursed as she remembered she had to work on her paper on Ionesco—it was taking her forever. She really didn't "get" him—absurd is funny, sure, but she didn't think his writing was such a big deal. She was a French major because she loved *France*, not because she really cared about modern French literature.

The buzzer surprised her. Almost 7:00 p.m. She was wary—sometimes addicts showed up at the clinic after hours, and a couple of times she'd had to call the police.

She pressed down the intercom button and said hello.

"Hi. This is Detective Willoughby of the Ninth Precinct detective squad. We're looking for a Barbara Wexler."

Surprised and worried, Barbara answered, "This is she."

"We're making inquiries into the death of the Hutchins student, and we're hoping you might be able to help us. I'm sorry to bother you so late."

She could hear his walkie-talkie crackling as he talked.

"Detective, I don't think I know her. I wasn't in any of her classes."

"No, ma'am, we know. But there's an issue about the pattern of facilities usage, specifically the Stevens Center gym on Thirteenth. We know you go there regularly, and we have a couple of questions. I promise it will only take a minute."

She hesitated; then she heard his radio again, and told herself to stop being silly.

"Of course, Detective. I'd be happy to help in any way I can."

She went to wait by the door. She smoothed her hair in the mirror—maybe he was cute. Maybe he was cute and *single*! She smiled; she could be such a damn *girl*.

She heard his steps coming up toward her on the stairs, and had to suppress a giggle of excitement.

The embalming room was larger than Jenner had expected. There were two stainless steel embalming tables, one of them piled with packaged shrouds and stacked white batting. Metal and glass cabinets ran along the pale green walls, signed inventory sheets taped neatly to their sides. There was a series of steel sinks behind the tables, and a large desk sat at the far end of the room.

The smell of formalin was fairly strong, but the ventilation system kept it from becoming overpowering. Dowling stood in the doorway, hesitant.

"Jesus, Bobby! Stop being such a pussy! She's already embalmed."

"Doc, I don't know what's worse, the smell of formaldehyde or the smell of decomp—"

Divell emerged from the corridor behind Dowling, pushing a gurney covered in plastic sheeting. The cop squeezed against the wall to let him pass.

Divell positioned the gurney between the two tables and then removed the shroud from the body. Jenner saw that the head had been skillfully reattached, the seams barely puckered by the twine suturing.

Divell sprayed a little water onto the embalming table where Jenner would work, a flat sheet of metal perforated with large drainage holes. He then leaned over and grabbed the girl's arm as Jenner lifted the head of the gurney, allowing Divell to slide the body onto the table.

The girl's condition was fair. The vascular access incision under the right collarbone was tightly sutured, there were barely visible cotton plugs in the nostrils, and, lifting up her lip, Jenner found a gingival suture lashing the mouth closed. The hair and eye makeup had yet to be done, but Divell's team had used a colored embalming fluid, foundation, and lipstick, and her face looked almost natural. The funeral director had done a good job, and Jenner said so.

The autopsy incision, too, looked as if it had been nicely sealed, but the chest was covered by a waterproof Inco Pad taped down along the edges, tacked with sutures at the corners.

Divell said in his deep voice, "Doctor, I see you're inspecting the materials and methods we chose to use for closure of the chest area. The injuries were somewhat unprecedented, and it became apparent that a complete cutaneous seal was impossible. We managed as best we could."

Jenner nodded, and Divell gestured to the head of the table.

"You have observed that Ms. Smith's head, previously severed from her body, has been fully reattached. The cranium has been stabilized on the neck through the use of a length of wooden dowel. Obviously, the neck incision will have to be concealed by careful clothing choice. But I feel that we have done the best job possible under the circumstances."

Jenner nodded appreciatively and murmured, "Indeed."

"Doctor, I'd like to ask you to preserve our workmanship as best you can, to whatever extent will not conflict with your professional responsibilities."

"I'll certainly do my best, Mr. Divell."

"I believe you, sir. The gowns, protective gloves, and disposable scalpels are to your left."

With that, Divell left the room; he didn't actually bow, but he gave the impression.


Ana gave the corkscrew another twist, which wedged the cork solidly against the neck of the bottle. Shit. Jun, her guardian for the night, was watching a video in the TV room with Kimi; she should have asked him to do it.

She pulled it out, but she'd shredded the cork. She screwed it in again as straight as she could, then tried wiggling it, but that just sent showers of shavings into the wine. Oh well. She'd just use the tea strainer when she poured.

She took the bottle, the strainer, and the glass, and went into Jenner's bedroom. She turned on his stereo; the CD was something soft and repetitive, and it sounded good in the quiet of his bedroom. She sieved herself a glass of wine, then went to the window. She sipped, looking out over the brick tenements north of Little Italy. Beyond NoLIta, the East River. And beyond that, Brooklyn. And beyond that, the rest of the world that wasn't New York City.

She lay down on Jenner's bed. She felt small on it, small and alone.

She wished he were there. She should talk to him. He was obviously pretty fucked up; maybe if she could get him to talk, he'd feel better. He'd feel better, and maybe be glad she was there.

She drained the glass, set the strainer on it, and poured another; she was feeling warm now, a little tipsy. She'd just about finished Jenner's whisky, so she'd switched to wine. And now she was getting drunk.

On wine—how fucking *grown up*!

She'd grown up in Orlando—Silver Lake, the nicest part, but still Orlando. Orlando was a party town, where everyone had a drug of choice, from the little kids tweaking on Coke and Skittles before their feet even hit the tarmac at Disney to lawyers doing rails of blow in expensive restaurant bathrooms. And she was one of them, too, a party girl. And proud of it.

She swirled the wine in the glass, watched the liquid slosh around. When she first started drinking, vodka was her drink. She used to sneak out at night to meet her friend Carmen, who'd wait for her at the end of the gravel drive, hidden behind the big magnolias in her Jetta convertible. They'd go to warehouse parties and dance all night to DJ Icy and Sandra Collins. Sometimes, for a laugh, they'd go to crappy clubs where the DJs played trashy Euro-trance; they'd let the businessmen buy them drinks, and then they'd dance with each other in white foam five feet deep, out of their minds on Ecstasy, laughing at the men who gaped at them as their wet clothes turned transparent.

And now . . . she was drunk on *wine*! She felt like she should be wearing pearls and a twinset. She smirked. One more glass.

She read the label out loud as best she could: "Puligny-Montrachet." She sipped, and even tipsy knew it was good; she'd remember it, maybe impress someone. She turned the bottle to read the back label.

"Whoa . . . forty dollars . . ."

Fuck. She didn't know it was that expensive; she hoped he wouldn't be pissed at her. She gulped it down, then lay back. The cat jumped up and rubbed against her, purring as she pressed his little head to her side. He climbed on her chest and nuzzled her chin until she giggled and pushed him away; later she relented, letting him curl up against her arm and tip his head on her shoulder.

She was starting to feel pretty wasted now. Drowsy.

The cat was asleep.

She would finish the bottle, then hide it so he didn't see.


Dowling had edged closer. Barely—he stood in the doorway, bracing for the worst. Within a few minutes, Jenner had almost forgotten the cop was there.

The original prosector's external description was adequate—hair and eye color, ears pierced four times on the right, twice on the left, small butterfly tattoo over the left pelvic brim.

Jenner was eager to see the wounds.

He started with the face, sponging off the foundation makeup, glad that Divell wasn't there to watch his work being undone. The face and upper neck were generally free of injury, but the lipstick wiped away to reveal discoloration of the lower lip. Jenner rolled the lip downward; on the inner surface, a split in the lip had been sealed with embalmer's wax, the tissue nearby discolored gray. He remembered Andie Delore's bruised mouth.

There was no way to be sure how she got the wound, whether she'd fallen forward onto the floor or if the killer had punched her in the face.

A straightforward fall would probably have caused bruising of the outer lip, nose, or cheek as well; it was likely a blow.

He imagined the girl at home, reading or watching TV when the doorbell rang. The unexpected caller would have surprised her, and yet she opened the door for him—did he use the cop line, or did he just quickly overpower her, punch her in the mouth, force his way in? The setting was remote, unlike with Andie Delore.

Jenner tore open a disposable scalpel package and cut the anchor sutures at the corners of the Inco Pad. He peeled up the horizontal band of surgical tape at the bottom and then lifted the pad upward, stripping it from the chest to expose the wound.

The chest and abdomen were soaking in cavity fluid, the formaldehyde solution used to preserve the inner organs. When Jenner uncovered the wound, the formaldehyde fumes rose in a vicious blast; the two stood back for a while, nostrils burning, eyes watering, until Dowling found the extractor fan switch.

When the room had cleared, they went back to the body.

It was an extraordinary injury. Two oblique, gaping wounds of the central chest, crossing to create an X shape. Each limb of the X might have been a separate wound, as the intersection point was extremely ragged; without knowing the inflicting weapon, it would be hard to tell.

He turned to Dowling. "Hey, do me a favor. There's a magnifying glass in my coat pocket—can you pass it to me?"

Jenner examined the wound more closely; under the hand lens, the edges of the wound looked striped. Jenner leaned back a little to get a wider view, and the striping pattern became more apparent. In the lower right limb of the X, he could make out a row of subtle, parallel, wedge-shaped abrasions along the wound margin.

"Bobby, I think we've got something here."

The detective stood behind him, peering over his shoulder.

Jenner turned his head. "You'll have to come here if you really want to see it."

"Why don't you just describe it to me, Doc?"

Jenner snorted, then said, "God, Bobby—there are gnats in Africa with bigger balls than you." He pointed to the wound. "These are patterned injuries here. They look pretty horrible, but they're shallow—they don't enter the chest cavity. There's no vital reaction here, either, so they were inflicted after death."

Dowling nodded. "Well, that's something, at least."

"I think they were made by some kind of instrument with moving teeth; inside the X, the teeth are moving, and they create this wide scrape along the side as they cut. Here's the important part, down here in the lower part. This row of parallel scrapes, about half an inch apart."

From behind him, Dowling muttered, "Great. I'll take your word for it."

"Well, you're going to have to photograph it, too. Shoot it up close to show the individual elements, but also far enough away to show the pattern. We need to see both the wood and the trees, okay?"

Armed with a purpose, Dowling became more comfortable. He popped open the clasps on the camera case, assembled the camera, and set about documenting the injuries.

"I'm seeing what you mean, Doc. Good eye. Any idea what he used?"

The flash went off again.

"Something between a large electric knife and a small chainsaw. Nothing too powerful, though, or the skin would be more chewed up. An electrical instrument would also explain that misty blood-spatter pattern. I think that he shut off the weapon before he pulled it out of the wound, which created the imprints of the teeth. Even if she were already dead, the speed of the tooth motion would likely spray the blood all over."

"How about a hedge trimmer? Would that do it?"

Jenner handed Dowling a short, L-shaped ruler, developed by the American Board of Forensic Odontologists to document bite-mark and other dental evidence. With the ABFO ruler in the shot, it would be easier to get a sense of the actual size and shape of the injury from the photo.

"You know, that actually makes more sense than an electric knife. The knives are designed to cut, to leave smooth edges, whereas a hedge trimmer is a much coarser tool."

"I keep telling ya, Doc—Mrs. Dowling didn't raise no cretin."

After Dowling had finished, Jenner turned his attention to the trunk. The organs were inside the torso in a bag; he removed them, and examined them on a side table. Jenner focused on the neck and the genital organs, areas where inexperienced pathologists tend to miss subtle trauma; there were no injuries in either region. She wasn't pregnant, and she had never given birth.

He turned her over gently. Her hair was long and dark, and Jenner gathered it in his fist and swept it upward. In the back, the suturing wasn't as neat as at the front—it didn't need to be. He cut the coarse embalmer's twine and carefully opened the suture line.

When the embalmer had attached the neck to the trunk, the skin had been partly tucked into the wound. As Jenner removed the sutures and eased the head forward, the wound seemed to blossom. The wound edges were clean, with little scraping; it was a high incision, running into the hairline of the nape of her neck. Jenner wasn't surprised that the original prosector had failed to shave the base of the scalp to examine it properly—forensic pathologists called it "the distraction of the dramatic": the guy had been so focused on the brutality of the injury that he'd missed the findings associated with it.

As the skin released from the wound, a neat row of dark figures unfurled along the upper margin of transection.

He turned to Dowling and said, "*Bingo.*"

He bent over the back of the neck with the hand lens. Now close behind him, Dowling blocked his light. "Move, please, Bobby."

Dowling came round to his side.

Under the lens, the figures turned into a little parade of black ciphers. The killer had taken his time, neatly engraving them one by one onto the skin. There was no vital reaction, no bleeding—this had been postmortem, done after death. They'd have to be—she couldn't have stayed still for this.

The markings had a leathery, dry surface, the skin burned to char. There were variations in the form of each repeated character, so he had done it freehand, rather than with a series of individual brands. The

elements of each cipher—verticals, horizontals, obliques, and curves—
were evenly burned, making the instrument unlikely to have been a
tool repeatedly reheated prior to application of each element; the only
instrument Jenner could think of that would produce burns of that
detail and consistency was a soldering iron, a very fine one, the sort used
in computer and electronics repair.

He leaned back and held the lens out for the detective to look.

Dowling asked, "What is it? Russian?"

"I don't think it's Russian. Greek, maybe?"

Jenner pulled a sheet of plastic wrap from his case. When Dowling had
finished photographing, he placed the plastic over the wound, and did
his best to trace the ciphers with a felt-tip pen. It was difficult, since the
head was now mobile, and the lower parts of the markings were caught
in the wound, and obscured by drying in the skin, but he did his best.

He held the sheet up to Dowling, who gave a low whistle. "Nice, Doc."

It was 1:00 a.m. They were almost finished. Jenner positioned her on
her side so that the embalmer could reseal the wound.

"Okay, Bobby. I need you to stand by the lights for a second. When I
say now, switch them all off."

Jenner took out his Maglite and turned it on, setting it so that the
light was soft.

"Okay, hit the lights."

He lifted her left wrist and slowly turned the hands under the dim
yellow light, inspecting them on both sides, first the palm, then the
backs of the hands, then the fingers, one by one.

"There they are."

When he turned the lights back on, Dowling saw Jenner was smiling.

Jenner showed Dowling the dental imprints over the bases of the
thumbs. He'd worried that the embalming process might have rein-
flated the tissues and destroyed the depressions, but there they were.
The killer's teeth were there, on the thumbs. Far too late for salivary
epithelial DNA, but his teeth were there. Even Dowling could make out
that overlapping incisor.

*I've got you, you bastard. You are mine.*

\*   \*   \*

Jenner sat alone at the desk, writing his notes. It was going on 2:00 a.m., and Dowling, after finishing the photographs and promising to have an odontologist document the bite marks, had headed home to the new Mrs. Dowling. Divell had taken care of the resuturing himself, and had done it surprisingly quickly; for a small man, he hefted the body about with ease.

Jenner was still writing when Divell left, admonishing him to "please be certain that you have extinguished all of the lighting prior to your departure."

Jenner wrote his last line of notes and then stretched, looking around. He liked the quiet. He tried to imagine what it would be like to spend an entire life working in a place like this; he couldn't.

On the wall opposite him was a promotional calendar from an embalming chemical supplier. In it, a gaunt Saint Dismas, the patron saint of funeral directors, knelt in prayer in front of the cross on which he would be hung, his eyes raised to heaven, his bony hands clasped fervently. Next to Dismas was a portrait of another patron saint of the funeral industry, Joseph of Arimathea, hands again pressed together, eyes locked on silver rays coming from a cloudy sky. No doubt accidentally, the two images had been hung so that both saints' lines of sight focused on an electric bug zapper high on the wall.

Jenner tilted the chair back and looked at them, amused.

And then stopped being amused.

The hands. The position of their hands. Praying fingers, the bases of the thumbs pressed together; Jenner could almost see the lips curling back, exposing the crooked teeth as they bit down onto the bound hands.

*Bingo.*

Exhilarated, he drove well over the speed limit most of the way back to the city. The traffic was surprisingly steady for the hour, an endless stream of tractor-trailers in both directions, all going too fast in the moonlight.

Jenner was sure he was right. The killer had forced both girls into a praying posture, bound their wrists together, then bit them.

Who prayed like that? Christians, obviously. Muslims pray with open hands, he thought. Jews? Jenner didn't know how Jews prayed.

But perhaps it wasn't a religious posture at all—maybe he wanted them to beg, to assume a universal position of supplication or submission. But that didn't seem right. A person could beg in any position, and this seemed too stylized to be anything other than a religious gesture.

Smith's family was religious. How do Mormons pray? Could this have been something related to Smith's family, enmity toward Smith's family?

But then how would Andie Delore fit in? Tony Delore had said he'd never heard of Sunday Smith. The Delores were Catholic, but Delore didn't strike Jenner as a religious man, and Jenner had seen none of the trappings of faith in Andie's apartment. The Russian triptych, but that seemed purely decorative.

He pulled back, trying to reestablish perspective. The million-dollar question was: How did he choose them? He went back to basic criminology, remembering the basic criteria for victimology drummed daily into the heads of police cadets around the world: Availability, Vulnerability, and Desirability.

Clearly, the killer had been able to gain access to both girls. Both had been vulnerable—he would have made sure of that. He'd probably stalked them for a while, learning their habits, confirming their access and their vulnerability. Desirability was the key.

What was it about Sunday Smith and Andie Delore that made him desire them? What characteristics did they share that made him track them, hunt them, butcher them?

They were both students at Hutchins. They were both female, both young, both had dark hair. Both were white.

He came back to religion. Neither seemed overtly religious, but what about the killer? Serial killers tend to kill within their ethnicity; do they also kill within their faith?

He reached the Lincoln Tunnel at 4:00 a.m., and was home before five. Jun was fast asleep in the TV room. Jenner shook him gently, then let him out, closing the door quietly behind him.

The loft was dark. He was exhausted, but too wired to sleep. He brushed his teeth and undressed quietly, and went to the couch; Ana had put away the sheets and pillow he'd been using.

He walked over to the bed and watched her sleep, curled onto one side, a pillow held to her breast, the cat sprawled against her shoulder. She was so lovely, her face soft, her hair tousled. She breathed out heavily and turned, and as she turned he saw her hand held a steak knife.

He sat down next to her, stroked her hair, and whispered, "Here, kitty. Let me take this." Her eyes flickered open and she smiled at him, and relaxed her grip on the knife.

She closed her eyes as he put his arm around her.


Jenner lay in bed, hands behind his head, looking up at the ceiling. Ana was telling him about her big plan for the day: she would spend it in the TV room watching *La Dolce Vita*—she was going to watch all the Fellini in his collection, because he was Andie's favorite director, and watching his movies made her feel like she was back with Andie, if only for a while.

Maybe she was safe now, Jenner thought. It had been five days since the murder: the killer would know that by now she'd have given any evidence she had to the police, would have given statements, looked at mug shots. He had little practical reason to interfere with her. Maybe just the threat, the terror swarming in behind the threat, maybe that was enough.

But this wasn't a normal man, a man who cared about "practicality." This man tortured, murdered, and mutilated without gloves; he knew he was leaving his fingerprints everywhere, and he just didn't care. This man would do whatever he wanted.

She was lying there with her arm on his shoulder, her other hand gesturing expressively as she talked at him. Looking at her, he knew his own motives were hardly pure. He'd grown used to having Ana around. No, that too was dishonest: he actively *liked* it. He liked being with her.

But when they caught the killer, when they killed the killer, when the killer killed himself, it would all be over. She'd go back to school; she'd see him from time to time, but it would soon begin to feel like an obligation to her. She'd feel weird about having shared his bed. At least they hadn't had sex.

*Would* she feel weird about it? He was almost twenty years older than her, more than enough to horrify her friends, enough to keep the guilt churning softly inside him. But she was very different from the girls he'd grown up with, so comfortable in her body, so unconcerned about showing it to him. Maybe it wouldn't feel at all weird to her.

He thought about the night before, driving back from Romen, the triumph of his discovery high in his heart, lying down next to her. He'd realized how much he wanted to touch her, to wake her up, stroke her, *own* her. He wanted her still, and he thought she might want him, too.

And then he recognized that all the way back from Romen, underneath all his excited speculation, he'd been thinking about fucking her, feeling that he'd really kind of *earned* it, hadn't he?

It was almost noon. He felt like a frustrated adolescent lying next to her, feigning politeness as he listened to her chatter, but covertly hungry and hard at the thought of her body.

This was ridiculous. He should get up.

He slipped out from under the covers, dragging the sheets over his lap. Ana clung onto him, giggling as she pretended not to let him go, her weight on his arm, dragging him back, making things worse. He waited a little; when it was safe, he stood up and pulled himself free of her grip.

He went to the kitchen and poured himself water. He watched her stand and wrap herself in the gray cashmere throw, then head into the bathroom. The sun, bright behind linen blinds, cast curious shadows on the living room wall; he thought about the markings on Sunday Smith's neck.

He took his scene bag, removed the tracings, and placed them side by side on his desk. The marks on Andie Delore's neck were repeated on the new tracing. They were the same alphabet, and it looked familiar. He was sure it wasn't Russian.

He sat at the desk. So what did he have? A religious element in the modus operandi, and an unusual character set. That this was some kind of writing with religious significance, maybe a scripture of sort, probably Christian given the praying hands. But what was it? Greek, Aramaic, maybe? What the fuck did Aramaic even *look* like?

He remembered a show of ancient manuscripts at the Metropolitan Museum of Art two or three years back, *Sacred Texts*, something like that. There would be an exhibition catalogue in the gift shop.

He showered and dressed. When he poked his head into the TV room, she was sprawled on the daybed, half awake in front of the TV, Marcello Mastroianni buzzing around Rome in his Triumph. She sent him on his way with a little hug, locking the door behind him. He told Jun he was going out, and then walked over to the Spring Street station and took the 6 uptown to Eighty-sixth Street.

He called Rad from the platform pay phone. The university provost, who, Rad observed, had known about the killing in Pennsylvania but hadn't made the connection, had been informed that the two deaths were linked; he would alert the student body. It wouldn't be hard—the news would rocket through the campus, and the tabloids, in their own special way, would make sure the rest of the city knew.

\* \* \*

At the Met, the vast banners draped between the tall Corinthian columns had never looked so vibrant. It was a beautiful day, and the sunshine and warmth had lured crowds of tourists out of their hotels. The souvenir sellers, like camp followers after an army, were out in full force on the plaza in front of the museum.

Jenner walked up the steps and into the echoing marble of the crowded entrance hall. The lobby was busy, and the gift shop busier than usual. He went through into the book section, quieter than the main room, but couldn't find what he was looking for.

He stopped one of the salespeople on the floor, but as he described the book he was looking for, the clerk stood there blankly. Luckily, one of the managers overheard.

"What you're looking for is *Sacred Rites, Sacred Writing*, sir. But I'm afraid we're out of stock. Manuscripts and documents don't tend to be big sellers, and the print run wasn't very big—I'm afraid we're not expecting it back in. Maybe you could find it on Alibris or eBay. I'm sorry."

Jenner thanked her. He'd try the main public library on Forty-second Street.

He walked out into the sun and made his way through the people sitting on the steps and the impromptu portrait photography going on in front of the building.

This was annoying. He needed the book quickly, and while the library would have a copy, who knew how long it would take to get his hands on it?

He looked around him. Everyone seemed so happy, thrilled at a gorgeous day in the greatest city on earth. Jenner relaxed a little. He should lighten up. Jun kept telling him that, and Jun was right. He decided to walk through the park.

Making his way through a knot of nursery-schoolers and their minders gathered around the bronze bears near the playground entrance, he headed through the Glade. At the Mall, he sat on a bench and watched the passersby strolling down the allée of elms.

It felt odd to sit outside. But apparently only to him—everyone he saw seemed cheery and bright.

He stretched back, tried to get himself into the spirit of the day.

He'd always liked the view over toward Central Park West, with its expensive doorman buildings capped with Gothic follies and strange ziggurats, like some lost kingdom in a Tarzan movie. It would be pretty great to live on the park, he thought. Although he could never live on the Upper West Side.

He stood suddenly. Simon Lescure.

Simon Lescure, the man who could solve his problems in a second, lived just across the park in a handsome white-stone town house on the corner of West Seventy-seventh.

Simon was one of Julie's publishing friends, one of the interesting ones. An absolute Anglophile, always immaculate in bespoke English suits, shirts, and shoes, Lescure was probably the most prominent lexicographer in the United States. He was a language pundit, a regular in print and on TV; and he lived a ten-minute walk from the Mall.

The elevator attendant, in navy blue livery, waited in the elevator, watching Jenner through the open doors until Lescure appeared at his door.

"Edward Jenner . . ."

"Simon! It's *great* to see you!"

They shook hands firmly. Lescure was clearly pleased to see him, although too polite to ask the reason for his unexpected visit.

As Lescure put away his coat, Jenner glanced around. He'd visited Lescure's apartment once before, for a party. The living room had a huge picture window with a beautiful view out over the treetops of the park, and the kitchen was the biggest Jenner had ever seen in New York. Lescure lived there with his wife and their three daughters, all of whom they'd named for characters in Willa Cather stories.

Jenner declined Lescure's offer of a drink, and sketched out his situation quickly, knowing it would fascinate Lescure.

Lescure savored the problem like a connoisseur inhaling the heady scent of a forbidden Cohiba. "Ah, Edward. Most intriguing . . . Most intriguing indeed!"

He removed his wire-rimmed glasses and, producing a linen handkerchief from his pocket, polished them with a flourish, then put them back on. "Come, Edward. Let's go to the library. I believe I can help you."

The library, at the end of a long hallway in black-and-white checkerboard tile, had an elaborate doorway framed by Ionic columns; Jenner remembered it as the coat room for Lescure's parties.

Lescure said, "Of course, this would be easier if you had the documents, the, uh, *evidence* in question. It's outside my area of expertise, but I do have some familiarity with ancient languages."

He stood in front of a bookcase, drumming his fingers on the case of a leather-bound encyclopedia, perhaps already anticipating the next lexicography conference, when he would tell the story of how he'd helped track a serial killer.

He shook his head impatiently, then paced along the crammed bookshelves, searching the rows with pursed lips and pointed index finger, finally selecting a volume.

"There you go, Edward. *Sacred Rites, Sacred Writings*. There are better references, of course, but that's the only one I have at home, I'm afraid."

He pulled over a chair for Jenner and then sat at his desk.

"If you see a text you recognize, I may be able to help you."

The book's designers had organized the plates chronologically, the earlier examples little more than flakes of papyrus with occasional legible figures. Jenner kept turning the pages. The exhibition had been global in reach, and there were examples of ancient documents from Korea, Japan, and China, as well as of Middle Eastern and European provenance. After poring over the pages for a few minutes, he showed Lescure the pages he felt were closest to what he remembered of the writing.

"Is it Greek?"

"No, Coptic. Interesting. Very interesting. Used by the Copts, Egyptian Christians. There are a couple of major forms—Bohairic and Sahidic—some minor forms, too, as I recall. Your error is understandable: the text is related to Ancient Greek. Alas, my Latin is strong, but I'm afraid I'm at sea with the Nilo-Hamitic languages."

He gave an elegantly hapless shrug.

Jenner thanked him, saying that even identifying the origin was a start.

"Well, of course, the person you need to speak with is my friend Patrick Sheehan, who's at Yardley College in Pennsylvania. He was actually one of the curators of this show. He won't just tell you definitively what it is, he'll tell you what it says and where it comes from. If it's ancient Coptic, there aren't many sources, and he knows them all."

Lescure seemed pleased. He polished his glasses again and said firmly, "Yes, Edward. Father Patrick Sheehan is your man."

The man lay on the floor, basking in the light streaming through the big casement windows. It was the first time since October that it had been warm enough for him to take down the heavy black cloth that sealed out the cold.

To sustain the experience, except for his hands, he hadn't washed afterward. He felt the sun baking the girl's blood onto his chest. He loved the way blood slowly crusted and flaked, the way it finally sifted off as powder. He'd learned to stay naked, to be *inside* the blood, for as long as possible afterward.

The days after a kill passed in a haze of indulgent pleasure. He felt agreeably spent. Relaxed. Mellow, almost. He looked at his Polaroids and wondered if they'd found the Wexler girl yet, what was left of her. This last one had gone well. No, this one had gone *perfectly*. He wanted them to find her; he liked thinking about that part. Liked it a lot.

For him, it wasn't really a killing until people *knew* about it. *That* was the completion—the moment when someone opens the door and discovers the body. He thought about the reaction, the horror. Nausea, even, if he'd gotten it right. He planned his work with his audience of one particularly privileged person—the Discoverer—always in mind. He thought a lot about the composition, particularly the color. He researched the positions, looking at paintings and drawings, and then did his own sketches. Sometimes he even planned the smell. He wanted the moment of discovery to be overwhelming, something that would stay with them for the rest of their lives. The last thing they thought about when they went to sleep, the image that woke them screaming in the darkest hours of the night.

He'd done his job particularly well with Barbara Wexler.

He thought about Ana de Jong. What would she have made of his night's work? Would she have worked with him? She could have helped bind the girl's wrists, perhaps held her down while he cut at her throat, made sure that her skin was properly lit to receive his text. There were many ways she could have helped.

FRIDAY,
DECEMBER 6

Jenner found Ana making faces at herself in the bathroom mirror. Looking for wrinkles, she explained matter-of-factly.

"You're twenty-one!"

She frowned. He sat on the tub and watched her put on eyeliner.

"Well, a girl has to look after herself, Jenner. Sooner or later, I'll need a nice, rich husband to look after me, and when that time comes, I'll have to be looking my best."

She laughed at his expression. "Jenner! I'm *joking*! When the time comes, any guy who wants to be my husband better be looking *his* best—"

The buzzer rang.

She wrinkled her nose. "Oh, my God, Jenner! *We* never had so many callers, and we were two hot chicks!"

Jenner went out into the living room, closing the door behind him. Garcia's voice shrilled on the intercom. "Jenner?"

"Come on up, Rad." Jenner pressed the buzzer to let him in.

"Naah, Jenner. You should come down. Ana with you?"

"Not right here. Why?"

"We got another one."

Hell. Jenner closed his eyes and leaned against the wall.

"Where?"

"Here. East Seventeenth. If we leave now, I can sneak you in before the ME arrives."

Roggetti nodded at Jenner as he climbed into the backseat.

"Hang on, Doc—you're about to learn why they call me Mario Roggetti."

Once they were on Lafayette, Roggetti hit the Wail button on the siren, and they plowed uptown, cars halting and turning, traffic parting, everyone hustling out of their way.

They cut over onto Third Avenue. At Seventeenth, Jenner was surprised to see they'd taped off the whole block. Cadets had been drafted from the Police Academy a few blocks away to handle traffic. A short Hispanic cadet motioned them to turn back onto Third, so Roggetti tapped the Yelp button a couple of times to put him in his place. He snickered as the recruit jumped, then quickly raised the tape to let them pass.

As he inched the car under the tape, Roggetti rolled down the window, leaned out, and called, "Hey, Sanchez! Diaz! Whatever the fuck your name is! In the future, try and watch just who the fuck you're pointing your dumb-fuck cadet fingers at!"

The cadet flushed and said, "Yes, sir!"

Garcia rolled his eyes. "Jesus, Joey."

"Just keeping the kid on his toes, Rad."

"If I hadn't been here, you'd have said 'your fucking spic fingers.' Pull over near the side of the park."

Across from the park, yellow crime scene tape sagged between the heavy black railings in front of a large brownstone. A uniformed officer stood at the bottom of the steps, impassively looking at the small handful of news cameras and reporters.

He nodded at Garcia and said, "Hey, Detective. They're on the third floor."

As Jenner followed the two cops through the clump of journalists, a hand grabbed his elbow.

"Doc?"

He turned to see Richie Parsons, the *Post*'s Crime Beat reporter.

"Sorry, Richie, can't talk."

"On the way out, okay?"

Roggetti stood holding the tape up, glaring at the reporters. Jenner shook his head and followed Garcia under the tape.

On the landing above the ground-floor methadone clinic, a young cop was bent over, hands on his knees, panting and ashen-faced, his older partner watching him with a look of vague distaste.

The stairways were warm, and the air on the third floor had the acrid smell of rotting blood. The crime scene unit was still processing the tiny apartment. Mike Seeley was in the living room, which was also the bedroom and the kitchen. He was sweating and clearly upset.

He nodded grimly at Jenner and said, "We moved the head. The super knocked it off the coat stand here when he opened the door." He gestured to a cheap wooden coat stand lying at his feet. The floor where the base had stood was a pool of deep brown blood; from the dried droplet spatter, Jenner realized that the head had been impaled on the coat stand, and set in front of the door.

Seeley seemed to be reading his mind. "Whoever opened the door looking for her was supposed to be staring right into her eyes," he said, opening the door partway to demonstrate. "Give them something to remember. It worked, too—super's an old guy, went to the apartment because of the smell, opened the door, and the head fell right off. The poor bastard's over in the ER at Beth Israel with chest pain."

Seeley pointed to the floor. "Head fell here—I was afraid it'd get damaged by some clown opening the door too fast, so I moved it to the end of the landing, put it on some plastic on one of the chairs. I don't think the uniform securing the stairway likes it too much, but I'm not about to screw up the evidence field inside the primary scene just because someone's feeling a little delicate this morning."

Seeley passed Jenner a pair of gloves. "We photographed the head in its original position, but I think it's all messed up because of the fall, at least in terms of spatter patterns."

Jenner, Roggetti, and Garcia walked back across the landing.

The head sat on sheets of cling film draped over a stack of cheap white plastic lawn chairs. It had been severed cleanly, the cut similar to Smith's, canted downward toward the right-hand side in front, upward toward the left. Smooth edges on the wound suggested a sharp edge on the blade. The cervical spine had been disarticulated right at the top: he'd opened up the back of the neck and cut the ligaments at the top, rather than wasting time and energy sawing through the bone. That was new since Romen.

He was learning.

Jenner gently smoothed the skin down at the base of the back of the neck.

"Huh." He turned to Rad. "No markings."

Garcia shrugged.

They went back to the apartment, stepped over the blood in the hall, and went into the living room.

The girl's naked body was in a big white armchair. She hadn't been tall—alive, her head had probably barely reached the top of the back-rest. Now her body seemed swallowed by the oversize chair.

There was a lot of blood: focal droplet spatter, with a large area of soaked-in blood over the back of the top of the chair. But what was most striking—the first thing they saw when they looked at her—was the thick bouquet of iridescent deep blue and green peacock feathers blossoming from between her breasts.

Roggetti spoke for all of them.

"*Fuck.*"

Jenner approached the body. Looking closer, he saw that the peacock feathers were the fletches of arrows, at least a dozen. The shafts of the arrows were light brown wood, each the thickness of a pencil, the fletches clearly mounted by hand. The arrows had to have been pushed into the chest, the shafts protruding about eight inches from the skin. Dark dried blood covered the margins, but Jenner thought he could make out small radial cuts or tears extending into the edges of the wounds; the arrows were probably tipped with broadheads, razor-sharp bladed heads used in bow hunting.

Rad touched his arm. "Jenner, you gotta keep moving. The ME will be here soon, and you need to be gone before he comes."

"Anything else we should see, Mike?" Jenner glanced around the room. "It looks like he did her in the chair, cut her from behind; I can't see blood elsewhere around the room, and there's heavy soaking in the back of the chair, with what looks like arterial arc spatter to her right. He may be left-handed. He's getting better at decapitation."

He stared at the torso in the chair. "And as for the arrows, Jesus, who the fuck knows?"

Seeley nodded. "I'm with you on all that, Doc. Rad showed me those Pennsylvania photos yesterday, and this thing is really similar. Not the arrows, I mean the level of violence."

Jenner bent to examine her wrists.

"Mikey, can you swab the backs of the hands for DNA? She's got bite marks here . . . see? Both hands, and controls from the upper inner arms. Let's do it here—they missed it in the morgue last time."

As he stood, Jenner realized he'd been smelling something strange in the room. Not the blood, not the early decomposition, something *under* the blood, something smoky.

"Can I turn her?"

"Just a couple more minutes, Doc. I need to get a bracketed set of her like this—the camera's been acting up. Tell you what, though—you can lean her forward and sneak a peek."

With Seeley's hands keeping the arrows in place, Jenner tipped her trunk forward. Her rigor was passing, the muscle tension readily releasing as she slowly folded, Seeley crouching with her.

Jenner muttered, "Jesus."

Her back was densely lined with text, the skin almost blackened under rows of hundreds of carefully burned characters.

Jenner shook his head. "Hours," he said softly. "It must have taken him *hours.*"

"Jenner, you think this is . . . uh, Coptic?"

Jenner turned to Rad, nodding. "It looks just like the other stuff."

He heard footsteps behind him as they eased the body back into position. Turning, he found himself looking straight into the eyes of Steve Whittaker, his normally pasty cheeks flushed. Ray Scales, the chief of detectives, stood next to him.

"Dr. Jenner." Scales sighed, glanced at Whittaker, then said, "I'm sorry, sir, but there's really no further place for you in this investigation. This is an NYPD matter. Roggetti, escort the doctor outside."

Jenner didn't argue—Scales was a boss, a by-the-book cop with political smarts, and it was in his interest to placate Whittaker. Still, the official rejection stung.

Seeley and Garcia looked away as Roggetti and Jenner moved toward the door.

Whittaker snapped, "Jenner! Hold it, bucko!"

Jenner turned, and Whittaker approached him, shoulders stiff, his index finger pointing at Jenner. "So help me God, if I see you at another crime scene, or if you come to the office, if I even *hear* you've been speaking with one of my employees, you'll be arrested so fast your head will spin."

"Nice seeing you, too, Steve."

They continued down the stairs, the blood pounding in Jenner's temples. When they were safely out of Whittaker's hearing, Roggetti snorted. "Good one, Doc!"

Outside, microphones and minicassette machines were thrust at them as the camera lamps flared on. Roggetti bawled, "Make way! Make way!" as he pushed through the scrum. As Jenner got into the car, someone was yelling, "How many body bags is she gonna need, Doc? *At least tell us that!*"


Jenner was still seething in the late afternoon when Jun knocked on the door. He peered over Jenner's shoulder, making sure Ana wasn't around, then said quietly, "Jenner, there's something you should see."

Jenner followed Jun into his loft, a vast white box with glossy walls, floor, and ceiling, every surface of which was encrusted with Jun's bizarre menagerie of pop culture artifacts, including an army of anime and video game figurines and a borderline pathological collection of ridiculous electronic gadgets.

The heart of the space was the workstation. All day long Jun wrote code behind ramparts of glowing flat-screen monitors and humming computers—sometimes for days at a stretch, eyes bloodshot, heart rocketing from all the Jolt Cola and herbal diet pills he'd slammed down. When he wanted to come down, he'd collapse in front of a vast wall-mounted Toshiba plasma TV, often watching it with three separate channels of picture-in-picture tiled down the right side.

Jun gestured at the TV; he'd been watching Tiger Woods playing in Bangkok on ESPN when he'd noticed the press conference on NY1. Jenner instantly recognized Scales at the podium. Roggetti, spit-shined and earnest as a choir boy, stood to his right, Whittaker to his left. Next to Whittaker stood a tired-looking man in a dark suit who Jenner didn't recognize. Rad Garcia was barely visible toward the back. The caption read "Live: Hutchins Murders Press Conf."

Jun pressed a button on his laptop-size remote control, and the chief's voice boomed out in five-channel surround.

". . . or contained. I stress again that this case is under active investigation, and that all potential leads should be immediately directed to the TIPS number displayed on the screen now, and on the NYPD Web site. I'd like to echo Provost Kleiber's cautions to the students, and to thank Hutchins for providing additional security in dorms and on campuses. Finally, in addition to the fifty-thousand-dollar reward previously disclosed, the Hutchins Alumni Society is offering a reward of one hundred and fifty thousand dollars for information leading to the arrest of the perpetrator."

The dark-suited man nodded.

"We'll take a couple of questions now." Whittaker moved closer to the podium.

"Dr. Whittaker?" The first question came from a print reporter Jenner didn't recognize, an older woman in a blue suit. "Doctor, had they been sexually assaulted?"

Whittaker leaned down to the microphone, paused dramatically, and then said crisply, "No comment."

"Doctor, is it true that all three were decapitated?"

"No, just two." Behind him, Chief Scales winced.

"Doctor, we understand that there is writing on the bodies; can you tell us what the writing says?"

Whittaker straightened up. "All three had text on their backs. The NYPD has determined that the writing is Coptic, a Middle Eastern cult. I encourage anyone having information about individuals who are able to write in Coptic to come forward."

Behind him, the chief of detectives' expression was dour.

"I don't mean to suggest that the killer is a practicing Copt," Whittaker continued hastily, "just that, as yet, we have been unable to interpret these writings. Although, of course, it's clear that the killer has some familiarity with the script. Next question."

A hand went up; Jenner recognized Richie Parsons by his Mets cap. As did Whittaker, to his apparent distaste.

"Mr. Parsons."

"Doc, when you say you identified the writing as Coptic, did you mean to say Dr. Edward Jenner identified the writing as Coptic? I understand he's part of the investigation, and my sources say he broke the code."

Whittaker flushed, a beautiful thing to behold on the huge screen. He leaned close to the microphone and said, "Dr. Jenner was briefly involved in the initial New York murder investigation as a retained observer. He has no part in this investigation, and has no relationship to my office."

Jun raised his eyebrows. "That true, Jenner?"

Jenner didn't answer.

Parsons wasn't letting up. "But Dr. Whittaker, it was Dr. Jenner who identified the writing as Coptic, true or false?"

"*No. Comment.* Next question? Anyone else?"

Whittaker's face was now flashing white on the screen as the TV lights glared off his sweating brow, his eyes searching desperately for the refuge of a softball question.

The vague satisfaction he felt at Whittaker's discomfort completely deserted Jenner a moment later, when Jun punched CNN up full-screen; they, too, were carrying the press conference live, sending it out across the entire country, around the entire world.

*Fuck.*


He told Ana in the evening. She was still avoiding watching TV, but he wanted to tell her before she found out some other way. She was stretched out on the sofa, reading a Calvin and Hobbes book; she said she couldn't concentrate enough to read a regular book. He didn't go into details, just that another Hutchins student had been killed, almost certainly by the same man who had killed her roommate.

She smiled wanly, then took the gray cashmere throw into the TV room. He watched her put Miyazaki's *Spirited Away* into the DVD player.

He gave her a fake grin. "Well, you're going to be seeing a lot more of me around the house! Apparently, they're going to arrest me if they find me 'interfering with the investigation.' "

She nodded distractedly and then said, "Jenner, if you don't mind, I don't feel much like talking. I'm going to watch Jun's movie."

He went to the kitchen and emptied the dishwasher, listening to her cry under the blare of the sound track, a soft sound like tissue paper tearing.

He knew what he had to do; he called Jun to say he'd be going out at around 2:00 a.m. Let them throw him in jail, take his license away—it would be a mercy killing, really. The girl deserved better, and he was going to make sure that she got it. He couldn't stop now.

Rad Garcia called at 10:00 p.m., apologetic.

"Jenner, I'm sorry about all this. We both know that if it weren't for you, we'd still be interviewing every damn male in the goddamn university, tracking down every phone number she'd scribbled for the last three months. Thing is, you shared your information, and the bosses think now they got enough to go forward from here. And they like you, most of them, at least, but they *need* Whittaker—word is he'll be chief in six months' time. You know how the game works."

Jenner snorted. "So, what are you doing with the skin text, Rad?"

"We're showing it to some guy at Columbia."

"Yeah, okay. Good. I hope he helps." He paused. "I'm going to meet with an expert on Coptic."

Garcia was silent for a second. "You sure you want to do that?"

"Sure. I copied those first letters as an authorized representative of the decedent's family and the second at the invitation of the Pennsylvania State Police. The NYPD doesn't have a say."

Jenner heard a woman's voice as Rad quickly covered the receiver. A few seconds later he came back on and said, "Okay. You do what you have to. Just remember: Whittaker's looking for any chance he can get to bury your ass."

Jenner cut down East Thirtieth toward the river. The southern sky was dark and heavy, but over Manhattan the night was clear and bright. He cursed his luck—the mortuary had closed-circuit surveillance over First Avenue and Thirtieth Street. He was pretty sure that if he could get into NYU Medical Center next door, he could get into the morgue through the back.

As he passed the security desk, he gave a casual smile and flashed his expired NYU photo ID, saying, "Hey, buddy. Cold night, eh?" The guard nodded, eyes fixed on his portable TV.

Jenner took the stairs to the second story, then headed to the men's room at the end of the corridor. He opened the window wide and climbed through, onto the gravel-topped roof of the classroom wing. He made his way to the end of the roof, which put him just above the alley behind the morgue.

Crouching, he realized that the drop was farther than he'd thought; it hadn't looked that high from the alley.

He landed hard. He stood for a second, feet stinging. His fall had sounded loud in the cold air—had anyone heard? He listened for a while, then cracked the door to the body-intake area; everything was quiet. Between deliveries, 2:15 a.m.: the techs were probably dozing in the break room.

He slipped into the corridor. The light from the morgue office was up ahead; Brooklyn Frank would likely be there watching TV. Jenner cut through the men's changing room to bypass the office.

He stepped through the locker room door, past the battered stalls and the old wooden cabinets, past the locker where someone stole his shoes once while he was doing an autopsy. Then, quietly, out into the corridor, safely on the far side of the office. He breathed a sigh of relief. He eased the swing door open, then slipped through into the dark corridor to the body coolers and the autopsy room.

There was a click as all of the lights came on. He straightened to see Brooklyn Frank and three other technicians standing in the corridor. They started to applaud, then all collapsed with laughter.

Frank pounded him on the shoulder, yelling, "You silent ninja muth-afucka!" Jenner shook their hands, everyone laughing and pounding him on the shoulder or slapping him on the back.

"How did you know?" Jenner asked Frank.

"Roundtree. He said if you didn't show up tonight, we could call him Captain Asshole for a year. Big drop from that rooftop to the alley, right?"

"You saw me?"

Frank turned serious. "We got a security camera back there. We would have nailed you in the alley, except then we'd be on video, too. You'll be fine as long as Dr. Whittaker never sees the tape. Another thing: we can't help you. Whittaker made a big deal about you. Tree said to do what we can, but don't get caught with you. Obviously, external only, right? And you have to be out of here by five a.m."

Jenner murmured his thanks.

"Aziz set the body up in the decomp autopsy room—you're safe, the back hall camera doesn't work. The head's in the bag."

He shook Jenner's hand again. "Good to see ya, Doc."

The techs filed back toward the break room, grinning and bumping elbows with him.


Her body was on the autopsy table, a black rubber block between the shoulder blades. He moved quickly—there wasn't much time, and he'd seen most of what he needed to see at the scene.

He hadn't noticed the abrasions on the left wrist, but they were consistent with the binding he'd documented in the other two cases. This time, Whittaker had been more careful: there was suturing on the hands where the odontologist had cut out the skin with the bite marks.

The arrows were gone, leaving an ugly cavity the size of his fist. The edges had radial cuts around the periphery, consistent with the bladed hunting heads he'd suspected, rather than the bullet-shaped arrowheads used in target shooting. There were no defensive injuries on the arms or legs, and the genitals were undamaged: the killer had had other things on his mind.

Jenner gently rolled her onto her side, propping her up with blocks against her chest and hip. The text was tiny, barely larger than newsprint, line after line, the tiny burned tracings filling up her back. To document it, he divided the back up into an imaginary grid of eight sections, then photographed it quadrant by quadrant, overlapping the shots to make sure he had it all. He checked the LCD viewfinder and tabbed back through the images to make sure they'd all come out; he could Photoshop them together to form a single detailed image of the entire text.

He removed the blocks and slowly eased her down onto her front. He pulled the sheet of plastic from his briefcase, then smoothed it carefully onto her back. He took his felt-tip pen and began to trace the patterns.

It was already past 2:30 a.m.

After the first few lines, his speed improved as he recognized recurring characters. He concentrated on copying the characters as neatly as he could. He stopped for a break a little before 4:00 a.m., went out to the loading dock and stretched his back. Frank raised the gate, and Jenner saw that the clear skies were gone; it was pouring now, the drops streaking golden rays in the light from the streetlamp in front of the men's shelter across the street.

He went back to work. Exhausted, eyes burning, back and hands cramping, he still had a third of the lettering to copy when Frank interrupted him just before 5:00 a.m. The photographs would have to be good enough; he hoped the text would be legible.

As Frank and Aziz took the body down off the table, Jenner held the plastic sheet in front of the wall-mounted light box used for viewing X-rays. It was insane, just insane. Hundreds, probably thousands of characters, tiny, ancient characters, burned into the skin of this poor girl. *Why?*

He waved the plastic to dry the ink completely before he put it away.

Somewhere in all those hundreds of lines, the key to it all, the answer to all the questions.

By the time he left the morgue, crouched down in the back of Frank's old Cadillac with the MORGMAN license plate, the rain was torrential. On 1010 WINS, they were talking about possible flooding on the FDR; in the East Village, some of the intersections were already partly submerged as fast-flowing runoff backed up in the blocked sewers. In the headlights, Jenner could see the sharp splashes of raindrops driving into the surface of the curb-high water.

Frank dropped him on Houston in front of Himali Restaurant and Goods, a twenty-four-hour Bengali hole-in-the-wall that catered to the cabdrivers refueling and retooling, a vestige of the times when there used to be three service stations at the intersection, now replaced by trendy furniture shops and a glass-sheathed Adidas store. He got a big tin mug of fantastically buttery lentil stew, at that moment the best thing he'd ever tasted. He made small talk with Mr. Ansari as he ate, one eye on the rain outside.

It wasn't letting up at all. He took off his coat and wrapped his briefcase with it, determined to keep the precious plastic sheet inside dry. With a nod to Mr. Ansari, he set off. He ran most of the way, his feet splashing freezing water, his shirt soaked through in seconds in the pelting rain.

His fingers were cold and numb, and he fumbled with the key, but then he was inside, the glass doors shutting out the rain driving against the roof of the shallow foyer.

Kimi was asleep in front of his door in one of Jun's big white leather armchairs, a Game Boy Advance on her lap. She wore a navy blue pinafore with white ankle socks and white platform wedges, her hair in pigtails with big blue velvet bows. Across the hall, the door was open and the lights bright in Jun's loft. Jenner woke her gently, and with a little difficulty.

She opened her eyes and smiled and murmured something in Japanese. Jenner winked at her, put his finger to his lips, "*Shhh!*" then softly turned the door handle and went inside.

He stripped in the bathroom, tossed his wet clothes into the hamper, then showered quickly, feeling the heat soak into his skin. He felt as he had the day he'd come home from the scene of Andie Delore's murder. It seemed like yesterday, it seemed like ten years ago. Not even a week since the whole thing began!

He put on a T-shirt and slipped into bed. She was warm and soft, and as he pressed against her, she turned to him and put her arms around him. Eyes closed, she whispered, "Hi."

He put his arms around her, too. She wriggled a little closer, tucked her head against his chest. He whispered, "Hi," into her hair.

She breathed out. "You feel good."

He smiled. "You do, too. Go back to sleep."

He fell asleep holding her, the sound of rain on the roof and beating at his windows. Warm, soft, dry, close.

He woke at 11:00 a.m., alone.

Through the big windows, the sky flashed. Then, a few seconds later, thunder. The wind had picked up, blowing the rain hard against the windowpanes. He could hear the spatter of water running off the ledge above.

He slid his hand to her side of the bed. Still warm.

Where was she?

He propped himself up on one elbow. There was soft yellow light coming from the bathroom.

"Ana?"

She came out and walked toward him in one of his T-shirts, a votive candle flickering in a cobalt blue glass cup in her hand.

She stood by the bedside, close to him.

"Hey."

He smiled up at her. "Hey."

She put the candle on the bedside table.

"I'm all better now, Jenner. Want to see?" She was speaking slowly, almost slurring her words. She looked him in the eye as her hand went to the hem of the T-shirt and lifted it up, showing him her belly. She wore nothing underneath the shirt. "See?"

He reached up for her and pulled her down to the bed. "I see."

She walked back from the kitchen naked, carrying a bowl of cereal and a spoon.

"Budge over, Jenner. Here, I made you gourmet cereal for looking after me."

He gave her some room, and she put the bowl down. Weetabix; he raised his eyebrows.

She frowned at him. "It's from Dean & Deluca, it cost a fortune, trust me: it's gourmet cereal. Jun said it was your favorite."

Jenner sat up, wondering where Jun had got that idea. She sat next to him; they shared the spoon.

When they finished the cereal, she climbed back under the covers, curled up against him. He looked over to the window; she'd raised the shades. Outside, the world was murky blue, the buildings across the street soft and blurred in the rain and the mist.

When he woke, she was leaning on one elbow, looking at him intently. "I feel different now. Do you feel different? It's different now."

"Yes, I suppose it is."

She rolled her eyes and punched him in the shoulder. "Jesus H. Christ, Jenner! Stop being such a *guy*! What, now you think I want to move in here and play house with you? I'm just saying I feel different. Don't you?"

"I *said* I did!"

"Seriously, Jenner, lighten up. Sometimes a girl just needs to get laid. That's all I'm saying."

Jenner felt a flush of embarrassment: he hadn't touched anyone, hadn't been touched by anyone, since Julie left. It had meant more to him than it had to her.

They lay under the big cashmere blanket on the floor in front of the TV. *La Strada* was playing soundlessly.

She stroked his hair.

"Jenner?"

"Yes?"

"You should tell me about it."

When he didn't answer, she rolled onto her back, away from him. "Jun really likes you, you know? He says you're great."

"He's a good guy. Really smart, too."

"He said things were hard for you after 9/11."

Here we go.

"Things were hard for a lot of people after 9/11."

"I don't care about a lot of people. Tell me about what happened to you."

"It doesn't make a good story."

"I don't care. Tell me about it."

He snorted. "God, what is this, a Julia Roberts movie? You get me to talk, and then I'm suddenly warm and lovable?"

She made a face. "Oh, I think you'd be pretty icky if you were warm. But you're actually already kind of lovable—in your own messed-up way."

He looked at her, lying there next to him, her arm across his shoulder, blue eyes serious and expectant. He breathed out.

"Jenner, you have to let it be over."

He shook his head. "See, that's just it—it's not over. Not for me, not for many people. Maybe it'll never be over."

"*What* won't be over? Your part in it is finished, Jenner. You've got to move on."

He closed his eyes. She was right.

And before he knew it, he was telling her about it, laying it all out, making his statement to her, just as she'd made hers to him and Rad a week ago. About working all those nights in the makeshift morgue on the sidewalk of Thirtieth Street, under the tenting and the high spotlights. About the flood of volunteers who came from across the country—ambulance crews, cops, firemen, sanitation workers, corrections officers, Salvation Army, anthropologists, so many volunteers. How they'd worked all day and all night for eight months, doing their best to identify the bodies, the limbs, the tiny fragments of tissue. About seeing the cadets, some barely out of high school, lining up to carry bagged remains to the X-ray unit or to the dentists.

It hadn't been like any other disaster. Usually, the pathologists had no connection to the victims, they could just concentrate on the work, on the science, clean and abstract, hidden away in the mortuary. But this time, there was no distance, no separation. Every night was an unrestrained parade of grief and anguish, a stream of stumbling survivors, cops and firemen, their backs broken by the searching, their hearts crushed by the finding.

Each time they recovered a member of service, the squad assembled and lined up to salute as yet another comrade was carried in, as yet another flag was taken off a body bag to be folded into a neat triangle. Later the silence of the arrivals would give way to the muffled sound of men sobbing quietly in the dark, hiding in the alleys behind the trailers.

Relationships started to fall apart because it was easier to let them go than to talk about it, replaced by pathetic affairs that died quickly in the middle of all the pain. And in summer, when it was finished—or rather, when it stopped—he didn't know what was left of him, didn't know what to do or where to go next.

She listened, stroking his hair. And she cried, and her tears made him feel foolish and weak. And she tilted her head against his, and held on to him, and held him under the blanket with her when he felt he couldn't stay there anymore.

\* \* \*

When it had finished, standing by that aching, empty space at Ground Zero for the ceremony marking the end of the recovery, dry-eyed as they led the riderless horse up out of the pit, he thought he was okay. That he'd got through it in one piece.

But he had stopped sleeping. On his days off, he walked through the city, away from his own little vortex, watching to see how it had changed. He became very sensitive to triggers—when a plane flew low over the city, he always imagined the trajectory continuing, smashing straight into one of the Midtown skyscrapers.

He slept less and less; nights gradually became tidal, the darkness rolling in quickly, then slowly rolling out, Jenner sitting wrapped in a blanket, staring at the paling sky through open windows. And eventually his career began to wind down.

One day, as the sun was beginning to show over the East River, Jenner gave up on trying to sleep and went in to the office. Whittaker was already there, triaging the day's autopsies. Apologetically, Jenner explained that he wasn't really sleeping, and asked for an easy day; he wanted to leave early and get a prescription for something to help him sleep.

It had been four years since Julie had chosen Jenner instead of him, but Whittaker never missed an opportunity for payback. There were five autopsies, and Whittaker could easily have cut him loose; he didn't even glance at Jenner as he assigned him two cases.

Jenner convinced himself he was getting a second wind during the first case, a jeweler who had dropped dead in front of his shop, but by the second, he could barely stand.

The decedent was a cachectic transsexual with advanced AIDS. She'd had the disease for almost fourteen years, and her physicians had sent her home to die, but the family demanded an autopsy, insisting that the public hospital had treated her poorly.

It happened right at the end. He'd completed the autopsy proper and was removing her breast implants so they wouldn't burst during cremation. The scalpel slipped from his fingers, almost numb under three pairs of gloves, the textured fingertips slick with blood.

The scalpel tumbled from the table, landed almost vertically, and then bounced back up off the floor toward him. There was a brief white flash of steel as he felt the blade slice through the leg of his scrub pants and cut into his skin.

He pushed back from the table, cursing, amazed by the freakishness of the cut. Fuck. He'd cut his hands before—they all had—but this just seemed incredibly unfair. Fuck. HIV. *Fuck.*

Tearing off his gloves, struggling to pull off the bunching, snagging gown, he went to the sink, jammed the hot tap on full, pulled up the pant leg, and began to squeeze the skin, milking blood from the fine half-inch cut, trying to wash out the tainted blood.

He called to Brooklyn Frank for bleach, but they couldn't find any. Finally, Antwon Terry found some powdered stainless steel cleanser, and Jenner slapped some onto the wound; it stung, and caked the blood almost immediately.

He tried gripping his hands around his upper calf like a tourniquet, but it made no difference. Then Tree came in with a brown plastic bottle of hydrogen peroxide. Jenner splashed it on neat, and it frothed the steel cleanser and burned like a bitch, but it felt like it was doing something.

"Go on, Doc. Put on some more. Use it up."

He sagged into a chair and looked down at his shin. He had rinsed off all the powder and blood, and the wound now barely fizzed with each new application, the edges pale and feathery, the surrounding skin now pink, the center of the cut liver brown.

"You okay, Doc? Was it HIV?"

Jenner looked up at Tree and gestured weakly toward the body. An old Public Enemy song ran through his mind, Flava Flav saying, *"Yo, Terminator—meet the gee that killed me."*

"I went over to the Bellevue ER, where they gave me a two-month preventative supply of AIDS drugs. And then I had to wait to see if I was infected. I was fine, but the medication made me really ill, and I became anemic. I stopped taking it after a month, but it took me months to recover from the anemia—months of pure exhaustion.

"I went back to work, but I was pretty much done, physically, emotionally. I kind of didn't know how to stop working. Didn't know what I would have done with myself. The deputy chief was fucking me over because his girlfriend had left him for me—each day, he'd load me up and sit around watching me burn out.

"And finally, I missed a murder. An old lady in her eighties, long history of heart disease, found fully clothed, lying on her bed. I didn't do an autopsy because she'd had heart attacks in the past. I shouldn't have been there, I knew I was too ill to work, really, but it was my call, and I chose to be there.

"Anyway, I looked at her under poor light, and I noticed her face was a bit purple, but I thought it was because of her position.

"I certified her death as due to natural causes, and would have sent her on her way if the morgue tech hadn't spotted a bruise on her neck. I did an autopsy and found the woman had been strangled. There were no external injuries on the neck—it was very subtle. But she'd been murdered, and I had missed it." He paused. "And the thing is, I just didn't care . . .

"The next day, I asked to meet with the chief and Whittaker to tell them what happened and to ask for a break. I figured Whittaker would push for my dismissal, but the chief would be on my side. And there was a lot of understanding about stuff in the post–9/11 period.

"But I realized I'd had enough. It was harder and harder just showing up at work each day. And not just because I was ill. I'd loved this city so much, and now it seemed like it was gone forever, and each day was just another day where something horrible could happen.

"I knew my work wasn't good for me, and I wasn't good for my work. So I went to the meeting, and I resigned."

"And that was that?"

"Some people tried to get me to stay, but they didn't understand where I was. I just couldn't be there anymore, couldn't do it anymore."

They lay there quiet for a long while. And finally he realized she was right: it *was* different now.

In the ruined factory on the river, the man was trying to get warm. The blankets hanging over the main window, sodden from the rain, kept pulling out their moorings, the brick so rotten it shattered when he tried to drive a nail with his nail gun.

He gave up and huddled in the corner, clutching his knees to his chest, all of his bedding wrapped around him as he tried to fight off the damp. He looked around the room. It was pathetic.

He'd been someone once, someone important. He had created FMed-base, an innovative database program, and for a while, his name appeared frequently in tech-sector newsletters and trade magazines. But just as quickly as he had risen, he had foundered, overtaken by younger, better companies with younger, better programmers.

In an instant it seemed as if all his success had just been illusion, his company just another entrepreneurial blip. After the long summer where his failure became too obvious for him to deny, he had given up. Early that September, he made his way to the same big glass building in downtown Manhattan where just three years earlier he'd signed his incorporation papers. The appointment was early, a quick mercy killing before his lawyer got on with making real money from real entrepreneurs.

The lawyer, impatient with his client's slow reading of routine documents, pushed his fountain pen into the man's hand and began to read aloud his own copy. The man sat silent at the conference table as his attorney went down the bankruptcy form, nodding his head slowly as he initialed each line, then signing and dating the bottom. The ink gleamed on the white paper, the bright morning sun gilding the final proof of his failure.

"You understand that with Chapter Eleven . . . ," the lawyer said, and then his voice was drowned out by the roar of engines and the clatter of the shuddering windows. He turned, confused, to the window just in time to see the impact. The man was falling to the ground when the blast hit, spraying the room with shards of tinted glass.

When he pulled himself to his feet, the lawyer was sitting against a partition, mouth gaping and shutting, blood pouring from his scalp. The man bent stiffly, picked up the bankruptcy papers, and went into the hall. At first he was deaf, but the roaring sound soon gave way to pandemonium, the sound of screams and car alarms. The stairwells were packed with panicked secretaries and lawyers.

On the street, traffic had instantly become snarled. He saw flames rolling up the sides of the tower. It was obviously impossible, some kind of illusion—special effects from a Hollywood B movie.

He stood at the corner for a while, leaning on a lamppost, his hearing fading out and coming back as he worked his jaw. He decided to walk home. He had just started east when the roar of the second plane flooded the area, followed by the explosion of its impact.

All the buildings in the area were emptying. Police and fire department and EMS vehicles were fighting their way through the gridlock. He reached the park in front of City Hall and realized he had to sit. He rested for a little, but the hysteria of the crowds upset him, so he stood again and moved toward the Brooklyn Bridge, dazed, his movements treacle-slow and painful.

He was on the bridge when the first of the towers went down. He didn't look, just saw the faces, heard the screaming, and knew.

When he reached the Brooklyn side, a Hasidic man told him he was bleeding, and wiped his wounds with a dishcloth wet with bottled water; it was nothing, scratches from the shower of glass. He blotted his injuries with the bankruptcy paperwork, then threw all the soiled papers into the garbage. He made to leave, but concerned people made him sit. He waited in the shade of the off-ramp for an hour, then continued on through the lazy flurry of paper and ash now floating down from the sky, walking toward the factory in Williamsburg that had housed his dead business, walking on toward home.

Jenner winced as he poured the champagne into the orange juice—a waste of a good bottle—but she wanted a mimosa, and so he'd made her a mimosa. And another. And was now working on a third. He misjudged, swearing as he lifted the dripping champagne flute up.

Alcohol or not, she seemed to be doing better. Lying in bed that morning, she'd talked about her future for the first time. She did want to go back to school, eventually. She'd take some time off, maybe travel, get it all out of her system. Maybe she could work for Uncle Douggie for a while; she was actually a pretty good photographer.

He wiped the counter, then put the glass down. He tipped a scoop of coffee beans into the mill and listened to her sing in the shower, a shifting, grisly medley of Coldplay and Britney Spears.

He pulsed the coffee, stopping when he heard a knock. Jun with more fucking bad news, no doubt. He opened the door to find Douggie Pyke, deep tan and weary, red-rimmed eyes. Jenner stepped back in surprise.

He walked past Jenner into the loft, sniffing. "Afternoon, Jenner. Am I in time for coffee?"

"Hey, Douggie. Just about." The shower was still on full blast.

"Can you believe this rain? I had to take the train up from D.C. They closed LaGuardia early this morning." His eyes scanned the loft. "Where's Ana?"

"She's just washing up, I think. How was your trip?"

Jenner heard her shut off the shower.

"How's she doing?"

"Good days and bad days. Pretty much how you'd expect. How was the trip?"

"Rough—D.C. to New York was actually the easiest part. It took forever to get back to Yaoundé. On the trek back, we came across a poacher camp. I got some incredible shots of butchered gorillas, saddest thing I've ever seen."

Pyke walked over to the counter and peered into the mill. He popped the cover and sniffed it. "What is this? Kenyan? It's still way too coarse." He pressed on the cap, and the loud rattle of the grinding chamber filled the room again.

Ana walked into the room, naked except for a towel tied into a turban on her head. "Jenner, do you have any moisturizer? My face is dry as—"

Then she saw Douggie, pivoted and ran back into the bathroom, her arms across her breasts.

Douggie took his hand off the coffee mill. He looked at Jenner, then walked over to the couch and sat.

He didn't speak for a minute or so.

"So this is your idea of looking after her?"

Jenner said nothing.

"She's half your age."

"Douggie, I'm sorry, but you don't know what it's been like. You have no idea what's been going on."

"Oh, I think I have a pretty good idea." He stood and called toward the bathroom, "Ana? Can you get your things? I'll wait for you in my studio."

He walked over to the bathroom, tapped on the door, and repeated himself.

"I can't come out," she said. "I don't have anything to put on."

Pyke turned to Jenner.

"Get her some clothes. Tell her to get her things and come downstairs. She can stay with me now."

"Douggie, she's—"

Pyke cut him off. "I don't want to hear anything from you right now."

Jenner said, "Jesus, Douggie."

Pyke turned and walked over to him. "*What?* Go ahead, say something—I'm *this* fucking close to punching you in the fucking mouth."

Jenner winced. The notion was ridiculous—Jenner was more than a head taller—but Pyke was his best friend. And he was right.

He stayed silent as Pyke walked out of the room.

"Is he gone yet?"

Jenner slumped down onto the couch.

"Yep."

She came out of the bathroom, this time without even the turban. She took two steps toward him, then bent over double with laughter.

"Oh, my God! That was so *great!*" She couldn't catch her breath, holding on to the countertop with one hand, trying to straighten up, gasping. "You should have seen your face!"

She slipped onto his lap and put an arm about his neck. "You didn't think it was funny?"

She looked at his face and saw that he didn't, which set her off into fresh gales of laughter.

Jenner just sat there, mystified.

"Between you and Uncle Douggie, I feel like a Victorian orphan. Damn! I wish I'd thought of that bit in *Blue Velvet*, you know, when she walks across the lawn naked to him in front of all of those people?"

She put on a voice. "*Edward . . . Edward, my secret lover . . .*" And then, prodding him with her finger, "*He put his disease in me . . .*"

That set her off again, and soon Jenner was laughing, too.

"Seriously, though," she said, "I should stay with him. He'll get over it—he's just tired. He feels like he's let my parents down, what with you molesting me and all. I can tell. I promise I'll sneak up so we can hang out. And when we're fooling around, I'll be shouting out, '*But . . . but . . . I'm half your age!*' "

And she collapsed laughing again.

The phone rang.

"Father Patrick Sheehan for Dr. Jenner, please."

Jenner sat up guiltily, Ana sliding off his lap with a protesting squeak. "Good afternoon, Father. This is Dr. Jenner."

"Pat, Dr. Jenner. Unless you're about to ask me to hear your confession!"

It seemed Father Sheehan was the jovial type. "Hah. Nothing to confess, thanks. Simon Lescure told me you'd be back today. I'm sorry to interrupt your homecoming."

"Not at all, not at all! Simon tells me that you are involved in a most intriguing situation concerning some form of Coptic text. Very exciting indeed! I keep telling my students that the ancient languages live on among us, but they never seem to take it in. Nor any of the other pearls I lob at them, I fear!"

The priest insisted they meet the next day. Jenner thanked him, took his address, and hung up.

Ana sat by, smirking and sipping her drink.

"Oh, I think it's a little soon to be talking with a priest, don't you? I mean, I know I rocked your tiny world, but it was just one night . . ."

Jenner frowned up at her. "I liked you better depressed."

She smiled a little smile. "Oh, I've kept a little of that aside, just for you."

She stood, then paused to lean over him and kiss his cheek softly. She whispered, "Thank you," into his ear, then padded back to the bathroom, mimosa in hand.

MONDAY,
DECEMBER 9

They met in the stairwell at 10:00 a.m., before Jenner headed out to Yardley to visit Father Pat. She stood on the landing between his floor and Douggie's, in jeans and a baseball cap, hair gathered into a ponytail tugged through the cap's backstrap. She asked him how he was. He was fine, she was too.

He had to go: Roggetti was waiting downstairs. Rad had called the night before to tell Jenner that their Columbia guy hadn't panned out. Apparently, Whittaker had brought him to the morgue to read the text directly from the victim's back; the professor had barely crossed the threshold of the autopsy room before turning white and having to be helped out onto the street.

Roggetti would drive Jenner to meet Sheehan; he also had pulled Jenner's tracings from the earlier killings from the Evidence Unit. All of which was fine by Jenner—the tracings were better quality than the photocopies he'd kept, plus he'd save the money on the car rental.

Ana turned to go. Jenner said, "Wait! I have something for you . . ."

He sheepishly handed her the oblong box wrapped in sky blue tissue paper.

"What *is* it?" she asked, genuinely excited.

She tore off the wrapping and dropped it onto the stairs. She unrolled the tissue paper, and tipped its contents into her palm. It was a handsome Laguiole pocketknife—authentic, not a cheap copy—with a three-inch blade, a stubby smaller blade for scoring the caps of wine bottles, and a corkscrew. The handle was rosewood with ebony inlay, and it had the traditional Napoleonic bee at the base of the blade; he'd spotted it in the window of an antique store after leaving Lescure's apartment.

She looked at it, beaming. "You know the Chinese say, 'Never give a friend a knife'?" She curled her fingers around the elegant handle, then kissed his cheek. "Thanks, Jenner. It's beautiful."

*   *   *

Joey Roggetti was leaning against the car out by the back loading bay, whistling either Nirvana's "Come As You Are" or "Hava Nagilah," Jenner couldn't tell. Joey insisted on taking the Holland Tunnel; as they neared the entrance, the tuneless whistling turned into tuneless humming.

On the Jersey side, Jenner looked back at the city. He didn't often take this route, and wasn't used to the Manhattan skyline without the Twin Towers, like a face without a mouth.

Roggetti had tuned in WDHA, a classic-rock station, that day broadcasting live all day from Asbury Park. Springsteen's "State Trooper" came on, and Roggetti sang along, beating the rhythm on the steering wheel.

Old metal bridges carried them high over the barren marshes and derelict factories below, the blighted swamp between Kearney and Secaucus, New Jersey, the saddest place on earth.

Roggetti fell quiet until they reached Pennsylvania, his mood brightening after they stopped for coffee. Ten minutes from Wilkes-Barre, he found a station playing the Stones; he kicked the car up to seventy-five and hit the cruise control. He hummed the verses to Tom Petty's "Free Falling," and sang along with the choruses. Jenner watched the countryside: empty snowy fields, low gray fencing, small industrial buildings and warehouses.

Yardley had the cheery air of a college that had long ago embraced its mid-level status, contenting itself with the ambience, if not the academic achievement, of the Ivy League. The buildings were brick, solid and handsome, set around large, snowy lawns with a central gazebo and beautiful oaks and elms, an elegant, winter-bare forest.

The holiday break was approaching, and the air was festive. From the gazebo, a choir sang carols, and there was a long table where three young women dressed as elves sold mulled apple cider and baked goods for charity. In front of every dorm, groups of students were building large, complex snow sculptures—a Golden Gate Bridge, an airport with planes taxiing on the runway, a model of the United Nations, and the like.

"They take their Christmas pretty seriously here, don't they, Doc?" Jenner nodded.

Roggetti shrugged. "You want some cider?"

They walked down toward the table of elves, conspicuous in their dark overcoats and slightly wary expressions.

The cider wasn't bad. Hot and thick and sweet, heady with cinnamon and clove, the paper cup warm in Jenner's bare hands.

A snowball fight broke out near the UN; it looked like something out of a J. Crew catalogue.

"Dr. Jenner?"

They turned to see a spry older man with white hair, flushed cheeks, and bright blue eyes standing under the arches. He wore a dark brown hat tilted back on his head, Bing Crosby style, a clerical collar peeking through his unzipped green parka.

Jenner nodded. "Father Sheehan?"

"Yes. Kind of horrifying to watch, isn't it?" He gave a crooked grin.

Jenner shook his outstreched hand and introduced Roggetti.

The priest led them back to his rooms, on the ground floor of the dorm with the Golden Gate sculpture. As he closed the door to his bedroom, Jenner caught a glimpse of stacks and stacks of books, overflow from the book-lined study where they sat. The room had a warm, dry smell of pipe tobacco and firewood; it was almost uncomfortably cozy, with deep leather armchairs arranged by the fireplace, where the mantel held a collection of small carved owls in wood and stone.

Jenner and Roggetti sat. They had a perfect view of the quadrangle lawn. The sound of "Deck the Halls" rose from the gazebo.

"There's no escaping it, is there?" said Sheehan, wryly gesturing to the window. "At Christmas, the whole world turns into some gigantic, awful mall."

He set a tray of glasses with a decanter on a side table. "I stay sane by telling myself that at least it isn't 'It's a Small World After All.' Sherry, gentlemen?" He was already pouring.

The priest took a poker and nudged the logs in his fireplace, then sat opposite them. He waited until they had sipped before he drank.

"Now. Your problem, Dr. Jenner. . . . "

Jenner set the large manila envelope of photos on the desk.

Looking at Sheehan sitting in his chair, expectant, anxious to help, at the man's books and owls around the room, at the snowy lawns and trees through the windows behind him, Jenner felt like a vector of disease, carrying sickness and decay into the heart of the priest's idyllic little world.

He opened the fastening on the envelope, then hesitated. "Father. I'm afraid you'll find these photographs very upsetting; I've been doing this for some time now, and even I find them disturbing."

The priest smiled softly. "Ah, Dr. Jenner. I did two tours as an army chaplain on the USS *Repose* during the Vietnam War; I assure you, a hospital ship at war quickly hardens the fainthearted. I appreciate your sensitivity, indeed I do; if I have some problems with the material, I'll speak up."

Jenner nodded. He presented the cases in detail, as delicately as he could. Whatever carnage Sheehan had witnessed on the *Repose*, it had been in the context of military conflict, where historic momentum strips away the moral implications of the actions of individuals. The crime scene photos were something inherently more horrific, more intuitively repugnant: brutal acts of torture and dehumanization, committed by one man not in the name of country or survival, but in the name of personal pleasure. As he spoke, he tried to gauge the priest's reaction, trying to spare him the full horror of the case, yet not wanting to omit anything that might be important.

The priest's white head remained bowed, his fingers steepled in front of his forehead in concentration. There was no display of emotion, just an occasional nod as Jenner described the three victims, and the violent, ritualistic aspects of their deaths.

"In the Smith and Wexler murders, the heads had deliberately been positioned to shock whoever discovered them. In one instance, the killer poured milk on a countertop, then set the head into the milk."

At this, the priest's head jerked upward. Jenner immediately regretted having mentioned it, but when he looked at Sheehan, he saw that his expression was more grim than shocked. He nodded for Jenner to continue, lowering his head again.

Jenner told him what they knew of the killer's appearance from Ana's description, and his theories about the physical branding process.

"Which brings us to you . . ." Jenner trailed off.

"Which brings you to me." The priest sat forward. "May I see the texts, gentlemen?"

Roggetti produced a large folder from his briefcase. He stood portentously, aware it was his moment, and walked to the desk, followed by Jenner and Sheehan.

The detective removed the photographs, eight-by-tens on glossy stock, and set them out: a couple for Delore, several for Smith, and a slippery stack of more than two dozen for Wexler.

Roggetti said, "I also brought Doc's tracing of the first two, if that'll help."

The priest put on a pair of half-moon glasses, then leaned over the pictures.

After a few seconds, he switched on the desk lamp and wordlessly pulled a chair over to the edge of the desk, tuning out Jenner and the detective.

He squinted at the Delore photos for a second, then put them aside.

"*Khi ro.*"

Roggetti and Jenner looked at each other. Sheehan turned to scrutinize a 1:1 close-up of Smith's markings. He picked up a legal pad and uncapped a fountain pen; without looking at the pad, he began to scribble.

"Fascinating . . . ," he murmured.

Jenner peered at the legal pad, but the priest's scrawl was as illegible as the killer's texts. The room was silent except for the crackle and hiss of the fire and the scratch of Sheehan's pen.

Outside, it had turned dark. Through the window, Jenner caught glimpses of students carrying lit candles, a soft stream of golden lights.

It was Roggetti who broke the silence.

"So, Father, is it Coptic?"

Sheehan ignored the question. He jotted a little more, murmuring words under his breath in a halting, arrhythmic manner.

He turned back to them.

"Yes, it's Coptic, but it's very unusual. The letters are poorly formed—skin would be a tricky surface, of course, but the shapes of the letter are uneven in a way that I don't think can be explained just by the challenge of writing on skin."

He tapped the first photo with his pen.

"It's hard for me to make these out. The first one, the single letter, seems straightforward. He's made a box, and written a single character in it; I think it's a *khi ro*, a Coptic method of referring to dates, specifically the Diocletian era."

Roggetti bobbed his head firmly, as if the Diocletian era was standard watercooler talk at the precinct.

Sheehan turned to reexamine the Smith photographs. Jenner knew that the characters would be hard to make out; abrasion from the neck wound, drying, and suturing had all disrupted and deformed the text.

Sheehan gestured to a walnut case on one of the bookshelves. "Detective, if you wouldn't mind, please pass me the magnifying glass that's in the wooden box there."

With the hand lens, he pored over the photograph for a long while, occasionally tilting it to lessen the glare from the glossy surface.

He put the Smith photographs down and shifted to the Wexler stack. When he saw the first image—a wide shot, taken in the autopsy room, of the decedent's back, the whole surface crowded with dense lines of text—he sat back in his chair and murmured, "My God."

He tipped his glasses up onto the top of his head and squinted at the text for a few seconds. Then he put the photograph back on the table, stood, stretched, and rubbed his eyes.

"Gentlemen, I'm going to need some time. The writing on the second girl is very hard to make out, but it looks like the first symbol is the *khi ro* again. I don't know how much of the rest I can decipher, but I'll do my best. The final victim . . . well, I'm hoping that text will be the most legible."

He picked his sherry up from the side table and took a sip, then put the glass down on the desk next to the photographs and turned to face them.

"When you study ancient manuscripts, you spend most of your time alone. I'm afraid I've become accustomed to that solitude—I'll work better without distraction. No offense, gentlemen."

"Oh, none taken, Father!" Roggetti said.

"If you could leave a cell phone number, I'll call you when I have something. I'm going to take a little nap, then a shower, then I'll get down to work."

Jenner passed the priest a CD of his photos of Wexler, the tracing of her back, and a printout of a spreadsheet he'd made to compare the murders, bloody nightmares sanitized into a neat grid. Three columns for the victims' names, then row upon row of specific data—date of discovery, estimated date of death, injury pattern, family history, academic record, everything Jenner had been able to think of. The priest raised an eyebrow: it ran almost five pages.

As they shook hands, Jenner said, "As soon as you have anything for us, even if it's only a vague feeling, please call. I know you understand how urgent this is."

He waited in the doorway for Roggetti to say his farewell.

The detective clasped Sheehan's hand firmly and said, "Thank you on behalf of the New York City Police Department, Father."

Roggetti shook the priest's hand, but didn't release it. "Father, I'd appreciate it if you could offer up a prayer for us, for God to give us help in catching this perpetrator."

Jenner paused, uncertain as to whether the priest would say the prayer at that moment, on the doorstep. But Sheehan was already closing the door, saying, "I'll do that, Detective. And may God watch over you and guide your steps."

Before Sheehan could close the door completely, Roggetti slipped his other hand in to clasp Sheehan's, uttering a final, earnest "Thank you, Father . . . Thank you," the mist of his breath hanging in the light from the lamp overhead.


In the dark of Pyke's loft, Ana lay in bed, staring at the pitch-black void of the ceiling somewhere overhead. She concentrated on not blinking, letting the tears well up and slip out by themselves, feeling them trickle over her cheek and down onto the pillow.

She snuffled and turned to reach out for her drink, but her grasping fingers knocked the tumbler off the bedside table, and it fell to the ground with a dull thud.

The tears coming faster, she slipped out of the bed, feeling the whisky-sodden carpet underneath her feet as she scrambled to find the cup.

Empty.

She cradled it in her palm, sank back against the mattress, and cried hard, her shoulders heaving as if invisible wings were struggling to lift her up.

It had really happened, all of it. She *wasn't* going to pass out and wake up hungover in their Cancun hotel room, and she would never again flop down on Andie's bed to howl about a date. Andie was dead, cut into pieces, buried in the ground. She was dead, dead forever, and all the whiskey in the world couldn't change that.

And the man in the window, the man who hacked apart her best friend just for fun, the man who smiled down at her as Andie's blood dried on his skin: that man had said that he would find her, and he would hurt her.

And no matter what Jenner and Roggetti and Garcia said or did, she knew that he would act. He would find her, and make her scream and make her bleed. He would hack her apart, and she would be dead, and they would bury her, and all the whiskey in the world couldn't change that.

TUESDAY,
# DECEMBER 10

A little after 1:00 p.m., they broke for lunch, gathering in Pyke's kitchen to wait for the delivery from the *cuchifritos* joint on Rivington—a salad for the prosecutor, roast pork and black beans and plantains for the rest of them.

Madeleine Silver was on the phone to the DA's office, hand over her other ear to block out the kitchen noise. Garcia was disassembling Pyke's Italian stovetop espresso pot, determined to show him how to make a perfect Cuban coffee, a *cafecito*.

Pyke was still frosty, but when the chief of detectives had Garcia interview Ana a second time, he didn't stop Jenner from sitting in. She was sitting blearily across from Jenner, reading the manual to her new cell phone, a gift from Pyke.

Garcia's old partner claimed Rad could talk the juice out of an orange; twice a year he taught interrogation at the FBI Academy in Quantico. Every time Garcia went to Quantico, he came back making the same *Children of the Corn* jokes, swearing to God that every single student at Quantico was a blue-eyed blond from Des Moines or Salt Lake City. Jenner, too, had lectured at the academy—it *was* a little *Children of the Corn* there.

The delivery man's buzzer interrupted a debate over coffee grinding. They ate at the table, Ana wordlessly moving to sit next to Jenner. She spilled her plantains out of their paper cup into the bag, watched it turn chestnut brown as it soaked with oil, then hungrily ate the *maduros* piece by piece, spearing them with a plastic fork and blotting them on some napkins, to the evident horror of ADA Silver.

The questions started up again, Rad promising they'd finish at 3:00 p.m. Ana's answers were unchanged; perhaps there was nothing more to get. As far as study habits, the task force had found no overlap between the victims (subjects, timetables, facilities, professors). Now Garcia was asking Ana about drugs.

She shook her head firmly. "Andie just wasn't into drugs. I always had pot, and I don't think I've ever seen her take more than two hits in the time I've known her. I mean, she could be kind of wild, and you'd think that with her dad she would've acted out more, but she wasn't like that. She didn't go on about it or anything, it was just her personal choice."

She watched the detective scrawling his notes.

"Seriously, Rad. She didn't touch anything, not even for a headache. She used to get really bad cramps, and she wouldn't take anything for them. The only time I've ever seen her take any drug was last summer, when she was doing the Lupron shots."

Madeleine Silver leaned forward and asked, "Lupron? What is that? Steroids?"

Ana leaned forward, tapping her pencil against the table. Then she gave a little shrug and said, "It's a fertility drug. Andie's dad wanted her to take some responsibility for her life, but she didn't want to get a job—she figured she'd fall behind in school. She tried to make a little extra money here and there. For a couple of summers, she was an egg donor. Like, for infertile couples?"

"Where did she do that?"

"I don't know, some clinic in SoHo, I think. A couple of them advertise on campus—they pay you seven thousand dollars. It's a lot of money, and it's not really that hard, just kind of gross. She had to inject herself in the stomach every morning for a few weeks to release the eggs. She got hot flashes from the Lupron, but she was basically okay."

"She did it twice?"

"Yeah, maybe three times, I think. The money made a difference, but for her, it was more than that, y'know? She liked helping the couples— they can be really desperate. I heard this pre-med student at Columbia, really beautiful and a major athlete, got thirty thousand for her eggs. The egg donor people just *love* the colleges—good gene pool. A lot of girls do it. Who doesn't need money?"

"Can you find out the name of the clinic where she went? I assume it wasn't one of the university clinics."

"No, I don't think so. I mean, maybe it's in her diary. I don't think they do it in a university clinic, I just think the egg donor people advertise on campus."

Jenner interrupted. "Are any of those medications still around? The bottle would have the pharmacy address, and maybe the prescribing doctor."

She shook her head. "I doubt it. I'm pretty sure they only give you exactly enough."

Rad stretched and pushed away from the table. "I'll see if Barb Wexler was a donor. We'll go have another look in the apartment—I doubt she'd have told Mom and Dad."

There was an urgent knocking at the door. Pyke let Jun in.

"Hey, Jenner. There's some guy trying to call you. He's been phoning every five minutes or so—I just missed the last call. You've got at least ten messages on your machine."

Joey and Rad came upstairs with him. He was about to hit the Play button when his phone rang again.

"Dr. Jenner, thank God! It's Patrick Sheehan. I think I have something."

Jenner said, "Hold on, Father—I'm going to put you on speaker. I'm here with Joey Roggetti and Lieutenant Rad Garcia—okay, go ahead."

"Hey, Father," said Roggetti.

"I'm pretty sure I have it. Almost positive . . ." He paused. "One thing. Sunday Smith—is that her real name? If it is her real name, does she have a middle or confirmation name? Specifically, is she a Katherine?"

"Father, it's Joseph Roggetti. I'm dialing the Pennsylvania State Police right now. Please go ahead."

Roggetti walked away from Jenner and Garcia, cell pressed to his ear.

"Jenner, can you get on the Internet?"

"Sure. Where should I go to?" He sat at his computer.

The priest spelled out the Web address for a Catholic church in Chicago.

"Okay," said Jenner. "I'm there now."

"Can you see the calendar? Click on that."

The screen filled with a grid listing church events and feast days.

"Are you on? I'm kicking myself for not seeing this right away. When you told me about the murder of Sunday Smith, I knew there was some-thing there. I just didn't make the connection until this afternoon. The *milk*, you see? Go to November twenty-fifth."

Jenner tabbed back a month and read out loud. "November twenty-fifth, canned goods drive collection one p.m. to five p.m., five thirty p.m. mass Father Wulstan, feast of Saint Katherine."

"Yes. Also the day Miss Smith was murdered."

"As best we can tell, yes."

"Okay, click on the link to the feast day."

The linked Web page was in German—*Katherine von Alexandria*—and came up slowly: the image of a woman in stained glass, a sword held up in her right hand and what appeared to be a broken cartwheel tucked under her left arm.

"You see the picture? This is Saint Katherine of Alexandria, a fourth-century martyr. She converted the emperor's wife to Christianity, so the emperor first had his wife killed, then Katherine. He ordered that Kather-ine should be crushed between two cogged wheels, but when the wheels touched her body, a bolt of lightning from heaven destroyed them, and killed her executioners. Then Maximus ordered that she be decapitated, but when her head was cleaved from her body, milk spouted from her neck."

*And there it was.* Jenner imagined the sunlight streaming into the Smiths' kitchen, illuminating the girl's head on the countertop, the milk clotting around it. He remembered her body on the embalming table, violated by the gaping X from the toothed weapon—the cogged wheel.

Jenner asked, "What about Andie Delore, Father?"

"Yes. November thirtieth, the feast of Saint Andrew. Andrew was scourged with seven whips, then crucified on a saltire cross—an X-shaped cross."

Jenner sat back in the chair and breathed out.

"And Barbara Wexler?"

"Saint Barbara's feast day is December fourth. Like Saint Andrew, she was whipped, but when the lashes touched her skin, they were divinely transformed into peacock feathers. Then she was decapitated."

Jenner imagined their bound hands, their praying hands, their martyred hands.

Rad leaned forward, closer to the speaker.

"Father, this is Lieutenant Garcia. Could you tell us what you learned
from the writing? What did it say?"

"Lieutenant, the writing is from a hagiography, a text describing the
lives of the saints. I'm afraid I made a mistake when I looked at it earlier;
the text I had translated as a reference to the Diocletian era, the term *khi
ro*? It is indeed used colloquially to refer to that time period, but its direct
translation, the literal meaning of the letters, is 'in this time of martyrs.'
I believe that that first symbol, which is repeated in all three texts, is a
simple declaration of intent."

"He's initiating a new era of martyrdom," Jenner murmured.

"Yes, I think he is." The priest paused. "After the *khi ro*, the text is purely
hagiographic. The first killing, the line reads 'Katherine of Alexandria, in
her wisdom, in her nobility, in her purity.' "

"The second is truncated, but it begins, 'Andrew, fisherman.' Saint
Andrew was one of the original 'fishers of men,' Jesus' twelve apostles."

"And on Barbara Wexler's back?"

"I'm still translating this, but it's an extensive passage from a source
similar to the previous two. There are a couple of things that are quite
striking about it, though."

He paused.

"First off, this text gives us the most information about the writer,
since it's the longest. I don't think the person who wrote it is genuinely
versed in Coptic. The symbols are poorly formed, but they are consistent: I think he's copying from another text.

"Students of alphabets often practice by copying older texts, but I
think I can be more specific in this instance. It's not a very big world, the
world of ancient manuscripts—everyone knows everyone else—and I
remember, about fifteen years back, a theft at the Parler Collection. This
was before I was at Yardley.

"The Parler Collection is owned by the library at Deene's College, in
southern Pennsylvania. It stuck in my mind because of the accusations

made by the Ancient Languages Department at the time. It was sad—it's not a top-tier school, forgive me for saying so, and that collection was a source of pride.

"Only a single manuscript was stolen, which was odd, particularly because it was hardly their most valuable. They had pieces going back to the fourteenth century, but the stolen manuscript was less than two hundred years old, a minor Napoleonic-era transcription of a now lost Coptic hagiography. The department head claimed that it had been transcribed by Jean-François Champollion himself—one of the original translators of the Rosetta stone—but the claim was ultimately discredited."

"What was the other thing, Father?"

"I'm not finished with the translation, but there's one thing that's really odd: the last two lines of the text are not Coptic at all, but Cyrillic."

"As in Russian?" Jenner asked.

"Well, most likely Russian. I don't speak the language, but I did recognize one of the words. *Skoptsi*."

"What does that mean?"

The priest paused.

"It's bizarre, Dr. Jenner. The Skoptsi were a nineteenth-century Russian mystical sect. The members castrated themselves as an act of self-mortification and a symbol of their commitment to God."

It was dark again.

It happened so quickly now, the brief gasp of daylight, muffled in early winter haze, suffocated before earth or skin had time to warm. The days were getting shorter. His days were getting shorter.

From the windows of the old factory, the man watched the bow lights of a tugboat passing soundlessly down the center channel of the East River. The crew had draped a snaggletoothed string of Christmas lights along the cabin, and he could make out the silhouette of a Christmas tree.

On the far bank, heavy traffic on the FDR was a glimmering ribbon of white and flickering red lights. It was almost pretty.

A sharp pain shot up from his right hand, and, lifting it up, he saw blood flowing freely from his fingers; in the dim light of the window, the blood was dark and thick, like blackstrap molasses. He'd been distractedly kneading the window ledge, and now, looking down in the half-light, he saw the night reflected in small glass shards on the sill.

He licked his fingers, and then blotted them on his pants. The whole room smelled of rust, of rotting iron, of his blood. His sense of smell was growing stronger. Or, at least, his sense of blood.

For a long while, he watched the cars on the expressway across the river, the traffic on the river.

In his workshop, he had books on forensic science. He'd read chapters—entire books—on the subject of blood spatter; he found the literature facile and lifeless, not animated by any real *feeling* for blood. He had insights no forty-year veteran criminalist could understand; they prided themselves on their scientific method, but it was he who was the real empiricist.

It amused him, pleased him, that now they were studying *him*, examining what he'd done, trying to understand what he would do next. Right now, in some crime lab, scientists in white Tyvek jumpsuits with masks and eye shields would be scrutinizing the arrows, maybe fuming them to find fingerprints, poring over the crime scene photographs, trying to interpret the blood spatter *he* had released. They were his archivists, a team of experts whose sole purpose was to bear witness to his work.

The newspapers were even better. The *Post* was the best—he was headline news now, big red *New York Post* headlines, his exploits splashed on the front page every day. In the *Post*, off-the-record comments from unnamed police sources gave reporters license for graphic descriptions of what he'd done. Their columnists railed about the cops, and called him a "fiend," and insisted that he was too smart to be insane, and that the only punishment for a "sicko" like him was death. They'd even given him a name—"the Inquisitor"; he didn't much care for it, but was proud to have earned a title. He was considering sending them a letter, maybe fill them in a bit on some of his earlier work.

He pulled his coat tighter around himself against the cold.

The first one he'd killed in New York was the son of a man who owned a bodega only a few blocks from the factory. The man had come across him on the path along the waterfront as he was walking back to the warehouse the day Dr. Zenker had told him he was dying (when he heard the prognosis, relief had washed over him, his fear replaced by a sense of clarity; even the knobs of tumor rotting his liver seemed to bother him less).

He was halfway to the factory when he saw a fat Mexican kid, maybe sixteen, dressed like a waiter in white dress shirt and black pants too tight for his girth, smoking a joint as he leaned against a sagging brick building.

The boy had watched him approach from a distance. The man saw him scan the area, checking to make sure they were alone. The man was immediately intrigued—this might be interesting.

The path took him within twenty feet of where the boy stood. Curious, he made eye contact, looked at him and nodded.

The boy straightened up and grinned. He had dewy brown eyes and a barely pubescent mustache.

"Hi."

The man nodded again and kept walking.

And that would have been it. Except the boy, bored perhaps, with nothing better to do, said, "Hey, mister. You wanna date?"

The man stopped. He turned to look back at the boy. Encouraged, the boy had smiled again and said, "You wanna date? I suck your cock real good."

The man hesitated for only a second. The boy, smiling widely now, gestured him forward. The man walked up to the grinning boy and hit him as hard as he could in the face.

The boy fell to the ground, gasping, blood pouring from behind hands pressed to his face. The man pulled him up to his feet by his hair, and then marched him toward the pier of his warehouse. The boy was begging and moaning, becoming frantic when the man dragged him past the tall grass, out of sight of the path. He saw the boy was going to start screaming, so he punched him hard in the face again to shut him up.

Then he pulled him down to the water and held his head under the water until he drowned. The boy's thrashing churned a thin scum of foam that lasted on the gray water for a while after he stopped, eddying around the boards that blocked access to the pier from the river.

Killing him felt good. As he held the boy under, kicking and splashing, there was a sudden rushing sensation, like a huge electric current, blasting out of some reservoir in the center of his being. The feeling was extraordinary, roaring out through his hands, a crackling discharge around his victim's neck. He could feel the boy's life force gushing back into his own body, replenishing him to overflowing, obliterating any fear, any weakness.

In an instant he knew that if he died with enough of this energy, he would transcend death to live on as some kind of blessed being, a king, a saint, an angel. For a second he saw himself there as if from a distance, from up in the rafter space over the enclosed pier, holding the boy's neck with both hands, kneeling on his back as he kicked futilely; he could see his own life becoming more vivid as the boy's life faded away.

He pushed the body into the water, and the little porker bobbed up, rolling over smoothly so that he was faceup. He was going to walk the body out to the water, push it down underneath the boards, and let it float on down into the harbor—no one would have seen him—but he caught sight of the rusting iron chain wrapped around one of the pillars. The tide was fairly low then, and his feet pressed on a slimy carpet of ooze and brick debris as he towed the boy back, deep under the overhang into the dank ammonia of a thousand rats' nests.

He arranged him with his back against the pillar, hooking the arms around the chain; as the water lapped up against the building supports, the boy rose and slipped, rose and slipped. It looked like the boy kept standing to say something and then changing his mind, over and over. It was good to see, but he realized the body needed more support, so he came back later and secured it with telephone cable. That had worked nicely. He didn't want the boy to drift away, he wanted to watch him change, just as any parent wants to see his child grow.

When he finally went back inside, he was aroused, and his mouth and fingertips were tingling. It was a new sensation, and he wanted to see his face and fingers, so he went to the mirror by the sink. He didn't look any different, really. Face blotchy from the effort and the excitement, hair damp against his scalp.

The calendar from St. Anthony and St. Alphonsus hung from a nail by the mirror, and as he wiped his face with a dishtowel he saw it was the feast day of Saint Florian.

He stank of stagnant river water, of the pier under the warehouse, of rotting mud and diesel oil, of soap scum and rat piss. He stole his water from the fruit packers by Manhattan Bridge (a long walk back, in the dark, a fifty-pound tank of water over one shoulder); though water was precious, he needed to wash. He filled a basin and, kneeling down, wiped himself all over with a cool cloth. He did a thorough job of it, even used some of his precious hand soap, collected in an empty Snapple bottle from the men's room in the Long Island City Costco.

As he scrubbed himself, his knees burned as they had so many times before, kneeling by the altar, listening to Father Martin give the sermon. He'd grinned at the thought of how shiny and pink he was then, young and full of some kind of potential, and at how different he was now, grown and kneeling naked on the floor, a man who could kill, a man who fed on death.

The boy probably went to Anthony and Alphonsus; lots of the Mexicans from the area did. He could even have been an altar boy.

Then, all of a sudden, it had hit him. *Saint Florian.* Saint Florian, martyred as a young man. Saint Florian, scourged and drowned, chained to a millstone.

He felt all the tension go from his limbs, and he slumped to the floor facedown, his arms spread. Again he seemed to float above himself, look down on his body. There was a smell of narcissus, and the room filled with white light, irradiating his body, healing his body, cleansing his soul.

WEDNESDAY,
DECEMBER 11

Ana lay across his bed, watching him dress.

"I thought you weren't supposed to be involved anymore, Jenner."

"I'm not."

"So why are you going to Pennsylvania? Why don't you stay here with me?"

"Because Rad and Joey say the chief of detectives says he wants me to go."

"Well, what about Dr. Whittaker?"

"He's not invited."

"Hmmph. And for that you're leaving me all alone, all by myself?"

She lay back on his bed, languidly stretched her arms up until her sweatshirt rode up to uncover her panties.

"I have to go."

She rolled over fluidly and got up on her knees.

"Stay, Jenner. Please."

He ruffled her hair, then lifted the bag onto his shoulder. "I'll call you from the road."

She pouted. "Uncle Douggie was right about you."

"You should've listened to him."

"I did! But I wore him down until he said I had to make my own decisions. You see, *he* cares about me . . ."

Jenner shrugged. When he turned to go, she called out, "Jenner!"

She came up to him, slipped her arms around him, and said, "I can't believe you're going."

He kissed the top of her head. She leaned into his kiss, then pushed him away with a soft punch. "Well, just fuck off and go then."

\* \* \*

Rad was leaning on his car in front of the building, all sunglasses and smile, sipping from a Styrofoam coffee cup.

"Edward! Good to see you!"

"You're unpleasantly chipper this morning." Jenner tossed his bag into the backseat.

"The kids are with their uncle Ricky this week." The smile broadened. "You should try the love of a good woman, Jenner. Do you a power of good."

Jenner sighed. "Ah, someday, maybe. Someday . . ."

Garcia climbed into the driver's seat, adjusted the rearview mirror, then took off his gloves.

The passenger-side door was still locked; Jenner tapped on the window. Ana suddenly burst out of his building, past the super, down the steps to the sidewalk. Jenner's sweatshirt came down to the middle of her thigh; her legs were bare underneath. A pair of Jun's sneakers dwarfed her feet.

She breathlessly pressed her new cell phone into his hand. "Take this, okay?"

"It's okay. I can use Rad's."

"No. I want you to have *mine*."

Her eyes were so earnest that he gave in, slipping the phone into his coat pocket with a grin. He leaned to kiss her, but she pushed him away.

"*Whoa!* What do you think *you're* doing? I'm still pissed at you!"

She gave Garcia a nod, then looked down Crosby toward Chinatown, and back up toward Houston. Her face was serious. Jenner smiled and said, "New York City, just like you always imagined it?"

"Not funny, Jenner. It's weird to be out."

"Good weird?"

"Weird weird." She shivered, and looked back at the building. "I should go in." She gave him a peck on the cheek, started to pull away, then kissed him hard.

He stepped back, pushing her toward the doorway. "Enough!" he said. "I told you: *Never in front of the cops!*"

She walked back up the stairs, then slipped past Pete into the entry foyer.

He got into the car. Rad sat there, eyes straight ahead, face straining to look innocent. He put the car into gear.

"You know, Jenner, there may just be hope for you yet."

As they drove up Crosby, they passed a white van parked across the street from the Lightbulb Factory. A man sat quietly behind the wheel, a large digital camera on the seat next to him.

They made good time to Romen. It was a different car, a beige Crown Vic that still smelled of the factory. Rad drove, keeping the radio low as he brought Jenner up to date on the progress of the investigation.

There had been little: if Father Sheehan's epiphany had made the killings comprehensible as a series, the task force hadn't been able to develop much practical information. Worse, every lead had crumbled the moment it was nudged. The curator of the Parler Collection was fairly new, and her predecessor had died a couple of years previously. The Deene's Ridge police department had never solved the manuscript theft, chalking it up to a prank that had gone too far. Detectives on the Inquisitor squad at South Homicide had quietly started looking into Hutchins's Comparative Religion Department, both faculty and students, and at that moment, Father Sheehan and Joey Roggetti were charting a calendar of upcoming feast days of martyrs.

The night before, Jenner had stopped by the Barnes & Noble in Union Square and picked up books on martyrdom and saints. The color illustrations reveled in pain and spilled blood, celebrating the saints' suffering as much as their faith. The methods of torture and execution had an abstract ingenuity that was almost playful, as if thought up by twelve-year-old boys.

Jenner had been astonished by the sheer number of saints. On any given day, there were a good dozen to be honored, both familiar canonical names as well as a vast litany of obscure saints. Many had been martyrs; Jenner told Garcia he'd figured that four or five martyrs were celebrated each day of the year.

Rad shrugged at Jenner's statistic, and fiddled with the radio dial until he found some eighties rock.

"I'm Cuban, Jenner. That's nothing! We've got all those saints, *plus* we've got Santeria stuff, you know, the *orishas*, our sacred spirits—Oshun, Chango, that whole deal."

"You think Chango knows you listen to Foreigner?"

"Chango? *Coño*, Chango *loves* Foreigner! Rush, too."

They drove in silence for twenty miles, then Rad said, "What do you think he chooses first, Jenner? Victim or saint?"

"Saint. You've seen how prepared he is. The tool he used to cut Sunday Smith open? The peacock feathers? He plans it out a long, long time ahead. He *designs* them, collects and makes his props. He's like some kind of director, putting together a play."

Rad nodded. "But how is he choosing them?"

Jenner shook his head. He looked out of the window, silent. The sun was up, and much of the snow on the fields had melted and then refrozen, leaving patchy sheets of ice shimmering amid the winter stubble. He watched his breath frost the glass.

When Rad spoke again, his voice was hesitant.

"So, I was wondering . . . How are you doing with all this shit? How you holding up?"

Rad had never talked about emotional issues before, but different New York, different NYPD. And now Rad Garcia, one of the toughest guys he'd ever met, wanted to talk about *feelings*.

Jenner, despite himself, was touched. "I'm okay. It felt strange at first, but I'm remembering that this is something I know how to do, something I used to be good at." He paused for a second. "And I guess I'm not surprised Whittaker's screwed me. He's playing the game, making his move for the chief's job. He wants credit, so he took mine."

"Maybe so, Jenner. But the guy is an asshole."

Jenner grinned back at him. "Yeah. He's an asswipe."

"He's an ass*clown*."

Steve Miller's "Rockin' Me" came on the radio, and Rad cranked it up.

She sat on the bed and watched Pyke pack, then she made coffee in the kitchen as they waited for the car service to take him to Newark.

"Where is Bhutan? You really have the best job ever."

"It's just work," Pyke said. "You know I'd stay here if I could, but the photo editor has been setting up this project for years now, and I can't suddenly pull the plug."

She shook her head and told him she was fine. "I've got Jenner and half of the New York Police Department guarding me. There's nothing to worry about."

Pyke muttered, "Well, it's the 'Jenner and half of the New York Police Department' part that's worrying me . . ."

Smiling, she put a hand on his shoulder and said, "He's a decent guy. I know you don't believe it, but I think he really wants what's best for me."

Pyke said, "No, I believe that's what he wants . . . but the guy's a mess. I don't want him to take you down as collateral damage." He was quiet for a second, then said, "He really is a good person. And you need someone to be with you right now, and I'm running off and deserting you. Just be careful with him—for both of your sakes."

"Well, first off, I think I've been good for Jenner. I think he's doing better. And second: you're deserting me to work so that I can have this great place to stay in!"

The intercom sounded. They hugged, and she waited at his window and watched as he walked out onto Crosby. Pyke's assistant was waiting there, a tall young black guy with thin arms who fitted Pyke's bags neatly into the grid of aluminum camera equipment cases. Pyke did a quick inventory, then turned and looked up. He saw her, smiled and waved, then got into the car and was gone.

She turned to face the loft. It was so clinical, with its white walls and stacked white enamel filing cabinets, and techno-fetish-y stuff. Jenner's apartment was warm and soft by comparison, with wood and fabric and pale, natural colors. She'd go up there and hang out, maybe draw.

She opened a cabinet and pulled out a bottle of wine, then put it back and took the last of the whisky instead. She lifted the bottle to eye level and sloshed the whisky around.

It wasn't enough. It was never enough anymore.


The Smith farm sat in its own shadowy little valley. Though the sun was still bright on the surrounding high ground, the valley was a good ten degrees colder, and snow drifted deep in the sloping hollows behind the farmhouse.

The driveway dipped steeply down to the house, and hadn't been plowed since the last snowfall. As Rad inched the car slowly down the drive, a thin young man in a white short-sleeved dress shirt and a green hunting cap with earflaps came out of the house and watched from the porch.

They stepped through the snow to the house; Rad, his hand outstretched, said, "Mr. Smith? I'm Lieutenant Garcia, this is Dr. Jenner. I hope this isn't a bad time for you."

The boy shook his head. "Not really doing much of anything. My parents left this morning; I'm staying behind to close up the house and sort out the rest of Katie's stuff before I go on to meet up with my folks."

His eyes were pale blue, his skin dark tan. He wore a black name tag, ELDER JAMES SMITH. Jenner had seen the Mormons in the countryside in Thailand; he imagined the boy pedaling his bicycle through villages and rice paddies on his mission, a satchelful of tracts tucked under the neatly folded black jacket strapped to the rear mudguard rack.

He was about twenty. Standing straight, he seemed crumpled and careworn beyond his years. Beneath the tan, he was drawn, and, though he stood in front of his own home, he looked more than a little lost.

"Must be hard, all this," said Garcia.

The boy nodded, then turned and walked into the house. They followed him into the living room. The furniture was cheap and battered, and the floor was covered with thick shag carpeting; there was a faint smell of mold. In front of the cold fireplace was an old rocking chair draped with an ugly crocheted blanket; on the floor by the chair, Jenner saw a near-empty half-pint bottle of Mr. Boston vodka.

"So ask me your questions. Me, my mom, and my dad have been near Ban Long, Cambodia, since last November; my dad's mission president. We were away when Katie died. Sarah probably knows more than I do."

He gestured toward a small alcove with a table, where a girl with pale, waxy skin and lank blond hair sat, hands folded, shoulders hunched. Even with her head down, Jenner could see her eyes were swollen and red behind her glasses.

"That's Sarah. She was my intended up until about a week ago."

Rad suggested they talk in another room.

Elder Smith smiled thinly and said, "Well, sir, we got the living room, the hallway, the breakfast nook, and then we got the kitchen. I mean, we could go in the kitchen if that's what you want. I mean, if that's what you really want; Sarah and her family cleaned up in there, cleaned it up so nice you can barely even tell."

He looked at the girl balefully. "They washed it real good, but you can still smell it. You can't get the smell of blood out . . ."

He was tilting slowly backward, and Jenner saw he was drunk. Rad quickly stepped behind him, bracing for a fall, but the kid listed forward again and kept talking.

He was mumbling now. "Swear to God, I can smell it in my bed. The whole damned house. My sister's blood."

The girl was sobbing, listening to him. He looked at her, angry and confused.

Rad put a hand on the boy's shoulder. "Son? You been drinking?"

"Yep. I have. First time ever! And you know what? It takes the edge off. It really does."

Rad turned to the girl. "Miss, maybe you could take the doctor into the kitchen while I talk with your friend."

She nodded and stood, then stepped past him, avoiding looking at the boy. Rad steered him toward the alcove table. "Come on, son. We're going to sit down and talk."

In the hallway with Jenner, Sarah said firmly, "I'm not going in the kitchen. We can talk here, or upstairs, but, mister, there's no way I'm going in there."

Jenner nodded. "Upstairs."

She hugged her arms across her bony chest as she led him briskly up the stairs.

"This is Kate's room, here——" She pointed to the left at the top of the landing. "That's the parents' room, and over there is Jimmy's." Her voice softened as she looked at his door.

"Did you know Kate well?"

"We were the only two LDS kids in our class at high school, so we kind of ended up hanging out all the time. We were different. She said all the right things, and she dressed modest, but she got on better with non-Mormons than me. I didn't see it coming, though—all along she was planning to leave the church and move to New York for college. I think maybe her uncle helped her out. Her mother's brother—Mrs. Smith used to be a Lutheran, she joined the church when she met Mr. Smith."

"Did you stay in touch when she moved to New York?"

"No. When she got in to Hutchins, she started acting different, like a gentile. Changed her name, started wearing different clothes, not so modest. After she got her tongue pierced, my folks wouldn't let me hang out with her. Which was hard, because that was the only way I could see Jimmy."

She started to sniffle again, her narrow chest shuddering under the thin cardigan.

"It's really hard. I love him, but he's been gone a year, and soon he's going to be gone for another year. You know I only spoke with him one time while he was away? I know it's not his fault—you only get to call home twice a year when you're on mission. It's supposed to be to their folks, but President Smith let him use his Christmas call to call me. He writes a lot, too. But then I met a good man in Provo when I was at the Missionary Training Center, and I fell in love with him. I prayed on it, and I had to be true to my heart."

She wiped her face with her arm.

"I was going to tell Jimmy, but I couldn't do it in a letter or an e-mail. And then Kate died. It took them forever to reach the Smiths. The sheriff let my dad and my cousins clean up before they came home and saw it. They wouldn't tell me about it."

She began weeping convulsively. Jenner heard movement below, and the boy's head poked into the stairwell.

"Sarah . . . you all right?" His tone was protective, almost belligerent.

She pulled herself together and told him she was just sad.

Rad appeared behind the boy. Behind the girl's back, Jenner nodded at his raised eyebrow.

"I think I've asked enough questions for now. Thank you both. Miss, if you'd like to come down here, Dr. Jenner and I need to have a look in Ms. Smith's room."

It was a plain room. The powder pink walls seemed the only concession to girlish whimsy: no riding trophies, or photographs of friends, or stuffed animals, or posters of movie stars or boy bands. Two portraits of Jesus looked down on the bed from the wall above.

"Okay, Doc, what am I looking for?"

"Vials or packaging are really what we want—anything with a label. The hormone course lasts a few weeks, so she pretty much had to have injected herself at home at some point."

Rad opened the closet and began to go through the clothes heaped on the shelf. Jenner searched the bulky white chest of drawers; the top drawer had stickers of hearts and rainbows haphazardly stuck on its front. There was nothing to find in the underwear drawer, just plain undergarments. The middle and lower drawers held simple tops and pants, with a wadded-up stack of love letters pressed into the back of the bottom drawer. They were more than ten years old, probably a crush from Mormon camp or summer school or wherever it was that Latter-Day Saints kids developed their crushes.

Rad was going through the pockets of the coats and jackets in the closet. He called over to Jenner, "Hey, pull the lowest drawer all the way out and see if there's anything underneath."

There was; she'd kept her secrets in the well below the bottom drawer.

To Jenner's eye, the traces of her hidden life seemed more sweet than shaming; he could imagine how exhilarated and terrified of discovery they must have made her. There was a letter on yellowed paper, apparently from high school: a boy named Tom dreamed of undressing her and touching her breasts, and "between your beautiful legs." There was a half-smoked Marlboro and a ball of lacy black lingerie.

Jenner reached back into the recesses as far as he could, sweeping his arm from side to side in the dust. There was nothing at the back, but as he was pulling his arm out, he felt something cylindrical roll underneath it. His fingers scooped up a small glass vial.

He produced it with a flourish.

"Rad."

It was a couple of inches tall, and empty, with a metal cap, the center of which had a punctured gray rubber membrane. She'd peeled off most of the label: there was no way to confirm the contents, or the prescribing physician, but one torn edge still clung to the glass, and it had a legible logo.

He showed it to Rad. "This look familiar to you? APPDRx? I could swear I've seen it before."

"Is it the manufacturer?"

Jenner squinted at it. "No, this is the pharmacy's, I think."

"Local?"

"I doubt it—she wouldn't have risked filling it around here. Besides, drugs like Lupron and Pergonal are pretty specialized—they don't carry them in every corner drugstore."

Rad nodded in agreement. "Particularly out here in Mayberry. Okay, we need to get back to the city and go through a phone book. Should be pretty easy to find them. We'll talk to the pharmacist tomorrow morning—we won't make it back in time tonight."

"Will we need a subpoena?"

"Yeah, I guess. He'd probably give up the prescribing physician's name, but if this thing's going to stand up and walk in court . . ."

Jenner looked around the room again. It felt small and empty and unlived-in. Solid bed from the 1950s, ugly white dresser onto which she'd stuck heart stickers as a little girl. He wondered if she'd been punished for that.

How could people choose a life like that, choose a life like that for their children? Did little girls *like* being ascetic? Perhaps she didn't even realize how bare it was. Perhaps all the LDS girls lived like that. Perhaps she didn't see the room as cold and plain, but as warm and suffused with God's love.

He thought of his own loft, which was almost as bare. But his sparse was the stylized, materialist sparse, and the objects he owned, while few, were beautiful and luxurious. He felt vulgarly affluent and shallow.

Then again, she hadn't been happy with this. She'd rebelled. Stopped dressing modestly, pierced her ears and tongue, moved to Manhattan, been close enough to a boy that she'd bought sexy lingerie. Or close enough to another girl, maybe.

It sounded as if she'd blossomed in New York, with her tongue piercing and her new name. At least until the old name had caught up with her.

In the living room, Elder Smith sat in the rocking chair, his head in his hands. The former intended, now calm, stood next to him, her pale hand resting limply on his shoulder. Her attitude was maternal, controlled, and slightly possessive.

Rad and Jenner went into the kitchen. The room faced west, into the open valley. The late-afternoon sun was now rushing across the frozen fields, flooding the room with a nostalgic, golden light, making the linoleum surfaces and aluminum trim glow.

They knew the room from the crime scene photographs, but the photographs couldn't have shown what was now obvious to them as they stood there: the kitchen had been the heart of the house, this had been where they had *lived*.

With its warm, buttery yellows and whites, it looked like the sort of kitchen where Mom baked pies in a housedress and frilly apron, leaving them to cool by an open window. The appliances, with the exception of a KitchenAid stand mixer, all looked a good forty or fifty years old. The mixer's dough hook was attached; Jenner imagined the smell of fresh baked bread drifting from the kitchen, warming and redeeming the rest of the barren house.

That kitchen, he thought, might never smell of warm bread again; murder poisons a house, turns it toxic as a contaminated well. Mrs. Smith would never bake there again without seeing her little girl sitting on a yellow chair at the yellow table, coloring as she waited for the hot loaves to come out of the oven. He couldn't understand how President and Mrs. Smith, in their gadarene rush to escape, could have been cruel enough to leave their son behind in this charnel house.

Perhaps this was a religious thing; perhaps they really did believe that the girl was in a better place. Perhaps they'd achieved some kind of complete emotional separation from her death. But the boy was a mess, anyone could see it.

Jenner just didn't understand.

The kid was right about the blood, too. The smell of bleach, intense and corrosive, shimmered from the warming countertops and table and floor, searing his nostrils and catching in his throat. Beneath it, Jenner smelled her blood as a sharp wave of rust, choking and primal.

He thought the room through.

The head had been on the island in front of him; her trunk would have been at his feet. There had been arcs of blood spatter low on the cabinets, arterial spray. He would have plugged the saw or hedge trimmer or whatever he'd used into the socket by the toaster on the counter.

Knife probably his own, probably did her pretty quickly after she took him into the kitchen. She'd probably offered him coffee. She'd have walked in first, he'd have followed her, and *bam!* hit her before she knew what was happening. Cut her throat, held her as she went down to the floor—if she were over his knee, that would explain the low height of the arterial spatter.

Probably pulled her clothes off her once she'd stopped moving, and then got down to work. Stripping her in that narrow space would have caused the broad smears on the low cabinet by the hallway door.

He walked to the island, then paced back to the hall door. Five feet, give or take—less than two long strides. God, he must have moved quickly.

There were pencil markings going up both sides of the door frame that he hadn't noticed in the crime scene photos. They'd strung for blood spatter! The criminalists—probably hicks who'd seen a few too many episodes of *CSI*—had taken the time to figure the angle of each blood droplet, then used lengths of string to determine the point of origin. Amateur hour—even the quickest reading of the scene made the killing sequence obvious.

He knelt in front of the door and looked at the pencil markings. Then he read out loud.

"Kathy, July fourth, 1990. Four feet ten."

Oh. The marks weren't from stringing.

He put his finger to markings on the other side of the door frame. "Jim, October seventeenth, 1995, five feet one."

Her mother had probably stood just where he knelt, telling the giggling little girl to stay still while she ticked her height off on the door frame, her brother waiting for his turn.

"*The child I buried* . . ." There was a poem, he couldn't remember how it went. "*Rest in sweet peace* . . ." It wasn't coming back. The mother, measuring her little girl's growth in the safety of the kitchen; now, Jenner kneeling in the same spot to document her death.

And what of all the years in between? Her achievements, her suffering, her happiness, her life—all the things that meant so much to her? They meant nothing to him.

Her life, other than whatever she'd done, whoever she'd been to attract the killer, couldn't be important to Jenner. Her life was an impediment, a warm, sucking thing that held on to him and stopped him from thinking clearly, so he could learn who killed her, so he could stop that man before he found himself kneeling in the kitchen doorway of another dead girl, eyes burning again as he read out loud how tall she was when she was seven.

Jesus. Enough.

He looked up at Rad and said, "I don't need to see anything more here. Let's go."

Rad glanced at him, then looked away quickly and nodded.

Jenner went out to the car while Rad finished with the boy and the girl. He leaned against the hood, waiting, looking out over the valley. The snow over the fields sloping away from the Smith house was a billowing, drifting blanket of virgin white, the ground underneath it black, frozen, and dead.

The second he walked through the door into his loft, she threw herself at him, wrapping her arms around him and showering him with kisses. "You took *forever* to get back!"

She pulled his coat off, looked around the room, trying to figure out where it belonged, then shrugged and tossed it onto a chair, saying, "So I did something major this morning, right?"

"What did you do?"

She made a face. "Jenner! I went *outside*! I've been cooped up in here forever now; that was my first time going out because I wanted to."

He nodded; she was working up to something.

"So I made a decision: I want you to take me out tonight."

He'd never seen her so lively.

"Yes? No? Tell me what you think! Because I really want to go out."

He sat. "Ana, it's almost ten p.m. I'm pretty tired. It's been a long day."

"What you need is a drink. I'm going to make you a drink. What do you drink? Wine? Let me fix you something."

"I don't need a drink."

"A glass of wine it is."

She pulled a bottle from the refrigerator, a Kongsgaard Roussanne viognier.

"Is this any good?" She saw the price tag and whistled. "Eighty dollars for a bottle of wine? What, did *Jesus* make this or something?"

He stood, but she was already scoring the foil with her knife, forehead furrowed in concentration; she seemed so excited, he didn't have the heart to interrupt her.

She peeled the foil, then started twisting the corkscrew into the cap, then jamming it impatiently back and forth. He stopped her before she could do any more damage.

"Slow down!" he said. "Here, let me do it."

He carefully levered the remaining cork from the bottle and poured two glasses.

"Here." He handed her the glass and then hastily added, "No! Wait!" as she began to gulp it. "This isn't, whatever, Manischewitz or something! Slow down, take the time to taste it."

She put the glass to her lips, then lowered it a second to add with a smirk, "This better be some damned tasty grape juice . . ."

She sipped, then murmured appreciatively, "Oh, yum! That really is nice! Thanks, Jenner."

"My pleasure. I'm glad you like it."

"Yeah, but no way is it worth eighty bucks, dude!"

She was giggling again, perched on her chair; he scowled at her, then tipped a little more into his glass. He said, "I have to do some work first, but after that, I guess we could go out. What do you want to do?"

She sat next to him, took his hand, and looked him earnestly in the eye. "Listen, Jenner, this is important to me. I think it's time for me to start trying to be normal again."

He nodded. "Okay. So what do normal girls do?"

She stood quickly. "I want to go clubbing!"

He was surprised; he'd figured they'd walk a couple of blocks, then come home and fool around.

"Where?"

"In the East Village, in Alphabet City. Wednesday nights, my friend Anthony runs a party called My Favorite Cyborg at Industrial Crisis over on Eighth between C and D. It's pretty great—totally underground, great DJs playing minimal techno from, like, Berlin and Detroit. It's kind of an institution—you're not supposed to talk about it, because within a week the place would be filled with Guidos and their big-haired girlfriends fucked up on apple martinis and Ecstasy."

He felt old.

"C'mon, Jenner! Fair's fair! You just exposed me to your culture, now it's my turn."

"Okay. But I can't stay out too late."

She put her arms around him and said, "Awww . . . don't worry, old man. I'll make sure you're back by four a.m."

"One a.m."

"We'll see." She straightened up and took another sip. "I don't know how long I'll last, either."

She drained her glass, then set it on the counter. "Okay, you go do your thing. I'm going to make myself beautiful."

Jenner got out the yellow pages, opened it to the Pharmacy listings. It would likely be a downtown pharmacy, close to the school. Initials APPDRx.

He found it as soon as he ran his eye down the roster. Astor Place Pharmacy and Drug Rx. He knew it well, Eighth Street just west of Broadway. He called the number and got a machine; the store was closed, and would open at 8:00 a.m.

Fair enough. It would wait until the morning. He kicked himself for not recognizing it the moment they found the vial in Romen—Rad could have had someone get to the pharmacy before it closed for the night.

When the man was a boy, almost every night, he came home from school in clothes that were bloodied and torn, his lip split or his eye blackened.

And every night, Father Martin would set him right back up for another beating, telling him he had to try harder to get along. Father Martin's exhortations took into account neither the boy's uniquely flawed personality nor the rapacious cruelty of childhood. His altered physical condition marked him for a life on the outside: the testosterone replacement therapy after the accident seemed more a disease than a treatment, boosting his muscle mass, making his body hard and unusually strong, but cursing him with acne so disfiguring that at school he was universally known as the Zombie Prick.

The hormones gradually made him angry and aggressive; unable to deliver snide comebacks to the ceaseless taunts, he resorted to his fists. After nearly beating another student to death, the boy was admitted to the Central Pennsylvania Inpatient Mental Health Center. Father Martin visited him in his little cell; the boy's ankles and wrists were strapped to the bed with leather restraints. The priest made it clear that if he told the doctors any secrets, Martin would punish Oliver, the smallest of the children who lived with him at the rectory, the little kid who told people the boy was his brother.

He didn't tell the secrets.

At the center, his teachers encouraged his flair for math. He clung to the neat, reliable world of numbers and flow charts and symbolic logic the way a recovering alcoholic tethers himself to a higher power as he starts a life of sobriety. He was safe there. He never felt wronged by numbers—how could he? The numbers were what they were, and only what they were, and when they didn't give him the answer he wanted, it was because he had mistreated them.

Statistics, calculus, linear algebra—everything came to him readily in the unimposing sterility of the special school. Outside of the classroom, he developed a passion for cryptography, spending hours reading about the history of codes. From codes he moved on to the study of alphabets, and by the time he was sixteen, he was doing phonetic translations into Egyptian hieroglyphics or Japanese *romaji*. At eighteen, he created his own written language, a curious script made of bold uprights and circles divided by radial lines set at different angles, like tentatively sliced pies.

He was allowed to enroll at Joseph Baxter Community College in Berwick. For him, it was like a halfway house before moving on to Deene: a new start where no one knew about his past. During his time in the hospital, he had been treated by a kind dermatologist from Beirut, who'd put him on a regimen of antibiotics, gentle scrubs, and sunlight. When he was released, his complexion, though pocked, was free of the pustules of his youth. To the other students, he was just another farm boy trying to advance himself.

Still, he never mingled. Each night, he'd ride his bike back to the rectory and sit at the drafting table he'd made from an old door, drawing flow diagrams and crafting alphabets. And while everyone was impressed by his invented alphabet, they'd have felt quite differently had they been able to read it: the upright slashes and hacked circles drawn with soft charcoal pencil hid luxuriantly detailed reveries of torture and murder, the sort of things he'd dreamed about—and, on occasion, enacted—since the third grade.

THURSDAY,
DECEMBER 12

Ana told Jenner she'd take just a minute to put herself together, but it was almost two hours before she felt ready to go out. All the time—changing, doing her makeup, changing again—she'd been on the phone, talking excitedly with friends, arranging to meet up at the club. He knew it would be well after midnight before they finally left the loft.

She was getting better, feeling braver about things like going out. Earlier in the evening she'd been chatty and wired, more alive than at any time since her arrival in his world.

He'd thought of himself as looking after her, but now he accepted that it had been a two-way street, that she'd also been fixing him. Her problems—her *real* problems—had overwhelmed his, nudging him out of his little cell and pushing him back into the world, armed with a purpose.

Now she was feeling free, and happy, and it was mostly because of him. She was calling up her own friends again, making plans, getting ready to move on, ready to leave him behind.

From the bathroom, he heard her laugh. He imagined her stretched languidly in the vast tub, her lithe body hidden under a heavy blanket of bubbles, holding the phone with her right hand while she shaved her legs with his razor.

Her laugh, which he'd always liked, now sounded sharp and unreasonable. He felt he barely knew her, that it had all been some kind of front. That she'd been playing the victim to please him, to finesse a place to stay, someone to care about her.

The bathroom door opened in a billow of settling steam, and she breezed past him wrapped in a thick white bath sheet, yakking on her cell, barely noticing him.

Later, impatient with his frustration, she sent him down to grab a taxi, promising to follow in a second. He waited in the back of the chilly cab; when she hadn't appeared after fifteen minutes, he paid the driver and went back up to his loft, furious.

She was sprawled on the floor by the bed, surrounded by her clothes, crying.

He knelt beside her. "What happened? What's the matter?"

She sobbed, "Joey brought me my suitcase, but half of the clothes are Andie's . . ."

He didn't get it. "Can't you wear some of the clothes you have?"

"No! No. It's not that . . . We always shared clothes—that's why they were in my bag." She sat up, wiping her eyes with her shirtsleeve. "It's just that I can't believe she's never going to wear that ugly Beck T-shirt ever again."

He put an arm around her and stroked her hair. "I'm sorry, Ana."

She stood quickly, gathering herself. "No, I'm sorry for making a scene." She took his hand as he stood. "I won't be long now, I just have to fix my face."

"I like your face the way it is. But I'll wait here for you."

She wrinkled her nose at him. "I won't be long." She headed for the bathroom, then turned. "I think I'm a little drunk."

"No hurry, Ana. Take your time."

She slid in next to him, and told the driver to take Houston all the way to Avenue D, take the left on D, then drop them on the corner of Eighth.

He slipped his arm around her shoulders and held on to her as she chattered in his ear, his pleasure in the moment dreamlike. He let the words melt together, and savored the pressure of her shoulder against his chest, the sweet, slightly childish smell of her perfume, a smell of mango and lime and incense.

She kissed his neck.

At least for now, she was with him. The world outside the taxi seemed a thousand miles away, all those people not even real.

It was nearing 1 a.m., but the streets and sidewalks were jammed. People spilled out of bars and restaurants, forming into little knots to make where-next plans. They caught a red light at Ludlow, and he watched the trickle of the young and hip into and out of Bereket Turkish Kebab House, a late-night downtown staple.

To his right was the true Lower East Side, with its old tenements and immigrants and wholesale fabrics, to his left, the East Village, their destination. Specifically, the far East Village, Alphabet City, Avenues A to D, gentrification to poverty, renovated town houses to run-down high-rise projects.

He realized then that Ana had chosen the route to avoid her apartment. When he reached to stroke her hair, she turned and smiled brightly, brushing his hand away.

"Almost there!"

He nodded.

"C'mon, Jenner. It'll be fun! You'll see." She rubbed his shoulder, then leaned into the bulletproof Lucite taxi partition. "Avenue *D*, driver! Take the left—c'mon, you can make the light!"

They got out in front of a bodega on the corner of Eighth. Despite the hour and the cold, there were two old men in front of the store sipping from bottles in brown paper bags, watching the flow of kids out clubbing.

Industrial Crisis was a retrofitted supermarket with frosted glass windows painted with a 1950s realist graphic, a large black wrench that stretched across the entire glass front. The club was in the middle of the block; he wouldn't have noticed it if not for the glowing column of white light over the entrance. In front of the door, a small blond girl perched on a high stool next to a muscular black man in a bulky black coat, behind them a couple of smokers exiled into the cold. Ana grabbed his arm and dragged him faster. As they got closer, he heard the muffled, repetitive thud of a kick-drum beat.

"Oh, my God! *Katie!*" Ana threw her arms around the girl, pulling her off her stool.

"Oh, my God! Ana!" There were kisses and a long hug, and under the factory light fixture, Jenner saw they were both crying. Ana closed her eyes and rocked her friend from side to side as she held her tight.

Smiling, the black guy said, "Hey, Ana, welcome back." His accent was English, South London maybe.

Ana turned and hugged him with one arm, murmuring, "*Winston!*" Then, seeing Katie's smeared mascara, she pulled away, opened her purse, and began to wipe her friend's face.

"Awww, honey. I've spoiled your makeup." Katie began to wipe Ana's face, too, the two now laughing. Katie glanced over at Jenner, looking him up and down. "You must be Jenner."

He nodded. The girl came over, stood on her toes to kiss him on the cheek, then hugged him.

"Thanks for looking after Ana. She's told us all about you."

He flushed as he shook hands with Winston, then Katie took his arm. "Let's go inside."

Couples and small groups packed the dimly lit lounge just inside the door; beyond the lounge an archway led to the dance floor.

When Ana went to say hi to the bartenders, Katie grabbed Jenner's arm and held him back.

"Jenner, there's something I think you should know. There's a friend of Ana's here tonight who isn't good for her. They have a kind of fucked-up history, and she hasn't seen him for a while, and I think it would be better if she didn't hang out with him right now."

"What does he look like?"

"Tall guy, hair cropped short, black eyelets in both his ears, a black labret."

"A labret—a pierced lip, you mean?"

"Yeah, just below the lip. The eyelets are those washer things people use to stretch big holes in their earlobes. You'll recognize him."

"Okay. I don't know how much I can say or do about who she speaks with."

"She likes you a lot. Respects you. I mean, look, it's a pretty small club, they're going to see each other, and it'll be weird. Just don't let her stay talking with Perry for long. Get her to dance with you or some-thing."

Ana came back from the bar, happy. "Timmy's not spinning tonight?"

"Nope. Some guy from Philly, Little Daddy Cane. He's been playing strictly old-school breakbeat—it's been like 1998 in there all night."

She watched Ana take Jenner's hand by the wrist, then said, "You guys go for it. I've got to get back to the door before someone undesir-able sneaks past Winston. We'll catch up."

Ana blew her a kiss, then started leading Jenner toward the archway. Behind her back, Katie nodded at Jenner and mouthed, "Thank you."

It was hot and dark inside; it took Jenner a few moments to orient himself. The dance floor was packed and the music was roaring, impos-sibly fast beats skittering through the air, wind-up monkey drumming, buzzing snare rolls, and whomping bass that sounded like a hovercraft colliding with a Mack truck.

The banquettes against the walls were piled with coats and bags and the occasional person too intoxicated to dance. At the far end there were three table booths, a little elevated above the dance floor, with a DJ podium and bar along the wall to Jenner's right.

Ana, still tugging on his wrist, led Jenner through the club, scanning the room for friends.

Jenner spotted Perry immediately. He was holding court in the largest booth, wedged snugly between two pretty blondes and a pale redhead. He was sallow and wiry, with flushed cheeks and expensively unkempt lank black hair, his gaze casual and amused. It was obvious to Jenner that Ana and Perry had been lovers—how could they not have been? They seemed almost crafted for one another. He was maybe twenty-five—pretty much perfect for her.

Jenner watched as a boy in a black hoodie with RED HOOK across the back approached the table and tried to engage Perry in conversation; Perry just kept watching the crowd, as if looking for someone more interesting, eventually dismissing the kid with a glance and a flick of his wrist.

Jenner saw him catch sight of Ana, then Ana saw Perry, and looked away a little too quickly. When she looked back, their eyes met, and this time she didn't look away.

She turned to Jenner abruptly and said, "Hey, why don't you hang out here, maybe get me a ginger ale. Maybe you can find somewhere for us to sit."

When Perry saw Ana walking toward him, he said something to his retinue, and by the time Ana reached his table, the last girl had slipped sullenly off the banquette and disappeared onto the dance floor. Ana leaned over, kissed Perry, then slid in next to him.

Waiting at the bar for her ginger ale, Jenner couldn't see the booth through all the dancers. Occasionally, the flashing lights and the bodies on the dance floor would align, and he'd catch a glimpse of her leaning in against him. Perry was nonchalant, his arms draped over the back of the banquette. She was the one making all the effort, lips pressed almost against his ear.

Perry didn't seem to be buying it. His eyes were on the dance floor, watching the two blondes dance together.

Ana stood and took off her overcoat, and Jenner felt his heart lurch. Underneath she was wearing a tight Bathing Ape T-shirt she'd borrowed from Jun, and some kind of industrial pants in a shiny fabric, tight around the ass, looser in the leg. She looked beautiful and sexy, and Jenner fought the urge to leave when she sat back down next to Perry.

The ginger ale was taking forever.

She kept talking to Perry, pressuring him about something, but he wasn't budging. Jenner realized that she now had her hand under the table—she was touching him.

The drink came, and Jenner paid, leaving a too generous tip in his hurry to get back to her. He had to do something, had to intervene—Katie had said so. But it all seemed absurd—she obviously still had intense feelings for the guy. And why wouldn't she?

He made his way around the perimeter of the dance floor, back toward them. When he got close, Ana saw him and stood. She grabbed her coat and walked to him without saying another word to Perry. Perry looked him over indifferently, then returned to watching his blondes.

Everything was all right. He wasn't interested in either of them, apparently.

Ana followed Jenner's line of sight and said, "An ex."

She looked at his face, then, smiling, touched his hip. "Relax, you've got nothing to worry about. He's a prick."

Jenner smiled back. "I wasn't worried."

"Yeah, *right*! You should have seen your expression when I sat down with him!"

"Here's your ginger ale." He gave her the plastic cup. "I wasn't spying."

"Oh, sure!" She took a sip. "Whatever. I have to go to the bathroom, then let's dance."

He waited there at the edge of the dance floor, holding her coat and her drink.

He had nothing to worry about.

The man's testosterone arrived at the FedEx office in Greenpoint, Brooklyn, in the middle of every third month. He bought the ampoules of piss-yellow syrup from a gray-market supplier in Laredo, Texas, a front operation for a Mexican outfit across the border in Nuevo Laredo. He had to pay for it himself, since the HMO doctor insisted it was unnecessary and refused to authorize reimbursement. He wondered what Dr. Zenker would say if he knew, particularly after he'd carefully explained that the man's liver cancer was probably caused by the testosterone replacement therapy after the accident. Well, he already had the cancer, and the injections kept him feeling right, so screw Zenker.

The day before he'd felt too ill to pick up the package. Guts knotting inside him, he had lain curled on his mattress unable to stand for much of the day, clutching his belly in agony; he couldn't afford the Oxycontin anymore. He found Saint Elmo in the tattered copy of *Lives of the Saints* he kept in his sleep hole, and lay, hand pressing his throbbing stomach, looking at an old woodcut of the martyrdom of the saint, who had his innards drawn out on a windlass.

Today the pain had eased and he felt almost human again. When the sun was fully up, he'd walk into Greenpoint and pick up the package.

Ana was still asleep. Jenner gently freed his arm, careful not to wake her. In the dark, he pulled a T-shirt from the dresser drawer. His neck was stiff.

At the other end of the loft, he opened the blinds on the kitchen side. He put two Weetabix biscuits into his mug, sprinkled them with sugar, opened a bottle of milk, and poured it into the mug. He sat down at the table, tilted his chair back, and began to eat the cereal. He took time to savor the change from crisp to soggy, the sweet, granular crunch of the raw sugar. The coldness of the fresh milk.

He set the empty mug back on the table. Julie had given it to him, when things had been really bad for him. A hefty mug-shaped mug, the color of cream, with a Goethe quote in black type: *Nothing is more important than this day*.

It wasn't just his neck—his sides ached, too, and he felt his knee creak when he straightened it. He was getting too old to be going out dancing all night.

Not that he'd danced that much. By around 2:00 a.m., he'd had enough, and sat on a banquette with Simone, one of Ana's friends, listening to her yammer on about how she'd broken up with Jamie or Lesley or someone; it had been loud, and Simone was drunk, and Jenner couldn't tell whether she was talking about a girlfriend or a boyfriend, but she kept on talking, pulling herself close to him and yelling in his ear, smelling of alcohol and pot.

Ana stayed out on the dance floor, where everyone seemed to be dancing with everyone.

He loved watching her dance, her movements liquid and electric, the way her stomach flashed when she raised her arms above her head, her eyes closed, an ecstatic smile on her face, her body moving as just one more wave of sound. Every so often, she'd catch his eye, and her eyes and smile would widen, and he didn't care who danced with her, he knew she was going home with him.

By 4:00 a.m., she was the only person still dancing, spinning and dropping, always in the half shadow, cutting rhythmically into the light beam with a tan arm or a swirl of hair.

He watched her dance with the light, enchanted and proud.

In the cab home, she pressed up against him, held her bare arm to his mouth to have him taste her sweat. Later she looked up at him and urgently whispered to him to do it harder, her eyelids fluttering, her skin hot and flushed.

Jenner showered, kept the water hot, trying to melt the knots in his neck. He toweled dry and dressed, then reached Garcia on his cell; coming in from Queens, the detective was stuck in bridge traffic. They agreed to meet at the pharmacy at 9:15 a.m.

He looked around his apartment. The place was becoming a wreck—clothes everywhere, magazines and books all over the place, empty pizza boxes and Chinese food containers on the tables and by the daybed. Ana's early efforts at housekeeping had fallen by the wayside. He wasn't a great housekeeper, but at least he threw boxes in the trash, and stuck his clothes in the hamper.

He started to clean the place up. When he opened the stainless steel trash bin in the kitchen, he saw she'd been throwing garbage out, but hadn't separated the recyclables. He tapped damp coffee grounds off the empty viognier bottle and an empty can of Italian tuna. Reaching deeper, he found two more wine bottles; he couldn't remember drinking them with her. But maybe he had—he'd been drinking more since she'd moved in. One of the bottles still had wine in it; he rinsed it out, then placed it carefully into the blue plastic bag for glass, feeling slightly virtuous.

Recycling had been Julie's thing. It seemed like there used to be a lot more concern about the environment. Maybe after 9/11 everyone felt that all bets were off, that what might or might not happen to the planet fifty or a hundred years down the road really just wasn't that big a deal.

*Nothing is more important than this day.*

He looked over at Ana. She was sleeping on her side, a pillow clutched against her thighs. Her breathing was fast, and the one leg outside of the sheets twitched. It was like watching a cat dream.

God, what an asshole he was! Ana had lost her parents, she'd been there when her best friend was tortured and killed, and yet *he* lived every hour feeling sorry for himself.

Boo fucking hoo. Poor Edward Jenner.

Luba Andreyev, the day pharmacist at Astor Place Pharmacy and Drug Rx, found irritating Rad Garcia an entertaining break from the routine of torturing her assistant. A bleached blonde dressed for a cocktail party in a tight red top and black miniskirt under her white coat, she affected bored disinterest, but Jenner could see she was enjoying herself.

The detective explained it one more time: they had a vial of Lupron dispensed by the pharmacy. They needed to find out if the decedent and two other Hutchins students had received Lupron from the pharmacy, and the name of the prescribing physician.

"I am telling you that I cannot tell you. This is confidential. Like doctor and patient."

"As I said, the girl—all three—are dead. Confidentiality no longer exists."

The dispensing area was elevated on a platform; she leaned over them, like a presiding judge, and said, "I do not think so. I cannot provide you with this information."

"Is there a manager we could speak with?"

"No manager. I am the senior person in charge."

"We'd like to speak to the owner."

"Mr. Hussaini."

"If he's the owner."

"You may speak to him." She paused, looked at her French tips, then down to Rad. "He usually comes in around three p.m."

"Do you have a home phone number for him?"

"He's not at home. He is at Home Depot in Queens."

"Does he have a cell phone?"

"Yes."

"Could you give me his cell phone number?"

"His cell phone isn't working."

The detective sighed, squared his shoulders, and said, "Ms. Andreyev, is there some reason you don't want to help us?"

She yelped a laugh. "Detective! I would do anything to help the police! *Anything!*" She breathed sharply, as if pulling on a cigarette, and then gave a weary smile of helplessness. "But I cannot do what you're asking me to do. It is illegal. And unethical. Both."

"Hussaini arrives at what hour?"

"Usually three p.m. Although maybe later today—I don't know how long he will be at Home Depot."

Rad looked at Jenner, then back at her. He pulled out his notebook and made a show of writing her name.

"We'll be back, Miss Andreyev."

"Good-bye!" she said, cheerily.

She turned to face Jenner. He caught her attention; her eyes narrowed for a second, and she looked down at the counter in front of her, then back at him. She broke into a wide smile.

"I think you are very much in love!"

"I'm sorry?"

"You are in love, with the murder girl in East Village."

She looked benignly on his confusion for a moment, then said, "Here." She folded the morning's *New York Post* over and handed it down to him. "Lower part of page."

Below the fold, laid out like frames from a movie, was a series of photographs of Ana in front of the Lightbulb Factory. Ana in his sweatshirt and Jun's sneakers coming out of his lobby. Ana running along the sidewalk to him. Ana on tiptoe, kissing him. Behind his head, the banner for Khatchaturian Vintage Lighting was clearly visible. There was a small headline, INQUISITOR SURVIVOR ♥ CASANOVA CORONER, and the caption began, "Moment of Happiness for Tragic Co-ed."

Spirits sinking, he walked toward the back of the store, reading the story. Richie Parsons must have had someone staking out his apartment, waiting for her. He cursed himself for forgetting that murders have vibrant lives beyond the narrow parameters of personal tragedy and forensic investigation. It wasn't his first time in the main ring of a media circus; he should have been more careful, for Ana's sake.

He folded the newspaper and brought it back to Andreyev, who gave him another exaggeratedly tender smile.

He walked back down the main aisle. Ana needed her own razor. He stood in front of the display, a little surprised at the number of options; for no particular reason, he decided on the Gillette Sensor Excel for Women.

"Can I get you some blades for that, sir?"

He turned to find a young Indian boy in a black vest, pinned to which was a red-and-white name tag that read DEBASHISH and JUNIOR PHARMA-CIST.

He squatted next to Jenner and rummaged through the cabinet under the razor display stand.

His back to Jenner, he muttered, "Is she watching?"

Jenner looked around, casually, at the rest of the store. "Yeah."

"She's a real bitch!"

Jenner grinned. "Really?"

"You're with the detective?"

"Yes."

The boy looked up and said, "I read about this in the paper. I want to help."

Jenner thanked him.

"I fill the bottles for Luba—she pretends she doesn't know how to work the label printer. I don't know the patient names, but all the fertility drug prescriptions filled here come from the New Hope Clinic. Dr. David Green. I think it's very close. All of his patients are students at the university."

"Thanks, Debashish—you've saved us a lot of time."

Jenner heard the rapid click of heels, and looked up to see Luba Andreyev bearing down on them, a large metal clipboard in her hands, her caring smile replaced by a suspicious scowl. As she reached their aisle, the boy straightened up and said, "There. Ten replacement blades. Sorry about that, Mister—we carry so many different razors, and the guy who does the restocking can be a real mess."

"No problem. I'm just glad you had them. Thanks again."

He needed to find a phone and let Jun know about the photographs in the *Post*. He nodded at Debashish, and gave a brief nod in Luba Andreyev's direction before heading to the cash register.

He hoped he'd irritated her.

Green's offices were in a red brick Greek Revival town house on Mac-Dougal Street, just off Washington Square Park. The waiting room was all taste and money—Danish modern furniture in a neutral palette, the Oxygen network muted on a wall-mounted plasma TV behind the receptionist. It was like something out of a movie. Jenner wondered for a moment what his life would have been like had he gone into clinical medicine. Plusher, at least.

There were a couple of young women filling out forms; they barely glanced up as the two men entered. Each had attached a color photo to the front sheet. Both were college age and attractive, and the blonde wore a sweatshirt in the Hutchins blue and green.

The door to Green's office opened, and the man himself appeared in the doorway. He hesitated, unaccustomed to seeing men in the waiting room. He was handsome, well built and too tan for winter. The buttons on his immaculate white coat were tight knots of white silk, and his shirt was clearly bespoke, his initials neatly exposed on the left French cuff. The effect was so carefully composed that Jenner wondered if the lab coat, too, was custom-tailored.

The receptionist slipped over to Green and spoke to him in a hushed tone. With a decisive nod and a concerned expression, Green ushered them into his large office. The white desk and brown leather and chrome chairs seemed to float above the thick butterscotch shag carpet. Green sat and motioned to the chairs, but Rad remained standing; Jenner followed his lead.

"I understand you have some questions that might involve my patients." Green leaned back in his chair and placed the palms of his hands together, tapping the tips of his slender fingers together one by one, the picture of a contemplative man. "You must understand that there are confidentiality issues, particularly in this type of practice."

He leaned forward again. "Actually, would you mind showing me some kind of identification?"

Rad wordlessly shifted his jacket from his hip to reveal his shield and holster.

Green nodded slowly. "Now, how may I help you, gentlemen?"

"We're investigating this series of killings, all students at Hutchins College. We believe that some, maybe all, of the victims had been your patients at some time or another."

For a fraction of a second, Green looked completely caught by surprise, but almost instantly regained his composure; it was an impressive display.

"I saw something on the news, but I haven't been paying close attention. You have to understand, I see these girls fairly briefly and in a relatively focused way—I'm not their gynecologist, I don't really have a doctor-patient relationship with them. I certainly don't know all of the patients in my practice. Why do you think they were my patients?"

Rad glanced quickly at Jenner. "We've learned that at least two were egg donors. We suspect the third was also a donor. We know they got their medications from Astor Place Drug, and we know that you prescribe almost all of that type of medication sold there."

"My practice is fairly large—I see almost one thousand patients a year, and probably prescribe most of the fertility drugs dispensed in this neighborhood. But certainly not all, not by a long shot." He paused, thinking hard. "And the pharmacy told you this? They confirmed these were my patients? No, clearly not, or you'd have said so."

Jenner spoke up.

"We have Hutchins students injecting a regimen of Lupron and Pergonal, which we know was prescribed at a fertility clinic near the university and then dispensed at a pharmacy near the university. Yours is the most likely office."

Green, amused, looked at Jenner. "Excellent pronunciation, Detective! Do you have a medical background?"

"I'm a forensic pathologist."

"Ah." Green leaned back again, a slight smirk on his face. "Well, mine is probably the best-known office in the area, but I assure you, Doctor, I have plenty of competition."

He sat straight now.

"I'd like to help you, but I can't even confirm the names of these patients—if they were mine—without either permission from the family or a court order," he said, then added in an aside to Jenner, "I'm sure you understand, Doctor."

"I understand that that would be a practical approach. But it would save a lot of time if you could just say yes or no."

Green looked at Jenner. "Doctor, do you think these girls tell their families what they're doing here?"

"I'd imagine some do, some don't."

"No. They almost never do, I think. Almost never." He leaned forward again and said, "I'm sure it'd only take a short while to reach the families by phone."

"The family of one of the girls is effectively unreachable."

Green spread his hands with a look of helplessness.

Rad touched Jenner's elbow and told the doctor, "We'll be back with a court order."

"Fine," Green said. "In the meantime, I'll speak with my lawyer. If you give me the names of the victims, I can have my staff start the search."

He glanced at his watch, a pink gold Patek-Philippe, then turned to the computer behind him and began to peck at the keyboard.

Rad wrote the names down in his notebook, tore out the page, and slid it across Green's desk.

Green didn't turn around, and said nothing more as they left the room.

It took almost until 4:00 p.m. to push through the subpoena. Garcia tried to do an oral application for the warrant, but the logistics proved too much, so they went downtown to the courthouse. Pressure on the case was such that testimony in an ongoing buy-and-bust trial was interrupted so that they could appear immediately before the judge.

They were both smiling as they bounded back up the steps to Green's office, this time with another cop following close behind. The waiting room was quiet, the last student gone, the plasma TV off. The receptionist stepped into Green's office to notify him of their arrival.

He gave them a curt nod.

"Detective. Doctor."

Rad said, "Dr. Green, this court order gives us broad search and seizure powers in this office, extending to all computers in this facility, to any personal computers owned by you, to your BlackBerry and any other digital storage medium, including your cell phone, as well as to paper records maintained here or at any other location you do business, including at your home."

Green's pitch rose in indignation. "Detective, this is ridiculous! We just needed to ascertain your right for me to confirm the identities of three patients in my practice! Surely this is unnecessary."

"Well, sir, on discussion with the chief, it was felt that it would be appropriate for us to personally locate and view all documents as needed, since information was judged not immediately forthcoming, and since others in your patient base might be at risk. That's why we brought Detective Mason from Computer Crimes along for the ride."

"But it was a confidentiality matter! I had no choice!"

"We have complete respect for your high ethical standards, sir." He paused for a second to make sure that Green could sense his insincerity. "And we'd like to begin with the computer in your office."

"This is absurd. This is nothing but a petty act of harassment. You can begin the hand search of the paper files here, but I'm calling my lawyer to review this before you start infringing the privacy of my other clients."

Garcia handed him the document with a grin.

"Go right ahead."

Green snatched the paper and stalked off toward his office. Rad called after him, "You have five minutes." The thick carpeting smothered Green's attempt at a door slam.

The file room was surprisingly large. Gray enamel shelves filled with color-coded manila folders ran the length of one wall; a workstation with telephone, computer, and X-ray viewing box was set against the other.

Since the file clerk only worked two mornings a week, Angie Buonfiglio, the receptionist, did the database search herself, the door propped open so she could watch the waiting room. Rad spelled out the names as she typed, her long fake nails clattering across the keyboard. Andrea Delore and Sunday Smith (who'd given her first name as Katherine) came up right away; they had to try several different spellings before they located Barbara Wexler's record.

She jotted down the file numbers on a Post-it, stepped into the stacks, and within a couple of minutes appeared before them again, three folders in her hand.

She hesitated.

"I'm sorry, but I need to confirm it with the doctor before I can give you the records."

They followed her into the reception area, and Ms. Buonfiglio tapped on Green's door.

Rad nodded his head back toward the file room, and Jenner followed him. They spoke quietly.

"Jenner, was there anything about these killings to make you think they might have been done by someone with medical training?"

Jenner shrugged. "Whenever someone gets dismembered, the cops always say, 'It's so clean he must've had a medical background,' but the anatomy's not that hard. Someone with a sharp knife could inflict pretty much any set of wounds, if they put their mind to it. Dismembering can't be that difficult—anyone who's dressed a deer, even cut up a chicken, could do it. It's not like we take Dismemberment 101 in med school."

"No, but it wouldn't hurt to be familiar with a knife."

"Sure. But Green is mostly about syringes and hormones and micro-surgery."

"He's a pretty big guy, though, probably strong enough to take care of them."

The receptionist was still tapping at the door; Green wasn't answer-ing. Probably still bleating to his lawyer.

Rad shook Jenner's shoulder. "C'mon! Wouldn't it be great if it was this asshole? We nail him now, close down the investigation, you're a hero, I'm a hero, that obnoxious fuck goes to jail?"

He grinned, looking over at the receptionist by Green's door. It was taking too long. "Naah, I know, you're right. He doesn't really feel right to me, either. He's too slick. He's got too much . . . *stuff*."

Jenner nodded.

Rad looked over at Mason, sprawled awkwardly in a Jacobsen Swan chair, then back to Jenner. "I'll tell you one thing: I'd bet cash money this dude is into something bad. And I don't mean just wrong—every fucker walking down Broadway at any given moment has some secret or other jangling away in his pocket. But this guy is doing something nasty. I can just feel it."

He paused.

"I'm serious, Jenner. I don't know what he's into, but I'm going to tear this place up until I find it. And if I don't find it here, I'm going to tear up his house. Then his car, then his boat, and then whatever else that smug fuck owns, until I find it."

The receptionist was tapping again, saying, "Dr. Green? Dr. Green?"

Rad turned. "Starting right now—I've had enough of this." He turned and said, "Mason! Come on, we're going in."

"Please step aside," he said to the receptionist. "Green? Enough! We're coming in."

They waited for Green to answer the door, but there was no response. Rad rolled his eyes, then pounded twice on the door.

"Green!"

Nothing. He turned the handle. Locked.

He pointed at the receptionist and said, "Key."

She scurried to her desk and brought it. There was a click as the lock opened. Rad quickly turned the handle and pushed open the door into an empty room; Green had disappeared.

They rushed into the office, Rad heading for the door to the right; an empty exam room.

Jenner had taken the door to the left. The sound of running water came from a sink inside.

"Rad! Over here."

Rad called to Ms. Buonfiglio again. "*Key!*"

She said she didn't have one, it was the doctor's private bathroom.

"Not anymore."

Rad leaned back, lifted his right leg, and slammed his foot against the door by the handle. There was a crash, and a splintering sound, but the door held. He kicked it three more times before it swung open, falling off the upper hinge into the empty bathroom.

The open window, broad and low, looked out over an empty alley behind the building, a black Mercedes SUV parked against the rear brick wall under DAVID GREEN MD in stenciled white paint.

"Fuck!" He pounded his fist on the sink. "Mason! Call it in. Get the word out."

The sink had overflowed, and Rad, stepping backward from the window, slipped and almost went down.

"*Fuck!* Jesus, Jenner."

In the office, Green's neatly folded white coat sat on a leather daybed. The desk drawers were all closed, and the appointment book Jenner had noticed earlier lay there undisturbed. Behind the desk, his computer monitor was off. Jenner saw that the light below the screen was flickering.

"Rad! Behind you! His computer—the monitor's turned off, but the computer's on!"

"What?"

Jenner stepped over to the computer and ripped the plug out of the wall. The yellow LED on the front of the CPU went out.

"What are you doing?"

"I think he's trying to delete his files."

Rad looked around the room angrily, as if waiting for Green to tumble out from behind a piece of furniture so he could beat the crap out of him.

"*Fuck!*"


Jenner and Garcia watched Crime Scene processing Green's Mercedes in the alley. They'd started with Luminol in the cargo area just after dark, and were now vacuuming the front and back passenger wells as well as the cargo space. There was no evidence of blood; one of the detectives had commented on how immaculate the car had been kept.

Rad shook his head and drew on his stubby cigar. "Have to hand it to him, this guy is pretty cool—the average shitbird would just take off in the car, but Green remembers the LoJack." He sighed. "He may be tough to find."

Jenner needed a break. He walked out onto the street and crossed over into Washington Square Park. The evening chill and drizzle had left the park unusually quiet; in summer it was a riot of street performers and tourists, dealers and potheads. Now it was deserted, save for a few scattered figures making their way through the trees, huddled under umbrellas.

Jenner sat on a damp bench and looked out over the park. The wet surfaces of the memorial arch at the foot of Fifth Avenue glistened in the floodlights. The cold felt good.

He was surprised at how calm he was. Their first big break. A clear connection between the three victims, leading to a real suspect.

Which, he now had to admit, Green was. Still, as much as he disliked Green, Jenner had a hard time imagining him doing . . . those things. But what had he been expecting—some deformed half-man with a hook for a hand? The evilest men are often the most ordinary, quiet, average people barely noticed by neighbors, even as they spend their weekends hunting and killing. An English criminal profiler Jenner knew called them "Custard People."

But Green was completely different, a man with a big ego but with genuine achievements and, doubtless, social skills. People probably liked him—his patients, his staff for sure. His receptionist had seemed very close—she'd appeared shocked at his flight, and had resisted releasing the files even after she knew he was gone.

He'd skimmed Green's files on the three victims; they were unremarkable. There had been few visits—an initial screening visit, a checkup while they were on Lupron, then notes about the coordination of stimulation of egg release and harvest, and a final op note for the egg recovery. Green had located the eggs using transvaginal ultrasound; no incisions were made, and once he'd retrieved the eggs, Green had no reason to see the girls again.

Jenner stood up, his legs stiff and cold. He walked back to Green's office. Rad had left, but Roggetti was at Green's desk, going through the appointment book.

"Hey, Joey. Can I use the phone?"

Roggetti waved him toward the exam room; Crime Scene was finished in there, and had already dusted the receiver for prints.

Jenner closed the door and sat down on a steel stool. He wiped off the fingerprint powder, then dialed long distance, connecting to the office of the corporate counsel in Massachusetts; better that Delore learned it from him than on CNN.

With a couple of keystrokes, the man deleted the file for his next project from the database. An elaborate precaution, perhaps, but he wouldn't make the mistake of underestimating his enemies. Of course, the police would eventually have access to a remote backup of the woman's records, but with a bit of luck, they'd never discover the file was missing. He killed the modem signal and stood.

He looked down on his workbench, at all the elements and equipment laid out in a neat row. He'd spent almost an hour honing the curved scalpel blades—much harder than sharpening a straight edge. They were now razor sharp along their entire length, which was important if he was going to scoop out the little spheres cleanly.

He'd refilled a twenty-four-ounce Poland Spring water squeeze bottle with gasoline from the generator, but had a hard time getting the duct tape to stick. He'd ended up wrapping the nozzle with rags, then ducttaping the rags.

Then there was his standard kit—screwdriver, short pry bar, manacles, duct tape, rope. Soldering iron. It was the stuff he always brought, but it still gave him a thrill to see it all laid out like that.

And finally, the sword. He'd found it in an Atlantic Avenue antique store, and it cost far more than he could afford. It was a Freemason's sword; he thought the decorations on the handle made it look gay.

He picked it up, accidentally carving his thumb on the blade. Smiling a little, he sucked the blood off his thumb: with a blade like that, who cared if the handle was a little . . . flamboyant?

The candle flame guttered and died, and in the dark, he realized he was shivering.

He'd barely been eating, and he'd been rationing his gasoline for days now, trying to make it last as long as possible, only using it to power the generator for his laptop. He could always get more gasoline, but he didn't want to take the risk of siphoning gas on the street this close to a project.

Standing there hungry, shivering in the cold and the dark, feeling the cancer inside him, he knew he couldn't go on much longer. How much longer? Months, maybe. A year? The last time he saw Dr. Zenker, months ago now, the oncologist had been obviously surprised that he was doing so well. He wondered if he'd be alive in spring, framing the thought in the form of a question: Will I be alive on April 17? Will I be alive on May 1? He wondered if it would rain on the day he died. If it would rain on the day after. Where, exactly, he would die. In this room, vomiting blood on the filthy mattress? Gasping for breath on the loading dock under the gantry, the stench of brackish water and rat nests filling his mouth?

God, he was cold.

He thought about a time when he was nine, when he and his mom had been walking out near the farm and they came across a rabbit, its fur matted with drying blood, shivering under a hedge. His mom said the rabbit had been in a fight, probably with the cat, and that it was dying, and that when you find something dying, and it's suffering, God says it's okay to help it stop suffering. She'd reached under the hedge to pull it out, but it had kicked and struggled, and she had accidentally broken its leg. It began to scream, a horrible, whistling scream, and when she put her hands around its head to wring its neck, it bit her. She had killed it, then thrown the carcass to the ground. She headed back to the house, calling over her shoulder for the boy to bring it for dinner. When she had gone over the top of a hill, he had taken a stick and beaten the little body until the fur came off in clumps.

He wrapped himself in a blanket and lit another candle. He inspected his kit again, feeling a little warmer in the yellow light, a little clearer as he looked at the shiny tools, glinting, ready to cut, ready to carve, ready to impale.

Yes. He was ready.


Jenner walked home from Greene's office, cutting across Washington Square Park and then down Broadway into SoHo. The cold and drizzling rain felt good; he felt awake and alive. It was close to midnight when he pushed open the door; he was surprised to find the loft in darkness.

There was a sudden orange flare as a match blazed in Ana's hand. The flame floated between two candles on the table, the glow lighting up two placemats laid side by side.

She slipped her arm around his waist, and laid her head on his shoulder while he looked.

She'd set the table for two. There was a pitcher of orange juice, and on each placemat a bowl of Weetabix waited for milk.

"I made your favorite: breakfast!" She kissed him softly on the cheek, her lips hot on his skin. "Thanks, Jenner. Thanks for everything."

She pressed him down into a chair, poured milk on his cereal, then sprinkled it with sugar before sitting down next to him. She moved her chair closer and leaned into him.

He asked her what she had heard.

"On the news it said you found him, that it was that doctor."

He put his spoon down. "Ana, I'm not sure he's the guy."

"On the news it said he'd been arrested before."

"What?"

"He was arrested for some kind of sex thing a few years ago."

Jenner pushed back from the table and turned the TV to CNN just in time to catch the headline summary at the top of the hour; they'd found Green's old mug shot and captioned it "Inquisitor Suspect." The story led the broadcast, with a reporter live in front of Green's office running through the facts. Someone on the Inquisitor squad had discovered that Green had been arrested for sexual assault while at medical school in Mexico. There had been a date rape allegation, the case stalling out when the victim, another medical student, refused to testify.

He turned to her. "Does he look like the guy you saw?"

"Yes. I mean, I didn't recognize him just looking at his face, but now that I see him again, I think that could be him. It was dark, and he was . . . bloody."

Maybe he was wrong. After all, hadn't he always said that everyone has the capacity to kill?

"You finished? Come and lie down with me, Jenner. I want to lie down now."

He stood and stretched, and let her lead him to the bed.

FRIDAY,
## DECEMBER 13

Jenner and Father Sheehan sat at Green's desk with Angie Buonfiglio, the receptionist. The priest, clearly bemused to find himself in the office of a gynecologist, was doing his best not to look toward Ms. Buonfiglio, who was wearing the shortest miniskirt Jenner had ever seen over thick wool stockings and high boots.

For her part, Ms. Buonfiglio, who had been brought up in a respectful home off Arthur Avenue in the Bronx, seemed just as uncomfortable sitting next to Sheehan. She did her best to hide her legs under the desk and keep her arms folded across her chest when not typing. When the priest excused himself to visit the bathroom, she took the opportunity to find a lab coat to cover herself, after which things were a little easier.

The plan was Jenner's; Sheehan, in Manhattan for a doctor's appointment, had volunteered to come in and help. They were going to correlate patient names to upcoming saint days. Roggetti had argued it was a waste of time, that Green would be too busy hiding to kill anyone, but Jenner held his ground. They started with the calendar and cross-referenced it to the patient database.

Shortly after 10:00 a.m., the filing clerk, Adeline Calixte, arrived. A serious-looking Haitian woman, she immediately took control, forcing the nonplussed receptionist to one side and creating a new database from scratch in Excel. Her speed was impressive, and as Sheehan spelled out the names of martyrs for each date, the cells onscreen seemed to fill up miraculously with contact names and telephone numbers.

Joey Roggetti arrived, a little bewildered by the mix of people surrounding the monitor. He didn't do much, just sat and watched, occasionally sneaking glances at Ms. Buonfiglio, then trying to catch Jenner's eye to do the arched-eyebrows-and-subtle-nod-toward-the-hot-chick thing. Jenner rolled his eyes in response, which seemed to satisfy Roggetti.

They broke for lunch at about 1:00 p.m. Sheehan excused himself and was getting ready to head uptown when Garcia arrived.

"Father, Jenner. Ms. Buonfiglio. Ma'am. How's it going?"

Sheehan glanced over to the monitor. "The next few days are pretty light as far as concordance goes. No patient/saint name matches for today or tomorrow, one match on Sunday, a couple in the early part of next week."

"Good. Gives us time to catch up with him—don't go too far into the calendar. Hopefully we're not going to need it."

"We figured we'd stop when we get to one month out."

Rad nodded in agreement.

Ms. Buonfiglio leaned in and said, "That can't be right. You said there's none for today? That's got to be a mistake. Today's the feast of Santa Lucia—my sister's saint day. That's a fact."

Sheehan nodded. "Yes, the feast of Santa Lucia. We've cross-referenced Lucia, Lucy, Lucie, Lucille, nothing."

The receptionist was insistent. "No, that's definitely wrong. I know there's a Lucy—she was in on Monday to talk about maybe going for a third round. Black hair, said her family's from Sicily. Pretty name."

Mrs. Calixte turned and said, "Well, she's not in the database. Are you certain her name was Lucy?"

"Absolutely. Italian, baptized Lucia, goes by Lucy. I told her about my sister when I met her. She's got to be there."

"Well, she's not." Mrs. Calixte took her hands off the keyboard.

Angie walked quickly out to the waiting room and began clicking through the appointment calendar on the computer at her desk. There was a triumphant exclamation.

"Here! Here, you see ... Monday ... morning appointment ..." Her voice trailed off. "This just doesn't make sense! I *know* she was here, Monday morning."

"She's not on the list?"

"No. I know I'm not crazy. She came in the morning ..."

Jenner walked out of the office and stood near her.

She tapped the screen with one long fingernail. "This is where she should be, but she's not. Instead, it reads Baer at nine a.m., then Baer again at nine thirty a.m." She stood up, confident again. "Which I *know* is a mistake! If she'd needed a one-hour appointment, I'd have booked it as one solid block, instead of recording two half-hour blocks. Someone's messed with this list!"

Jenner looked at Garcia. Roggetti stepped forward and put a hand on her shoulder and said appreciatively, "Great work, Angie!"

She basked for a second, then sat bolt upright.

"Wait!"

She dashed out of the reception area, through the office, and into the exam room. There was a metallic clank, and she emerged waving a fistful of papers.

"I have it! The original list I print up for Dr. Green every day!"

She quickly looked through them, and then pulled out a single sheet with a flourish. The bright pink fingernail scratched across the page.

"Nine thirty a.m., *Lucia Fiore*." She slapped the page down on the desk in triumph.

"Can you get this record for us? It's very important."

"Of course, Doctor. It would be my pleasure." She shot a look at Mrs. Calixte, who continued to concentrate on the monitor. "My pleasure."

She held the schedule up and read out Lucia Fiore's medical record number in her clearest voice to the clerk, who typed it in and then turned back to her. "No record."

"Try it again! It's right here! It has to be that."

The second try was unsuccessful, too.

"This is *insane*! I know she's got a chart!"

Jenner said, "Maybe the chart hasn't been filed."

The receptionist flew to the stack of charts piled on a low table in the filing room. She rifled through them, pulling out folders randomly to gauge her position in the chronology.

Finally, she held up the folder. She slapped it down on Green's desk, in front of the monitor where "No Such Record" was still prominently displayed.

"You see?!"

*   *   *

Rad dialed Lucia Fiore's number on his cell; still no answer. Jenner, in the backseat, said, "It's on Elizabeth, should be just a little below Spring."

Roggetti drove. At a red light on Spring and Mott, he gestured up the street and announced that Martin Scorsese was born on that block.

Jenner said he thought Scorsese was born on Elizabeth.

"Nope. Mott between Prince and Spring."

Garcia sighed. "He was born in *Flushing*. He grew up on Elizabeth, that's where his parents were born."

He pointed ahead of them. "Joey, park on the far corner. We'll walk—here's as good a place as any."

Jenner handed the address to Rad.

It was a generic five-story apartment building in tan brick, with cheap white gauze curtains in the aluminum-framed windows. Two old women in matching tweed coats sat on a bench by the steps to the front door, in front of the display window of a new boutique. The mannequin in the window was silver, with a tiny bikini made out of what looked like silver dollars and Christmas tree icicles. The women watched Roggetti walk up and ring the doorbell.

No answer. He rang it a second time.

"Who you looking for?" said one of the white-haired women.

"Lucy Fiore. Two F. You seen her?"

"Oh, she doesn't live here anymore! She moved a month or two ago. Somewhere in the neighborhood, I think—she's still working over on Cleveland Place, at Caffe Vaporetto. I saw her yesterday."

"Thanks. You know where we could find her new address?"

The woman shrugged. "Well, you could try the post office, maybe. Or the café."

The second woman nodded in emphatic agreement. "The café."

Roggetti thanked them and rejoined Garcia and Jenner. "I still say this is a waste of time. She didn't answer her phone, she isn't home."

"Well, Joe, maybe she's home now. Either way, we have to let her know."

He was silent for a minute.

"So, Doc. How did Saint Lucy die, anyway?"

"Badly, Joey."

"Oh. Okay. No problem." He looked offended.

Jenner shook his head. "No, I'm sorry, Joey—I'm a bit preoccupied. Lucy was condemned to a brothel because she was a Christian. When the soldiers came to haul her away, they couldn't move her. Her eyes were so beautiful that they tore them out to disfigure her, so now she's the patron saint of the blind, and of eye doctors—in paintings, she's usually carrying her eyes on a little plate. Anyway, after putting out her eyes, they doused her with oil and set her on fire, but she wouldn't burn, so they killed her with a sword."

After that, they walked in silence.

Spring Street was rapidly gentrifying, and on every visit, Jenner saw a new boutique or trendy bar. Caffe Vaporetto was a small restaurant on Cleveland Place—the lone Italian place on the block, wedged in with a French bistro, a Mexican cantina, and a gourmet cheesecake shop. The owner was a pretty blonde, and Roggetti stepped up his pace when the barman pointed her out in the gloom at the back of the restaurant.

He told her they were looking for Lucy Fiore, that they were concerned for her safety, and she quickly found a cell phone number and street address.

"I was actually wondering where she'd got to—she has a paycheck here, and I thought it was weird she didn't show up this morning."

Roggetti dialed the number; instantly, there was a high-pitched chirruping from behind the bar. The owner reached down and held up a pink cell phone with a yellow plastic Pikachu fob. She opened and closed the phone quickly, cutting off the ring tone, a look of concern on her face.

"It's a five-minute walk to her place. She's on Mulberry between Grand and Hester. And please—tell her to call me, okay?"

She followed them out to the sidewalk and watched anxiously as they walked down Center Street. They were walking fast.

Rush hour was nearing, and traffic had slowed to a crawl. They hurried east along Broome toward the heavier side of the sky. No one spoke.

Making the turn onto Mulberry, the three men broke into a run:

ahead, on the far corner of Grand, people were coming out of the second apartment building down, coming out in a hurry.

They dodged traffic on Grand, Roggetti holding one palm up flat like a traffic cop, shield raised high in the other. As they hit the sidewalk of Lucy Fiore's block, the sound of a fire truck siren starting up floated toward them.

They ran up the stairs, Jenner stopping to check the names on the mailboxes. The stairwell smelled of smoke, and on the third floor, the corridor lights were off, emergency lighting now bathing the hall in a glowering red.

"She's 3G, Rad—make for 3G."

Rad pounded on the door, then leaned back and kicked it hard. And again. Roggetti slammed it with his foot until the door smashed open.

Smoke rushed into the hallway in a hot blast. They ran in, yelling her name.

Most of the apartment was burning, the flames spreading from the windows toward the doorway, across the floor, and along the cabinet fronts like a curtain. There was already more smoke than air. In the center of the room was the body of Lucy Fiore, twisting against a central column, engulfed in fire, the axis of the blaze.

Jenner, holding his coat up over his nose and mouth, ran to the sink and turned the water on full blast. He grabbed a coffeepot from the sink, filled it with water, turned, and threw it over her body. Then a second, and then a third, then Garcia and Roggetti were soaking her with saucepans from the sink, and there was a popping sound, then a whoosh as the overhead sprinklers kicked in and the smoke turned white, and she stopped burning.

There was a crashing sound as one of the windows smashed in. Two firemen appeared and one clambered through, dragging the hose, yelling, "Are you all right? Are you all right?"

He started to blast the burning wallpaper of the free wall, and Jenner stepped around to protect her body from the water, making a slashing gesture with his hand and shouting "Don't spray here!"

The fireman, initially confused, nodded, and gave a quick spray to the kitchen area. The ceiling sprinkler had doused much of the fire now; the hose had put out the major flames, and would now only damage evidence. He shouted something to his hose man, then passed the nozzle out through the window before beginning to open all the windows.

Jenner stood in front of the body.

He yelled into her face, "Lucy! Can you hear me?" He had to try.

There was no response.

Eyes burning, gasping for breath, he felt her neck for a pulse. As he lifted her chin up, the charred skin underneath fissured wide. There was no bleeding, and he knew she was dead.

She had been impaled, fastened to the pillar not only by loops of burned rope, but by a sword driven through her belly.

Rad grabbed Jenner and pushed him toward the windows, where Roggetti was already leaning out to gasp and retch into the fresh air. They were all three covered with soot, coughing up black phlegm, their eyes stinging and red-rimmed, their faces striped by tears.

The fireman signaled down to street level, where ambulances were arriving.

Jenner turned from the window; he had to see the body.

She was badly burned, her legs and lower body charred. If she'd been wearing clothes, they were gone now. On the floor, a broad outline of charring flared across the floor in front of the body; Jenner could make out an archipelago of splash burns leading from the main char site—evidence of some kind of accelerant.

Her hair was badly singed, and there were scattered erosive burns on her forehead. Underneath, interrupted by the burns, covering her forehead, was a band of Coptic lettering.

There was one more thing. He knew the answer, but he had to see for himself, had to know for sure. He went to the sink and opened the cabinet underneath, looking for gloves.

"Jenner! We have to go down to the ambulances."

Voice ragged, Jenner shouted back over the hissing sprinklers and sirens rising up from the street, "You go ahead, Rad. There's something I've got to see."

"Jenner! She's dead! Leave her—you can come back. Please, man."

No gloves.

"In a second."

He walked back to the girl's body and, fingers trembling, reached out to her face. Very carefully, desperate not to split the skin, he lifted the girl's eyelids. He stood in front of her, the tears now welling fast from his burning eyes as he looked into the empty sockets.

Behind the barricade across the street from the smoking building, the man watched with satisfaction as his creation played itself out.

He was calmer now. It had been several hours since she'd last been alive, during which time he'd worked on her—crafting her basic structure, bestowing the text upon her face, finally completing the transformation by relieving her of her vision.

Finishing her was easy: he doused her with gas, and when the bottle was almost empty, set it at her feet open, then tossed a match.

After that, he had walked down the stairs and out the front door, strolled down the street, and onto Hester. There he cooled his heels, leaning against the wall of a Chinese seafood packaging company until he heard the commotion on Mulberry.

Jenner's arrival with the detectives was a pleasant surprise. Apparently they were getting closer to him; the thought pleased him. That there was a team out there, whose purpose was to track him and interrupt his work. A challenge! He was grateful for this opportunity to watch his opponents in action.

He'd caught sight of them when he'd looked up Mulberry at the sound of the sirens. Jenner, of course, he knew; he was fascinated by the look of concern on the man's face as he ran to the Saint. This was the closest look yet he'd got at the Hispanic, who looked middle-aged, flabby and out of shape. But the younger one, the one he'd not seen before, Italian, maybe, was muscular enough to present a challenge, should it come to a confrontation.

When the time came, he'd do the Italian first.

He watched, neck craning up, mouth slightly open, just like the rest of the sightseers behind the barricade. The ladder went up, and the window was smashed, and the hose was turned on, and when the smoke turned into steam, the crowd broke into applause. He joined in, pounding his hands until they stung. When the fireman made them all move farther back onto the sidewalk to make space for the ambulances, he leaned over to clap the man's shoulder and say, "You guys are great!"

He clapped even harder when the firemen led the two cops out of the door and down to the ambulances, clapped until he wept. Their faces were black, their eyes pink holes with little white rivulets from their tears; the older one actually looked quite ill. As people saw him stumble, the clapping faltered, and everyone looked grim; the man mimicked their looks of concern, then smiled with relief as the cop gave the thumbs-up.

Looking up at the apartment windows, he realized he'd done everything with the blinds up. Had he been sloppy, or was this perhaps his hidden intention?

He wondered how she looked now, the Saint. Would her writing still be visible? He'd tried to splash the gas on her lower face and trunk, but the flames had probably spread to consume her. Why hadn't the sprinkler system come on sooner? There'd be more about that in the newspapers, no doubt.

Jenner appeared at the window, coughing. He hacked for a bit, and then spat black onto the ledge.

He watched Jenner, leaning out of the window, elbows on the wide sill, panting. Was he crying, or just exhausted? He didn't look like much; it seemed ridiculous that a man like him—fired from his office, it said in the *Post*—should end up with Ana de Jong.

But, of course, that was his own fault. He'd made the bed for them, and they'd tumbled in. Now they lay together, intertwined, knowing each other carnally.

He grew angrier. Why Jenner? The man didn't find him particularly good looking; he was unemployed and, from the way he was gulping air in the window, obviously not in good shape.

This was another excellent example of the fallibility of the theory of natural selection: Jenner, a demonstrably inferior male, could spread his seed through the girl, who was made of far finer clay. His genes would continue on, prospering without merit.

This was just ridiculous.

When he intervened, he would make sure that Jenner knew exactly what had happened, that Jenner understood that he himself was directly responsible for whatever happened to Ana. She would have to be taken from Jenner, ideally while they were together in his apartment. Now, *that* would shake him up a bit! A police source in the *Post* had described him as "reclusive" ever since the Twin Towers; well, this would help change his feelings about lazing around in that apartment . . .

It wouldn't be difficult. He'd discovered the super had a naughty habit of propping open the door of the loading dock in back when he was bringing garbage out; access would be a snap.

He realized he was staring at Jenner, and consciously broke his gaze. Jenner straightened, apparently having seen the Hispanic being treated in front of the ambulance. He disappeared from the window, no doubt on his way down to see to his friend. His *amigo*.

The man itched to do it.

Patience. It wasn't yet her time.

He could wait; it was something he was good at.


The chief of detectives arrived, and ordered Joey and Rad to the St. Vincent's emergency room over their objections. He took Jenner to one side.

"You okay, Doctor? You look as bad as them."

"I'm going with them, Chief." His voice was hoarse from the smoke and the shouting.

They watched as Garcia was lifted up into the ambulance, a green oxygen mask over his face. He saw Jenner talking to Scales, and gave a helpless shrug.

"Good."

The chief was silent for a second.

"You know, Jenner, you put me in a really difficult position on this. I know all about this beef between you and Whittaker, but the fact is, he has the power, and we have to work with him officially, and long after this whole mess goes away, we'll still be working with him."

Jenner nodded.

"You've been right all along. You've found things he's missed, you've figured out stuff he didn't, and today we almost got the guy because of you."

Jenner looked up at the gaping windows of the torched apartment. "Yeah. Almost," he rasped.

"Come on, Doc, get real! Sure, we'd have found this guy eventually, but you and Garcia and Roggetti have been on this right from the start. You tracked down Green, you found the girl, you almost stopped him. We're so close."

Jenner wiped his mouth. "You really think it's Green?"

Scales gave a decisive nod. "We've got more information. You know about the incident in Mexico, but we found out, back twenty-plus years ago, before he went to college, Green was convicted of sexual battery. He was working at a country club, fondled a girl in the crew room showers; she was thirteen at the time. But he was a minor—rich parents, good lawyer, different era—five years' probation, record sealed. The girl's family saw him on the news and called us up."

"I don't know, Chief. I'm still not sure."

"Yeah, Garcia told me the two of you don't like him for this. But I gotta tell you, the harder we look, the better he looks."

Garcia's ambulance was backing up. The chief waved at his driver, then said, "Anyway, what I'm saying is thank you. Garcia said you were the best, and he was right. I hope you'll continue working the case—we could really use you."

Jenner's eyes were burning from the smoke; when he reached to wipe them, his hand came back with an oily smear of soot.

"I appreciate it, Chief. I should go. I'll ride over to St. Vincent's with Roggetti."

"Wait a sec. I'm thanking you in private, because now's not the right time for me to express this publicly, but I'll work something out." The chief stepped back, then clapped a hand on his shoulder with a nod. "I want you to understand, that time will come."

Jenner glanced over at the ambulance, where Roggetti looked exasperated in the stretcher as the paramedic tightened the chest belt.

"Thanks, Chief. I should go." Jenner left him waiting for his car and walked to the ambulance, climbing in to sit next to Roggetti's stretcher.

Garcia, Roggetti, and Jenner met in the mid-afternoon on the brick plaza in front of the U.S. attorney's office, grimly shaking hands and nodding at each other. Garcia made a feeble joke about shitting black, but Roggetti didn't even crack a smile.

Rad rested a hand on Joey's back. "C'mon, buddy. We'll find him soon."

"We'd have got him yesterday if I hadn't slowed us down."

"Jesus, Joey. You didn't slow us down! You had your doubts, you expressed them appropriately. And we ignored them—also appropriately. Eh?"

Smiling, he shook Roggetti's big shoulder, but couldn't break the sulk. "C'mon. We're getting closer. We'll find him."

"What have we got to go on now? We don't even know if it's Green—what, he's on the run and he takes time out to punch someone's ticket?"

"I spoke with the Chief of D's last night," said Garcia. "He's ninety percent it's Green, but he doesn't want to take any chances. So he wants us to work whatever leads we want while the rest of the task force stays on Green."

Roggetti said, "If it's Green, we won't get any credit for the collar. It'll go to Pat Mullins and Ruben Santiago—and you know Pat won't share."

"Joey, everyone knows we cracked it. Besides, what, you really *want* all that paperwork?"

"It's not the paperwork, it's the boat! The sooner I make first grade, the sooner I get a boat." He was trying to hide a smirk.

"Hey! It's Joey! He's back with us!"

"I'm back working for my promotion. Come on."

The three of them set off toward One Police Plaza.

Joey turned to Jenner. "So, how's Ana? She good?"

Jenner thought for a second. "I don't know. She was passed out in front of the TV last night when I got home, and she was so tired I could barely wake her. She said she'd been watching the news all day, which probably didn't help. And this morning when I woke, she was still asleep. I think she's depressed—she needs to speak with a counselor."

They signed Jenner in, then went up to Computer Crimes on the eleventh floor. The lab was at the other end of the building, through a warren of offices, behind a white door posted ANALYSIS, the YSIS crossed out with a scribble of pencil.

Garcia turned to Jenner and muttered, "New York's Finest in action . . ."

Mason stood at the central workbench, jotting notes, while two task force detectives watched the oversize screen next to it. When he saw the door opening, Mason hastily shut down the show, triggering protests from the cops with him. Jenner recognized Green's computer next to the monitor.

"Anything good, Mason?"

"Well, yes and no. Nothing Inquisitor-related yet. Most of the data on the hard drive is corrupted, and the recovery software is pretty damn slow. But he screwed up: he used CD-ROMs for backups."

Mason pressed a button on the computer, and the CD tray slid out. He dropped a CD in and closed it. A window opened onscreen, a list of the files.

Mason murmured, "Pick a file, any file," and double-clicked at random. Windows Media Player opened up, low-res color video clearly shot in Green's clinic.

A girl on an examining table, apparently asleep. Green, sitting on a low stool in front of her, leaned back, took his scrub cap and mask off, and then his gloves. He turned and pointed something toward the camera; the camera zoomed in as he pushed the stool away and knelt down to lean forward between her raised legs, his hands moving toward her pelvis.

Mason hit Pause, saying, "After that, the thing writes itself."

Roggetti gave a slow whistle. The paused image on the screen hovered, Green clearly recognizable.

"The video lasts about twenty minutes. The CD has eight of these, and because the good doctor is a happy little grazer and takes off his mask, we've got beautiful portrait shots here he could blow up and send out as his Christmas cards . . . What's more, it's a CD-R, so I can pull the date stamps for the file creation from each one. And the CD itself is labeled in indelible marker . . . wait for it! . . . number 17."

Rad said, "Mason, bring in a female cop—enough with the peanut gallery here. Have her watch the videos and catalogue the times." He tapped the screen, pointing out a wall clock visible behind the victim. "Pull the appointment schedule from the office computer, and have the squad work up preliminary IDs on the victims. Then she and someone from Sex Battery can start with the notifications. Does the chief know?"

"Yeah, I called him. He was in a sec ago."

"And nothing from the hard drive?"

"Still working on it. The guy's got a zillion pirated Jimmy Buffett songs but, like I said, nothing obviously Inquisitor-related."

"Are there any straight photos of Green, where he's not busy committing a felony? Something we can use for an ID?"

"Yeah, I saw something."

Mason tapped at the keyboard, opening and closing folders, the screen finally filling with thumbnail photos of Green attending a medical meeting.

"Print one that shows him best?"

"Sure."

A few minutes later, they were leaving, the color print tucked in Rad's pocket.

"Let's see what Ana thinks."


They found her tidying the TV room, CNN on in the background, stereo blaring. She was flushed from the effort, her smile bright and brittle.

"Here they are! The Men Who Went Into the Fire!"

She put down the garbage bag and walked over to Roggetti, said, "I'm glad you're safe," then kissed him on the cheek. And then she kissed Rad's cheek and said, "You too," and then Jenner's mouth, a little longer. "And you."

Rad said, "How are you doing, Ana?"

"Me? I'm fine. Good." She nodded her head firmly. "I'm good."

She sat. "But you're the guys who went into the fire! How are you feeling?"

Everyone muttered they were fine, and then she stood, turning to Jenner to ask, "Would your guests like something to drink, honey?"

Roggetti asked for juice. She walked out of the TV room toward the kitchen, humming, leaving Rad and Jenner staring at the empty door frame. Rad turned to Jenner, eyebrows raised.

Jenner shook his head and shrugged.

Roggetti leaned forward and said "Whoa!" fumbling for the TV remote. Onscreen was a montage of video from the evening before, shot from a helicopter above Mulberry Street. There was video of Joey's stretcher being loaded into the ambulance, and Rad giving the thumbs-up sign to the crowd, and Jenner climbing in after him. The caption read "Fourth Inquisitor Victim."

"God! We look terrible!" Joey said.

The station cut away to a live feed from in front of the medical examiner's office, where Jacob Sarkies, MD, billed as "Forensic Psychiatrist, Tristate Forensic Task Force," was holding forth. Jenner had met the guy a few years back, when Sarkies was in the middle of his psych residency; he was still an obnoxious little prick.

"Robin, all the evidence we have so far is totally consistent with Dr. Green leading a secret life as the Inquisitor. There's a very high degree of correlation with the profile Tristate Forensics had generated—age, build, previous sexual history, previous failed marriages, even his having a large car in which to move victims and equipment."

"Doctor, isn't it unusual for a physician to be a serial killer?"

"Well, yes and no, Robin. It is unusual for a serial killer to be so highly functioning, but you have to remember that such men—and occasionally, women—range across the IQ scale.

"It also makes sense that he was drawn specifically to surgery. Surgery is a practice of medicine that demands an almost cold-blooded ability to shut down emotions like anxiety and fear. Surgeons tend to be strongly opinionated men of action, and work in an environment where there's a hair's-breadth difference between saving life and taking life. I've observed a tendency toward narcissism in surgeons, and narcissism is a most useful tool for the serial killer. Not to mention an ability to use a knife."

Sarkies allowed himself a small grin.

Jenner snorted and glanced at the cops. "Talk about narcissism, eh? You think that profile of his told him Green drove a Mercedes SUV?"

Rad said, "Probably told him the color, too."

"Well, Doctor, you've certainly given us a lot to think about. Thanks. Back to you, Mike and Jess."

Ana had come in with a tray while they were watching. There was orange juice for Roggetti, a two-liter bottle of Coke, a couple of cans of beer, and two airline mini-bottles of whisky that Jenner had swiped when he was upgraded to first class on a Chicago flight the year before.

Rad asked her to sit for a minute. She sat close to Jenner, her hand on his thigh.

"Ana, we'd like you to have a look at a photo, see if it looks like the man you saw. Do you think you could do that for us?"

"Absolutely."

Rad removed the photograph, placed it on the coffee table, and smoothed it flat.

It was a photo of Green with two older physicians, standing by a fountain in a resort hotel lobby.

"Could this be the man you saw?"

"I'm not sure. I only saw him for a second, and he was in the dark, and bloody."

"Take your time. No rush." He pushed the image closer to her.

"I guess he's about the same size, same age, roughly. As best I can tell."

"How about the face?"

He pushed the photo a little closer to her. She tilted her head from side to side, studying it.

"It's hard to say for sure . . . But, yeah, I think that's him."

"You're sure now?"

She leaned back. "Just about as sure as I can be. That's the man I saw."

Rad made a note on the photo and had Ana sign and date it. "Thanks. The DA will need to speak with you once we find him."

She nodded.

"And we'll find him soon. Every cop on the eastern seaboard is on the lookout for this son of a bitch. Don't you worry, we'll get him."

He stood. "C'mon, Joe, we gotta go."

"Okay. Seeya, Ana. Seeya, Jenner."

Ana started tidying again as soon as they were out the door. Jenner gently grabbed her wrist.

"Let's talk."

"Let me finish cleaning first."

"Cleaning can wait. Sit down and talk with me."

She stood. "No."

He looked up at her. "I'm worried about you. I thought you were doing really well, but I'm not so sure."

"Deal with it. I'm dealing with the things I have to deal with. This is how I deal."

"That's not good enough."

"Why not, Jenner? Because I'm not crying and holding on to you and making you the hero? I'm okay. You want to talk because you want to be the hero. And I don't want to talk because I don't need a hero—I hate you feeding off me like that."

She spoke so quickly and vehemently that he was stunned.

"Have you been waiting a long time to say that?"

Her lip quivered, and her eyes shone wetly. "It's not that I don't appreciate what you've done for me—I do, I appreciate it so much! And I'm so grateful for the way you've thrown yourself into this and worked to catch this . . . man."

She half-folded the dishtowel in her hand, then tossed it onto the coffee table, saying, "I just need to work through it myself. I need time without everyone asking me if I'm all right, if I feel okay, if there's anything they can do for me. I just need a break from being the *victim* all the time."

"Okay. I can understand that. But I just want you to know that if you need help . . ."

Her mouth set as she wiped her eyes with the back of her hand. She picked up the dishtowel.

"Message received, hero."

She took the tray and left the room.

He woke early and alone; Ana had slept on the daybed.

He was stiff, every joint locked, every muscle knotted tight. Worse, in the bathroom cabinet, he couldn't find the Vicodin tablets he thought he had left over from his back injury. He made do with a couple of Tylenol and a long soak in a hot bath.

When he got out of the tub, he changed into his sweats and did some stretching excercises. Then he peered out into the loft. She was still asleep, clutching a pillow under her head, another wedged between her thighs.

He wanted to talk to her, but after the night before, he didn't think she'd want to talk like that. And some of what she had said was right.

The TV was still on, still on CNN Headline News. David Green's face filled the screen, and then the image cut away to a shot of NYPD patrol cars on a dark tree-lined street, their turret lights casting red shadows across the big lawns and old oaks. He turned the volume up a little.

". . . in the early hours of this morning. The doctor, primary suspect in New York's Inquisitor murders, was arrested after an anonymous tip led police to the New York suburb of Cos Cob, where he was found hiding in the hot tub enclosure at a house belonging to his ex-wife."

They cut to a bedraggled Green being led away by two Emergency Service Unit cops, his hands cuffed behind his back; as the camera tracked him into the cop car, it looked like he was crying. News helicopters followed Green as he was transported back into the city, the flashing lights of the four-car motorcade glimmering rubies in the predawn gray.

Jenner looked at his watch. A little after 11:00 a.m.; Green would have been processed by now. He changed the channel; the local stations were broadcasting live from in front of the DA's office. He called Rad's cell, but got dumped into voice mail. The same with Roggetti. Maybe they were interviewing Green.

He called Manhattan South Homicide. When someone finally answered, he could hear they were watching the same station as him. He was told to hold for Garcia, then the receiver was put down on a desktop with a loud clatter. The task force office sounded like a gospel service, call-and-response shouting at the TV and occasional applause.

Roggetti picked up, ebullient. "Jenner! Top of the morning to you, my Irish friend!"

"I'm not Irish. Celebrating, Joey?"

"Yes, Doc, indeed we are. You heard we got Green, right?"

"Yes. I'm watching the news now. I still don't think he's the guy."

"New witness."

"What?"

"We got a new witness. A lawyer who lives on the uptown side of Tompkins Square Park puts him running across the park that night."

"He sure?"

"She. It's a female. And she's sure it's him."

"Huh."

"Wait—I'm handing you over to Rad. Take care, Doc!"

"You too, Joey."

Rad came on the line. "Hey, Jenner. So what do you make of this?"

"Is this new witness credible?"

"Far as I can tell. Corporate lawyer, dresses well, talks well. Coming home from her office, sees the guy running through the park. Runs right past her. Timing makes sense, too."

"I guess I was wrong." He paused. "What's Green saying?"

"He's not talking. He's waiting for his lawyer."

"Yeah, figures."

Another whoop went up in the background.

"Okay, Rad, well, congratulations, I guess. Let me know if anything new happens."

"You got it. Nice work, Jenner. We did good."


She was still asleep. He switched the TV off, then put a note that read "WATCH THE NEWS!" against the coffee jar. He dressed slowly, hoping she'd wake; when she didn't, he went across the hall, where Jun and Kimi were about to go out for dim sum. He walked with them, quiet as they chatted.

The thing had ended, they'd crossed the finish line, but there was no feeling of victory. It wasn't so much that he'd been wrong about Green—he'd been wrong before. But now everything was coming to a close, and things between him and Ana were completely fucked up.

They went to Jing Fong in Chinatown. It didn't look like much from the street, but a long escalator ride landed them in a vast dining hall, like some of the mega-restaurants Jenner had seen in Hong Kong. After lunch, they walked in Chinatown for a while. Then Jenner excused himself, leaving Jun and Kimi to watch old Chinese women doing tai chi in the park behind the city jail. He walked up to Houston Street, and ended up at the Landmark cinema, where he watched a slight French movie.

When he got home, she was waiting for him at the door. She kissed him, murmuring, "I'm sorry," into his ear as she held him hard. Her skin was hot against his.

She pulled away and took his wrist.

"I got you something!"

She made him sit at the table, then put a box with white tissue wrapping paper and a red bow in front of him.

"Open it!"

It was a cell phone. He smiled.

She sat on his lap and put an arm around his neck, and launched into an animated description of everything she'd done after she'd seen the news. Shopping, mostly. Phone calls. Lunch with friends at Dojo on St. Marks. Bought him a phone at Mondo Kim's.

The buzzer rang.

"That'll be our dinner."

"What did you order?"

"Chinese."

"I had Chinese for lunch!"

"Shaddup! The Chinese have it breakfast, lunch, and dinner every day!"

He handed her his wallet and headed for the bathroom. She'd put his pajamas out on the granite counter. He took a quick shower and dried off, then dressed again.

She'd set two places at the table, and had put all of the food into serving bowls. There were lit candles, and next to a white bowl of persimmons in the center of the table, his new phone was charging in its dock.

There was no sign of her.

He called her name. No answer.

He went to the TV room, knocked on the door, then pushed it open. The room was empty.

He called down to Douggie's apartment, and hung up when he got the machine.

He checked the toilet, and the walk-in closet.

Heart pounding, he left his apartment and rapped on Jun's door. No answer.

He went in.

She was sprawled on Jun's big white couch, eyes closed.

He stepped quickly to her, and she sat up dopily.

"What is it?"

"Sorry. I got worried because I lost you."

"I just came over to Jun's to get a bottle of champagne. I must have fallen asleep."

"Apparently. Do you still feel like eating?"

She sighed and said slowly, "Yes. I'm a bit washed out, but I want to have dinner with you. Let's go."

But she didn't eat, just poked at the food with her chopsticks. She was subdued and taciturn; Jenner hadn't understood until now just how emotionally exhausted she was. After dinner, she wanted to watch a movie, but after choosing *Battle Royale*, a violent Japanese action movie, she stretched out next to him and promptly fell asleep. She slept for the length of the film, through the gunfire and the explosions, and when it finished, he didn't have the heart to wake her. He draped the blanket over her and went to bed alone.

He'd been asleep for only a few minutes when she woke him, standing naked by the bed, holding a candle. He smiled up at her and lifted the covers.

"Hey. Come in, you'll get cold."

"First, look." She gestured toward her stomach. "I'm all healed now."

The wounds on her stomach were now clean red scars, like a triplet note on a piece of sheet music.

"You know, they're actually kind of cute. They'll be pale in a few months. Now get in."

She had one knee on the bed when she dropped the candle, spattering hot wax onto the blanket. She clumsily put out the flame with her hands before the blanket burned.

"Oops."

Jenner sat up. Gouts of dark wax were crusting on the blanket surface.

"You okay?"

She nodded. "Just cold. Let me in."

She slid in next to him, curled up against him, and fell fast asleep almost instantly.

He stroked her shoulder, then slipped his hand down her flank, let his fingers stroke across her stomach. And then stopped.

He reached to the bedside table and turned the light on, lifting up the sheets to look at her. Drying wax was spattered across her belly and thighs, her skin under the rinds of set wax angry and red.

She had burned herself, and hadn't even noticed.

"Wake up."

He forced her up into a sitting position, half asleep, her slack body sliding back to the mattress.

"*Ana!* Wake the fuck up."

He shook her. Her eyes flickered slowly.

"What? I'm up, Jenner."

He turned on the light.

"Open your eyes and look at me."

She kept her eyes shut, so he held her head steady and opened her lids with his thumbs; under the lids, her eyes were moving, the pupils tiny little dots in the blue of her irises.

He let her back down, slowly.

"Oh, Jesus, Ana. You're doing heroin, aren't you?"

Her head was on the pillow again, her eyes closed.

"No, Jenner, I'm not. Swear to God . . ."

"You can't even keep your fucking eyes open."

She was half asleep again.

He threw the blanket back, pulled her arm toward the light, looking for injection marks. She resisted feebly. Both arms were clean. He moved her lips as if he were handling a rag doll, examining the rest of her body—her inner thighs, the backs of her knees, her feet. He breathed out again. No needle marks.

He went into the bathroom, grabbed the little steel trash pail, and tipped it into the sink. An old toothbrush, pieces of dental floss, a toothpaste box from Fresh. Then he found it: tucked into the toothpaste box was a translucent paper envelope the size of a postage stamp. A smudged blue ink imprint on the front read "Steppin' Razor."

He emptied the medicine cabinet, placing the contents neatly onto the countertop. The Vicodin was gone, as was his Ambien.

He went to the kitchen, opened the wine cupboard, and didn't need to count—it was clearly depleted.

It was barely past midnight; Jun would still be up.

He knocked on the door. Jun answered in a ratty T-shirt and sweats.

"What's up, Jenner?"

"Ana has a problem."

Jun opened the door wider and gestured to the couch. "What do you mean?"

They sat, and Jenner said, "I think she's been doing heroin."

Jun nodded slowly. "Probably."

"You knew?"

"Well, not heroin. But I know she's been drinking a lot, and I think there's stuff missing from my medicine cabinet. Anything to get numb, I figured."

"Why didn't you say anything?"

"I wasn't sure. I mean, I wasn't even sure about the medicine cabinet, but it all makes sense." Jun leaned back. "Where do you think she got it?"

"I don't know. She was in the East Village yesterday . . ." It wasn't like the 1980s, when there was a dealer on every corner, but over on Avenue D, if you knew where to go, people still sold heroin hand to hand.

He thought back over the last two weeks. Everything was coming together. When did it begin? Wine, first. Vicodin and Ambien, all laid out right in front of her. She'd had plenty of time alone, when he was out running around like a boy scout. But the heroin?

Then he knew: Thursday night, the club. That was why she suddenly wanted to go out. And that guy Perry in the club—when she'd reached under the table, it wasn't to touch him, it was to cop.

He shook his head. "I should have talked with her, made her see a shrink or something."

"Her choice, Jenner." He stood up. "What are you going to do?"

"I don't know."


Later, he sat at the foot of the bed and watched her sleep. Everything was finished, all the work was done. The cops were putting the last touches on the paperwork and turning back to more routine crimes, the girls were dead and buried, the families getting on with their grieving. Everyone had a role to play, and knew how to play it. Except him.

What was he supposed to do about Ana?

\* \* \*

The man closed the *Post* and looked at the front page again. INQUISITOR INTERROGATED. An unflattering close-up of his old client, the usually dapper Dr. Green in filthy khakis and a stained sweatshirt, looking like some bum scraped off a heating grate. Green wouldn't like that—he was always such a little fashion prince.

He was surprised that he felt no jealousy, no anger at the misplaced credit. His calm was an epiphany, of sorts: it meant that he was actively evolving, operating above the level of ego in a kind of rarefied space only accessed by those who had obtained pure and esoteric knowledges.

Credit was unimportant. All that mattered was that he was doing the work, transfiguring the Saints, creating the beautiful shrines. That his work was immediately torn apart by the police was irrelevant: the important thing was that they had existed, that he had created moments of transcendence, of radiance, of perfect grace. Ecstatic moments where flawed women had been reborn in sainthood, wherein he himself had been cleansed and purified.

They'd realize soon enough that Green was as capable of doing this work as a puppy was of sinking a battleship. Particularly when they saw his next project.

He powered up his laptop and modem, dialed in on the stolen phone signal with a free starter AOL account, then reached his destination. He'd created a camouflaged virtual server on the Hutchins Museum of Military History server, tucked away behind the firewall he'd designed for the college. Today his signal seemed stable. An FMedbase administrator screen came up. He tabbed down to his gateway into Green's clinic, and hit the Access button.

Nothing happened.

He hit it again.

Again, nothing.

He ran the diagnostics program. Error message: "No Such Server."

Ah, of course. The police would have impounded the office computer, and were busy sieving it for kiddie porn, or whatever Green's particular thrill might be. The New Hope Clinic had automatic remote backups to a data storage facility somewhere in the Lehigh Valley in Pennsylvania, but he didn't have a chance in hell of hacking his way through their security.

He had an instant of unfamiliar panic. What would he do? Those were the women he'd chosen, whores whose threadbare integrity allowed them to sell off the fruits of their womb, to scrape sacred life out of their harlot bellies in return for blood money. They barely deserved the redemption he offered, the rebirth through suffering in the radiant image of pious, glorious martyrs.

He went to his washbasin. In the mirror fragment, his temples were atrophied now, his face gaunt. He picked up the shard, angling it down at his torso; the muscles now seemed bound to a brittle armature of eroded bone, the muscles thickening as the scaffolding on which they hung wasted.

But it was an illusion caused by his weight loss. Inside his skin, he could feel his strength surging. The muscle and sinew were rock hard, the bone underneath strong as marble.

So. One more. One more shrine. He was to do one more. Then he would be finished. Then he could rest.

Ana de Jong.

He was ready for her now.


Jenner was sitting by the bed, waiting for Ana to wake, when Rad called to tell him they'd located a possible secondary scene: Green had a small apartment on East Seventh, and Crime Scene had found a concealed remote camera system. Rad asked Jenner if he wanted to come along for the search.

He did. He needed the time to figure out what he was going to say to her. Waiting for Garcia, he continued his search of her clothes and her bags, and found another bag of Steppin' Razor, full this time. He tossed it into the toilet and flushed, standing and waiting to make sure it disappeared. Then he flushed again.

He recognized Pat Mullins's bullet-shaped head at the top of the stoop. It was a brownstone between Second and First, not as classy as he would have expected from a guy as affluent as Green.

"Hey, Pat."

"Doctor. Nice to see you out." He nodded at Rad and Roggetti.

Jenner said, "Nice work on getting Green."

Mullins responded with a wink, saying, "Piece of cake, Doc."

"Is he saying much?"

"Not a peep. He's got Barry Haimlisch, who's shut everything right down."

Jenner remembered Haimlisch. "I've met him a couple of times. He's sharp."

Roggetti said, "Well, good for him. The case against his client is pretty much open-and-shut."

"Maybe," Rad said.

"What? You don't think so?"

"Too soon to tell, Joey. I mean, SexBat, sure. But the Inquisitor stuff? The case is still pretty circumstantial."

Mullins shrugged. "We'll see. In the meantime, let's see what we got here."

As they walked inside, Rad said, "I was talking with Woody Milwood over at the crime lab, and so far they've got no fingerprint matches between Green and any of the scenes. Not a one."

Mullins shook his head. "Maybe he's got an accomplice. Look, even if we don't have good evidence on the Inquisitor, we've got plenty to send his sorry oral-sodomy-committing ass to jail, and that ought to loosen him up a bit. No pun intended."

Rad grinned. "You backing down on this, Pat?"

"Nope. I think we got the guy. I'm just being . . ." He searched for a word, then found it. "Keeping my mind open."

The second-story floor-through had been chopped in half; Green's studio apartment was in back. The kitchen opened into the living room area, filled mostly with a low platform bed with an ugly maroon quilt.

Green had barely bothered to decorate. A framed poster of skiers at Jackson Hole on one wall, on another a blowup of a photo of a generic sunset over a generic beach somewhere, Mexico, maybe.

In an armoire in the corner, tucked between the TV and a mini stereo system, they found one of the small cameras; the second was hidden in a low bookshelf among medical journals and the occasional textbook. One of the crime scene detectives opened a small wood box on the lowest shelf and spilled its contents onto the bedside table—some condoms, a pair of handcuffs lined with matted fake leopard fur, and a small brown plastic vial of Viagra.

In the armoire, Green had a stack of CDs—Kenny G and Phil Collins, Sade and Enya—as well as *The Notebook*, *The English Patient*, and *Jenna Jameson's Wicked Anthology* on DVD. Roggetti, poring through the bookcase, pulled out a black plastic album and opened it to show the others a collection of DVD-Rs numbered with black marker ink. Roggetti selected one, put it in the DVD player, and switched on the TV.

There were a couple of flashes onscreen, and the video began. A girl on the bed, Green on his knees between her legs, her hands on his head.

Someone said, "Turn up the sound!" and Joey looked over the remote for a few seconds before the volume suddenly leaped to a buzzing roar, the girl's moans over the white noise echoing in the room. Roggetti turned it down a little.

It looked consensual; the others nodded when Jenner said so. He doubted they'd find anything else there, so he told Garcia he was heading home. He left them watching the TV.


Ana's clothes were folded neatly and stacked on the table. He heard water running in the bathroom.

When she came out, her eyes were heavily lined with black, her mascara was thick, and her lips glossy. She looked older, almost old.

He sat down and watched as she put a big Urban Outfitters shopping bag on the table and began stuffing her clothes into it. When it was full, she set an X-girl bag next to it. She turned to him and said, "You feel sorry for me, Jenner? Is that it? 'That poor orphan girl, the horrible thing that happened! And now she's all fucked up and . . . oh, my God, *look! She's on drugs!*' That it, Jenner?"

She turned away and began cramming socks into the bag.

"Ana, please. I'm not judging you. I can't imagine how hard all this has been on you. I think you've been incredibly brave."

"Was that what you were thinking while you were fucking me?" She struggled with the zipper of her cheap plastic makeup bag, then threw it down, turning to focus on him. "No, really, tell me what you were thinking—I'd really like to know! 'I'm helping her now, I'm doing this for her own good? This oughta make her forget her dead friend!' "

He looked away.

She was done packing.

"And now you're blue because your little orphan bitch is doing smack? You're afraid it's your fault, right?"

He didn't look up.

"Answer me!" she screamed. "Don't just fucking sit there, say something, say anything. Take a fucking *risk!*"

He looked at her, but didn't speak.

She grabbed a candlestick and hurled it at his head. He threw up his arm, knocking it away.

"Fuck you! Fuck you, you fucking *coward!*"

She lifted the bags, one of which immediately broke at the handle and spilled her things onto the floor. She collapsed to her knees, sobbing as she tried to gather the clothes together in her arms.

He watched her crawling under the table, her flushed face streaked with mascara. A pair of socks, rolled into a ball, skittered out of her reach, and she sank onto her clothes, curling up and crying freely.

He knelt down to help her up, but she pushed him away. She stood and ran to the sink, pulling out a garbage bag. She scooped most of her clothes into the garbage bag, then spun it shut and picked up the shopping bag. She put the bags on the couch, then put on her coat. Shouldering her bags, she turned to him.

"I don't need your help, Jenner. You need mine. *You need mine!* So fuck you, fuck you, fuck you, good-bye."

She slammed the door.

\*   \*   \*

At twilight, around 4:00 p.m., he walked to Williamsburg, to Dalrymple's Food Discount, and spent the last of his money. He'd been trying to keep pure by eating only vegetables and grains, but decided he needed more protein, and calcium for his bones, so he allowed himself organic milk and beef, despite the expense.

Back at the warehouse, he unpacked his groceries. His kitchen area was as cold as most refrigerators, but he kept food in an old steel toolbox because of the rats; the meat went out on the window ledge in a metal biscuit tin.

He boiled some cauliflower. Eating at the bench, he leafed through the Dalrymple's flyer by candlelight, imagining what he would buy if he had a hundred bucks to spend.

It was a holiday season flyer, and the cover—an old illustration, maybe from the fifties—showed a family gathered around for a Christmas dinner. The fireplace in the background had stockings and swags of holly, and the mom was hefting an enormous turkey onto a dinner table filled with decorations and side dishes as the dad and the brother and the sister looked on with enthusiasm and delight.

The children would have already got their gifts—kids got the presents in the morning, he knew. They wake up and come down and there are presents from Santa under the tree and in the stockings, and then Mom and Dad come down and give them more presents. After church, the women cook dinner.

His Christmases had been different. He would wait all day on the bench by the farmhouse door for the church people who brought them a turkey, not wanting them to come in and see his mom and dad passed out at the kitchen table.

He finished the cauliflower and leaned back.

He needed a van.

TUESDAY,
DECEMBER 17

She came in just before dawn. Jenner heard her let herself into the loft, the scratch of her keys settling on the table. She slipped under the sheets and lay against him; when she lowered her head to his chest, he felt her tears on his skin.

He figured she was high, but he didn't care. He would help her get through this, get straight.

She was asleep. He looked at her face, now without makeup.

She was beautiful.

He would help her. He would get her help, and everything would be fine.

To his surprise, she was up before him. He found her in the living room, tapping numbers into his cell phone's memory.

"Here," she said, handing him the phone. "I want to test it."

She opened her phone up and showed him. "Look, you're on speed dial."

Jenner's phone rang, an irritating high blurting.

"Now you do me. Just press two and hold it."

He pressed the key; her phone played a little snippet of music.

"I like yours better."

"We can change the ringtone."

He pulled the juice out of the fridge and poured them each a glass. He put one down in front of her and waited. She was studying her phone intently.

"Ana?"

"What?"

"What do you want to do?"

She was still looking at the phone. Just when he thought she wasn't going to answer, she said, "To kick. To kick it."

"Will that be hard?"

"Maybe."

"How long have you been doing this?"

She shrugged. "Long enough that when I'm not high, I really *want* to be high."

"Since Thursday?"

"This time."

He looked at her.

"And before?"

"On and off. Once in a while."

He sat next to her.

"Snorting?"

"Uh-huh."

She was concentrating on the phone now.

"Injecting?"

She turned quickly to him and said, "Oh, my God, Jenner! Of course not!"

"So how are you going to stop?"

"I'll just stop."

"And that's it?"

She smiled at him sadly. "No. You'll help me."

He put an arm around her. "When did you last get high?"

"About nine a.m. I used up the last—you didn't find everything, by the way. But it's finished now."

"Is there anything I should get?"

"I don't know. A *TV Guide* and some ice cream?"

"Cherry Garcia?"

"Sounds good."

He put on his coat, and she grabbed his arm and looked him in the eye. "Thanks, Jenner. You're a good guy."

The phone rang. Garcia.

"Jenner, the chief is holding a press conference in about twenty. I think he's going to release information about the Green case, and I thought you should be there."

He looked over at her. "In twenty minutes?"

"It's at One Police Plaza. Five minutes by cab from your place, Jenner. If that."

"Okay."

He told her and said he didn't know what to do, and she said go, and he told her he'd be back with the ice cream in about an hour.

Roggetti, Mullins, and Garcia were onstage, flanking the Chief of D's, standing back by the flags. Jenner was surprised at how small the room was, too small to deal with the crowd of reporters. The room buzzed with at least a dozen languages, and Jenner saw cameras with battered stickers from Japan's NHK, the BBC, and RAI from Italy, among others.

Scales put his papers on the lectern and scanned the crowd, nodding at Jenner. He tapped on the microphone, then began to speak.

"I have a brief prepared statement, after which I'll refer all questions to the public affairs officer."

He cleared his throat, then continued. "I'd like to announce that this morning a grand jury indicted Dr. David Green for seventeen counts of oral sodomy, twelve counts of sodomy, and two counts of sexual battery on a minor. At a hearing immediately afterward, he was denied bail on grounds that he is a proven flight risk. He has been remanded into custody until his trial."

He paused. The reporters listened, pens poised above steno pads, microcassette and minidisc recorder microphones pointed at the chief.

Scales breathed in, then said, "Dr. Green is no longer considered a person of interest in the Hutchins student homicides."

Etiquette immediately collapsed, the reporters rising to their feet, shouting questions and waving microphones.

The chief nodded grimly. "Ladies and gentlemen, thank you for coming."

He started off the platform when Richie Parsons, in the front row, shouted, "Are you telling the people of the City of New York that you have no idea who the Inquisitor is?"

The chief stopped, weighing his options.

He turned, walked back to the lectern, and began to speak, the AV tech turning the microphone back on midway through his first sentence.

". . . all must be considered. Dr. Green was only a person of interest in the Inquisitor killings, never a suspect. This confusion rose up out of rumors tossed around by the media, something out of NYPD control.

"Rest assured: we have strong leads, and all of these leads will be explored to the fullest extent possible. We are confident that we will have the perpetrator in custody soon."

He switched off the mic at the lectern, then added an unamplified "Thank you" before leaving the conference room, followed by Garcia and then Roggetti and Mullins, the three detectives looking very somber.

Jenner caught up with them outside on the plaza, and together they walked over to Duane Street for coffee at the Courthouse Diner.

Jenner asked, "What happened to your new witness?"

Pat Mullins said, "The lawyer? Turned out she was a psycho. Hasn't worked in a couple of years—went schizo. Her current residence is an assisted living facility a couple of blocks north of the park, but she's circling the drain, and smart money says she'll be locked up or on the street in the next year or so. She tried to bite Ruben during the photo lineup."

Jenner asked, "So, what's next? What do we have? Rad?"

Rad shook his head. "There's not much forensics. No, wait, it's actually the opposite—we have *all* the forensics in the world. We got fingerprints and bite marks, we got blood. But none of it's in any database. His blood doesn't ring any bells at CODIS, and we've got no suspects for a DNA comparison. Everyone at the clinic comes up clean—we're pretty much at square one again."

Jenner leaned back. "Okay. We know the link—Green's clinic. Is it the clinic, is it the clinic database, is it prescriptions he wrote . . . ?"

Rad stopped stirring his coffee. "We figure someone outside has access to the database. Mason said a real hacker would have had no difficulty at all getting past the firewall on that database program."

Jenner said, "It's got to be someone outside the clinic—they could access and change files like the appointment calendar, which was electronic, but couldn't get rid of the hard-copy stuff printed out in the office."

They all nodded, and Mullins said, "But where do we start? Is it because they're egg donors? Because they're Hutchins students? Why those four?"

Roggetti added, "And who's next?"

They were all silent for a while.

Jenner's cell phone rang. It was embarrassingly loud.

He opened it.

"Hello?"

There was no answer.

"Hello?"

He looked at the phone, then shrugged. "I don't know how to use this thing. Ana gave it to me. She's sending me a text message—this is her cell number here, but she's added 911 at the end."

Rad looked at it.

"That means 'emergency.' We'll run you up." Rad grabbed his coat. "Yo, Mullins—Dr. Jenner, Detective Roggetti, and myself are forever grateful for your generosity."

They left Mullins signaling for the waitress.

In the car, Jenner dialed her number, but kept being told, "The customer you are calling cannot be reached at this time."

He turned to Joey and said, "Faster."

Joey hit the siren and they pulled ahead, racing up Centre.

Rad said, "What's going on? Should I call for backup, Jenner?"

Jenner shook his head; she was probably starting to withdraw. "I don't know. No, I don't think so."

They flew past Canal Street.

He leaned forward to talk to them. "Look, I should be straight with the two of you. This whole thing has taken a real toll on her. I found out last night she's been doing heroin. We had a fight, and she ran away. She came back this morning, and she's trying to get straight."

"That's rough." Rad nodded. "Poor kid."

Jenner tapped Joey's shoulder and said, "Take the left onto Prince and right on Crosby—you can park in the lot round the back."

Roggetti pulled in near the back loading dock, next to a graffiti-covered delivery van. Jenner had the door open before the car stopped, the detectives following him a second later.

"We'll come up. You might need some help," Rad said.

Jenner impatiently pushed the call button for the service elevator. The door was propped open with a garbage canister—Pete was bringing down the trash.

"The stairs," Roggetti said.

As Rad opened the stairwell door, there was a clang and a hum from the elevator behind them. The broad door opened, and Pete backed out onto the dock, pulling a cart stacked with garbage bags past them as Roggetti held an arm out to stop the door from closing.

When Pete's cart had cleared the door, Rad and Jenner got in, Roggetti following. As the door closed, Jenner noticed movement in the bags.

"Rad!" he shouted.

Rad turned to step out, and the man wearing Pete's uniform leaned in and slashed hard and fast at his face; Rad fell backward, his hands waving at the blood pouring from his neck. Roggetti and Jenner tumbled out of the closing door; catching Jenner down on one knee, the man brought the back of his fist down hard onto the back of Jenner's neck.

Jenner went down, vision blurring as Roggetti struggled to pull out his Glock. The gun was tucked out of sight on his hip, under his jacket, the backstrap still snapped shut; he didn't have a chance. The man switched hands with a metal weapon—something with a long, thin silver blade, a knife or screwdriver—and swung it backhanded into Joey's neck, burying it deeply.

Roggetti grabbed at his neck, choking. A blow to his abdomen dropped him; he lay writhing, his hand desperately slipping at the bloody handle in his neck.

The man squatted next to him, and with one swift move pulled the screwdriver out, tossed it into his right hand, and then, pinning one of Roggetti's shoulders down with his knee, started methodically stabbing him in his neck and upper chest. Roggetti was bleeding heavily now, rocking slightly with the stabs.

The man half stood and used his foot to turn Roggetti, now gasping weakly, onto his front. He calmly pressed one foot on the back of Roggetti's head to steady it, then drove the screwdriver into the base of his skull.

Jenner struggled to stand, his feet slipping from underneath him in the slick of Roggetti's blood. The man saw him on all fours and kicked him heavily in his left chest. Jenner felt his ribs buckle.

"Stay down, Doctor," the man said. "I'm pretty sure I just broke at least two of your ribs. If you move again, I will kill you. Stay down, I'll let you live. Move, I'll do you like I did him."

Jenner lay there, curled up and fighting to breathe, unable to straighten from the pain in his chest, Joey's blood smearing his face and hair.

The man turned to the cart and swept a couple of garbage bags off the stack. The next bag was open, and he tore it down to reveal Ana de Jong, her arms bound with clothesline, her mouth mummy-wrapped with duct tape.

As soon as the daylight hit her, she struggled frantically, eyes bulging. He lifted her easily, as if he were tucking an attaché case under his arm, then put her down on the edge of the loading dock.

"Wait just a second," he said. He slipped off the dock and started to walk toward the van.

"Oh, wait! Your friends . . ." He turned, stepped back to her, and gently rolled her over so that she lay facing Jenner and Roggetti. Her eyes widened, and she started to scream into her gag and twist against her bonds.

The man wiped his hands on his Carhartt jacket, then walked to the van and opened the back doors.

Jenner tried to move toward Ana, but he couldn't catch his breath; he just lay there looking at her, shaking his head as he looked into her eyes. She was screaming, her face red from the effort, tears flowing down over the duct tape into her blood-soaked hair.

The man walked back to the dock. He nodded at Jenner and said, "I'll be taking her now. Good-bye."

He swung her down off the ledge and carried her, cradled in his arms, to the van. He had just put her in the van when the elevator door opened again.

Jun Saito, covered in blood, stepped out, glanced at Jenner and Roggetti, then shifted his attention to the sound of the van door slamming shut.

He immediately brought up his pistol and started firing from the dock, holding the gun with both hands as he walked toward the ledge, shooting. The first shot smashed into the left rear window; the second skimmed over the man's shoulder.

The man sprinted to the front of the van and got in. He fishtailed out of the lot as Jun jumped down to follow, still firing.

It took all of Jenner's strength to gasp out, "No! Ana's in the truck!" and once he'd said it, he couldn't get back the breath he'd lost.

Jun watched the van drive off, then closed his eyes. He turned to Jenner.

"License begins ALHR, New York State license. Remember that, Jenner."

He scrambled up onto the ledge and looked into Jenner's face keenly.

"You okay, Jenner?"

"Can't breathe . . ."

"ALHR. I need you to remember that, okay?" He pressed Jenner's shoulder. "Kimi's dialed 911, they're on their way. I can hear them."

Jenner could, too, a siren echoing from the firehouse a few blocks away on Lafayette.

"Wait here. I'm going to check on your friend."

Jenner twisted his head to his right. Jun was standing there, looking down at Roggetti. The cop was no longer moving his limbs; soft tremors ran down his body every few seconds.

"Jenner. Can you hear me? Do I take out the screwdriver? Will that help him?"

"No . . . leave it . . . ER . . ."

The elevator door opened again, and he saw Kimi kneeling next to Garcia, crying and shaking as she pressed a heavily bloodstained white towel to his neck, her arms and shirt glossy with the detective's blood. His leg stuck out of the elevator, and the door kept opening and closing on it.

He couldn't tell if Garcia was alive or dead; his face was pale, and as the world began to move away from him, Jenner saw that there were beads of sweat on him, like fake dew on wax fruit.

The sirens grew louder, and there was shouting, "Drop it! Drop it!" then he heard more screaming, Kimi, maybe, maybe even himself, no, not him, his breath, he couldn't get his breath, ALHR, he wasn't breathing, and then everything went black.


Ana woke in darkness, pain roaring across her chest as if her breastbone had been split with an ax. She was partially suspended. Her head hung forward, her arms angled back and up, her shoulders straining as if they were about to pop out of their sockets. Above the rope chafing her wrists raw, her hands were numb and her fingers wouldn't move.

She started to retch, the spasms that racked her chest tearing at her arms. The retching subsided, leaving her hanging, shivering. Her whole body was icy. She straightened her legs, and the pain in her wrists and shoulders eased as she took some of the weight off.

She tried to stay calm and think clearly.

What did she know?

She was still dressed, and it didn't feel like anyone had messed with her clothes. Jeans, panties, a bra, T-shirt. Her new sweater.

Okay, she was clothed, she was okay so far. Socks, no shoes. Okay so far.

Where was she? One step at a time. Think. Okay, she was in a room, but it had no windows, or else the windows were heavily shaded.

She was bound. Wrists behind her back, pulling upward. By what? Rope, not handcuffs. Coarse natural rope, not smooth synthetic.

What else? She was close to a wall. She wished she could see more. There was no light.

Where was she? She was against the wall in a room. The room was cold. She concentrated. The room was colder toward her left than her right. Was there a window there? Door? Fireplace?

She couldn't tell. She leaned back. The wall was icy cold; brick, she thought. It smelled of burned charcoal. She felt the floor with her feet. Planks, wood planks. Wide.

So. She was tied up in a brick room with broad floorboards. A loft? A warehouse?

She tested the bonds of her wrists; her hands were tingling.

She straightened up as best she could, then leaned to her side as far as she could, until her face pressed against the brick. It smelled of damp and mildew, and she felt an oily smear on her face. She kept rubbing; in some parts of the wall, the plaster was missing.

She slid one foot out, balancing on the other leg, sweeping it slowly across the floor again. In some areas, the wood was spongy, splintering softly when she pressed hard.

So. An old warehouse. Damp. In the basement? Near a river or pond or lake?

Wait—was she still even in the city?

She listened hard, straining to catch city noise. Traffic, sirens, yelling, loud music—all of the things she'd complained about when she first moved to New York, she was desperate for them now.

She could hear nothing.

She breathed deeply. It smelled wet, and it smelled moldy. *Dank. Dank* was the word, she thought. It smelled dank.

And she had figured out that she was in an old, probably abandoned, warehouse, in a room where all light had been blocked out, and the warehouse might be near water. Maybe outside the city.

Okay. Good, she was thinking, she was using her wits. That was good. She could feel her nerves jangling, but she was keeping it together. Just by thinking about things, by being rational, she'd made herself centered in this place. And she'd done it all just by thinking about what she smelled and what she heard.

Then she heard something else: a thrumming noise that gradually grew louder into a crescendo, then was abruptly interrupted by a high-pitched shrieking sound.

And *that* sound she knew instantly.

And she had figured it out: she had been trapped by the monster who had drilled her friend's flesh and then nailed her to a wall, and torn apart three other girls for kicks, and killed Joey Roggetti and Rad Garcia, and he was sharpening a knife outside her door. She was in a room in the middle of nowhere, where no one would hear her scream when he began to hurt her, and no one would help her when he started to cut her, and no one would find her body unless he wanted them to see what he'd done to it.

## A
*LHR.*

When Jenner woke, it was light.

He was in a bed, a hospital bed. There were three other beds in the room. One with a young black man in it, asleep, the other two old Hispanic men, also sleeping.

He turned his head. Through the window, he could see the East River beneath him: a tugboat pulling a barge heading upstream, a Circle Line tourist boat sliding slowly out of its path toward the Brooklyn side of the water. The crumbling piers and factories along the riverside urban neighborhoods of Greenpoint and Williamsburg across the way.

Bellevue Hospital. He was in Bellevue.

He moved to sit up, but the left side of his chest felt like a slab of crushed meat and mangled bone. He caught his breath sharply, and waves of pain spiked from his belly through to his back. He lay still, gasping.

On the monitor next to the bed, he watched his heartbeat, regular, sinus rhythm ninety beats per minute.

He could feel layers of tight cloth beneath his blue hospital shift. He slowly raised his right hand, tugged the gown open: under a clear film dressing, a rubber tube entered his chest, partially hidden by a piece of gauze lightly stained with blood and Betadine. How odd to be seeing his own chest tube, after removing hundreds from the battered and bloodied dead over the years.

A Filipino nurse came into the room holding a clipboard and a pen attached to a lanyard around her neck. She noticed him awake and gave him a sympathetic smile.

"Good to see you awake, Mr. Jenner."

He nodded, mouth dry. "What day is this? How long have I been here?"

"Don't you worry about that now," she said, smiling. "You just rest and get better now."

"Nurse, please, I need to know: what day is this today?"

"Well . . . this is Wednesday. You came in yesterday afternoon."

She pulled the top blanket up, saying, "You're a lucky guy! You had rib fractures, and a tension pneumo. You know what that is?" as she tucked it tighter around his waist.

He nodded, but she continued.

"That's when there's a hole in the lung, and so air gets out and fills up the chest and the lung collapses so you can't breathe. So yesterday in the ER, they put a tube in your chest to suck out the air."

She inspected the suction bottle next to his bed. Then she lifted his gown. On his solar plexus, there was a rectangle of gauze taped down with bandages.

"Just checking for bleeding. They were worried you had an injury to your spleen; that's a little organ like a sponge filled with blood, just below your ribs on the left. So they did a laparotomy. That's when they make an incision to look inside to see that you're okay. And you were fine, no laceration or rupture."

She smiled brightly down at him. "And no bleeding from the wound. I think you're a lot better now!"

She jotted some notes onto the clipboard and again told him he was a lucky guy, a very lucky guy, then put a thermometer in his mouth. "You ready to eat something?"

He pulled the thermometer out. "Do you know anything about my friends?"

Her face clouded. "Oh, I think you have to speak to Dr. Kahn for that."

"Please, tell me."

She hesitated.

"Please. I think one is dead."

She shook her head sadly. "I'm sorry. I read in the papers today that two men died."

His head sank into the pillow. Rad, Joey, dead.

"And the girl?"

"Oh, Mr. Jenner. You really need to speak with Dr. Kahn. And some policemen are here to talk with you. They're waiting for you."

He caught her wrist with his hand.

"Please tell me: did they find the girl?"

She looked around quickly, then leaned in.

"The Hutchins student?"

He nodded. She shook her head. "They don't know where she is. She's gone. The newspaper said a man in a white van took her."

He let her go and lay back. She fluffed his pillows and started to leave, then turned to him.

"Dinner isn't until four thirty p.m. I could bring you some fruit salad, if you like."

He closed his eyes.

Jun was standing by his bed, face pale, dark shadows sagging underneath his eyes.

"Hey, Jenner. How you feel?"

"Okay. Any news of Ana?"

He shook his head. "From what they're saying on the TV, they've got no leads. They found the van over in Queens, parked by a cemetery near the Kosciuszko Bridge. It was stolen in Williamsburg that morning."

Jenner nodded.

Jun looked awkward. "You need anything, Jenner? I would've been here sooner, but they only just let me out of jail."

"*What?*"

"It was nuts yesterday. I swear to God, they came *this* close to shooting me, because I had the gun.

"I kept telling them what happened, but they wouldn't listen. So I went through the whole thing—on my knees, handcuffed. They roughed me up a bit.

"It was insane. FDNY arrived first, and they're looking at the detectives, and they pronounced Detective Roggetti dead at the scene, and then there's almost a fight when the cops show up, so they end up taking him to the ER in an ambulance, but he was just pronounced dead when they got him to the ER. But at least they got Garcia in okay."

"What do you mean?"

"They got him to the ER, and then to the OR really quick."

"But he's . . . he died. The nurse said he died . . ."

Jun looked confused. "No. I mean, he was in the ICU. On the news they say he's critical, but Detective Santiago said the surgeons said he would be fine."

Jenner thought for a second. Two men died. Then he understood.

"Pete?"

"Yeah," Jun said. "They found his body in the basement."

Jenner turned away. Joey was dead. Pete was dead, killed for his work clothes and passkeys. Rad nearly killed. Ana gone.

He looked up at the ceiling and put his hand to his forehead. It was his fault. If only he'd been quicker. There were probably many things he'd overlooked.

Jun ignored Jenner's tears.

"Kimi was screaming at them, telling them I wasn't involved. But they busted me for unlicensed possession of a firearm. They let me go early this afternoon, but they kept my gun."

"I'm sorry, Jun."

"No worries, Jenner—you think I'd only have one?"

Someone came into the room; Jenner turned to see Pat Mullins standing there. He looked awful—unshaven, the same clothes Jenner had seen him in the morning before at coffee.

"Hey, Doc. How you doing?"

"Okay, Pat."

"Look, I have to ask you some questions, okay?"

Jenner nodded, then asked about leads on the abduction. Mullins shook his head no.

"How's Rad doing?"

"He's pretty banged up, but they think he'll be okay. Guy cut his throat, he lost a lot of blood. It took them eight hours in the OR, but they patched up all the jugular veins and the carotid arteries and all. They have to do tests to see if he has nerve damage when he comes around, but the surgeons said to be hopeful."

Mullins looked quickly at Jun, then back at Jenner. "Okay, Doc. Questions; I'm afraid your friend can't stay."

Jun asked again, "Anything you need, Jenner?" then disappeared when Jenner shook his head.

Mullins had Jenner describe what happened as a continuous narrative, then questioned him on the details.

It wasn't easy, but Jenner was surprised by how much he remembered; it had all happened in two, three minutes at most, from the moment he saw the movement in the garbage bags to when he passed out. He was quite lucid up until the killer put Ana in the van; after that, his recollection was vague.

By the time he was done answering Mullins's questions, he was exhausted. He lay there while Mullins finished his notes.

There was talking in the hall. Jenner saw what looked like a ward round—probably a surgical fellow and a couple of the trauma surgery residents.

Mullins stood and said, "I'm sorry about all this, Doc. Really I am." He paused. "I'm glad you made it through."

He stood there.

Jenner said, "Pat, is there something else?"

The detective glanced into the hall.

"Actually, Doc, there sorta is."

He moved closer to Jenner, and sat down again in the chair by the bed.

"This is hard for me to say, and I'm guessing it'll be harder for you to hear. I respect you, Doc, you know I do. And I know you were trying to help. But you can't be involved in this case anymore."

Jenner struggled to pull himself up, wincing as he sat straighter.

"Pat, I've been with this case since the beginning. They'll be letting me out soon. There must be some way you can use me? I don't want to help, I *need* to help."

Mullins sighed. "Doc, I'll level with you. There's a lot of . . . *emotion* in the department right now. You know how it is after a cop gets killed. And I think what's happening is, because we don't have a suspect, and we don't have clues, a lot of people are blaming you."

Jenner lay his head back on the pillow and looked at the ceiling.

"Now, I know you were only trying to help. But people are saying that if you hadn't been mixed up in this, if you hadn't . . . hooked up with that girl . . . none of this would have happened. Everyone says that girl should have left town. But she stayed with you.

"And at the end of the day, a good man is dead, Garcia's in the ICU breathing through a tube down his throat. And he got the girl."

He stood up, picking up his coat and folding it over his arm. "What I'm saying is this: stay away from the case. If you have a good idea, call me or Ruben Santiago. But if you physically get involved, if you show up at a scene, or start questioning witnesses, or stuff like that, the way some of these guys are talking . . ."

He put on his small porkpie hat, then turned and said, "Seriously, Doc. For your own good."

"Ah . . . Mr. . . . no, *Dr.* Jenner! I'm Dr. Kahn. How are you feeling?"

Jenner had been wrong—not just the fellow, but the attending surgeon himself was leading the ward round.

"A little sore. What do I have?"

"You're a medical doctor, right?"

Jenner nodded.

"Okay, good. Your ribs on your left side took quite a pounding. Full-thickness fractures with moderate displacement of the ninth and tenth ribs in the anterior axillary line, hairline fractures of eight and maybe even seven. You had a tension pneumothorax; they did a needle thoracostomy in the ambulance—saved your life, probably—and then we put in a chest tube because it didn't look like you were reexpanding properly.

"We were a bit worried about your spleen, so we did a minilap—I extended the incision over a bit and got a really good look. Your left chest and abdo wall are just one big hematoma, with kind of amazing bruising of your peritoneum, but I think we're okay. We're going to keep an eye on you for a day or two—you know how easy it can be to miss an intra-parenchymal splenic lac. And we don't want you bleeding out into your abdomen the minute we boot you out of here, eh?"

He was cheery, dark, with a ruff of jet black hair poking out of his shirt collar.

"We'll see how you are tomorrow evening, and if your spleen looks okay on the CT Friday morning, out you go. That chest tube can probably come out tonight after a follow-up X-ray. Good enough?"

Jenner nodded. "Thanks."

The surgeon wagged a finger at him.

"Now, when we kick you out, you take it easy. We don't want you doing yoga, or going to the gym, or any other physical exertion. Two weeks of rest, in bed or sitting, until we know you're out of the woods, eh? I've been caught by surprise by a delayed splenic rupture two weeks after the injury—don't let that be you, okay, deal?"

Jenner nodded again. "Thanks, Dr. Kahn."

Kahn turned to the second-year resident and said, "Where's the guy with the liver? How's his 'crit doing?" and they left.

A nurse's aide plugged in Jenner's phone and searched the bag holding his things for his address book.

He was about to give up after the sixth ring, when Sheehan answered. "Ancient Languages, Father Patrick Sheehan speaking."

"Edward Jenner, Father."

There was a brief silence, then the priest said warmly, "Oh, Dr. Jenner! It's good to hear your voice! I've been so saddened by everything that's happened. Truly awful. Detective Roggetti was a man of . . . tremendous character. A colorful figure indeed, with a good heart. And Detective Garcia? How is he doing?"

"They say he should be okay."

"That's just grand. Grand."

They were quiet for a second, and Jenner felt the yawning distance between his room in Bellevue and Sheehan's in Yardley, two hundred miles of wet highway and snow-covered pasture between him and the book-filled study on the beautiful, wintry quadrangle.

"And yourself, Edward? How are you feeling?"

"Ah, a bit . . . beaten, really, Father. I'll be okay."

"Of course you will!"

"Father, there's something I need to know."

"Yes?"

"I need to know the first possible date where it's the saint's day for Anne, or Ana, or Anna, or anything like that."

The priest was silent for a moment. "I was hoping that you'd be able to put this aside for a while. Why not let the police look after things until you get better?"

"Please, Father. Is there anything you can see that sticks out?"

The priest sighed. "I looked last night, actually. There is. The feast day of Saint Anastasia."

"And when is that?"

"In our calendar, Anastasia's feast day falls on the twenty-fifth of this month. On Christmas Day, Jenner."

The man brought things for her, things she needed to stay locked in the little room. A blanket, a candle and matches, water and bread, an empty pail, some newspaper. When the door opened, she was barely able to see into the gloom of the room beyond, his silhouette a harder shadow against softer ones.

He said, his voice calm and matter-of-fact as a secretary running through her to-do list, "I'm going to handcuff you. Don't be a stupid little bitch. If you try to kick me, I'll break an arm. If you try to bite, scratch, or hit, I'll break both your arms. If anything you try draws blood, I will cut off your right hand with an ax.

"Understand that I find you intriguing, but you have little actual value to me. You are little more than an afterthought. If at any point I suspect that you're planning something—to escape, to send some kind of message, to injure me, anything—I will kill you immediately. Got it?"

Fighting the desire to scream, she whispered, "Yes."

He moved quickly about her—he obviously knew the room well, and was used to working in the low light. When he moved near, she could smell him, a curtain of mold drawn over a wall of fetid sweat.

She made herself not flinch, holding still while he put on the handcuffs and let her slowly down onto the ground.

He said, "I'm going to cuff your ankle first, then your wrists. So you can put your hands in front for me to recuff them."

She nodded.

"I can't hear a nod."

"Yes. Sir."

"Good."

She drew a sharp breath at the cold metal against her ankle, then he clipped the handcuff on, squeezing it tight until it was crushing her skin.

"Please, this hurts a lot."

"It'll stop you from running. As soon as I've done your hands, it can come off."

"Please, hurry. Sir."

He was fast. And very strong—he rolled her over as if he were flicking a pencil across a desktop. He gripped her numb hands, and she felt the cuffs encircle her wrists. Then he popped the cuff off her ankle. The blood flooded back into her foot; she wept from the rush of pain.

"Your hands are cold; you may have frostbite. I want to see them in the light."

He held her wrist loosely.

"I'm going to light a candle. Close your eyes. If you open them, I'll stick my thumbnails through your eyeballs."

She closed her eyes tightly. She remembered the photos of the girl from Pennsylvania, and knew he would do everything he said he'd do.

There was the crisp snap and sharp, sulfurous smell of a match strike, and behind her eyelids the world glowed golden brown.

She felt her hands being moved as if from a thousand miles away.

"They're a bit blue, but it's not frostbite yet. When I leave, you should rub your fingers if you want to keep them."

She began to sweat, her heart pounding in her chest, thudding freakishly heavily against her breastbone.

"There's food, water, and a candle. If you need to go to the bathroom, there's a bucket, and newspaper for wiping. It'll be a little tricky at first, but you'll get the hang of it.

"You may open your eyes when you hear the door bolted."

He was gone.

In the candlelight, she saw that she'd visualized the room fairly accurately, except it was smaller than she'd imagined. The recognition flared in her as a small ray of hope.

The brick was dirty, slippery with damp and mold, and years of leaks had left puddles all over the floor; in some areas the floorboards were clearly rotten.

She rolled to her right. There was the door. There was very little light beyond it; he seemed to live in the dark. Or maybe there was no electricity: that would explain the candles.

What was the time? She felt her right wrist; she was still wearing her watch. She should save the candle. She puffed and blew it out.

She moved the matchbook nearer, pushing it against the cup that held the candle. Then she lifted her cuffed wrists to her face and pressed the illumination button on her watch; the dim orange glow was a warm sphere of light in the cold shadows.

Eight p.m.

The room went dark again.

In the pitch-black, the cold rushed at her. Her sweat dried quickly, and now she felt her skin prickling, the hairs rising up along her arms.

She rolled onto her back and lay still, looking up into the dark. As she lay there, she felt pressure against her butt. She tilted her hips, felt it again. There was something in her left back pocket.

She rocked back and forth, feeling its shape.

It was the French knife Jenner had given her, with the small blade and corkscrew. She'd become so used to carrying it that she'd forgotten it was even in her pocket.

She reached around to see if she could dig into her pockets with her hands, but she couldn't twist far enough, even when she turned her jeans to the right in front to bring the pocket closer. She tucked her knees to her chest, lay on her right side, and wiggled, trying to shake it loose. It was deep in the pocket and wouldn't come out.

She felt around with her hands. The floorboards in this area were soft and uneven, with a hole a little less than a foot long; if she could slide the side of her hip against the lip of the hole, she might be able to get some leverage on the knife, force it up and out of the mouth of the pocket.

It was worth a try.

She wriggled into position, lying on her left over the hole. Pressing her hip into the hole, she dragged herself into a ball position, scraping the pants against the rim as she bent. She could feel the knife, immobile under the fabric, slipping past the rim.

She tried again, and this time felt it budge.

Again, and the knife began to loosen in her pocket.

And again and again, the knife now clearly moving.

She kept wriggling, heart beating faster, panting from the effort. One more push ought to do it.

She pressed down firmly, then curled up and, as she did so, felt the knife slip smoothly upward in the pocket. She felt it reach the pocket opening, but instead of sliding out onto the floor, the knife tipped backward and fell through the hole, into the bottomless darkness beneath.

She rolled onto her back, breathless and in tears. The muscles of her back were locking down, going into agonizing spasm.

The door flew open, and the man came in quickly.

"What are you up to?"

She didn't say anything.

In the dark, he walked toward her and kicked her, a glancing blow to her hip.

"I said, What are you up to?"

Tears welling, she said, "Nothing, sir."

"Shut your eyes, I'm turning on a flashlight. Same rules—you peek, my thumbnails will be the last things you ever see."

She closed her eyes, and felt the flashlight beam playing on her face. She was flat on her back, the hole between her shoulder blades.

She felt his hands on her pants, and tensed. He patted down the front pockets, then turned them out, first the right, then the left. Then pulled her hip up and patted the empty rear pockets. His hand then swept down her back on each side, pausing to rub the catch on her bra strap. There was nothing to find.

He rolled her back down.

"I'm watching you all the time. If you do anything, I'll know it. If you give me a reason to kill you, I'll do it."

He left her lying there, crying, as he slid the bolt into place.

The chest X-ray was fine, his lung fully expanded. They removed the chest tube, sutured the tube site closed, and put on a fresh dressing.

In the early afternoon, a police artist came to his room, and they worked up a composite sketch. There was no point in Jenner looking at the mug books—if his fingerprints weren't on file, there would be no mug shots.

Later, they let him take a wheelchair to his repeat CT scan. He lay there, breathing and not breathing as instructed, for about twenty minutes. On the way back, the nurse's aide who'd accompanied him asked if she could stop at the bank in the lobby; he told her he was fine, and that he'd make his own way to the ward.

As soon as she was out of sight, he wheeled to the express elevator and rode up to the tenth floor. The SICU was an array of individual bays surrounding a central monitoring station, each bed easily curtained off from its neighbors. The patients all seemed inert, unresponsive, as nurses and therapists revolved busily around them, their worlds limited by the blue draperies, computer monitors, and equipment stands.

It was only because of the cluster of uniformed cops gathered around his bay that Jenner was able to recognize Garcia. His face was grotesquely bloated and pale, his lips swollen, his puffy eyelids taped shut. Fine tubes ran from the mesh of sutured wounds and surgical incisions on the side of his neck out into pear-shaped drain reservoirs half filled with bloody fluid. A pale corrugated hose led from the center of Rad's neck to a bedside ventilator, his chest rising and falling to the machine's rhythm.

When he wheeled closer to the bed, one of the cops, a younger white man with brush-cut hair, his badge number hidden under a black mourning band, stood in his way.

Jenner said, "He's my friend."

The cop nodded. "We know who you are."

Behind him, Jenner recognized Jimmy Haley, who he'd worked with after 9/11, before he made sergeant.

"Jimmy, please."

Haley looked down at Jenner, shaking his head. "God, Doc. You look like shit."

The other uniformed officers looked at Haley. He thought for a second, then said, "Fuck it," and told them to stand down.

With the cops looking on, Jenner wheeled his chair to the bedside, stopping next to the ventilator. He sat there watching his friend sleep.

It was quiet for a while, but eventually the cops started talking again. Cars, mostly, and what the PBA was going to do about the overtime situation. Later, an anesthesiologist in blue and green scrubs stopped by to check the vent settings. He looked down at Jenner with interest.

"Were you the other one?"

The other one?"

"The other Inquisitor victim."

Jenner lowered his head.

"How are you doing?"

"Okay. How's Detective Garcia doing?"

"Much better than he looks. Not out of the woods yet, but he should be fine. You guys came to the right place—you get shot or stabbed in New York, Bellevue's the place to go. The vascular surgeons did a great job on his neck—we'll get rid of the trach soon."

"Thanks."

Jenner sat slumped by the bed for a while, watching Rad's chest rise and fall to the ventilator's cough and hiss, watching the green trace of his heartbeat march across the monitor, trying to persuade himself it wasn't his fault as he twisted and burned inside.

Behind him, there was the noise of creaking chairs as the cops stood, then quiet murmuring.

"Dr. Jenner."

He turned to see Dulcie Garcia, Rad's wife, standing with Izzy, her eldest son; he hadn't seen her since the party when she joined the DA's squad. In the blue-white glare of the X-ray box, her face was gray and unreadable. He'd never seen her in glasses before; her eyes, distant behind thick lenses, were puffy and red.

Her son was like a young Rad, the same easy burliness and gentle manner. Crossing himself, he slipped onto the chair next to the bed, leaned forward to grip one of his father's hands, then began to pray silently, his lips moving quickly as his forehead sunk to his dad's hand.

It was Jenner who broke the silence. "I'm so sorry, Dulcie. I just talked with the surgeons, and they say he's doing great, that everything should be fine. They're taking out the trach tube tomorrow."

She nodded, distracted. "They told me."

"How are you holding up?"

She was quiet for a while, watching her son plead with God for the life of his father. When she finally spoke, it was with sadness and reluctance.

"You know, I'm not one of those cop wives who spends every second of every day worrying about where her man is, and if he's okay. I know Rad doesn't take unnecessary risks. I know he's careful, he won't make a dangerous move without backup. When he started on the job, he promised me he'd always play by the rules, and I was okay with that; you play by the rules, you don't get hurt, because your buddies always got your back. And he kept his bargain, and he always played by the rules."

She was choosing her words carefully.

"But he's been working with you. He likes you, you know? Says you make him think different, that working with you makes him a better cop. And I like you, too, Jenner. I like you because you make my husband feel good, and I like you because you seem like a nice guy. And we were so sorry for you after all you went through."

He was touched. "You know I feel the same way about him."

She held up a hand to stop his interruption. "But, the fact is, you're not a cop. You're a nice guy, but you're not a cop. You don't think like us, you don't look like us, you don't work like us, and in the end, you can't do what we can do. And one of the things cops do is protect each other. We watch out for each other.

"And I know part of why Rad likes you so much is that you're not a cop, but it's also why I always worried about you. I knew you'd make him play by different rules, and I worried.

"So now he's played your way, and this is what's happened. Joey's dead, Rad's half dead. I'm not saying it's your fault . . . No, wait, I am saying that. That's just what I'm saying. I think Joey and Rad got into trouble because they were playing by your rules, running around, chasing your leads, no backup, no safety net. And that's why they got hurt."

He looked at the blanket on his lap. "None of us . . . I had no idea that something like this was going to happen."

"No, of course not, Jenner. You couldn't. You just follow the clues, wherever they go. And once you were . . . seeing that girl, you didn't look around, you didn't watch out, you just ran after the clues. You shouldn't have been involved, and you shouldn't have dragged Rad in, and you shouldn't have dragged Joey in."

She looked down at him.

"I need you to stay away from Rad. Let him get better. Don't make him think about this stuff. He needs some time, time to stay with his family, time to get well again. Please. You owe him that."

Jenner nodded, then turned his wheelchair and headed toward the elevator bank, behind him the rhythmic peeping of monitors and the whispered words of the boy's prayer.


Something inside her was slowly tearing. Twisting, clawing at her guts, trying to rip its way out. She lay there pulling herself into a ball, her cuffed hands awkwardly rubbing her belly for relief. She'd chewed the collar of her T-shirt until it was thick with spit, desperate not to cry out, terrified that he might come back in. She couldn't stop herself from retching, and had to use the bucket repeatedly.

Afterward, she lay there on the floor, crying and shivering. Wishing she had just a taste of heroin, wishing she were warm and high.

She couldn't lie to herself anymore: she was in withdrawal. How long had it been now? Two days without heroin? She squinted at her watch through puffy eyes. A day and a half, almost two. Her skin, hot and flushed hours ago, was now cold and clammy. There was no heat left in her body at all, her skin pale blue, her lips dark and dried. Already dead.

Jenner. What would he do? She screwed her eyes tight, imagined him lying in his TV room watching Japanese movies, that cat sleeping by his side. Maybe ordering dinner. Or having some of the Weetabix from Dean & Deluca.

No, wait. He was in the fucking hospital, maybe on life support. If he was alive at all. He'd been so weak on the loading dock. Maybe he was dead, or paralyzed.

She rubbed the goose bumps on her arms and tried to scrunch herself into a ball, but the heat just poured out of her; she imagined it as a spreading puddle draining out of her onto the floor.

Everyone was leaving her, one by one. First her parents, and now Jenner. Her uncle. The cops. And they'd just been trying to help her. Really, she should have just stayed and waited for him in the backyard, let him climb down the trellis and kill her after he'd finished butchering Andie. Then they would all have been fine. Jenner, Joey, Rad Garcia.

And what difference would it have made? She'd have lost two weeks, two lousy weeks in which she managed to hook up with Perry and start doing H again, this time kind of seriously. You go, girl!

The candle had rolled under her; touching it, she felt a sudden desire for light. She felt around her for the matches, but had the shivers so bad she couldn't strike the match.

She rolled back down to the floor and cried until the cramping started getting really bad. She needed to use the bucket, but she was afraid he'd come in, so she put it off, and put it off. Then she could wait no longer, and clumsily tore her jeans down with her cuffed hands to squat in the dark corner, crying from pain and humiliation and self-pity, crying because she didn't want to die, crying because no one would come to find her.

D r. Khan squinted at the grid of CT images on the viewing box. "You see here, Doctor?" he said to Jenner, tapping one of the scans with the tip of a gold-cased mechanical pencil. "Your spleen. See how it isn't all the same shade? It may be nothing, but there may be some bleeding in here. You got a good kick or two in the ribs, there, and that's a great location to pound on if you want a splenic injury."

Jenner nodded. "I've seen sudden death due to delayed splenic rupture a few times—guy sent home as okay after a fight, then slowly bleeds into the spleen until it finally ruptures and he quickly bleeds out. The CT is equivocal?"

Khan nodded. "It might be nothing. I just can't tell without doing serial scans, and even then there'd have to be some time between scans for me to be comfortable to make a reliable diagnosis."

"Are you keeping me in here?"

"Oh, I don't think that the management would go for that. You're a doctor—physician monitor thyself, eh? Go home, come back in three days or so for a follow-up. By then it should be pretty clear whether it's growing or not. How are you walking?"

"Slowly. My chest hurts a bit, so does my side. My stomach wound feels okay, though. The chest tube site itches a bit, but that's it."

"Par for the course. You feel ready to go home?"

"I've felt ready to go home since I first woke up in Bellevue."

"Good, good. That makes two of us! Ha ha. Come see me in outpatient clinic Monday afternoon; let's get a repeat CT first. The ward secretary will set it up."

They shook hands.

Khan turned to go, but stopped and turned back to Jenner, holding up an admonishing finger.

"I want to make this crystal clear: if you've got a slow bleed into your spleen, even slight pressure can make it worse, or even burst it. Strictly bed rest until you see me Monday, eh? And even if the Monday scan looks good, minimal activity for the next couple of weeks. Check your blood pressure every four hours or so; blood pressure goes down, pulse goes up, worsening pain in your abdomen or flank, call 911 and come in by ambulance. Got it?"

Jenner nodded.

Khan smiled again.

"Okay, Doctor. Liberty beckons . . ."

Jenner thanked him again, then dialed the Ninth Precinct one more time to see if there'd been any news of Ana.

Jun brought him clothes; the ones he'd been wearing had been impounded by the crime lab. They walked slowly together through the corridors, went down in the elevator, and out into the cold air. It had snowed all night, and Jenner was surprised to see the scrappy hospital lawn blanketed in white.

At the curb, Kimi was waiting in Jun's Lexus, the inside lights on, the car glowing as if radioactive. He opened the passenger door, and "Baby One More Time" boomed out. Kimi yelped when she saw Jenner, then her face wrinkled and her eyes filled with tears as she looked at him. "Jenner! How do you feel?"

He smiled at her. "Good."

Dabbing her eyes, she turned to Jun and spoke in Japanese for a few seconds.

"She's going to ride in the back with you while I drive. We'll get you up now, then you can go onto the seat yourself. Go slow, eh?"

They helped him in, then Kimi climbed in next to him and gave him a careful hug. "Oh, so good to see you, Jenner!" she said, squeezing his hand and holding it in her lap. She wiped away her tears, then leaned forward to tell Jun to skip ahead to "Oops! I Did It Again!" and sang along, clutching Jenner's hand tight all the way home.

There were vases with flowers outside his front door, and cards leaning against a lit devotional candle. Behind them, the front door and inside frame were sooty with fingerprint powder. Inside, though, the apartment was spotless.

Crime Scene had been all over it. They'd taken the bathroom door, which had been torn off its runners: Ana had been able to make it to the bathroom, which was presumably where she'd called him from. Then the man had broken through—it was probably over in seconds.

"We called your housekeeper to come by and clean after the cops left. She didn't want to be paid, but I insisted."

"Thanks, Jun. I'll pay you back."

He nodded, then put the bag of Jenner's pain meds on the coffee table, along with the crime lab receipt for Jenner's vouchered clothes.

Jenner eased himself into the big chair. Jun set a glass of water on the coffee table nearby, then stood awkwardly.

"You want Kimi and me to hang out with you? Or maybe come over to my place—we're going to get sandwiches from Balthazar and watch *Alien Resurrection*."

Jenner smiled. "Thanks, Jun. I just want to chill here."

"Sure, Jenner. I understand." He turned. "Call if you need anything." He closed the door softly behind him.

Jenner listened for the sound of Jun's front door closing, then pulled himself to his feet. He walked stiffly to his desk and went through the stacks of books until he found Alban Butler's *Lives of the Saints*. He opened to the Anastasia entry, and read; he needed to know what would happen to her if he didn't find her before the twenty-fifth.

National said they wouldn't have a car for him until 11:00 a.m.

SATURDAY,
# DECEMBER 21

He woke at 6:00 a.m., and soaked in the bath in the dark, Brian Eno's *Music for Airports* playing softly. He felt the muscles in his left side loosen in the hot water, but they knotted up again when he stood to get out of the bath, a harsh stabbing pain radiating along his flank.

He sat at the table and inflated the cuff around his arm, his eyes on the dial as he deflated it. He pressed his fingers to his right wrist and counted for fifteen seconds. His blood pressure and pulse were okay.

He looked at his chest in the mirror. He'd taken off the dressing before getting into the bath; now his torso looked like sunset fighting a storm, pale pink and red stripes over his ribs livid against the glowering purple bruise that was his left side.

It hurt more when he looked at it, so he quickly dressed the chest tube site and shrugged his shirt on. He buttoned it gingerly, looked at himself in the mirror, and said out loud, "Good as new!"

It didn't work. He took a Tylenol Number 3, brushed his teeth, then finished dressing. He had some cereal, then packed an overnight bag.

He sat in the armchair to rest, and watched TV. Outside a church in Queens, several hundred cops in dress blues were getting into formation, lining up along the procession route. They were several deep along the path to the front door, where the body would be carried. There was a large civilian turnout; he tried to spot anyone who might be one of Joey's relatives, but it began to drizzle, and he couldn't see faces after the umbrellas came out; they were probably inside. He turned off the TV when the mayor arrived, a little before 10:00 a.m.

He couldn't do anything for Joey, other than nail the man who'd killed him. But maybe he could still do something for Ana. He couldn't let himself slow down now, couldn't stop to wallow. No more thinking about victims, no more thinking about loss, no more thinking about the days ticking away, counting down to the twenty-fifth, the feast of Saint Anastasia.

He e-mailed Jun to say that he was going out of town for a couple days, and not to worry, that he'd be careful. He tried to say thanks, but the more he tried to express, the slower he got, so he deleted it all and wrote, "Thanks. For everything."

Then, just for the hell of it, he called the Ninth Precinct. He left a message on Pat Mullins's voice mail that he was going to Pennsylvania to see if he could get any more information about the text, and could Pat call him if they found anything. He read the number of his new cell phone, squinting as he struggled to decode Ana's scrawl.

He carefully pulled his coat on, checked to make sure he'd packed his painkillers, and went down to find a cab.

It was a long shot, he knew, but it was the only lead he had. The police had already made inquiries, and reached a dead end. But, at the time the detectives had called around, the theft of an old manuscript from a college in the middle of nowhere had hardly seemed critical; no one had gone out to the location to ask in person.

Interstate 78 was a long crawl from the Delaware River Bridge until well after the Hamburg exit. Traffic finally eased when he got onto the westbound I-76, but the sky was dark before he reached Deene's College.

The school was on the border of Somerset County, pretty as a picture, with hills and valleys blanketed with handsome old-growth forests. The local joke was that it was a beautiful place to be dirt poor; the cool climate made for miserly farmlands where backbreaking work produced heartbreaking yields.

At the front gates, a worn white billboard with uneven black lettering announced "DEENE'S COLLEGE, founded 1978, Achievement Through Excellence," lack of ambition passed off as lack of pretense.

Behind the sign was a small tan-brick building that did double duty as security post and information center. He couldn't see anyone inside, but the lights were on, so he tapped on the window; he was answered by the sound of a flushing toilet. A beefy young man with a pink face emerged. He wore gray pants and a white shirt labeled "Wharton-Somerset Private Security," and was hurriedly wiping his hands with ragged paper towels.

"You caught me off guard."

"Sorry to bother you."

He eyed Jenner up and down.

"The school is closed until January seventh."

"I'm looking for the Security Service," Jenner said, flashing his shield, wondering if he was breaking the law.

The man looked at the brass badge and murmured, "New York City . . ." He straightened up, suddenly helpful. "Well, you got me tonight. How can I help you?"

"About fifteen years ago, you had a theft from the collection of ancient manuscripts. A fairly valuable document was stolen. You ever heard of that?"

"Can't say that I have—fifteen years is a while ago. Mostly we just deal with drunken freshmen vandalizing Mr. Deene's statue during rush week, the occasional mopey girl who takes a few too many pills, stuff like that."

Jenner pointed toward the green computer screen in the room.

"Would it be on there?"

The man laid his palm softly on the monitor. "Nope. This only goes back about five years, six tops. Wouldn't be in it."

"Okay. How about security officers? Anyone been working here long enough that they might remember it?"

The guard put his hand to his chin, his expression clouded with doubt.

"Naah . . . fifteen years is a long time to stay at Deene's . . ."

"No one at all?"

The man shook his head.

"How about your boss?"

He brightened.

"No! But he got the job after his brother retired, and his brother lives real close."

He thought the guard was reaching for a pen to write down the man's phone number, but the man surprised Jenner by grabbing his jacket and coming out of the booth.

"C'mon. I'll take you to him," he said, jiggling the door handle to make sure the booth was locked.

Jenner thanked him, and unlocked the passenger side of his car.

The guard thrust out his hand and said, "Tommy Anderson."

They shook hands, then Anderson started glancing around the car, as if expecting to see a head, or body parts or something.

Jenner said, "Relax, it's a rental."

Anderson seemed a bit disappointed. He leaned toward the windshield and said, "Okay, in about a minute College Drive'll cross Oak, then Wireless Road. Go past Oak, then take a right on Wireless."

The college's buildings were low and nondescript. The dorms were mostly paired semi-detached town houses; in one area, there were three-story apartment-type complexes around a tiny swimming pool, the pool area surrounded by chain-link fence.

Anderson tapped on the window and said, "Two years ago, at Halloween, we had a sexual perversion incident right behind the gazebo over there."

He sat back in the seat. "Guy completely ass-naked except for a face mask and flippers—you know? For scuba diving? He jumps out from behind the gazebo and exposes himself to some Chinese exchange students. *Girl* students."

They crested a ridge and drove downhill, into a valley; the road ahead, the trees ahead, dissolved into thick fog. Jenner slowed, and turned off his high beams.

They crept forward slowly, the lights carving tunnels into the shifting mist ahead. Anderson put one leg up onto the dashboard and glanced at Jenner.

"You should wear your seat belt—you have to be careful on these roads."

"I do usually. I had an accident; it hurts to wear the belt."

Anderson nodded slowly and looked ahead. He started tapping the dashboard rhythmically.

"I bet you see a lot of weird shit."

Jenner shrugged, keeping his eyes on the road.

"What's the most messed-up thing you've ever seen?"

Jenner looked at him briefly. "A David Hasselhoff music video—apparently he's huge in Germany."

Anderson snorted. "No! I meant at your work! I once saw this movie where . . . ," and he launched into an impenetrable description of a slasher film.

As they neared the bottom of the hill, the fog became paler and paler. They reached a bend at the bottom of the hill, and they were bathed in light; it was like floating inside a big white cloud.

Jenner squinted as Anderson pointed in front of them.

"That's Bill Johnson's house. That's where we're going."


Bill Johnson lived in an old Airstream trailer at a sharp bend in Wireless Road at the bottom of the valley of Deene's Holler. After the second time his trailer was hit by a car, he petitioned the county for road signs. They'd put up a STEEP INCLINE sign, and a zigzag sign, and Johnson paid for a CHILDREN PLAYING sign out of his own pocket.

After the third time his home got hit, Johnson bought spotlights from the same company that set up the college sports field. Now the glare from thousands of watts of bright light irradiating the chrome-bright Airstream trailer was dazzling; had Johnson come out to see who his visitors were, Jenner might have mowed him down without even seeing him.

Jenner parked the Taurus at the foot of the lighting rig and got out, stiffly. He blinked a little, holding his palm like a visor to shield his eyes. Anderson stood there, a little smug in aviator sunglasses.

"Yo, Bill!"

There was no answer.

Tommy walked to the open door of the trailer and rapped his knuckles on the inner screen-door frame.

"Bill!"

Behind the screen, the door opened. A man in a ratty plaid bathrobe stood there, leaning on a walker.

"Heard you the first time."

"Sorry." He gestured to Jenner. "This man is an ME from New York City, working on a murder. He wants to know about a valuable book stolen from the college a few years back. Fifteen, was it, sir?"

"Yes, about fifteen. An old manuscript."

Johnson reached his arm behind the door frame, and the brightness eased. He pushed the screen door half open, then turned and painfully began to push his walker into the dark of the trailer, muttering, "Come in," as he disappeared.

It was Jenner's first time in a trailer; it seemed neither smaller nor larger than it had appeared on the outside. The air was heavy with cigarettes, the curtains yellowed from years of smoke.

"Sorry about the light. Idiots take that turn way too fast, and when the fog gets bad, I turn the lights up all the way. Probably take you five minutes to roast a turkey up there on that main light trestle."

Johnson eased himself into a lounge chair. Jenner saw that he was wearing a nasal cannula, attached by a thin tube of green plastic to a cylinder of oxygen behind the chair.

"So, Bill, this is Mr. Jenner, and—"

"*Dr.* Jenner. He's an ME—that means he's a medical examiner, and that means he's a doctor."

He turned to Jenner. "I think I know what you're talking about. Maybe fourteen or fifteen years, someone stole an Egyptian document from the Parler Collection. That it?"

"Yes, that's it."

Johnson leaned back in his chair and began to struggle with the cannula, tugging it awkwardly to get it past his big ears.

"Damn thing keeps getting caught."

He leaned forward, picked up a Marlboro 100 from a box on the coffee table, flicked open a gray metal Zippo with a sharp snap of his wrist, fired up the cigarette, then leaned back again, inhaling with obvious satisfaction.

His lips were the color of liver, his face bluish. He coughed a little, then put the cigarette down and reached for the cannula. Holding the nasal prongs to his lips, he turned the tap on the canister and sucked down a blast of oxygen.

He looked at the two of them as they watched him.

"Bastards should make a mask that gives you oxygen while you smoke, fer chrissakes."

Tommy Anderson nodded in vague agreement.

"Doc, what you think? Think I should quit?"

Jenner shrugged.

"That's what I say! I been smoking since I was twelve, I worked in the mines until I was thirty, of course I'm gonna have emphysema! Had it when I was forty! And I've almost made it to seventy, so screw all those sanctimonious bastards who told me I had to quit."

He took another hit of the cigarette, breathed out, then had a coughing fit, the phlegm rattling coarsely in his chest. He was breathless in seconds. He sat there, breathing in short gulps against pursed lips, his eyes watering with effort.

He caught his breath for a few seconds, then began to speak.

"So, Doctor, sure, I remember that. Not much else happened at the campus in my time there. We knew who did it, too, but they never could arrest him. No proof, no witnesses, no statements, no nothing."

Jenner sat up a little straighter.

"You knew who did it?"

"Sure. God, I can't remember the name, but it was a student. Funny kid, some poor orphan kid. Weird kid. I can't remember how we knew it was him, but we were pretty sure about it. We interviewed him, even called in the state police. But the kid said it wasn't him, and we had nothing on him, and we had to let him go. What the hell was his name?"

Jenner said, "Do you have any notes or records from back then?"

"Sure! It should all be on the computer in the security office."

Anderson said, "No, sir! Computer only goes back, maybe, six years!"

Deep into an inhale, Johnson rolled his eyes. He breathed the smoke out smoothly.

"You ever wonder what that folder labeled 'Archives' was for, Tommy? You should click it sometime . . ."

He pushed forward and grasped the walker. He gasped and puffed as he pulled himself to standing.

Jenner stood, ready to help.

"No, Doc, I got it, thanks. I can do this . . ."

He shuffled over to a desk, empty except for a bulky old laptop. There was a silver metal decal on the top: PROPERTY OF DEENE COLLEGE.

The man opened up the screen, then sat down, panting.

"Sir, if you would be so kind as to pass me my gas . . ."

Jenner wheeled the cylinder to the desk and helped Johnson arrange the cannula around his head. Johnson settled the prongs inside his nostrils, then nodded, and Jenner turned the knob to start the flow of oxygen.

His stubby fingers were surprisingly fast on the keyboard. Jenner recognized an old-fashioned text-based telecom program in the active window. A speaker turned on with a tinny click, and then there was the very loud sound of a touch-tone phone being dialed. There were a few seconds of shrill electronic honking, and then the connection was established.

The screen displayed an ASCII mosaic banner reading "DEENE/ADMIN/ DATABASE."

Johnson tapped in his password.

"Now, let's see . . . I remember the year and the month—half the student body was still drunk because we beat the Halsford team for the first time ever that weekend."

He tabbed through a few screens, then stopped.

"Okay. The week before. Nothing much during the week . . ."

He tabbed onto another screen, this one promisingly full of text.

"Okay, here's the game. Lots of drinking, a little vandalism, and we found out about the theft on Monday morning, I think . . ."

He tabbed to the next screen. The ledger was blank.

"Huh . . ."

He tabbed forward again, followed the ledger down on the screen with a finger, then checked the date and started tabbing back through previous dates.

Then forward again.

He shuttled back and forth for a few minutes before turning to Jenner, drawing a long draft of oxygen before saying, "So, someone's deleted the ledger for the week of the incident."

He smiled weakly up at Jenner.

"Sorry, Doc. Looks like someone's beat you to it."

Jenner said, "Is there a hard copy of the ledger?"

"Nope. I don't think the administration even knows they have this much."

"Can I look on the original computer?"

"Don't see why not. You some kind of computer whiz?"

"No. But this is my only lead."

Johnson lifted his arm weakly.

"So, Doc—you going to tell us what's this all about, anyway?"

Jenner glanced at the TV set in the corner. "You been following the Inquisitor case in New York at all?"

"The guy killing those students? Sure—you think it's connected?"

"Yes. It looks that way." Jenner looked Johnson in the eye and said, "He's abducted a student; unless we get to him first, he's going to kill her on Wednesday."

Johnson had caught his breath again. His face was set, serious now. He pursed his lips for a few seconds, then exhaled in a weak, breathy whistle.

"Well, I'll tell you what you're gonna do. You're going to help me over to my chair, then you're going to drive a few miles down to Accident, Maryland; there's an okay motel about eight miles out of Accident. Tonight, I'll make some calls, and if there's a way to get the information, we'll figure it out." He breathed in deeply through his nose. "I can't promise anything, but God, we'll do our best."

*   *   *

The man listened, ear pressed against the door. She was finally quiet.

She wasn't what he'd expected, not by a long shot, not at all what he'd thought she'd be like after seeing her from the window.

He stroked his thigh, the muscles cramped and aching.

Unreliability was a big issue for him. When he selected a target, he stuck to it. You had to *commit* to a target, always. His algorithm was specific: select, locate, track, survey, prepare, isolate, access, execute, document, exit.

The man knew how to commit.

When he'd finally seen her in the flesh in that courtyard on Seventh, gasping and trying to stand after falling off the trellis, like a pretty little kitten stunned from its first big fall, he'd found her terribly appealing.

He knew now that a lot of that had been the situation. She'd seen him at his peak, ecstatic, exhilarated, wrapped in a crusting carapace of her friend's blood. She'd seen him as no other soul still living had, seen his true self revealed. And, naturally, it had made him imagine certain . . . possibilities. Now he felt a little foolish.

In taking her, he'd also wanted to show them what he could do, show the world his strength, his courage, his resolve. The newspapers were turning him into a cartoon—that name "the Inquisitor" was a joke! What if it stuck? What did "Inquisitor" even *mean*?

Well, they knew about his power now. He'd read an interview where the head of the Patrolmen's Benevolent Association said that the dead cop "fought like a lion"; he'd laughed out loud at that. The man just lay there and gasped like a pig while he got stabbed! It had taken, what— twelve, thirteen seconds to kill him? He was a big guy, he went down hard, he bled quick, and he died fast. End of story. Some lion!

It had been *easy* for him to take her. And that was why he took her. And he took her because he found her intriguing. And he took her because he wanted Jenner to suffer.

Jenner! No matter how much a mess the girl was, she was too much woman for Jenner. The man clearly didn't know what to do with her. And he might be a doctor, and he might have book smarts, but Jesus! The man couldn't take a punch!

He thought of Jenner lying there helplessly, wriggling a little in his friend's blood, staying down when told to stay down, just like a dog. Like a pussy.

He sat there, grinning now, in the dark outside the girl's room.

But she didn't behave like he thought she would. She'd been docile and obedient, but not terrified of him, of what he could—probably would—do. He'd hoped that that situation might have emerged—what was it, Copenhagen syndrome?— where she developed a fondness for her captor. He felt himself blush.

She wasn't like that. She played it safe, did just as she was told, didn't resist his anger. And then, once he had her in the room, and everything had calmed down and the situation was established and it was time to get to know her, she had been sick. Retching and puking, sweating and moaning.

At first he thought it was because she knew he was going to kill her, but it got worse, and he realized it wasn't fear at all. It was drugs. She was coming down from drugs. Heroin, he was pretty sure.

He had no respect for people who did drugs. If you cannot master your urges, if you cannot respect the temple of the body, you forfeit your humanity, you become the beast that has somehow wandered into the cathedral.

That boy he killed had been that way. Peddling his ass to buy drugs, trying to drag the man down with him, trying to make him wade in that stinking pit of degradation that was his faggot life. He'd killed the boy out of anger—no, *outrage*. Outrage that the boy could even have *dreamed* that someone like him would do the things he was proposing.

It had been an act of kindness, releasing the boy from the moral and physical squalor that was his earthly life. And now again, this girl, again the drugs.

He pressed his ear to the door again, and heard nothing. The crying had stopped, the moaning was over. He imagined her lying there in the blanket, her breathing slow and even, her body calm, her mind at peace.

She was quiet now because the drugs were out of her body. The process had been hard on him, but it was finished now. She was herself again. But what self was that? At what level did she understand what he was doing?

He knew a way to find out.

When he opened the wooden box of mementos he kept under his desk, he was impressed by how full it was. On top was some sentimental stuff he'd been looking at the day before—a certificate for good drawing he got in the fifth grade, and a couple of photographs of the set he'd designed for the drama club production of *Our Town* when he was at Deene's. Underneath that layer, the old papyrus sheets had crumbled so badly that they now lay like a low stack of leathery yellow cards in the vellum he folded around it. He put the parchment to one side to remove his trove of Polaroids, as many as fourteen or fifteen from each Saint.

He spread them on the table, as if playing solitaire. He loved the photos, loved being able to fold the entire little scene into his palm—setup, execution, final image. It was like being dealt a good hand in poker.

He chose four or five of the most spectacular—pictures where the participants' reactions were really clear, final photos of each tableau so you could really see what was going on. He swept them up into a little deck, then looked for something to hang them with. He didn't have any thumbtacks; nails would have to do. Besides, nails were symbolic.

He lit a hurricane lamp and walked back down the corridor to her door. He slid the bolts one by one, then stepped inside. She was lying where she always lay.

He didn't care if she could see now. She was weak—she'd been ill for a day and a half, and hadn't eaten much since, and had thrown up what she'd tried to eat. He looked at the loaf; black and gray mold spread across the corner where she had nibbled it—if it was, indeed, her eating it and not the rats. She was weak, and no threat.

If she joined him, she joined him, and if she didn't, she would die, so either way, it wasn't an issue.

She didn't move. In the shaky yellow light, he could tell she was awake, but she stayed turned away from him.

Good enough.

He put the lamp down on the floor. He held nails between his lips as he worked, the Polaroids in his hip pocket. He kept half an eye on her: as he began to hammer the first into the door, she stiffened, but did not turn.

It didn't take long—a few taps were enough to drive a nail through each photo into the wood. Nailing them, of course, interrupted some of the Coptic he'd copied in waterproof marker, but the dense writing filling the white borders of each Polaroid made a handsome frame, and almost looked better with the nail.

When he finished, he stood back and looked at the door.

It was an impressive sight, by any reckoning. Twenty Polaroids, each with its filigreed mantle of Coptic text, nailed to the black door in neat columns.

He looked down at her, and nudged the lamp a little nearer to the door. He decided to leave. He'd come back for the lamp later, after she'd had a chance to look at it by herself. She was shivering now, and he knew it wasn't the drugs anymore.

By the time he reached his workshop, she'd begun to wail, hysterical shrieks that ended as choked sobs.

No. She was not at all what he'd thought.

They smoke at breakfast at the Gap Weekender Motel, just outside of Accident, Maryland. They smoke in the bedrooms, they smoke in the bathrooms, they smoke in the concrete breezeway in front of the long blocky slabs of sagging plasterboard and concrete that constitute each wing, and they were smoking in the motel's diner.

Jenner was the only person not smoking. The two men at the other end of the counter were using the fatter one's plate as an ashtray, now a small heap of mangled butts and gray ash smearing through the yellow streaks of clotting yolk.

From their conversations, most of the men in the room were there to apply for work at a new federal prison just over the state line in Hazelton, West Virginia. The prospects, at least the ones at breakfast, were burly and heavily tattooed.

He ordered more toast, and watched the waitress scoop out a glob of concentrate for his second glass of orange juice. He was moving slowly: the muscles in his chest were still cramping, but he felt a bit better than the day before.

What was Ana doing now? Was he feeding her? Probably—he'd want her in shape for her ordeal on the twenty-fifth. The day before, thinking over the crime scenes in a travel-plaza Arby's near Paxtonia, Jenner had realized that, beneath the injuries, all of the victims had seemed pristine, almost polished. It was clear that the defilement of something beautiful and pure made the act somehow more *worthy* to him, a richer sacrifice. He'd take good care of Ana.

Johnson had called at 8:00 a.m. to say that Jenner should be at the counter at nine. It was now nine thirty, and still no sign of him.

He peeled the foil cover off a butter packet and spread some on his toast.

The phone rang, and a second later the waitress called him over.

Everyone watched him walk around the counter to the phone. He turned toward the milk dispenser to talk. Bill Johnson's voice, slightly hoarse; the quiet hiss of the oxygen made him sound a thousand miles away.

"Mornin', Doc. You checked out yet?"

"I was waiting for your call."

"Okay, well, Deene's College's Finest is about to deliver: I got you a name, I got you a location, and I even went so far as to get you an interested contact in local law enforcement."

"That's great. Where is it? Nearby?"

Jenner could hear the tinny scrape of the tubing against the receiver as Johnson sucked in his breath.

"Nope, Doc. Maybe sixty, seventy miles north of here. In some town I never heard of named Snowden. The sheriff will meet you in some other town I never heard of named Houtzdale."

"Why is the sheriff interested?"

"Search me. My brother said we should call the county sheriff, give them a heads-up that you'd be coming. About ten minutes ago I got a call back saying they'd be glad to help you, and to meet the sheriff at the junction of Route 53 and McAteer Street in Houtzdale; they'll be expecting you about noon."

He paused, breathing heavily.

"He said to take 219 up—you can pick it up in Somerset. He'll take you on into Snowden, I guess."

The cannula tubing raked across the mouthpiece again. He was speaking slowly now, the words spilling out in the gasps between sharp breaths.

"Okay, Doc. It isn't even ten a.m., and I've already had enough excitement to last me a year. Good luck with them in Snowden."

Jenner could hear that he was about to hang up, and quickly said, "Wait! Mr. Johnson, you said you knew a name?"

"Oh, sure, sorry, Doc. My brother remembered this morning."

He was gasping again.

"The guy you're looking for, name of Farrar, Doc. Robert Farrar of Snowden, PA."

* * *

The orange light of her watch face flared up in front of Ana's eyes.

A little before noon, Sunday, December 22, it said.

The orange died out, the watch face glowing dimly for a couple of seconds before drowning in the dark.

It would be light outside. Sunny, maybe, one of those brilliant, cold December days where the buildings seem hard-edged and sharp in the sky.

Or maybe it was gray, maybe rainy. Drizzling. Pouring. Pouring rain, people scurrying along under umbrellas, waiting under awnings for the storm to ease up. But there would be light.

Three shopping days left until Christmas. Xmas. Three days till Xmas. People running around to parties, last-minute Xmas shopping. Where did the poor go at Xmas? Uptown, she guessed. The outer boroughs. Presents from the Salvation Army or something? Something like that.

But at least they could walk outside, be outside in the light. They could walk into Grand Central, see the light streaming through those big windows into the vast concourse.

How long had she been here? She couldn't remember. Was it already a week? She didn't know.

She was losing it. She'd been lying in the dark, starving slowly, her body slowly shutting down. She still had a good bit of the candle left, but she wasn't using it because of what he'd put on the door.

And now she was clean. She was herself again, sober. No drugs, nothing but pure sensation and emotion.

Even in the dark, she knew what was up there on the door, looking down on her. She'd seen them all, crying and terrified, pleading into the camera as he clicked the button. Seen Andie. Seen them before he did what he did, and seen them afterward, butchered and posed, still looking at the camera. The last one was barely even recognizable as a face, just a bloody mask with empty eye sockets and weird symbols burned into her skin.

She couldn't look at them, and she was afraid to touch them because of what he might do to her if she did. So she stayed in the dark. She could cover them with the blanket, and have some light for a while, but it was too cold. Not moving, not walking, just lying there, she could feel herself slowly freezing, every muscle stiff and weak, every joint aching.

She didn't care now if she lived or died. He was only keeping her to kill her. When she'd been sick, he brought her water, once even a battered tin pot filled with water so that she could wash herself. Now he was treating her differently; he'd been expecting something from her, she could tell, but he wasn't anymore. Had she screwed up an opportunity to save herself? If she'd acted differently, would she be all right now? What had he wanted?

It wasn't sex—he could have taken that at any time. He knew it, and she had accepted it.

So what *did* he want? What else was there?

She thought of Jenner. A week ago, a year ago, a lifetime ago. She didn't think he was dead. She hoped not. He had been nice to her. The cops were dead. Rad. Funny Joey Roggetti. Dead because of her.

Soon she'd be dead, too.

Fuck it. Maybe it would be quick.

Jenner's car crept past the stretch of low clapboard and brick buildings that made up downtown Houtzdale. At the intersection of 53 and Mc-Ateer, he saw the Houtzdale PD black-and-white, hazard lights flashing, behind a silver gray F-150; the officer was leaning against the pickup's side window, chatting with the driver.

Jenner pulled in behind the truck, and walked up to introduce himself.

The cop looked him up and down, then nodded his head toward the pickup and said, "These are the guys you want—I'm just saying hi."

He tapped the roof of the cabin and said, "Andy, Don. Take care," nodded at Jenner, then left.

The door swung open, and a young man climbed out.

He shook Jenner's hand and said, "Andy Slater, Doctor. Pleased to meet you."

Gesturing toward the cab, he said, "My dad, Don Slater. He used to be chief of police in Altoona; before that he ran the volunteer police department that covered most of the rural parts of Clearfield County."

Jenner bent a little, and saw a tall man, clean-cut and somber, sitting in the backseat, expressionless in aviator sunglasses.

"Doctor. Welcome to central Pennsylvania. You want to get in, we'll take you where you need to go."

Jenner said, "If it would be easier, I can just follow you in my car."

"No need. We're heading a bit off the beaten track, don't want you getting lost. Besides, your car will be safe here—anyone who got sprung from Houtzdale Correctional has already hopped the eleven a.m. bus and is long gone."

He was grinning slightly, his tan face barely lined.

"Besides, we have things to discuss." The grin faded.

Jenner climbed into the passenger seat and found himself awkwardly positioned in front of the older Slater. His side still ached, and turning was difficult.

They drove north through the town, over a bridge, across railroad tracks. Don Slater stayed quiet, his son filling up the silence with a running commentary.

"That's Beaver Run, the stream. First Commonwealth Bank up ahead there."

The buildings quickly fell away, leaving Andy Slater with little to say. The snow was heavier up here. They were in farmland again, boxy red barns floating on a sea of white, like Monopoly hotels spilled onto a big sheet of cotton wool.

He had started up again, "So, we're on the edges of the Allegheny Plateau—" when his father interrupted.

"So, Doctor. I understand you're making inquiries about Robert Farrar. That correct?"

"Yes, sir."

"And this is in reference to those New York City murders, the students?"

"Yes."

Don Slater took off his sunglasses. His eyes, blue-green and clear, were watering slightly.

"And he's, what—a suspect in the killings?"

"Possibly."

The older Slater nodded slowly and tucked the sunglasses into the breast pocket of his heavy jacket.

Jenner asked, "Can you tell me what he looks like?"

Slater shook his head. "I'm afraid not, Doc. I haven't seen him in more than twenty years. We'll see if we can find a photo of him for you."

He watched the fields go by for a while.

"Y'know, Doctor, in any given situation, there's not just a right way and a wrong way. There's a thousand different ways, each of them with different degrees of rightness or wrongness. And the rightness or wrongness of a particular choice sometimes isn't really clear. You try to make the best choice you can on the information you have available, and you hope it works out."

He ran a hand over his hair, smoothing it down.

"The thing is, even if most of the choices you make will work out, sooner or later you'll find out you made a wrong one."

Slater's manner—the unhurried speech, the calm, clear-eyed gaze—was reassuring. This, Jenner was sure, was a man who would help him catch his killer. He let some slack into his seat belt and turned gingerly toward him.

"To understand this better, you've got to understand a bit of the history. Where we're going now didn't used to be part of Clearfield County, it was its own little county, a hundred square miles of some of the worst farming land in the state, with three towns—Psalter Brook, Barretsburg, and Snowden—each with a population less than two hundred. When I was a kid, we used to make fun of those kids because they were dirt-poor. The *real* dirt-poor—forget crops, the soil on that land couldn't support weeds, even.

"But the families never left. Generation after generation just stayed on in the failed farms of the generation before. These families got increasingly isolated, kept to themselves, living the barest existence, not trusting anyone from the outside, not asking for help for anything.

"When I was a cop around here, we wouldn't hear a peep out of Barretsburg County, not a peep. And because there was only me and another guy, that was okay with us. From time to time you'd hear rumors about some guy smacking his old lady around, but if there was no formal complaint, there was no grounds for intervention, so we just let sleeping dogs lie. As they say, don't poke a skunk."

The land was hillier now, the snowy fields dotted with pocket forests of hickory and oak. Seeing Jenner looking toward the woods, Slater said, "There are forests all over this area, and some of them offer pretty good hunting. Which was how I first met Bobby Farrar."

He leaned back with a slight sigh and slipped his sunglasses back on, even though the afternoon light was now wan and gray. He sat silently for a minute, his face set in a slight scowl. Then he began.

"About twenty-five years back, a couple of hunters from Pittsburgh were hunting elk around here. Cold fall day, not having much luck. They're starting to talk about calling it a day, when all of a sudden, in the middle of the woods they came across a kid, maybe ten years old, half naked, kneeling in a clearing.

"They call to him, but he doesn't hear them. He suddenly pitches forward, and he's lying on the ground, pounding the dirt in front of him. As they get close, they can see he's covered in blood. In front of him there's a dead dog, a collie, I think it was. The kid has stabbed it to death—killed it and skinned it. And in front of the carcass there's this sort of altar, a pile of rocks and branches, and on top of it he's put candles and the bones and skulls of some dogs."

They had crested the top of the range of hills and now were going down again, into a valley. The sky had darkened, and Jenner saw the first flakes of snow drifting down. In the valley, the air was heavier, colder; in some areas the drifting snow almost buried the fencing along the roadside.

"They approach the kid, and even though they're standing next to him, he doesn't respond. So one of them reaches down and flips him over, and the kid just lies there stiff in front of them, pounding the air like he was still pounding the ground. They said his eyeballs had rolled up inside his head, and that he'd pissed hisself.

"After a while, he slows down, and seems to be going to sleep. It's fall, October or November, so they can't just leave him there like that, so one of them wraps him in his jacket, and they bring him out of the woods, taking turns carrying him.

"The first house they come to is so derelict they don't believe anyone even lives there. But people do, and it turns out it's the boy's house. The father is drunk, threatens the hunters with a shotgun, the mother is wailing, takes the boy and begins to wash him down. And they're trying to tell the guy his son needs to see a doctor, but the father keeps swearing at them there's nothing wrong with his boy, and then the mother starts screaming they hurt her son, and she jumps up and grabs a big knife, and they run.

"They notify us, we respond to the farm. Father's sobered up a bit, lets us into the house. The mom is sitting on a ratty old couch, holding the boy all wrapped up in a blanket, rocking him back and forth.

"The boy isn't much to look at, scrawny and all, but they're obviously giving him food to eat, and he's clean—of course, his mom has just washed him down. I give him a look-over, and he seems to be okay. He has a couple of welts on his leg, but his dad said he fell while climbing a fence, and I don't push it.

"The whole time, the boy won't say a word to us. I ask to see where he sleeps, and they show me his room. It's filthy, piled up with household junk, no toys. On the walls, they put up pictures from an old children's Bible—David and Goliath, and Daniel in the lions' den, and so forth. Big picture of Jesus with his chest open, pointing at his burning heart.

"I talk to them about taking him to the hospital to get him checked out, but they say that's against their religion, that God will provide, and stuff like that. And then I ask them about the altar, and the mom starts screaming it's not true, and the dad gets pretty upset and tells us to get the hell out.

"So we leave. The hunters are waiting for us up on the road, and they take us down into the woods. It gets dark early in the valley, and mist forms pretty quick. And I tell you, I'm not much for creepy stuff or ghosts and so forth, but walking through those woods in the dark, the mist settling in all around us, going into the clearing and seeing what this little boy had done . . . well, I tell you, it was the goddamned *eeriest* thing I've ever seen in my life. The hunters—two big guys from Steel-town, both with guns, one an ex-marine—don't want to come into the clearing. And I can't say as I blame 'em.

"My partner shines the flashlight on it, and I look for anything that looks human, and far as I can tell, there's nothing there. So I kick over the altar, and we throw the dog's body onto the pile. Jerry brings down some gas from the truck, and I set the whole thing on fire, burned the altar in the clearing.

"I didn't think I put that much gas on the pile, but I tell you, those flames were shooting up so high that I was afraid that the trees were going to burn. We back away, I watch from the edge of the clearing, and when it settles down a little, we begin to walk back up the hill to the road.

"The moon is out now, and the woods look all golden from the fire, and there's this big plume of smoke you could see for miles. And as we're walking up the hill, I hear it. I hear this . . . howling. This shrieking sound, echoing through the valley, just howling and howling . . .

"And I knew it was the boy."

The snow was coming down heavier now, and Andy Slater turned on the windshield wipers. The light from the high beams seemed almost solid, given mass by the rushing snowflakes.

Don Slater squinted into the snow, trying to recognize the land-scape.

"About ten more minutes to Snowden. He lived on the other side of the town."

His expression seemed to have softened, and he was sitting less stiffly in his seat.

"Anyway, we got out of there quick. I guess I made some mistakes. I didn't report it to anyone—there really wasn't anyone to report it to, unless I wanted to drag in Clearfield PD. I didn't make them take him to a doctor. I did check at the school: his teacher said he was a poor student, prone to daydreaming, but nothing irregular. And he occasionally had bruises, but boys play rough."

He paused, looking out over the fields.

"Really, it was a different time back then."

He looked at Jenner again.

"But I'm starting to think I made my biggest mistake that night when I got home: I told my wife.

"I know you know how it is, Doctor—you can't help but talk about the things you see with the people who care about you, particularly the bad things, the really bad things you need to get off your chest. And my wife was a good listener, and a good person.

"The next day, she took it on herself to contact the priest in Snowden. She was a Methodist, like many folks around here, but Barretsburg County is the exception that proves the rule. Welsh Catholics originally settled it back in the early eighteen hundreds, and the church in Snowden was pretty much the only Catholic one for maybe twenty miles.

"You see, she thought the boy might have a religious problem, and if he wasn't going to go to a hospital, maybe the family would let him see their priest.

"Now, I don't pretend to be an expert on the Catholic Church, but I've been thinking that for a priest to be sent to a church in the middle of nowhere where you have a population of maybe three hundred and fifty people in the entire county is not what might be called a *reward*.

"I knew the priest was pretty new to Snowden, maybe three or four years out of Pittsburgh or Philly, I don't remember which. Everyone knew he'd taken in a couple of orphans from Barretsburg. At the time, I didn't think anything about it, you know, just good deeds and all. There was some whispering, but I just figured it was Protestants gossiping about the Catholics.

"Anyway, my wife calls up the rectory and tells the priest the story, asks him to go check on the Farrars. So he does.

"The next week, the boy goes to live with the priest, staying in the rectory like the orphans. And, you know, I was actually kind of relieved when I heard that—I was pretty sure Bobby was no stranger to his daddy's belt.

"And for a while, I think he did okay. But then, middle of winter, I get a call from the hospital ER up in Clearfield. Someone driving on the Psalter Brook road has found Bobby Farrar walking along in the snow without shoes, no coat. They pick him up and they see he's bleeding from his groin area, so they take him to the hospital. In the ER, they find that he's got a huge gash in his scrotum, and one of his testicles is missing. The bleeding has pretty much stopped by itself, so the surgeons clean up the wound and sew in a fake testicle and patch up the other one. He won't say a word about what happened. Actually, he won't say a word about anything—doesn't say who did it, doesn't say it hurts, doesn't say, 'Where's my mommy?' He just sits there, lets them examine him."

Andy Slater tapped his hands on the wheel.

"Up ahead there, Doctor, at the far end of the valley."

Through the snow, where the dark sky sank into the shadow of the valley, Jenner could barely make out the silhouette of a steeple.

"Snowden."

Don Slater leaned forward.

"Can you see it? I can't make it out, myself. But it's the Church of St. Stephen. The rectory where Bobby Farrar was living when it happened is right next door.

"I went there straight from the hospital. I knew the kid was mentally disturbed, and figured he'd done it to himself, but I needed to document the circumstances as best I could.

"This road we're on, the snow was so deep I almost couldn't get through. That night, driving into Snowden, inching down this damn road, taking every curve at less than five miles per hour, sure I was going to run off the road and roll my truck down the hill, what really struck me was that when I finally got down into the town, I didn't relax at all. Not a bit.

"There's only maybe fifty houses, if that. I could see people were in them—there were parked cars, and lights in some of the windows, and smoke coming from some of the chimneys. But all of the blinds were shut, all of the curtains drawn.

"There was something about that town that felt . . . sick. Diseased. And later on, I figured they had to know. Some of them, definitely. All of them, maybe. They knew, and they just didn't want to get involved."

They could see the steeple clearly now, low and black at the head of the valley. The road dropped down toward the town in a long sequence of hairpins and cutbacks. Andy Slater slowed the truck to take the first turn.

"Anyway, I pulled up to the rectory, and Father Martin was waiting at the door. Tall, thin man, looked like he'd never experienced an emotion in his life. What's the word—*gaunt*. He was gaunt, like some monk starving himself in a cave or something. But there's something else to him, some smugness, some satisfaction, some weird, dark pleasure.

"He says he isn't even aware that the boy is missing. No, he hasn't heard the phone ringing. Doesn't ask why the kid was in the hospital thirty miles away. Takes me to the dormitory. Turns out there are four other little boys living there. It's barely six p.m., but the other boys are already in bed, and the lights are off.

"Around Bobby's bed there are pages covered with calligraphy, even with little paintings for the first letter, like from medieval times. No books, no toys—Father Martin says he doesn't have any toys, and they never asked him for toys, and that Bobby likes to copy old documents, that it calms him down. He says Bobby is working on a copy of the Magna Carta. He asks the other boys where Bobby is, and one of the kids says they saw him praying in the room where they get dressed before the mass.

"So we go down to this small room that gives out onto the back of the altar in the church. And in one corner, there are spatters of blood, and a pair of boy's underpants soaked with blood, and there's one of those hooked knives carpet layers use. The walls are white wainscoting, and I can see spatters of blood flicked up onto them, all at a pretty low level. I figure he pretty much had to have done it himself, kneeling. Hooked the knife under, and—"

"C'mon, Dad. Enough."

"Just watch the damn road, Andy. I'm going to tell Dr. Jenner everything I saw. And I'm going to tell him everything I've thought about or suspected since then, because I don't know what's important and what's not. And if I don't know, you sure as shit don't. So shut up and drive."

Andy was driving a little fast, the wheels slipping occasionally in the snow.

"Take it easy, Andy. Concentrate."

He leaned back in his seat again.

"The priest said he had no idea what this was about, that Bobby had never been anything other than polite and well behaved. He'd been applying himself in his studies, and putting on weight. He let me question the other boys, who were maybe nine to twelve, something like that, and they all said they didn't know anything and Bobby hadn't said anything.

"And he never did. His parents didn't utter a peep. After a couple of days in Clearfield, the hospital staff found a bed for him up north, at Warren State Hospital, a mental facility. I think he was there for a couple of months, supposedly the youngest patient ever there. They turn him out, and he goes back to live with his folks again, carrying a big paper sack full of tranquilizers.

"After that he doesn't speak with anyone, doesn't say a word, except to Father Martin. After that, all I know is gossip, and not even direct from Snowden people, who still don't talk about it. But supposedly Bobby's dad gets really pissed off about how close he is to the priest. And it soon gets back to him that everyone in the county knows about his son and what happened. He starts drinking even more, and he's a mean drunk; there was a story that one time Bobby's dad made him walk into town in one of his mother's dresses to buy salt and sugar—don't know if it was true, but it sure stuck.

"I get a couple of calls out there, have to calm his dad down. I take away his shotgun, figure it'd be safer like that. I see Bobby in the house, or in the fields, or near the woods, but whenever he sees me, he turns and walks away. And I let him walk.

"Then one day, maybe a month after I hear the story about the dress,

I get called to a fire in Snowden, and I respond to find that it's the Farrar farm. Bobby and some of the people from the village are standing outside, and there's obviously no way to do anything—place went up like it was made out of kerosene-soaked kindling. And then, when the house is engulfed in flames, I see Mr. Farrar through the window, completely on fire, this screaming ball of fire banging around inside. It's too hot to get near the building, and I try to pull Bobby away, turn him so he can't look, but he breaks free and runs down by the paddock and stands there, kind of hopping from one leg to the other, watching his dad burn until I physically catch him and drag him off.

"Someone from the coroner's office comes in from Barretsburg, looks the place over the next day, decides it was a heating oil explosion. I'm with him, and I see there are large nails in a row near the front doorjamb, and when I ask him about them, he says that sometimes heat in a fire makes the wood shrink and forces the nails up, that this is just because of the fire. I got the sense that he doesn't want to make an issue of it. No one did, really—afterward, I find out no one ever called the fire department on it."

He paused. "You ever see or hear anything like that? The nails coming up because of a fire."

Jenner shook his head. "It doesn't sound right to me."

"Anyway, Bobby went back to live with Father Martin. It was kind of a community decision—I think people actually felt he was better off without his mom and dad. And the kid *wanted* to go to the rectory. I didn't fight it. I mean, how much worse could it be than with a father and mother like Bobby's?"

The road leveled off as they entered the valley floor. The road ahead to Snowden was hidden under a couple of inches of snow, untrammeled by foot or tire.

"After that, things were pretty quiet. Bobby seemed to settle down after his parents were gone. I know Father Martin kept a pretty tight leash on him—he never went out to the parties, didn't go to his own prom. They sent him to a special school, but he didn't really make friends, just hung out with the other boys in the rectory.

"None of them mixed with the other kids, really. They were a little pack, playing only with each other, walking through town as a little group, all dressing alike. At the time I thought they just wanted to keep to themselves, that maybe the other kids were mean to them. Later I found out that the other Snowden kids weren't allowed to go to the rectory, or play with the boys that lived there. There were never any allegations of abuse at the time, although I had my suspicions."

He looked out into the onrushing darkness, silent.

"After a while, I move on, and lose track of Bobby Farrar. Then, about five years back, I get a call from the Philadelphia PD about a murdered male prostitute they'd traced back to Clearfield; they wanted me to help make notifications. Turned out it was one of the rectory kids from Snowden. It happened after Father Martin's first stroke, so I took it on myself to make the ID. I went to the rectory, got photos of the kid, then drove up to Philly.

"I hadn't seen the boy in more than ten years, so I go to the place where he'd been living, see if I could find more recent photos. Crummy apartment in the worst part of North Philly.

"He was living with another of the rectory boys. The other kid's home when I get there, but he doesn't want to see his friend dead like that, so I get some photos of the guy with and without makeup to take to the morgue.

"Just as I'm about to leave, I see a framed document on the wall, with Egyptian writing, and he sees me looking at it, and he says that Bobby Farrar made it. I ask what ever happened to Bobby Farrar, and he says Bobby was the only one of them who made good. Says he went to Deene's College, then got rich from computers. I was kind of surprised, but the kid said it was all Father Martin, that Father Martin had really made Bobby work hard, made him the man he was supposed to be.

"Then he gives this kind of smirk and says, 'Like he did for me and Olive'—his friend's name. I didn't ask what he meant, I just wanted to take care of things and get back home. I felt bad for him—it looked like they were living on soup—so I gave him twenty bucks and told him to take care of himself, and then I left."

He fell silent.

The truck purred slowly through the dark village.

Andy Slater pointed up ahead.

"That's it."

The black stone of the church and steeple glistened in the truck's headlights, the roof sheathed in an envelope of snow. Next door to the church was a house made of the same black stone, with a carefully lettered sign that read "Rectory of St. Stephen's Church, 1824."

Slater pulled the truck over and let the engine idle for a few seconds, watching the snowflakes twisting through the beams. Then he shut it off and turned to Jenner.

"We're here. This is where Father Martin lives."

The snow crunched softly under their feet as Jenner and Don Slater made their way to the heavy oak door. The rectory was on the edge of the cemetery, and Jenner could make out the white silhouettes of row after row of curved and flat-topped headstones, an occasional cement cross looming among them.

Slater used the old bronze doorknocker, and a few seconds later, the lights in the entrance hall lit up. The door opened, and standing in front of them was a young priest with freckles and unruly red hair, the sleeves of his cassock pushed up to the elbow, wiping his wet hands with a towel.

"Good evening," he said, his expression neutral and sincere, ready for whatever type of crisis into which he was about to be thrust.

Slater introduced himself and explained that he and Dr. Jenner, an investigator from New York City, would like to speak with Father Martin.

The priest, who introduced himself as Father Dominic, ushered them into a living room and said apologetically, "You mustn't have heard. Last month Father had another stroke; the poor man has lost his speech. We have a board and some magnetic letters so he can communicate, but even that is hard for him."

He sighed and sat in an armchair opposite them, his voice quieter.

"In truth, he's doing very poorly, and isn't expected to live much longer. Weeks, maybe days, the doctor said. On top of it all, he's developed a very painful eye infection, and so we've been giving him painkillers to keep him comfortable. I'm afraid he won't be able to help you. But perhaps I might be of some service. I've been here more than a year now, so . . ."

Jenner said, "Father, we're trying to gather information about Bobby Farrar. I think he was a little before your time."

"The lad who painted the rectory sign? We have some of his artwork here—he was a calligrapher, you know? We have a wonderful copy of the Magna Carta he did when he was young, and some Egyptian papyruses, and even one of his paintings."

"Have you seen him recently?"

"No, I've never met him. In fact, I know he hasn't been here for years. Until two or three years ago, Father Martin told me, he would send postcards and paintings every month. Then they just stopped. It was sad—Father had so enjoyed hearing from Bobby."

Jenner asked, "Do you have any of the paintings or the letters? Do you know where they were sent from? I'd really like to see them."

"Oh, I'd need the envelopes for a return address, and they're long gone. New York City, though. The paintings were of New York City—skylines, parks, river views, and the like. I'm no expert, but I thought they were rather well done."

He gestured to the closed door across the room.

"Father has one of the larger ones framed in his bedroom across the way. I put the rest in storage in the garden shed. It won't be easy to reach—the drifts are about four feet against that door."

He paused, then continued slowly, "If you would be as quiet as possible, you could look at the painting on Father's bedroom wall. You could stand at the doorway—I'd rather you didn't actually go inside. But we should wait a little. I've just given him his new Fentanyl patch, and that usually puts him out.

"Let's give the man some time to drift off. Some coffee? I was heating up some dinner when you rang—just soup, but if you'd care for some, you're welcome to join me."

Both men thanked the priest, and declined.

"Is there anything you can tell us about Bobby Farrar, Father?"

Father Dominic stood and went over to the fireplace, prodding at the logs absentmindedly with a brass poker.

He shrugged. "I'm afraid not, really. He was very close to Father Martin. I know he had some . . . emotional difficulties . . . when he was younger. And I know he'd been injured—Father Martin told me he used to have to give the boy testosterone pills, because of his injury.

"Martin was quite proud of him; I get the impression they had quite a mentor/protégé relationship. I know that he did well in high school, particularly with extracurricular activities—he was a gifted artist. He used to stage the annual crèche for St. Stephen's, and he designed sets for the high school drama club. Very accomplished!

"Then he went on to college, and took up computers, and did very well for himself. Martin had a theory that Bobby's interest in ancient languages gave him the edge over his colleagues, his fascination with symbols and syntax; I could see where that sort of skill set might come in handy for a computer programmer.

"After college, he founded a software company, and developed a database system for medical and insurance records. Hugely successful, made him a fortune. He created databases for some of the biggest schools in the Northeast, I believe.

"But I'm afraid that's all I know. He ended up in New York City, as I said, but Father has had no news of him in some time."

He paused.

"May I ask . . . Is Mr. Farrar in trouble?"

Slater spoke up. "Just routine inquiries, Father. Routine inquiries."

The priest nodded. "Ah. Routine inquiries. Very good."

He glanced down at his watch.

"It should be safe now. The drug eases the pain for a few hours, but he wakes at the drop of a pin."

He stood, and they followed him to the bedroom door, where he turned and put a finger to his lips. He gently turned the knob and pushed the door to Father Martin's bedroom open.

The ceiling lamp, apparently on a dimmer circuit, seemed to cast more shadow than light. The room was a sickly green in the weak light.

Jenner could hear the rattling tide of Father Martin's breathing. The old priest was half hidden behind the door, the foot of his hospital bed sticking out beyond it.

Father Dominic pointed at the far wall. There was an ornately framed, large-scale watercolor, painted almost exclusively in shades of red. In front of a long-haired, bearded king on a throne was a kneeling man with a silver halo, arms lifted, palms upward in supplication, eyes raised to heaven. Two Roman soldiers held him down by his shoulders, while a third squatted in front of the kneeling man, a short, curved blade in his hands. The man with the knife was carving symbols across his victim's forehead; thick crimson rivulets covered his face like a net.

The priest closed the door.

Don Slater touched the priest's arm and said, "Father, what was that painting of?"

The priest smiled a little. "Striking, isn't it? It's a portrait of Theophanes. In Constantinople, sometime in the eight hundreds, he spoke out against the Emperor Theophilus, who had insisted that religious images be destroyed. When Theophanes refused to shut up, the emperor had his men cut a long verse onto his face; supposedly it took them two days to complete it."

"Father Martin tells me it was Bobby's absolute favorite subject to paint." He grinned at them. "What *is* it about young people that draws them to the macabre?"

They sat down, back in the living room.

"Father, can you think of any other place where some of Bobby's letters might be? Perhaps in Father Martin's room?"

"Well, I suppose it's possible. But I'm afraid we really can't go looking through there tonight—the man needs his sleep. I'm very sorry."

Jenner glanced at Slater, then looked at the priest.

"I have to tell you that this is a matter of life and death. Mr. Farrar may be involved in the killing of a series of university students in New York City, and we believe that he may have abducted a young girl. Our backs are against the wall here."

The priest nodded gravely.

"With all due respect, Doctor, Father Martin hasn't received a letter from Bobby Farrar for some time now. It seems very unlikely indeed that there'd be anything of relevance to the current situation in old letters. I'm happy to give you access to the shed, but, as I've said, you're going to need several men to dig it out if you're actually going to get in. I'm sorry, but I can't let you into Father Martin's bedroom tonight."

Don Slater began to speak, but Father Dominic silenced him with a wave. "I'm sorry, but he's a dying man, and suffering terribly. You're welcome to wait until he wakes, but that may not be until morning."

Jenner nodded.

"I understand."

He leaned back, then turned to Slater.

"I should probably be getting back to New York. Do we have enough time before we head out for a cup of coffee?"

Slater said, "Up to you, Doctor. Shouldn't dawdle too long, or we'll never get back up out of the damned valley. Pardon my French, Father."

The priest stood with a smile.

"I'm delighted to have the company. Sometimes the rectory seems a little too quiet, with just Martin and I. And I rarely have visitors—too new in Snowden, I guess. It'll take me just a couple of minutes."

He made for the kitchen. Slater stopped him, saying, "Sir, my son's outside in the car—mind if he joins us?"

"Good heavens, no! Bring him on in—we don't want him freezing out there."

The priest went into the kitchen, Slater through the front door. Jenner stepped quietly into the hall. He probably had about four minutes, five if he was lucky.

He reached for the bedroom door handle and was about to turn it when he heard the priest call out, "Doctor, you're in luck! I have some Starbucks Rift Valley blend! You'll feel just like you're in the city—"

Jenner stepped back into the living room. "Sounds great!"

He returned to the bedroom, turned the handle, and slipped inside, closing the door behind him.

The old priest lay there in the bed, his breathing regular and dry. He was tall and thin, his bones almost visible through translucent skin, his shriveled hands clawing the sheet to his neck. There was water and a medicine bottle next to the lamp on the bedside table.

Jenner scanned the room. The bookshelves were packed, but scrupulously neat. The desk, though, was covered with papers, apparently a way station for the priest as he sorted his mail. Jenner started to sift through the memos and calendars on top of it, then turned his attention to the drawers, quickly tugging them out one by one. In the lowest drawer, he found what he was looking for: a small wad of postcard-size linen stationery, bound with a purple silk ribbon. The topmost was a view of Manhattan from the Brooklyn Bridge in maroon ink.

He closed the drawer, and straightened. There was a click, and the bedside lamp flooded the room with light.

Father Martin was sitting propped up in the bed, his fingers trembling against the switch on the lamp cord. His face was thin and pale, the cheekbones prominent, his hair a brush-cut ruff of white. His eyes were unblinking, bright green blue, his left eye deeply crusted and bloody.

Jenner walked to the bed, flashed his shield, and said, "You'll have these back within the week. You should get some rest now."

He reached over, tugged the switch from his hand, rotated the lamp so the priest couldn't reach the switch, then turned it off.

Then he turned his back on the upright shadow in the bed and left.

The two Slaters were standing in the hallway, Andy confused, his father unruffled. Don gestured to the living room, and they sat without talking. Seconds later, the priest walked in with a tray holding a large French press coffeepot, cream, sugar, mugs, and a plate of Pepperidge Farm Milanos. He nodded a welcome to Andy Slater, and then started to pour.

\*   \*   \*

Where do you go when your body's there, but you aren't? In the days lying in the dark, shivering under the blankets, Ana slipped away, her body
now just a beaded curtain wrapped around her, her spirit slipping past
the silvery chains, leaving them swaying as she left.

She didn't look down from space and see her body; it wasn't like that,
not at all like that, not mystical and groovy and life-affirming. But there
was tranquility in the absence. She would go back to Florida, back to
Silver Lake. Lying by the swimming pool with Carmen, her hair smelling of chlorine, her skin warm and tan.

And she would be okay for a while, remembering the heat and light
on her skin. But then it would abruptly break, and she'd feel herself
tumble out of space back into her body, jerking into consciousness with
a gasp, sobbing as she found herself on the mattress in the freezing dark,
the coarse blanket chafing as she tried to get warm.

When she was awake again, awake and fully conscious again, it was
hard, because she'd start thinking about what the man was going to do
with her, and she'd lie there feeling her tears cool as they coursed down
her filthy cheeks.

She'd once read that people who set themselves on fire don't feel
anything because they're in some kind of trance state. When he killed
her, she wanted to be in a trance state. When he started cutting on her,
or drilling her, or whatever he was going to do to her, she wouldn't be
in her body. She was going to leave it; not so much leave it as disappear inside it, find some spiral staircase inside herself and walk down it,
go down deeper and deeper inside until she was gone, like one of those
monks burning in kerosene.

The thought of being deep inside herself, locked away inside, far from
him, made her warm again; and then she could think about Silver Lake,
and Carmen, and the sun. At least for a while.

J enner had left one of the windows open in his loft, and the room was freezing; in the lamplight, he could see his breath fall and disappear.

He threw down his bag and went to the kitchen. Three messages. His cat paced on the counter, purring, while he played them back.

The first was Rad, voice creaking and painfully slow. Rad had passed Jenner's information on to the Inquisitor team; they'd located a software business address for Robert Farrar and a handful of residences for the name. They were checking the residential addresses, and an ESU team was responding to the software company address.

The second was from Pyke, a terse request for news, for anything Jenner had heard. The third had come in just before he'd walked through the door.

"Doc, it's Pat Mullins. Rad asked me to follow up with you."

There was a loud grinding crackle and then a silent pause; Jenner imagined the glove covering the mouthpiece as Mullins spoke with someone on the ESU team. He came back on the line, sounding tired and pissy, and Jenner knew his leads hadn't panned out.

"Evening was a bust. Six Robert Farrars in the five boroughs, contiguous New Jersey, Westchester, Nassau, Suffolk, and whatever the hell that southernmost county in Connecticut is, Fairfield, I think. We identified a software company he was a partner in, went belly up not too long after 9/11. In association with that, we found a residential address for Robert Farrar; he'd moved from the place, like, three years ago. No forwarding address. We're following up on that now."

In the background, Jenner could hear chatter, and imagined the strike team back at the station. Hanging up the body armor, locking the guns into the cages, bitching about the evening, about his bum leads.

"Took an ESU team to Williamsburg, to the office address. It's a ret-rofitted factory; the whole building's used by technology firms and the like. Got the building manager out of bed, he says the guy moved out of there a year or two ago, when his business went bust. So that's a whole night, nothing to show for it."

Noise welled up in the background, and Mullins paused for a second. "So, yeah. A bust. But, anyway, thanks, Doc. Take care." He paused a second, then added, "Sorry."

Then a click, and the loft was silent again.

Jenner looked again at the postcards he'd stolen from the dying priest. A waste of time—various watercolors in Farrar's weird maroon color scheme, just views of the Manhattan skyline, the correspondence a couple of years old.

He threw them down on the table and started to undress.

So, that was that. Driving through the snow, he'd imagined Ana being rescued, Farrar shot dead. By the time he reached New Jersey, the fantasy played in an endless loop, slow motion like the climax of a Peckinpah movie. The shadowy figures of the ESU team slipping around back of a suburban house, or a burned-out warehouse, flash-bangs in, cops through every door and window. Farrar going for his gun and being blown away, every person in the room emptying his assault rifle or handgun clip into him, shredding the monster until what was left would have to be scooped into garbage bags and carried to the morgue. Ana would be tied to a chair in the corner like a silent-movie heroine, weak from hunger and fear, and when the cops pulled down her gag, she'd ask for Jenner.

So much for that.

He felt like his chest was slowly caving in. He'd found the guy, but there was nothing he could do. He'd blown his last chance with the cops. Sure, they'd work his leads, and if the leads paid off, they'd bust Farrar, but Jenner was history. If they ever thought of him afterward, the thing they'd remember was how he got Joey Roggetti killed. How he dragged them from their homes a couple of nights before Christmas to chase down shitty leads in Brooklyn in the freezing cold.

Jenner lay down on his bed, staring at the ceiling. After a minute, he rolled carefully to his right and picked his book of saints, a mass-market

paperback published by a Cistercian press in England. The entry began
blandly enough:

> Anastasia d. AD 304, tortured and received the Holy Crown of
> Martyrdom at Palmarola during the Diocletian Persecution, after
> refusing to renounce her faith.

But Jenner knew that they always hid the *really* horrific deaths behind
banal descriptions. He made himself read the whole text one more time.

> Saint Anastasia, on discovering that all the confessors had been
> butchered by the emperor, wept openly in the Roman court. When
> asked why she was crying, she said she wept at the loss of so many
> of her brethren. She was then interrogated, and revealed herself
> as a Christian. When Diocletian couldn't persuade her of the exis-
> tence of the gods, she was sent to the holy man Upian. When Upian
> failed to get her to renounce her faith, he sent three pagan women
> to seduce her. When she rejected them, Upian attempted to force
> himself upon her; he was immediately struck blind, then collapsed
> and died, convulsing in agony. The prefect of Rome then tried to
> starve her to death, but she miraculously survived. Finally, she was
> led to the island of Palmarola for torture and execution. Her breasts
> were cut off, she was burned on a bonfire, and then decapitated.

Religious myth is fluid, the stories changing with the century and the
chronicler. Farrar would piece together the cruelest version, distill the
most horrific interpretation. It wasn't a story from almost two thousand
years ago anymore: it was real, and it was actually going to happen.


The Ambien Jenner took worked too well: he slept until the early afternoon, waking with a start to the ringing phone. He hadn't closed the
curtains; the sky was tarnished tin, the room shadowy and somber.

He was too stiff to reach the phone, but when he heard Rad struggling to speak, he pulled himself out from under the blankets and picked up.

"Rad. I'm here."

"Hey. Jenner. Good to speak to you."

"How you doing?"

Rad coughed, and muttered "Ow" under his breath. "Hangin' in there. Okay."

"I got your message last night. Thanks. And Mullins called to say the warehouse was a bust, and the residential addresses, too. Anything else turn up?"

"Naah. They think he's the guy. Farrar." He was breathing a little heavily. "They confirmed he designed and installed the databases at Hutchins, and at New Hope Clinic. Figure he has backdoor access. Computers—"

Jenner said, "Yeah. That's pretty much what we figured. Anything else?"

"No . . . Keep you informed . . ."

"Okay, Rad. You take it easy, okay?"

"You too, Jenner."

He was about to hang up when he heard Rad say, "Jenner."

He answered.

"Jenner . . . you did good. You got everything right, all along . . . I appreciate it."

"Thanks."

"No, Jenner, wait."

It was painful to listen to him.

"Look. They'll get her, okay? They'll find her."

"Thanks, Rad. I hope so. Thanks."

There was a clatter as the detective hung up.

He put on a robe and drank some water. He put fresh food in the cat's bowl and took care of the litter. He went into the bathroom, brushed his teeth and splashed water on his face, then went back into the kitchen. The Weetabix was finished, so he fixed a bowl of Raisin Bran, then took it to the table and sat, looking out over the East River. He spat out the first mouthful of cereal; the milk was clotted and bitter. How could he not have noticed? He picked up the bottle—expired five days ago.

He sat, the taste of spoiled milk in his mouth, staring out the window. The Lower East Side, and Brooklyn beyond, the low mosaic of dense buildings, a few boats on the river, and on the other bank the warehouses of Williamsburg, like an old Dutch engraving.

The phone rang. Dan Israel from the DA's office. More bad news—he should stop answering the phone.

Apparently, Father Sheehan, who was enjoying sudden celebrity in ancient language circles, had given an interview to the *Times*. Trying to share credit, the priest had cited the tracings Jenner had made of Barbara Wexler's back. When Whittaker read the article, he'd discovered that Jenner had seen the body at the morgue; he'd had the surveillance video pulled and reviewed by Security. They'd identified Jenner breaking into the office early that morning, coming over the rooftop next to NYU Medical Center.

Whittaker had turned the tapes over to the DA's office and was demanding that charges be pressed. Jenner's actions were technically a class D felony, and the evidence against him was strong. Dan and Ken Salt had arranged for Jenner to quietly appear before a friendly judge the following day; both felt that it would be best to plead guilty. Conviction could carry a sentence of up to seven years in prison, but given the circumstances, Jenner would receive a fine and probation.

If Jenner didn't make his court date, a warrant would be issued for his arrest. If he pleaded guilty, the fine wouldn't be large, and the probation wouldn't be long. But there was something else: the felony conviction would go on his record, and Whittaker would be lodging a formal complaint with the state licensing board. A felony conviction made it quite possible that Jenner's license would be suspended or withdrawn, particularly with Whittaker's growing influence in Albany.

Jenner thanked Dan and hung up.

\*   \*   \*

After he'd showered and dressed, he called Rad at Bellevue. A nurse's aide told him that Garcia's wife had had the phone removed from his room.

Jenner broke down and called Pat Mullins. Some news, no real progress. Every trail for Farrar had gone cold. They'd located the former CEO of Farrar's software company in a federal prison in South Carolina, doing time for embezzlement. He'd been interviewed, and had volunteered that there was something wrong with Farrar physically—he needed to have regular hormone shots—but something even more wrong with him socially. The man said Farrar straight out had no idea how to communicate with other people.

They'd done a broad-area canvas through the neighborhood around Farrar's old company in Williamsburg; other than a lot of bums, the search had been negative. Since they had no photograph of Farrar, it had been a shot in the dark at best. Besides, who'd hang around in the place where their life's work went belly-up?

Looking for a photo, they'd run a DMV search; they'd just now located a record for him in Pennsylvania. His full name was Robert Sebastian Farrar, age thirty-five. They had requested the photo from his expired driver's license; more than ten years old, but better than nothing. They were considering doing another sweep through Williamsburg, this time with the photograph.

The Pittsburgh-based forensic unit was in Snowden at that moment. They'd shoveled their way into the storage shed and were going through its contents. A Questioned Documents specialist on the team had been faxed copies of the text on Barbara Wexler's back; he was currently working a comparison to the painting in the priest's bedroom. Document examiner or not, Mullins said, it was pretty much a slam dunk, given the case history and the subject matter of the painting—the man having text cut into his face.

They'd subpoenaed the phone records from the rectory in Snowden, but he figured that was likely a dead end.

"And that's about it. When we get the photo, it'll go out to the media. He'll be on every TV in New York tonight, and on the cover of every newspaper in the country tomorrow morning."

He was silent for a second, then continued, a little softer.

"Look, Doc. We'll find him. Probably by tomorrow morning it'll be all over. Once his photo's out, someone'll drop a dime. You'll see. Leave the worrying to us, okay?"

"Thanks."

"We'll take care of this. You rest up. How're the ribs?"

"Fine, Pat. They're fine. Thanks for being straight with me."

The detective hesitated a second, figuring out how he was going to say what he wanted to say.

"So you should rest up. And . . . Doc, look, it would probably be better if you didn't call me on this line. My battery's almost dead, and with things going the way they are, everybody and his brother is calling me. If anything happens, I'll let you know right away, okay?"

"Okay. Thanks."

The line went dead.

He sat at his table and watched the fading light die out over the water. He couldn't even think. No bright ideas, no sudden inspiration.

Jenner paced the loft, measuring out the room in long strides, wall to wall. He was losing his mind; he had to get out. What could he do? Where could he go?

He couldn't stop thinking about her, the image in his head throbbing between life and death. Ana bound to a chair, alive; Ana butchered and burned, dead.

He would go out. He had to get out.

He couldn't stop imagining her dead, imagining that Farrar had killed her and butchered her and burned her. Jenner didn't have to shut his eyes to see how she would look now, her hair singed to bristle against her blackened scalp, the splitting of her baked skin, the wounds he'd inflicted . . .

He had to stop. His clothes felt strange. Not too tight, not too loose, not itchy, just . . . strange. Hanging on him like body armor. The elevator door opened, and he was in the basement; he'd pushed the wrong button. The basement hallway reeked of rotting fruit and roach spray; it never had when Pete was alive.

He rode back up to the lobby, but there was nowhere for him to go. Why would he go out? He would stay home. He should stay home, in case someone called.

He checked his mailbox, clogged with junk. Flyers, mailings from real estate agents, menus, bills. There was a small gray cardboard box of new checks, and a plastic-wrapped sample issue of a new lifestyle magazine for rich New Yorkers. He was going to toss them out then and there, but the elevator opened, and he climbed in, his bones aching.

He threw the mail on the table, then opened a bottle of wine. Glass full, he sorted the mail, threw out most, and took the check box over to the desk where he kept his checkbooks.

He opened the box, and was surprised to find it was packed with newspaper. He looked at the front of the box and saw there was no bank logo, no return address.

The hair on the back of his neck began to prickle.

It wasn't newspaper, it was a supermarket flyer, carefully folded. It smelled funny, but the newsprint wasn't running, and the paper was free of oily staining or powder particles that would suggest an explosive charge.

Completely focused now, he went to the bathroom and found his manicure set, a gift from his mother when he started medical school. He sat at the desk and gently picked up the paper using a tweezers and a clippers. The papers came out as one, and he saw that the inner pages of the flyer had been carefully folded to create a small packet the size of a thick sausage.

Holding the packet with the tweezers, he swept everything off the desk. He covered the desktop with a clean sheet of drafting paper, then carefully set the little packet down in the center, switching on his desk lamp.

The wrapper was in black and red ink, a flyer from Dalrymple's Discount, a budget market chain with branches in poorer neighborhoods throughout the Northeast.

He opened the drawer and pulled out his camera. He photographed the wrapped packet, rolled it, and photographed it methodically on each side. On the underside, where the flyer had been tucked under into folded points, he saw russet staining, possibly from the red flyer ink running.

He carefully folded open the points, then the wrappings. The package had been made by simply rolling and folding the flyer around its contents. It was a page from the butcher's section, with kitschy illustrations that looked like they'd appeared in Dalrymple's holiday catalogues since the early 1950s: turkey, ham, lamb, and an image of a family at Christmas dinner. Inside the layers of paper there was a wadded-up clear plastic bag; he slowly unrolled it with the tweezers.

At first he thought they were two pale green olives. Bemused, he nudged them toward the opening of the bag; they rolled out onto the paper and lay there, and the sickly sweet stench of putrefaction rose from the bag, quickly engulfing the room, and he knew then that he was looking at the eyes of Lucia Fiore.

The man was gone, she was pretty sure of it. He went out most nights—he brought fresh newspaper every morning, usually the previous day's *Post*, and he had to be getting it from somewhere. She had heard the creak, and then silence, and she was left alone in the dark and the cold.

Her candle was gone now, used up; he wouldn't give her another. She had begged, but he'd just closed the door without saying a word—he hadn't spoken to her since the first day.

It was a bad sign that he was avoiding making any connection with her. She wanted him to talk—she'd read that it's harder for killers to go through with it if they see you as a person. Then again, she'd also read that it was an inability to feel empathy that allowed them to torture and kill.

She struggled to sit. She was weak now, she realized. He'd stopped feeding her—another scary sign. Before, he'd been feeding her nothing but bread and water, and once, pretzels. It was some kind of sick joke, she thought—cartoon prison food. Maybe it meant something to him. Bread and water. And salt?

Whatever it meant, he was weakening her. It was a struggle to get upright on the mattress now, wriggling on the rotting ticking, pushing herself up onto her hips with frozen knuckles—he checked her wrist bindings several times a day, making her hold her hands like she was praying as he tied her wrists tightly with coarse rope.

The effort to sit up—just to sit up—left her breathless now, and it took a few seconds for the dizziness to fade. But being upright, difficult and unstable as it was, made her feel a little better.

She listened for him.

Nothing. She'd learned that before his absences there'd be a metallic creak—a door or latch or something. When he left he'd be gone for up to three or four hours. As soon as he came back, he'd rush to check on her, his precious treasure.

It disgusted her. It was like Hansel and fucking Gretel, the witch poking them through the bars of their cage to see if they were fat enough to eat.

He'd been growing increasingly suspicious. Several times that day, he'd burst through the door without warning, blinding her with his flashlight. But now she heard the sighing squeaks of the floorboards outside her room as if they were notes on a piano, and she knew the tune his feet played, and she'd hear him coming and quickly cover up what she was doing.

Because she *was* doing something now: she was escaping.

It was his own doing: she'd found a way out because he hadn't given her another candle. That morning, rolling around on the mattress to find a position to ease her numb shoulder and arm, she'd knocked the stub of remaining candle into the hole in the floor.

The feeling of loss was devastating. It was only a one-inch cylinder of wax, and she'd been hoarding it so resolutely that she might never have lit it, but now it was gone, and she would be left in pitch-black until he killed her—for the rest of her life. As she felt herself disappearing into the dark, she realized she'd heard a soft *thunk* when the candle fell through the hole.

It hadn't sounded like the stub had bounced off something so much as it had landed on something.

She rolled to her side and stretched out her hands, sliding them across the floor until she found the opening. The air was cold—maybe colder even than in her room. She'd just assumed that the hole led through to the floor below, but perhaps she'd been wrong.

She reached out, letting her hands slip down into it. She leaned forward and wedged her arms into the void up to the elbow, and felt her fingertips touch cold, damp debris and wood.

There was a crawlspace under the warehouse floor.

It wasn't deep, sixteen inches if that, but if she could get into it, she might be able to crawl through it until she found a way out. If the air inside the crawlspace was that cold, maybe the wood of the ceiling below had holes in it. Maybe even a trapdoor that let out to the floor below.

But how could she get into the crawlspace? She could barely get her arms in to the elbow—what was that, an eight-inch diameter? But if the wood was softened by age and rot . . .

She pressed the wood as hard as she could. Her heart sank—it felt pretty sturdy. Stroking the floorboards around the hole, she found them all quite solid, the edges of the hole smooth with age; maybe there'd been a pipe or something. But perhaps, if she could get enough leverage on the individual planks, she could somehow pry them up.

She hooked her fingers around one plank and tipped backward, hauling on the wood as hard as she could, but it didn't budge. When she finally brought her hands away, they were raw and wet, and she could feel blood on her fingers, scraped on the splintering edges.

But she didn't cry.

She felt around, trying to get a sense of what it was like in the space beneath the floor. There had to be a way.

But even if she got into the crawlspace, what then? The subfloor was damp and soft—would it hold her weight? So what if it didn't! She'd fall through to the next floor, maybe twelve feet or so. She doubted that the fall would be more than maybe fifteen feet, and it might hurt, and she might be stunned for a bit—maybe even knocked out—but she would live.

She imagined herself lying half-conscious on the floor, fragments of rotten wood around her. Sunlight from big factory windows flooded the floor, and it was warm. She'd lie there for a second, get her bearings. In the light, it would be easy to undo the knots. She imagined pulling herself to her feet, then making her way to the window. She'd slip onto the fire escape, and creep down to the ground. And then she'd run, and someone would find her and she'd be saved.

She just had to get through the floor.

But how?

There was nothing in the room, just the mattress, her toilet bucket, and newspaper. The bread plate and the plastic water bottle. Nothing she could use for a lever or a pry tool.

She couldn't stop to think about that now. Keep moving.

She reached back into the crawlspace again, patting the subflooring. Her hands brushed something loose. She grasped it and passed it between her hands, feeling the smooth surface, the row of metal bumps of the edge of a corkscrew.

Her knife. She'd dropped it the first day, and now it had come back to her.

She lifted it carefully through the hole and held it in her right palm. With some difficulty, she managed to open the blade with her left. She held the open knife in her hands, pressing the blade flat against her thigh, showing herself it was real.

She had a weapon.

This time, she cried.

Farrar walked briskly down Greenpoint Avenue, the length of plastic hose shoved back into his pack, swinging the five-gallon canister of gas—filled to the brim, an easy fifty pounds in weight—by his side as if it were filled with cotton candy. He felt a bit like vomiting. His mouth and nose still burned, and he kept on raking up phlegm in the back of his throat. The gas he'd spilled while siphoning made his shirt stink like a service station, which didn't help.

But he had plenty of gas, and that was what mattered. More than enough for the generator and the girl.

He looked at his watch. After midnight! Just twenty-four more hours.

Good.

He didn't like keeping the girl. Well, he liked parts of it, but there was something about her that wasn't right. She didn't behave like the others, who had begged, cried, even offered actual sex if he'd let them go.

Sure, this girl had cried, and yesterday she'd begged for another candle, but still: she wasn't like the others.

There was something about her he didn't trust. Sometimes she was completely immobile when he went in, just lying there in the dark, eyes closed. She knew that she wasn't to look at him, but the fun part was that he got to look at her. He knew it got to her. He'd sometimes just stand there, looking at her on the mattress, letting the light play up and down her shivering body, knowing she could feel the movement of the flashlight beam through her eyelids, that she knew he was standing there, looking at her.

But at other times, he could almost *feel* her thinking. Plotting. Scheming. Waiting for him to let his guard down. Maybe he should tie her ankles.

But that would be an admission of weakness. He wasn't afraid of her—what could she do to him? She had no weapon, and he'd been feeding her what the Blessed Anastasia had eaten when she was in the convent. Now he'd stopped her food, as Publius the Prefect had punished Anastasia at Diocletian's request. She would grow weaker. The ankle bindings were unnecessary.

He stopped short, stunned to see himself on TV. There he was, in the display window of Walkuski Brothers Electronic, his face filling a twenty-seven-inch Sony television screen surrounded by glittering garlands of red and green tinsel. It was his face of twelve years ago, from his driver's license. How on earth had they got that? And then, underneath, his name appeared on the screen.

For a fraction of a second, panic rose into the back of his throat, and then, just as quickly, there was a rush of satisfaction.

*Recognition.*

They knew who he was! Everyone knew that it was he, Robert Farrar, who had done these things. That he could strike at will, reach in among them and transform their daughters, slay their sisters, even murder their guardians, throwing cops aside as if he were brushing lint from his sleeve. His name would be on the lips of the city by morning. No! Not just the city, the entire country, maybe the entire world . . .

Their nameless dread now had a face, had a name.

His name.


Crime Scene left Jenner's loft at about 5:00 a.m., after taking endless pointless photographs of the box and wrappings lying on the kitchen counter. They clearly didn't want to screw anything up, but still, what did they think they were doing? Back at the lab, the criminalists would photograph everything all over again, until the ink on the wrapping was just about starting to fade from all the flashes.

When they'd gone, the exhaustion and the wine overtook him; he passed out in the chair at the kitchen table. He woke to the cat trying to climb onto his lap, his claws digging into Jenner's thigh as he sank back to the floor.

It was already after 2:00 p.m. Angry with himself for sleeping at all, he headed to the shower.

There was no return address on the box. Farrar had used self-adhesive stamps for postage. The ink of the postal franking was barely visible, obscured by the dark blue sky through which Santa's sled flew on the fifty-cent stamps. In the shower, it occurred to him that maybe he could find something if he played around in Photoshop.

He put on his robe, sat at the table, and uploaded the photos from his camera to his laptop. He'd photographed the box before Crime Scene had arrived, bracketing with shots from different angles and different illumination of the postal stamp.

He opened the images in Photoshop, lightened them, and then bumped up the contrast. The image went grainy, and the numbers and letters started to swim on the screen, but he was pretty sure that the zip code ended in 378.

He went online and looked through a zip code database for the city. Manhattan ran 10001 through 10286, Staten Island 10301 to 10314. In the Bronx, the numbers began at 10451, while Brooklyn numbers started with 112. He saw that 11378 was the post office code for Maspeth, Queens.

He looked up the Maspeth post office on an online map. It was close to the Brooklyn border, near the high ground of the Olivet and Mt. Zion cemeteries, among the first sights a visitor saw on a cab ride from the airport. It was pretty close to the intersection of the Brooklyn-Queens Expressway and the Long Island Expressway, and so was easily accessible from anywhere in Brooklyn, Queens, the Bronx—the whole of Long Island, if Farrar was using a car.

But was he? He'd never got a New York State license, and he'd stolen the van he used when he took her. He probably mostly took public transportation, or traveled on foot.

He looked at the map again. Farrar was likely to be in an area where Dalrymple's distributed flyers. On the Dalrymple's Web site he found a branch in Williamsburg. He printed out the map in large scale, drew an X at the Dalrymple's in Williamsburg, and then marked the Maspeth post office. Then he marked the address he had for Farrar's old business.

There were, at most, three miles separating the widest points on the map. And, he remembered, Farrar had stolen the van in Williamsburg, and it had been recovered in Queens, just under the Kosciuszko Bridge. Another X at the bridge. The marks now clustered on the Brooklyn/Queens interface. Greenpoint or Williamsburg, Jenner figured.

It made sense that Farrar would stick to Brooklyn. He probably didn't know the city that well, but he'd have been familiar with Greenpoint and Williamsburg from having worked there.

It was almost 5:00 p.m. He should get moving.

He went to change, threw his robe on the ground, and stopped, catching sight of himself in the mirror. The ugly bruising on his chest didn't seem to be improving. Black threads poked through the crusting incision where they'd put the tube in to reinflate his lung; looking at it, he felt his side begin to itch and burn.

As he gingerly put his T-shirt on, he heard his phone ring. He ran to the desk, snatching the receiver up just as the answering machine came on. *Please, God, let it be Mullins with good news.*

"Dr. Jenner?"

He recognized the voice instantly, the familiar thin, self-righteous tone: Steve Whittaker. He fought the urge to hang up.

"Yes."

"It's Dr. Whittaker."

"What is it, Steve?"

Whittaker snorted. "Well, *Edward* . . . I was calling to see if you'd heard from the district attorney's office yet." He paused. "What, did you think I wouldn't find out?"

Jenner sat. "It's more like I didn't care if you found out."

"Always ready with a snide comeback! Well, I have some news for you—let's see if you have a snide answer for this." He paused dramatically, and then finished in triumph: "I've petitioned the state oversight board to have your license revoked."

Jenner was silent.

"Not so glib now, eh?"

"Sorry, Steve. I was just putting on my pants." He fastened the button and stood. "Yeah, I know, some friends in the DA's office gave me a heads-up. Is there anything else? I'm in a bit of a hurry."

"Well, I think they'll agree with me that any forensic consultant who'd break into a secure facility doesn't have the integrity necessary to practice medicine in the Empire State."

Jenner shrugged. "They may well." He grabbed his sweater. "Hold on a sec—I'm just putting my sweater on."

He put the receiver down and slipped into the sweater, then picked the phone up again.

"You still there? Sorry about that." He fixed the collar. "Now, where were we?"

Whittaker's pitch was rising. "You know you won't be able to practice in New York, right? You do understand that, don't you?"

Jenner sighed. "Well, I probably needed a change of scenery anyway."

Whittaker seemed pleased. "You might want to consider working as a coroner's pathologist in the South. The pay's not great, but I think it'd be good for you to have a coroner overseeing your work, making sure you don't screw up . . ."

Whittaker paused expectantly. Was that all he had?

Jenner said, "Yes, I've always liked the South. You know I trained in Miami, right?" He wedged the phone against his shoulder while he fastened his watch. "Well, Steve, thanks for calling. I should scoot—there's something I've got to take care of."

Whittaker was sputtering on the other end, and then Jenner had had enough.

"Hey, you ever wonder why people hate you, Steve? It's not because you're an asshole—people forgive assholes all the time. And it's not because you're a manipulative, backstabbing prick. It's because, at the end of the day, you're nothing. You'll do whatever it takes to get ahead, but there's nothing inside you—no kindness, no joy, no compassion. Nothing but ambition, nothing but the drive to claw yourself up on top of other people.

"At the end of the day, what they can't forgive is that you happily mess around with their lives, when you don't have one of your own. 'A petty little man'—that's what Julie called you. Did you know that?"

Whittaker struggled to formulate a comeback, finally spitting out, "Well, I don't see Julie with *you* now, do I? What does that make you, Jenner?"

"It makes her too good for the both of us. But we knew that, didn't we?" Jenner laughed. "Since we're talking about Julie, I should come clean. Remember the office party to celebrate your promotion to deputy chief? Well, that was the first time she and I hooked up. We knew you'd never walk out on a party in your honor; Julie had the key to your office, so we fucked on your desk."

Whittaker squealed, "That's a *lie!*"

Jenner, wrapping his scarf around his throat, said, "No, Steve, it's not. Remember how you came in the next morning and you couldn't figure out how your Hopkins diploma just 'fell off' the wall? Well . . ." But Whittaker was already gone.

He crossed the hall to Jun's apartment and knocked. He heard giggling, and after a brief delay, Jun answered the door barefoot, in sweatpants and a loosely buttoned white shirt.

"Jenner."

"Jun, sorry to bother you. I need to go to Brooklyn; I'm pretty sure that Farrar is around there, somewhere in those old factories and wasteland along the water in Williamsburg and Greenpoint. I'm going to walk around, see if I can see anything."

"Why don't you call the cops?"

"After last night? They think I'm a jerk—no way they'll take me seriously. Besides, I'm pretty much grasping at straws."

Jun shrugged. "You sure you're well enough? What did they say at Bellevue?"

"I skipped my clinic appointment."

Jun shook his head. "Jenner, this sounds like a really bad idea."

"I can't just sit in my loft doing nothing." Jenner paused, then said, "Look, I'd like to borrow your gun."

"God, Jenner. This is *insane*." He leaned back against the door frame and sighed. "Okay. Let me get dressed."

Before Jenner could argue with him, he stepped back into his apartment. There was a muffled discussion in Japanese. A couple of minutes later, Jun opened the door and said, "Come in, I'll just be a second."

He disappeared into his bedroom. Jenner eased himself into a chair by Jun's desk. Kimi came out of the kitchen with a glass of water for Jenner. She put a hand on his shoulder as he drank, and said, "Please be careful."

Jenner nodded.

"And don't let him get in trouble with the police again, okay, Jenner?"

A few minutes later, Jun emerged, now in tight black leather pants, a white turtleneck, and trendy nerd glasses with thick black frames, a virulent orange faux fur coat draped over his arm. He checked himself out in the mirror, nodded in approval, then turned. On his bookcase was a large diorama of Godzilla rampaging through a train yard; Jun lifted the plinth to reveal a hidden compartment from which he pulled a black semiautomatic.

He showed it to Jenner. "It's a Smith & Wesson ten-millimeter pistol, just like the FBI."

"Ah, just like the FBI. Better than the nine?"

"They think so." He held it up. "Ten in the magazine, one in the chamber. This one's a bit finicky—be careful with the magazine release safety: if the magazine slips down even a little, the gun won't fire."

Jenner nodded vaguely.

Jun said, "Okay, now, this is cool." He flicked a tiny button on the trigger guard, then lifted the gun and pointed it at the far wall; a bright red bead of light appeared on a Transformer model on the shelf.

"Crimson Trace laser sights in the grip. It senses when you're aiming, and turns the laser on. With those sights, a Sunday school teacher who's never even *seen* a gun could take out a bad guy at ten yards."

" 'Take out a bad guy'? Been hanging out with cops?"

"Smith & Wesson puts on training sessions; in the coffee breaks, it's all about shooting bad guys . . ."

"You sound like an infomercial. Where's the safety?"

"Right here. This way, the trigger won't pull, to fire, like this. Sometimes you have to squeeze pretty hard."

Looking at his watch, Jenner nodded. "We should get moving—it'll be dark soon."

Jun lifted up his shirt and wedged the weapon into the band of his pants. He frowned, pulled it out, put on his coat, and pushed it into the pocket. He shrugged.

"What else? It's not too bright out—I'll bring a flashlight. Cell phone. MetroCard, iPod. I can't think of anything else."

"I can't either."

Jun paused. "Remind me again why we're not just calling the cops?"

"And tell them what? There must be hundreds of burned-out buildings and empty warehouses along that stretch. Anyway, they don't want to hear from me—I sent them there once, and I wasted their time. They remember things like that."

"So, what do we do if we find something?"

"*Then* we call the cops."

She could kill him. Wait for him to come to check on her, maybe make some noise to bring him closer, then just stab the knife into his face or his neck or something. God, how she loved the idea of slamming the knife into his chest with two hands, the look of stunned horror on his pocked face as she drove it in, seeing him stagger back as she pulled it out and stuck him again, his shirt filling with blood, his hot red blood spattering out of him, her wrists slippery with his blood as she kept on stabbing and stabbing and killing him. Maybe she would castrate him as he was dying, just hack his stuff off with her knife. She would stand over his dead body and spit on him. *I spit on your grave.*

But she knew it wouldn't go that way. She was weak, he was powerful; she was bound, he was fast; she was lying down, he was standing; she was in the dark, he was blinding her with that goddamn light. He'd see her coming, grab her arms, and take her knife away. And then he'd hurt her.

And he was up to something. He kept making short trips, coming back and moving things. That morning he'd been using the grindstone for hours, sharpening things. Whatever it was, it was going to happen soon.

She had to escape.

No matter how she tried, she couldn't cut her bonds. When she held the knife in her hands, she couldn't reach the ligature with enough pressure to actually cut into the coarse braid. She tried pinning the knife between her knees and rubbing the rope against it, but the knife kept slipping down, and it was hard to get it back. She was afraid she'd knock it away from herself and he'd come in and discover her trying to writhe her way over to it.

She decided to make her hole to get into the crawlspace first.

The floorboards that abutted the wall by her back were short; they'd been laid last, she figured, cut down from longer boards to fit. If she could pull up three of them, she thought she could get down underneath.

The rusting nails had rotted smooth by the passing years. Finding the nails by touch in the pitch-black, stroking the floor with the backs of her bound hands, was almost impossible, but it occurred to her that all she had to do was find one nail at one end of the plank: the other nails would be neatly arrayed in a line across the width of the board.

Getting the nails out was like trying to scoop baby powder with a twenty-pound pry bar. She had to dig around the nail heads with the blade, then lever them up with the back of the blade, usually finishing pulling the nail head out with her fingers. Sometimes the rusted heads broke off; those were almost impossible to pull out, but when she pried up the first board, the broken nails offered little resistance as the board rose.

She almost yelled in triumph when the first came up. Her shoulders shook a little from the effort, and she teared up, but she felt her energy surging as she started on the second. She worked faster now, her fingertips torn and bleeding, the sides of her fingers cut repeatedly as the knife slipped through her awkward grip.

The second board came up in a sudden shower of wood particles and dust that made her cough explosively. She heard his footsteps sprint toward the door.

She let the plank slide back into its position, covering the debris with her newspaper, and turned flat onto her back, putting her hands on her belly.

She heard him flick the catch, then closed her eyes, burning with wood dirt, as he threw the door open.

Her eyelids lit up yellow as he shone the light at her.

"What are you doing?" His voice was almost a scream.

"Nothing. I . . . I think I'm getting sick."

She heard him sniff the air.

"I smell blood."

"I'm getting my period. I need some . . . pads . . . or some cloth."

He was silent for a second. She had to have blood all over her T-shirt from her bleeding fingers.

He sniffed again, then said, "Use newspaper. You won't be here much longer, anyway."

The light went off her face, then flickered back onto it; he was looking around. She held her breath, then spoke again. "Please. I really need cloth. I have very heavy periods."

"I don't care. Use newspaper."

He sounded disgusted; he quickly pulled the door shut behind him, and she heard the latch close.

She almost laughed—she could read that fucker like a fucking book.

Farrar didn't trust her at all. And he didn't like that she was bleeding; for reasons he couldn't explain, it repelled him. *Disturbed* him. There was something unclean about it, unhealthy, unholy.

He was glad it wouldn't be long now. He was going to take his time with her, start in the late morning, stretch it out over the day. She was tough, and even though she now looked thin and drawn, he figured she'd go the distance.

He hadn't settled on the final details. He'd sharpened every cutting tool he had, from the hooked carpet knife he'd used to mortify himself for Father Martin all those years ago through to an ax—not the little hatchet he'd used on the Chinaman, but a full-sized ax.

He could do it almost any way he wanted. With Anastasia there was plenty of room for artistic license. He had starved her, of course, had fed her bread and water and salt. Now it was a simple question of how to cut her, where to put her up, where to burn her. Ideally, she should be found while she was still in flames. Night would be best, but the location was important, and he still hadn't figured it out.

He leaned back against the girl's door, listening. He could hear nothing, but he was sure the little bitch was up to something.

The bells at St. Stanislaus were tolling half past four.

Of course. St. Stanislaus. Behind the old granite church, there was a small cemetery with a large oak tree, hidden behind high, graffiti-covered walls. He could prepare her in the warehouse and then, when it was dark enough and late enough, move her to the church in the handcart, under a tarp. A couple of tarps, maybe, to stop any blood from soaking through. There would be risk, but at that time on that night, it would be fairly small.

He began to pull lengths of four-by-four together, laying out the main upright and the crossbeam strut for what would be the cross, checking the proportions.

It looked good. It had come together like something that was just meant to be.

He started up the generator and listened with satisfaction to the coughing roar as the nail gun compressor warmed up.

As Jun closed his front door, Jenner heard the muffled sound of his phone. Perhaps they'd found something . . . He hurriedly opened the door and picked up.

"Jenner, it's Dan Israel. You were supposed to be here at the court-house by three p.m.! You've got about fifteen minutes to get here, other-wise the judge will leave, and you'll be completely screwed."

"Sorry, Dan. I don't have time."

"Make the time! You don't show up, they'll send out a bench warrant and bring you in in cuffs. It's really important that you make it down here."

"I understand. I just can't make it."

"Maybe I can get the judge to stay a little longer, until a little after five o'clock."

"It's not going to happen, Dan. I really appreciate your help, but I just can't come down."

As he hung up, he heard the buzzer for the building entrance. He grabbed his coat and nodded his head toward the elevator.

"We'll get it on the way out."

When the elevator doors opened, they found a tall black woman in a FedEx uniform in the lobby, running her finger down the occupant list, a small package in her hands.

"You know what apartment Dr. Jenner is?"

He identified himself and took the package, looking it over warily. She waited for him to sign, glancing around the small lobby, once again cluttered with flyers. She tutted and said, "You guys need a new super. I was so sad about Pete—he was such a nice guy." She took the receipt and went out onto Crosby.

He turned to Jun.

"It's from Snowden, where Farrar comes from."

Don Slater's handwriting was surprisingly precise, with fat, looping o's and a's written with a fountain pen.

Dr. Jenner. Father Michael found these in drawer of writing desk after you left. Please forward to appropriate local agency when you have examined. Best, D. Slater.

It was a small sheaf of watercolors on the same heavy cream card stock he'd seen in Father Martin's drawer. More views of Manhattan, the skyline rising across the water. They were well done, the buildings readily recognizable, the outlines of the skyscrapers and bridges not weakened by the softness of the brushstrokes.

"They're not bad," murmured Jun.

Jenner was about to stick them in his mailbox when he stopped, looking at them more closely.

"Look at this . . . He's not dating them, but you can see these have the World Trade Center, while *these* . . ." He fanned the cards out on the lobby table, separating several of them. "These don't."

Jun said, "So these ones are more recent?"

Jenner nodded, scanning them more carefully.

"Wait a second . . ." He pointed at one of them. "Look—here you can see the Cortland Iron Building—you remember it? That huge fight between the preservationists and the developers, then six months ago, the developers demolished it during the night?"

He held up two of the views. In the first, the Cortland Iron Building, a battered brick warehouse with original painted advertising still visible along one side, was in the near foreground; in the second it was gone, replaced by low fencing covered with some kind of netting, reduced to another pile of rubble like the warehouse across from it.

"Father Dominic was wrong about when the letters stopped—Farrar was here, at this location, within the last six months."

He turned and walked to the elevator, turning to add, "We need an address for the Cortland Building; I'll go online. If we find the view in the postcard, we've found him."

And she was through.

She pulled up the last plank, rolling to lift it across her body. Her clothes were torn, her hands raw, every muscle was quivering, but she could get out of the room. She could escape.

She wriggled back onto the mattress and reached for the water jug.

Don't want to get too dehydrated. She drank, then forced herself to finish the bread from the morning.

She flashed her watch. Six o'clock.

She breathed out. The crawlspace couldn't be much deeper than a foot. Sixteen inches at the most. She could get into it, but the floor above would be right on top of her face, pressing down on her.

She imagined writhing her way under the floor, slowly being buried alive under rotting wood and the grime of a century, her every movement spraying more dirt into her hair and eyes and mouth, packing her nostrils and closing her throat. She wanted to be sick.

She drank more water.

She would crawl down into the hole, she would pull the mattress over it, and she would crawl or wriggle or writhe as long as she had to. She would escape.

But what if she got stuck? She imagined herself panicking, screaming as her mouth filled with dirt, her chest unable to suck the thick air down into her exploding lungs. Then the feeling of his rough hands as he grabbed her wrists and dragged her back.

Oh God—could *he* fit into the crawlspace? He was muscular, but he was wiry. He might. It would be a tight fit, but he might.

She took another gulp of water, then drained the bottle.

She breathed in, and then out, wriggling until her back was against the wall. She tucked her knees up, and then twisted to her left, easing her legs down into the hole. Her feet disappeared under the floorboards as she let her legs straighten, pushing herself gradually away from the wall.

Her hips started to slip under the floor, catching a little on the edges. Her back slid down the wall, shoulders scraping. Her knee locked as she tried to straighten, and there was sharp stinging as her stomach scraped across the broken nails. But she was now sitting in the crawlspace, her neck and upper chest and arms still in the room.

She stopped.

Had she heard him?

She listened.

Nothing.

Nothing at all.

She didn't like that. When he made noise, she knew where he was—his fucking grinding wheel was like the bell on a cat. But it was quiet, the building silent except for her panting. He could be moving toward her on tiptoe, ready to drag her out.

Then she thought of something worse: what if he'd been expecting her to do this, and was waiting under the floor for her? Waiting for her with a knife, or a cattle prod or meat hook or something.

Tears streamed down her face. She was losing it—the notion was ridiculous. She had to hold it together.

God, give me strength!

She closed her eyes and thought it again. God, give me strength. I'm scared and I'm all alone, and it's dark, and he wants to hurt me, and I don't know what I'm doing. Please help me. Jesus. Please help.

She thought of all the bad things she'd done, the lying, the cheating. The drugs. The men. The women. And she thought about how far she was from everything, just floating in this death-filled black void, trying not to die, trying to stay alive just a bit longer. The tears came faster now.

Help me, Jesus.

Her frozen fingers interlaced as she let her head bow down. Help me to find strength. Help me fight back. Help me to live. Let me live. Let me live and I will be good.

Her hands relaxed into the bonds, and as the tension in her muscles dropped, she felt the bonds slip a little on her forearms.

They were looser. She might be able to get them off.

She tugged them apart, worked her arms together and then apart, trying to coax some more give into the ropes.

She knew she had to leave right then, get out while she could. She could work on the bonds inside the crawlspace. Now she had to get out, go, start crawling. Because she was going to escape. She was going to get away, and lead back men who would kill this man.

The fucker. The fucker. The fucker. He was not going to kill her.

Time to go.

She stiffened her arms and swung them forward. With shaking fingers, she flashed her watch one more time, shone the feeble orange light around the room, fixing it in her memory. It would give her drive, it would push her on. The light failed and she pressed it again, turning her wrist now toward the door. The pictures.

There they all were, the girls he'd taken, the girls he'd taken and cut up and butchered and killed. Andie. All of them.

She was different. He was not going to kill her.

She slipped completely under the floorboards, sliding along, letting her arms follow her in an almost graceful curve, Ophelia sinking into the annihilating crawlspace.

She was escaping. Time to go.


Jenner couldn't get through—the Inquisitor Task Force line stayed busy. He finally reached the desk sergeant. Jenner tried to give his information, but the cop wasn't interested.

"Sorry, sir, Dr. Jennings, but we have a situation right now. There's been an incident at the Union Square subway station, and we're having a Level Four contingency response. If you have information for the squad or the Task Force, please call back and leave a message on the voice mail."

Jenner felt cold. An incident at Union Square requiring an All Hands response—*now* what?

He shook himself. He was out, he wasn't involved, it wasn't up to him to make decisions, to set up triage, to worry about the implications. Not his problem. He had to find Ana.

He turned to Jun. "Where's your car?"

"At the Lexus shop over on Eleventh Avenue. Routine maintenance."

Jenner shook his head. "We'll get a cab."

On the street it was mayhem. Ambulances were snarled in the jam of last-minute shoppers, and the air was filled with honking horns and yelping sirens. People streamed from the subway entrances as police officers waved away confused commuters.

On the corner of Houston and Crosby, they asked a cop directing traffic what was going on.

"Explosion at Union Square. They're shutting down the subway. Bridges and tunnels will probably be closed, too."

He turned his back to them, pointing both arms at a white box van idling at the light. He yelled, "You! *You!* Keep it moving! Wake up, buddy! I'm talking to you! Keep moving!" pointing his fingers at the driver and jerking both arms toward himself as he urged the van forward into the gridlocked intersection.

It was hopeless. Even if they could find a taxi, the streets were so choked now that nothing was budging.

He turned to Jun. "We have to walk. We can cut through the Lower East Side, over to Delancey, then go across the Williamsburg Bridge. Keep an eye out for taxis—maybe we can get across the bridge before they close it to traffic."

They walked quickly, setting off down Lafayette. After about twenty minutes, Jun spotted a livery cab that had just dropped off a passenger, an old black Lincoln Town Car with T&LC plates.

Jun waved at the driver, who flashed his lights. He was the tiniest Haitian man Jenner had ever seen, completely bald, without eyebrows, his trim little frame clad in a boxy black suit. The passenger-side window slid down smoothly. He leaned slightly toward them.

"Where do you want to go?" He had a thick accent, and pronounced the syllables with elaborate care, as if he was rolling marbles in his mouth.

"We need to go to Williamsburg. Down to the waterfront near Greenpoint."

The driver casually looked Jenner up and down, his eyes narrowing as he saw Jun and his expensive orange fur coat.

"That would be one hundred dollars."

Jun said, "But it's a ten-minute drive!"

"Not today. Today it is not ten minutes. It is not twenty minutes. It is maybe thirty minutes, if we are lucky. Maybe longer."

Jenner said, "Jun, it doesn't matter. We need to get there."

They got in the car.

"Please pay now."

Twenty minutes later, they were still inching east on Delancey. At Suffolk, the traffic ground to a complete halt. The blare of horns became deafening; drivers and passengers were getting out of their cars to peer ahead.

Jenner stood next to the Lincoln in the crook of the open door. To his left, a turbaned Sikh was talking into a cell phone next to a yellow cab with its Off Duty lights lit, gesturing to the unseen listener as he stared toward the bridge.

Jenner tapped him on the shoulder.

"Hey, do you know what's going on ahead?"

"Very bad! Bomb at Union Square. National Guard close bridge. No one can leave now! All bridges, all tunnels."

Jenner felt faint. He tapped on the livery cab's roof.

"Jun! Get out. They've closed the bridges and the tunnels. That explosion at Union Square was a bomb. They're shutting down Manhattan."

Jun climbed out and slammed the door. "What do we do?"

"We walk. They've got to be open to foot traffic."

Jun nodded. Jenner was already on the median, walking toward the bridge.

Behind Jenner, Jun looked back and slowly raised his middle finger to the livery car driver, now completely locked in immobile traffic. The little man shrugged, smiled softly, and held the one hundred dollars up, fanning out the twenties and waving them gently.

Farrar stood back and admired his work.

The stubby cross was finished, the four-by-fours nailed securely together. He'd kept the upright to almost seven feet; if he sank it fifteen inches into the ground, her feet would be supported a couple of inches off the earth. He would begin working on her up in his room, where he had all his tools, then carry her down to the courtyard. There he would put her on the cross and move her out of the warehouse buildings in the handcart. He would cover her with the tarps, toss on some junk, and any passing driver would dismiss him as just another homeless man with a cart out gathering scrap metal.

He looked out toward the river and realized that it had gone dark some time ago. He pulled his coat around himself, feeling the night's chill. The ground at the church would be frozen now; he'd need a tool to dig with if he was going to get the upright securely planted. For a second he wondered whether it was worth the extra effort, but he caught himself with a grin. As Father Martin used to say, "If a thing is worth doing, it's worth doing right." At least the bastard was right about something.

The streets would be empty when he wheeled her to the church, but when the first flames rose and the alarm was sounded, a crowd would quickly gather in the churchyard and witness it before the cops shut the scene down.

The thought warmed him. He wished he had a shovel, but it was something he'd never needed—he didn't bury his prey. His eyes lit on a five-foot cast-iron rail, an upright from a segment of Victorian fence he'd found near the Gowanus. He picked it up, felt its weight. It would do nicely.

He powered up the old generator, went back to his workbench, and began grinding the tip of the pole to a sharp, chisel-like edge.

Midway through he paused, turned, and made a few jabbing motions with the sharpened rail. It had a satisfying heft; it would make digging a posthole in the frozen cemetery ground as easy as scooping melted ice cream.

Holding the iron bar at its center, he spun it around like a windmill, his movements smooth and powerful. He was delighted—it really was the perfect size for him. He could put it to use for far more than just digging in the dirt.

He went back to sharpening it, relaxed at the thought of the pleasures the next twenty-four hours would bring. He thought about the girl lying in her little cell, listening to the grinding.

The National Guard blockade of the Williamsburg Bridge was utter chaos. The sergeant in charge, a pale young man who couldn't have been twenty-five, had stationed most of the men out on the bridge roads, waving back the approaching cars. Apparently following an established contingency plan, his men were detaining and searching vehicles SUV-size or larger. The combination of cars being turned back into the unyielding knot of blocked traffic, and larger vehicles being waved forward, only to be stopped for searching, had locked the intersection cold. The whole mess was made worse by the thin stream of inbound cars still filtering across from the Brooklyn side, blocking one possible exit for the cars trapped on the bridge approach.

Drivers were becoming increasingly upset, blasting their horns and shouting at each other. The blare of horns was punctuated by the sporadic crunch of low-speed impacts as drivers pushed and pulled their way through what was now something between a parking lot and a demolition derby, trying to get up over the median and back onto westbound Delancey Street.

In the crush of people squeezing onto the bridge's pedestrian walkway, Jenner could only spot Jun ahead of him because of his bright orange coat; any other day, he'd have given him hell about it. The press of bodies was becoming frightening; each surge carried him a little further forward, almost lifting him up off his feet. He kept one hand firmly on the wallet in his pants pocket and let the swelling crowd motion bear him toward the checkpoint.

He wondered if Jun could see him, knew how far behind he'd fallen.

The crowd's movements had become bizarrely random, buoying him forward, then carrying him back, to the left, to the right, with no net forward progress. There was yelling from the front of the line, and finally a guardsman made an announcement, his voice tinny and indistinct through the megaphone.

The sergeant had instructions to let no one pass; he moved onto the roadway, megaphone at his side, shouting across the full width of the inbound and outbound lanes at the men now stationed there, standing sullenly behind pale blue NYPD barriers, automatic rifles slung across their chests.

Jenner spotted Jun ahead and shuffled through the throng toward him. There were police helicopters above now, and looking over the crowd, he saw lights in the sky over the Brooklyn Bridge. Apparently all the bridges were cut off.

The subways were closed, the bridges were closed. The city was on fire, and they were stuck.


It was a nightmare, far worse than anything she'd imagined. She should've known right away: when she first went under, she felt herself starting to suffocate as she wriggled through the dirt and grime caked under the floorboards. She was on her back, the mattress pulled onto the hole she'd made, being swallowed whole by the dark. Grit was spattering from the flooring above her face, raining into her nose and eyes.

She had to turn over, get herself facedown, protect her eyes and nose and mouth. But when she tried to tilt to her right, her shoulder pressed up against the floorboards above her. She hunched her back and twisted more, tried to screw her torso around, but she couldn't do it.

She started to lose it and pushed harder, twisting her hips, trying to lengthen her torso, desperate to turn over. In an instant she was wedged, her left shoulder up against the floorboards, her right arm crushed underneath her, unable to move forward, stuck too tight to turn back. She panicked, flailing with her legs, clouds of choking dust eddying around her. Her head was thumping up against the joist, sending down showers of rotten wood and dirt, spilling into her ear and down her neck, edging her into hysteria.

She tried to regulate her breathing: breathe in for a count of five; slowly breathe out for a count of six. She calmed, and as she did, she could feel her position easing. After a few minutes, she was able to relax enough to let her left shoulder roll back down flat.

She lay there, thinking for a while. Then made her decision: she'd have to go back to the room.

She wriggled backward to the hole, arms stretched toward it, then pushed the mattress up and out of the way, raking her back against the edge as she pushed herself up into the room again.

She lay on the floor, panting. Here her breath came easily; cold air that had seemed dank an hour earlier now tasted clean and sweet. Lying on her side, breathing deeply, she shook as she imagined herself crawling back down into the asphyxiating crawlspace.

Then she heard him outside. Grinding. Grinding something, sharpening something. Something he probably was going to stick into her.

And she stopped crying, and got onto her hands and knees, and put her arms forward into the hole, and then her face, and then dragged herself forward, back into the void.

At around 9:30 p.m., the helicopters overhead stopped circling and moved off in formation. Looking downtown toward the harbor, Jenner saw the helicopters at the Brooklyn Bridge follow them. He and Jun were only a few yards from the barricades when word finally came through that there had been no bomb, that it was an explosion in an electrical substation that had ignited a Downtown 6 train. Several people were injured, some critically, but any wider implication to the blast had been ruled out.

Within minutes the crush at the walkway entrance was unbearable. The guardsmen hurried to remove the barricades, but they were too

slow for the crowd; Jenner saw beer cans and plastic cups flying overhead.

Just as the bottleneck seemed on the verge of going out of control,
an ESU van arrived, and a half-dozen cops in helmets and body armor
climbed out. Their sergeant spoke quickly with the National Guard sergeant, then started shouting out commands. Some of the guardsmen
were redeployed onto the bridge to help get the cars moving, and the
cops began funneling the pedestrians onto the walkway.

On the bridge, the path was wider, built to carry both bicycle and foot
traffic. Jenner turned back to look at the city. The sky was dark, the skyline crenellated by blocky office buildings, their facades grids of light and
dark metal. Beneath him, Delancey Street was all lit up for the holidays.
Looking uptown, he couldn't see any flames or smoke. There were sirens
everywhere, but they seemed to be responding to the chaos at the bridge;
he couldn't make out anything happening up toward the Union Square
area.

Jenner looked over to Brooklyn. Once they crossed the bridge, it was
probably only a couple of miles to where Ana was.

If she was even there.


They hurried across amid a streaming tide of people carrying briefcases,
Christmas gifts, shopping bags. There was little chatter on the bridge, the
crowds moving quickly and quietly, occasionally turning back to judge
the distance from the Manhattan anchorage, now lit up with spotlights,
or to search the skyline for smoke.

As they passed the Brooklyn anchorage, wrapped in scaffolding as part
of the never-ending structural work, floodlights came on, illuminating
the girders and meshwork and throwing shadows on the fabric netting
billowing and slacking in the wind.

The crowd spilled off the bridge onto Continental Army Plaza. Traffic on
the Brooklyn side was light; apparently word had got out about the bridge
closures, or they'd shut down the Brooklyn-Queens Expressway. Helmeted

cops were moving the cars and trucks forward; a platoon of National Guardsmen was assembling in front of the mounted statue of Washington.

Jenner and Jun headed away from the main mass of people, back toward the river; soon they were walking on empty streets. As they walked, the battered tenements gave way to old brick Victorian factories and warehouses. Nearer the waterfront, there were signs of gentrification, with billboards attached to the scaffolded facades promising expensive condominium loft developments. Downriver, toward DUMBO, cranes dotted the bank, tearing down the old and decrepit to better house the new and luxurious.

The neighborhood was desolate, and they were quite alone as they walked down the middle of the road, their shadows shortening before flipping and lengthening as they passed under the streetlights. Jun was tense, his hand hovering by his side as he scanned the empty side streets.

On Kent, they turned north. At the corner of South Second Street, Jenner paused under a streetlamp to check Farrar's small painting.

"Is this the area?"

Jenner shook his head. "No. It's a bit nearer to Greenpoint, maybe another mile."

They walked on the sidewalk now, neither speaking.

Farrar wasn't sure if he could wait until midnight to begin; the urge to start, to pull her out and start, was overwhelming. His eyes scanned the room, a final check that everything was in place.

He'd arranged large red and white pillar candles around the center of the room; this would be his main work area, the broad expanse of floor in the middle of which lay the cross. He'd laid kindling at the foot of the cross to make sure she knew what was coming.

He'd set his equipment out on a folded black towel on a large tin box. This project was a fairly simple one, and didn't require any complex instruments or elaborate props. The worn lid of his boxed set of six surgi-

cal knives lay open, showing off the deep indigo velvet lining, as luxurious now as it had been when it was made back in the nineteenth century.
The scalpels were unusually long, each with a traditional blade on one
end and a different tool on the other. In a catalogue of antique surgical tools, he'd discovered that one of those implements was a curette,
although he wasn't sure what curetting was. Of course, the intended
function of the implement was irrelevant; he had proven himself skilled
at improvising novel uses for the most obscure tools. The set was the best
thing he'd ever bought on eBay.

He checked to see that he had film for the Polaroid camera (he'd
never made the switch to digital, which was too clean, too *immediate*—he
liked the slow evolution of the image on the Polaroid, the way the shapes
gradually came into focus, the way a dark blur resolved itself into an
open mouth, for example, the red deepening behind).

Satisfied that everything was in place, he headed for her room; it was
time she learned what he would do to her.

She'd thought it would be easier. Even though her frame was slight, the
space was too tight for her to crawl on her hands and knees as she'd hoped.
Instead, she had to drag herself along, pulling herself forward with her elbows, and wriggling in a side-to-side motion, like some kind of lizard.

In the pitch-black, she had no sense of how far she had gone. Worse,
with all the wriggling, and after changing direction to get around a large
clay pipe, she'd become disoriented.

She lit her watch again, peering into the crawlspace ahead of her. The
orange light didn't reach far, dying into shadow a couple of feet ahead.
She couldn't see the next column, but assumed they'd be evenly spaced.
She was a couple of feet in front of one column: if she moved straight
forward, eventually she'd hit a wall.

Now her plan seemed like the worst plan in the world. There wasn't
going to be a hole in the planks, the floor wasn't going to give way and
pitch her into the room below, and freedom. Instead, she would crawl

under the floor for hours, maybe days, slowly dying of fatigue and hypothermia. She imagined herself curled up in the fetal position to keep warm as the life slowly flickered out of her. Imagined her body, shriveled like an old leaf, being discovered a couple of years later when the building was torn down or gut-renovated during conversion into expensive lofts. Imagined her death depicted in a cutaway diagram in *USA Today*, her body a little cartoon outline in blue, buried in the floor.

Then she heard his footsteps, felt the floorboards sag as he walked across the floor—*over her body*. She lay still, flattening her belly into the dirt, right cheek down, listening, hiding as if he might see her. Her heart was banging so hard in her chest, she could barely hear.

The footsteps stopped, then receded back in the direction from which they'd come.

There was silence for a second, and then the footsteps again, slow this time, interspersed with a slow grating noise; he was dragging something across the floor.

He reached his destination, let the object down with a heavy thud, then was still for a second.

Then he walked back over her, sending little showers of filth onto her hair and back.

She knew where he was walking: he was heading in the direction she'd come from. He was going to her cell. He was coming for her.

Astonished, Farrar scanned the empty room again, the beam from his flashlight jumping around crazily.

Then he saw it: over by the wall, a small hole through the floorboards, about a foot and a half wide and ten inches deep. She must have been hiding it with the mattress.

The hole was small—too small for him—but there was no other way out. She had to have gone through it.

He thought it through, considering her options and probable outcomes as if she were an SAT question. He was surprisingly calm.

If she'd gone through the floor, she'd have to come out at some point. Where did she think she was going? He'd explored the factory pretty thoroughly: there were no other holes on this floor. He was pretty sure that the ceiling of the floor below was intact, but he would check. So she had two options: come back up out of this hole, or make a new hole.

But how had she made this one? He squatted to examine the floor. The boards were rotting in the area, and the nails had largely rusted away. Still, it couldn't have been easy to get the planks up. Well, whatever: somehow she'd managed to get herself under the floor.

As he stood, he realized that there was also a third possible outcome: she could die under the floor.

The last one, of course, was an option for her, but not for him.

How could he get her to come out?

He remembered a biology class in fifth grade when they had walked onto the school's back lawn and poured bleach onto the ground. Within minutes, dozens of worms were writhing on the earth, obscenely pink against the emerald grass, the glistening mucus of their surfaces foamy with irritant secretions.

He could certainly do that. He'd downloaded recipes for making vesicant gases, chemicals he could release into the crawlspace to make her skin blister and bubble, leave her eyeballs opaque and leathery. But would he be able to control the gas? There would be a significant risk to him. And while gassing her might be satisfying, he wanted her beautiful for the transformation.

He relaxed. He had a full day to play with her: it would be like playing Whack-a-Mole at the fairground. He would use his new cast-iron spear—it was sharp and heavy enough to go right through the floorboards. And even if he did impale her, he could still use her.

He went into the main room and picked up the pole. He held it horizontally, loosely in both hands, bouncing it a little, feeling its mass. Where to begin?

He paused for a second, then ran across the room almost to the door of her cell and drove the bar into the floor with all his strength, as if he were pole-vaulting. The tip of the heavy rod slammed through the wood with a splintering crunch, and plunged into the subfloor.

There was a muffled moan of surprise and fear; he couldn't pinpoint the origin, but the pathetic little shriek made him laugh out loud. He knew he hadn't hit her.

Time to go again.

He sprinted diagonally across the large room, raised the pole to shoulder length, and brought it down in an arc to plunge through the floor.

He straightened and stood there, leaning on the pole as he ground it in the hole, smiling happily in the candlelight.

In the glow of Jun's flashlight, Jenner squinted at Farrar's painting, then peered down toward the river, a glinting black ribbon at the end of the derelict street.

They were there. To their left was the scaffolding and tarp material in the big lot where the Cortland Iron Building had been. None of the buildings on the street were visible in the painting, but the view of Manhattan across the East River—up toward the Empire State Building on Thirty-fourth, now lit in Christmas red and green, the slender, hubcap-shouldered spire of the Chrysler Building on Forty-second, the slanted top of the Citicorp Building on Fifty-third—aligned neatly with those in the image, like a jungle treasure map in an old adventure serial.

Jenner felt his stomach tighten. They were well away from the houses and the tenements, with their warmth and light and people; the worn streets of the waterfront warehouse district were desolate and dark. In some areas, old cobblestones poked through the battered road surfaces. The only light was back at the intersection, where a bare bulb in a protective wire cage dangled like a hanged man from a small plywood yardarm on the front of a small storage facility; as the breeze picked up, yellow light flickered weakly on the roadway, making the melting snow glisten.

Jenner looked down at the picture.

"Yes. I think this is the street."

They stood together looking toward the water. Callyer's Slip was a dark street of ramshackle warehouses, their leaking roofs covered with corrugated metal sheeting, closed off from passersby with roll-down steel security gates. Both sides of the street had been fenced off behind tall poles and barrier fencing, with coils of razor wire running along the top. In the middle of the block on their right was a vacant lot, a demilitarized zone between buildings that were derelict and those still clinging to life. Beyond the empty lot, opposite the remains of the Cortland Iron Building, Jenner could make out an enormous old warehouse, staggering on sinking foundations and sagging arches, its windows gaping black shadows in the rotting masonry; it seemed to reach all the way down the block to the river.

The wind picked up again, and he saw Jun was shivering.

"Hey, Jenner—you know, there aren't any phones near here. Last one I saw, like, on Quay Street, about half a mile back, the phone was torn off."

"It's okay—I've got my cell phone."

"Have you checked it? I'm not getting a signal down here."

Jenner took it out and handed it to Jun. Jun flipped it open, shut it, and reopened it. "One bar."

He put it to his ear. "No signal."

It began to rain, a fine misting rain that chilled their skin and beaded on their clothes. Jun put his hood up. Jenner turned up his collar and said, "I think it'll be down toward the end, one of those abandoned buildings by the river. It would be safe for him—most days, this street's probably pretty dead by four p.m. Maybe we'll get a signal nearer the water."

They started toward the river, their damp footsteps ringing off the corrugated metal sheeting covering the windows of an old garage.

\*   \*   \*

Ana lay on her belly, panting, face flattened in the oily grime, feeling the pain howling in her thigh from where he'd speared her, feeling the stickiness of the blood soaking her pants.

How long had he been hunting her? An hour? It had to be more. It felt like forever.

He'd sliced across her right leg. She was so cold now that her wound was going numb.

How badly had he got her? She thought it was just shallow—surely it would have felt much worse had he got the spike deep in her. She wished she could look at it. Or maybe not.

He'd developed an attack pattern: before each strike, he'd talk to her, murmur things to her, things she couldn't hear with both her hands pressed hard over her ears, blocking him out, trying not to make a sound. Then he'd take a couple of steps back, and sprint full speed across the room to slam the pole through the floor into the crawlspace.

At first, she'd panicked and scrambled away, but then she realized that, after each attack, he was staying stone silent, listening for her to betray her position. There'd be a pause, then again he'd come tearing across the room, and she couldn't tell where he was coming from, where he was going to, and she didn't know if she should move, didn't know if he'd figured out where she was, and then there would be a horrible crash as the pole smashed into the crawlspace, spraying splinters and dirt everywhere.

Eventually he got her. She'd felt the weapon, sharp as a knife, heavy as lead, carve across her thigh and into the floor underneath her, felt the searing sting, felt the warmth of her blood spreading across her skin. Reached down her leg, touched her fingers to the hole in her pants, to the wet gash of torn skin and flesh underneath.

As she lay there smothering her sobs, he padded back to the other side of the room for his next run-up. She thought his strikes had been random: she'd been too quiet for him to figure out her position. She decided not to move, expecting his next strike would be well away from that spot.

But then she realized that her blood would be on the pole. Would he see it? She imagined him getting ready to run, holding it up, and then spotting blood on the tip.

She had to move, but her body had lost the ability. Her muscles were exhausted, her legs wouldn't budge. She forced herself to imagine the spear plunging into her, through her filthy shirt, through her skin, shattering ribs to impale her heart, imagined it as painful as sticking her fist into a deep fryer.

That was enough. She dug her elbows in, forced herself forward. She dragged her injured leg behind her, pulling it as if it were a bundle tied to her waist by a length of cloth. And when she moved, she wasn't numb anymore. It hurt. It hurt, it hurt, it hurt.

She pitched forward, and for the first time let her face sink down fully into the layer of grime. She lay there. She felt her scalp tickling, and when she reached up to her hair, her hand came away wet and sticky.

Blood. She must have hit her head.

She closed her eyes, let her arm drop down. She lay still, panting.

Then she heard him taking his wind-up steps. He paced back a couple of paces, then . . . nothing.

She heard a dull, metallic thud, as he let the handle of the pole hit the ground.

He'd spotted the blood, of course. He was looking at her blood on his spear, knowing he'd hurt her.

She heard the steps again, getting closer. Walking over her. He was going to inspect the hole he'd made, see if he'd killed her.

She willed herself to stop breathing.

Then, in the silence, she heard something strange, a dry, rhythmic sound. She closed her eyes tight and listened harder.

It came again. Little breathy puffs, repeated in short cycles.

And then she knew exactly what he was doing—she could almost see him lying there, body stretched out on the floor next to the hole he'd made when he'd hit her, poking his nose into the hole and sniffing. Sniffing at her blood, as if she were some kind of animal.

And once again, she told herself that she was going to live. She was going to live, if only to see this man die. She wouldn't wait for others, she'd do it herself, she'd kill him herself. Kill him like the animal he was. She would kill him for taking her, for killing Andie, for killing Garcia, for killing Tony Roggetti and maybe Jenner, too.

She pushed herself up and began to pull her body forward.

For him, the smell of blood had the sort of warm, centering effect that the smell of baking bread had on others. He lay with his face near the spear hole, breathing in the smell, wet and primal, like rust-stained wood.

He was calmer. What had he been thinking? He mustn't damage her badly, not yet.

He could tell from the scent that there was not a lot of blood; he didn't think he'd inflicted a mortal wound. But he could have, and that would have been bad. What if she'd died before he could kill her properly? He cursed his childish rush to instant gratification.

He rolled over to peer into the hole. There was nothing visible beneath it, and he could hear nothing. There was just the smell of blood.

He rolled onto his back, feeling a heat spreading over his middle. It appealed to him tremendously, her being trapped underfoot. He wanted to play with her a bit longer while she was down there. Eventually he'd winkle her out of her little hidey-hole, and then turn her out in ways she couldn't imagine, not even in her worst nightmares in her cell.

Over on his workbench, he could see the silhouette of his nail gun. If he could get the nail gun underneath the floor . . .

As long as he avoided her head, it would be fun. The gas-powered compressor was old and noisy, and the noise coming from a supposedly abandoned building might draw attention. Still, tonight the risk seemed pretty low, and if there were a more worthy project, he couldn't imagine it.

He ran his finger over the tip of the pole, touching the traces of the girl's blood. He rubbed some onto his upper lip, felt the intake of his breath draw her smell up into his nose, into his sinuses, warming it, making the little molecules of blood dance in the inner chambers of his head. Under closed lids, his eyeballs fluttered up inside their sockets.

Jenner stood looking down to the water. There was nothing. The street was dead, the buildings still in use—legit auto body shops to full-on chop shops, Jenner figured—closed down tight as a drum, the abandoned buildings all dilapidated beyond the point of habitation. No movement, no light, no heat.

They stood by the lot, against the fence, its base plastered with trapped scraps of newspaper and fluttering plastic bags. The light from their flashlights played across the field, a blighted wasteland of illegally dumped trash, covered with a spotty layer of grimy snow and punctuated by the shells of old appliances.

He could hear Jun's teeth chattering; the guilt he felt angered him.

He'd dragged Jun out for nothing. He'd been wrong about the street— no, not wrong about the street, it was certainly the street in Farrar's picture, but he'd made the jump to believing that this was where Farrar would have the girl, and then another to thinking that he would just walk down the street, find the girl, and save her.

He'd read too many books, seen too many movies. Who was he kidding? This was real life, and there was no sign of Farrar, no sign of Ana. Even if there had been, Farrar would have killed them before they got anywhere near the girl, would have cut him in two without blinking an eye; Jenner would never forget how the man had moved on the loading dock on Crosby Street.

Why had he even thought he had a chance against him? Not in this world, not in the real world.

They walked down to the waterfront, in front of the vast factory. At some point, a fire had stained the brick around the windows with thick smears of soot, and through the empty ground-floor windows Jenner could make out much of the collapsed roof, snow-mounded piles of rubble and broken joists.

He realized how tired he was. This was pointless.

"We'll go down nearer the river, and if we don't see anything else, we'll head home and . . . figure out our next step."

Jun nodded. They moved in silence, neither really focusing on the buildings around them anymore, the last walk a glum gesture, a symbol of what they'd tried to do for her.

They walked the high fencing and razor wire the entire length of the ruined factory, all the way to the waterfront. The fencing ran out over the water along a concrete jetty; at the end of the jetty, one side of the pier sagged into the water.

Across the river in the mist, the buildings of Manhattan were spangled in light, below them the cars on the FDR a glimmering necklace.

Across the street, a crane sat among the heaps of crushed brick and metal and glass in the Cortland Iron Building lot. The views from the condos that would go up here would be amazing. Large Dumpsters sat on each side of the gate, resting like barges on mud turned pink from brick dust. The brick mud flowed out of the entranceway all the way to their feet, a river of pulverized building.

Jun looked down and cursed. "Great! These are Prada. I paid four hundred dollars last week at the SoHo store—I'll stick to Payless in future."

He leaned against a fence pole and began wiping brick mud from his shoes. Jenner, watching, straightened.

"Jun. I wasn't wrong. This is the place . . ."

"What?"

"When she was talking about the night her roommate died, Ana told Rad the man had pink mud on his boots. We're standing in it."

Jun pointed his flashlight at their feet.

"Jenner, it looks a little pink, maybe, but there's nothing around here. It's dead."

They stood there in silence. Maybe Jun was right—there was crushed brick around the entire city.

Then, from somewhere far behind them in the dark heart of the ruined factory, they heard a gas engine start up.

"So, what do we do?"

Jenner said, "We . . . we have to get a closer look. If it's anything, we'll call the police, okay?"

Jun pulled out his cell phone, flicked it open. "On what? We still don't have reception."

"Maybe you should wait here. I'll go check it out, and signal you if we need to get the police."

"Jenner, what is this, Boy Scout camp? 'Signal' me? I'll come with you. If we actually find something, then I'll go for the police."

Jenner nodded.

"I think we can get past the fence over there on the pier."

Out on the concrete jetty, the engine was louder across the water.

The factory was much larger than they'd imagined: the burned-out brick shell that ran along Callyer's Slip was just the southern-most wing of a larger complex. Behind the boarded-up waterfront facade, they could make out an old loading dock under a high arch-way, and beyond the dock a central courtyard, piled high with bricks and refuse.

The chain-link fence in front of the warehouse ran along the jetty for some yards. Jenner grabbed the fencing and tugged it hard; the mesh rattled, slightly loose against the uprights, leaving enough space to wedge a foot underneath onto the concrete. There was room for them to move along the fence on the water side all the way back to the riverbank. They made their way along the pier, clinging to the slippery fence with aching fingers. Jun made it to land first, and stood, stretching out a hand to Jenner. The mesh recoiled with a tinny spring as Jenner stepped onto the hard ground.

Jun said, "There's got to be another way. I can't believe he's been get-ting in and out along that fence, climbing along the pier every time."

Jenner looked into the dark ruins and muttered, "We should keep it quiet. Who knows if he's watching out."

Jun shrugged. "Who knows if it's even him."

They looked up at the hulking factory. The building was actually four huge wings around a central quadrangle. Caked black soot from the fire surrounded almost all of the windows; none had glass. Part of the facade along the waterfront had collapsed, and much of the roofing was gone. The boat slip ahead was under a broad Roman arch, its width spanned near the top by a rusted iron gantry, the loading dock and landings beneath sheathed in shadow.

They made their way along the narrow embankment, the path overgrown from years of neglect. They kept their flashlights off, the walkway barely visible in the dim light of the damp night.

They turned the corner and moved toward the dock area. Under the big arch, the sound of the engine grew louder, rattling around the damp walls. The path ahead disappeared into the dark recesses of the slip. Jenner wrapped the flashlight in his scarf to dim it, and shone the faint beam in front of them; it was better than nothing. They moved toward the sound, toward the center of the factory.

Jenner came to a stop.

"Fuck."

On the far side of the gantry, the walkway was blocked by a ten-foot-tall fence, the top heavily garlanded with razor wire. The fencing looked new, probably put up when they'd fenced off the waterfront for demolition and new construction. It ran several feet out over the water to an upright that had also been wound with razor wire. There was no give to the fence when he pulled on it, and in the light of Jenner's flashlight, there was not enough room to get under.

Jun nudged his elbow and murmured, "Look."

Jenner followed the beam of Jun's flashlight in front of them. Jun slid the light along the upright for the gantry. He was right: it looked climbable.

\* \* \*

Farrar was ready: time to make things a little more interesting.

He dragged the rattling compressor over to the big windows, careful not to burn himself on the hot engine. It was an ancient Rol Air, the housing battered and the thick rubber air hose chewed up and frayed. He'd soldered the safety lock so that he no longer had to press the nail gun against a surface to fire it: now it was point-and-click.

Smirking at his own geeky joke, he glanced around the room. The floor was now pocked with gaping holes; using the sharpened bar and his hatchet, he'd enlarged many of them so that he could get his nail gun down into the crawlspace. In the far corner, working under cover of the noise and vibration of the compressor, he'd pried up several floorboards to create the hole through which he'd eventually extract her.

He fought the urge to whistle.

The compressor had probably done its job by now. It took a little while for the old machine to build up a head of pressure, but once it had, the gun could fire a three-and-a-half-inch roofing nail right out the other side of a two-by-four.

He knew very well where she was—over by the two big windows at the end of the long room, opposite where he needed her to go.

He hefted the nail gun, the hose draping over his arm like a python. It felt good, an extension of his hand, the tubing one of his arteries blasting air down to the gun in his fist. He would take one shot at close range, just the one, for fun; the chance that he'd hit anything vital was small. One close-range, then after that he'd take his time, herd her toward the exit hole with more distant shots, wounds meant to puncture, to goad, not to kill or maim. But the first one, that was a freebie, that was just for kicks.

With the compressor roaring away near her head, she wouldn't hear him coming; even so, he stepped softly as he walked across the floor. The surprise would be part of the fun, her discovering he knew exactly where she was.

Standing by the engine, he picked up the nail gun. He studied the floor in front of him, tried to visualize her lying underneath his feet.

After a few seconds, he bent over and pressed the muzzle of the nail gun to the wood.

He breathed in deeply, closed his eyes, and held his breath. Then he squeezed the trigger.

There was a surprisingly loud bang as the nail shot right through the rotten floorboard, and an immediate yelp of pain.

On his knees now, he listened excitedly for her movements, trying to figure out which way she was moving, but he could hear nothing but the noise of the compressor. Swearing, he grabbed the machine and quickly dragged it to the other side of the room. He dropped to his belly and crept across the floor as slowly and quietly as he could.

He could hear her under the floorboards, snuffling and gasping. She was moving away from the stairway, he thought, moving along the window wall, dragging herself through the crawlspace, whimpering like a bitch as she crawled.

He pressed his face to the floor, his ear over one of the holes, trying to get a sense of how far she'd moved.

A bit farther, she'd moved a bit farther.

He crawled forward, nail gun in his left hand, the stiff hose scraping the floor as it dragged behind him. He moved toward the far wall and placed his ear over the nearest hole.

It was silent. She was holding her breath, the bitch was holding her breath!

Or dead, it occurred to him. She could be dead. The thought unsettled him, the idea that after all his planning, his building, the wooden cross ready for her body, his beautifully chosen site, after all that, her pointless attempt to get away might spoil his project. He had such little respect for her now that he could just *spit*.

He listened, holding his own breath, like a doctor being careful not to mistake his own pulse for that of his patient.

Silence.

Then there was a quiet rustle, the faintest sound of fabric brushing wood. She was alive!

He closed his eyes tight to listen, pressing his head down against the floor, trying to seal his ear against the hole.

The corkscrew drove right through his cheek, goring the roof of his mouth as she punched it into his head, ripped it back downward, hooked his face down against the dark hole. Howling in pain and shock, he tried to push himself up, but she fought him, twisting her fist away from him. He finally jerked to his feet, tearing his cheek wide open.

He staggered through the room in agony, his fingers struggling to press the torn flap against his face, his wrist already slippery with blood.

He ran back to where she was, stood over her body, and stomped the floor with his boots, screaming wetly at her, telling her how he'd open her up and show her her insides, how he would let the rats eat her guts until she begged him to kill her, his bloody spit spraying onto the floor.

And when he calmed to quiet sobbing, he heard another sound, a sound he'd never heard in any of the projects. A sound he hadn't heard since he was a boy.

She was laughing at him.


Jun was waiting for Jenner on the gantry landing, catching his breath, when they heard a gunshot, clear and sharp. Jenner ignored it and kept climbing, the muscles on his side shrieking from the effort.

Jun knelt and reached out to Jenner, pulling him up onto the landing. "You hear that?"

Jenner nodded. "I'll go across first."

They had made their way to the top of the steps to the gantry crossbeam when they heard the screaming.

"Christ, Jenner! What is that? Is it her?"

"Just keep moving. If it can take my weight, you'll be fine."

His heart was racing. The screeching cut through the throb of the engine, echoing through the archway like some Halloween-house sound effect.

The gantry in front of him was badly rusted, but it had hefted thousands of pounds in the past. Besides, if he fell, it was a twenty-foot drop into water, not onto the glass-strewn rubble on the bank.

The howling ringing in his ears, he edged out onto the span girder, steadying himself against the curve of the arch overhead as he moved, shimmying sideways, telling himself the screaming was a man. The air near his head reeked of damp and ammonia.

He moved along the gantry over the slip, his feet sending scatters of rust pelting down into the water.

"Keep going, Jenner. You're almost there."

The girder rim felt soft underneath his foot as he passed the halfway point.

"Jun, shine your flashlight at my feet. It's rusted pretty bad."

The screaming stopped. The engine sounded louder as he crossed, thicker.

The beam at his feet revealed flaking leaves of rusted iron, barely held together by a peeling layer of paint. He scuffed at it with his foot, then pressed softly.

"It's rusty, but I think it's solid—maybe you should cross on the other side of the girder."

He wrapped his arms around the chest-level upper girder and continued, placing his feet carefully before gingerly easing his weight down.

When he reached the gantry deck on the far side, he turned and was surprised to see Jun already almost halfway across behind him. He stood on the deck, catching his breath as he lit Jun's path.

Jun eased past the central girder, clinging to the upper girder tightly as he edged across.

"Damn. It's even more rusted here. I'm going to cross over."

He pulled himself onto the upper girder, hugged it with his arms, and slipped over onto the other side, gently letting his feet down onto the girder rim.

He breathed out, gave Jenner a nod, and continued.

With his first step, a broad slab of rusted iron broke from the girder beneath him, pitching him down into the abyss. Jenner saw him hit a crossbeam, then spin off, hitting the water with a huge splash, and disappearing under the surface.

Jenner clambered down the gantry anchorage as quickly as he could, dropping the last ten feet.

"Jun!"

He shone the beam of light over the water. Nothing. How deep could it be?

"*Jun!*"

He tore off his coat, and was about to dive when Jun broke the surface, choking and gasping, spewing water, blood flowing freely from his head, black and glossy in the night, brilliant red under Jenner's bare light.

Jenner knelt at the edge to reach for him.

"Over here! Jun!"

Jun swam toward him, then shook his head violently, turned, and began to swim away.

"Where are you going? You're bleeding . . ."

Jun put his hand to his head.

"My head hit something." His breath was a mist over the surface of the water. His teeth were chattering. "I think I'm okay . . . fucking coat almost drowned me."

He brushed a hand to his head, saw more blood.

With some effort, he paddled back toward Jenner's outstretched arm, but before he reached him, he stopped.

"Take my hand! Come on!"

Jun shook his head, spitting out the foul water as he struggled with his waterlogged coat. He finally pulled free; he lifted his arm and pushed the pistol up onto the landing.

"Jenner, take the gun! I've got to get out of the water. I'm going to try to swim back past the fence here, get the police. You have to go ahead."

Jenner watched his friend as he swam unevenly toward the far side of the loading dock. From somewhere in the building behind him, he heard more gunshots, the reports echoing over the loading dock.

Jenner turned to the sound of the shots, took a step, and then looked back to Jun; he seemed to be slowing.

Jun yelled, "*Go!* I'll be all right. Find Ana!"

Jenner moved toward the courtyard, trying to decide which way he should head.

From the corner of his eye, he caught movement in the water and spun around, the gun in his hand raised.

Lashed to the pilings of the landing was a body, waist deep in the water, rolling with the slip's soft current.

*Ana.*

In the light of his flashlight he saw the body of a young adult, the face and upper torso nearly skeletonized, the skull spackled with putrid white flesh where the skin hadn't rotted through, the scalp hair short and black.

It wasn't her.

He stepped backward, staring at the piling. The body was loosely tied, perhaps deliberately, so that it could move with the tides and the waves. The dead reanimated.

No time for this. He turned and went into the courtyard, toward the gunshots, the pistol clenched tight in his fist.


She couldn't win. She couldn't win. She was going to die now.

She barely heard the shot as another nail hit her thigh. Almost unconsciously, her body twitched and began to move, dragging her with it.

She must be pretty messed up. Her elbows were raw, the skin of her back scraped bare against the trusses, raked by nails, her scalp and hair crusted with blood. And God only knew how her legs looked! She giggled at her vanity, the tears building in her eyes.

There was another bang, the burn of another nail, her left calf this time, she thought. Again her body lurched forward. Dragged a few more inches, then slumped.

She was done. She had nothing left. It was all gone, spent on trying to escape this fucking monster and his fucking castle.

Her eyes burned.

She lay half-conscious, waiting for the next nail, unable to move. She couldn't hear him anymore, couldn't feel the vibration of his approaching steps—she was close to the engine now, and the noise was deafening.

She wished she could turn over, so she could die on her back, looking up through the floorboards, through the roof, up through the sky to heaven.

She let her cheek down into the filth—what did it matter now? The cold helped her body fall away from her.

She said her prayers. God bless everyone she knew. Mom and Dad. Gram. Uncle Douggie. Rad and Joey. Andie. The tears were back. Jenner. She told herself she'd see her mom and dad soon. And Ana; God bless Ana.

Who was left to go to her funeral? Jenner. Would he visit her grave? Kneel down in the cemetery, put flowers there or something? He'd do that. He was good. Jenner was good. He would kneel down by her grave, a hand on the headstone.

Here lies Ana de Jong, born . . . Wait . . . when did she die? She snuffled a little, and slid her wrist, painfully slowly, in front of her face, fumbled at the button.

The orange light flared in her face, blinding her for a second.

Her eyes adjusted slowly.

Twelve-oh-three a.m. December 25.

Wait . . . Still holding her watch in front of her, she pressed the button again to make sure.

Yes, Christmas.

She straightened her arm, and the orange glare lit up the face of Robert Farrar, lying right next to her under the floor, bloody teeth smiling through what was left of his mouth.

Jenner knew the building as soon as he stepped into the quadrangle—sheets of clear plastic covered the windows on the top floor, while all the other courtyard windows either gaped empty or were sealed with sheets of painted plywood.

To reach the main entrance, he had to clamber over the heaped debris in the courtyard. There was a big handcart leaned up against the sealed doorway; he tipped it aside to climb through the large hole smashed through the concrete block.

He took the stairs as quickly as he could, wary that his footsteps might be heard above the engine. He was out of breath; he would take a couple of seconds to pull himself together on the first landing where the stairs turned to the left.

He stepped quietly onto the landing, one hand on the balustrade. The floor immediately collapsed, his legs dropping out from underneath him, his hip slamming onto broken flooring, sliding down into darkness. The gun spun out of his hand as he slipped, desperately trying to anchor himself on the stairs with his elbows. He grabbed hold of a railing in the dark, legs kicking the air wildly as he swung by one arm, then gradually pulled himself up onto the remains of the stairs. He crawled upward on his belly, checking that the runners underneath him were solid, before pulling himself to a kneeling position.

He lay there stunned and breathless, his left arm throbbing as if it had almost been torn out of its socket, tears in his eyes. He'd lost his gun.

The flashlight beam spread across the step in front of him; he picked it up and shone it onto the landing.

It hadn't been an accident: the floorboards near the continuation of the staircase were intact, and the boards that had collapsed had fallen as a single panel. He shone the light inside the hole: under the stairs, a handful of stakes and metal poles bristled upward, their crudely sharpened tips pointing up, ready to impale anyone who tried to climb the staircase.

Jenner looked down at his leg and saw blood soaking through near his left calf. Christ.

He had to keep moving.

He scanned the floor around the spikes, looking for the gun. No sign of it, nor on the stairs. He pulled himself closer to the railing and shone the light down onto the floor below. The pistol lay on top of the rubble.

He stepped awkwardly over the gaping landing and limped slowly down the stairs to pick up the gun. Then he went back up again, this time testing each tread with his hands before stepping on it. On the top floor, he pressed himself against the wall, unsure whether Farrar could see him, unable to trust his footing, wondering what other little surprises the man had in store for unexpected visitors.

The shooting had stopped.

Jenner knelt, and peered cautiously around the corner. The factory floor stretched away in front of him. He could see no movement.

The vast room had been partitioned off with clear plastic sheeting framed clumsily with two-by-fours; a flap of untethered plastic stirred at his approach—the entrance.

The inner room was ringed with lit candles, the flames flickering with the breeze as the plastic flap slipped shut behind him. On the floor near the entry lay a wooden assembly; coming closer, he saw that it was a human-size cross.

He held the gun, felt warmed by its weight, by how solid it felt in his palm, pointing, ready to kill. He pressed the button, and a red dot magically appeared on the floor in front of him; he aimed at the wall in front of him, the fine red beam faint but reassuring. It occurred to him that he didn't know if the safety should be in the forward or back position; too late now.

A gas-powered air compressor rattled away in the opposite corner; maybe his arrival hadn't been noticed.

He quietly took another step forward. He paused, listening. He could hear nothing over the compressor engine; but then, if Farrar was around, neither could he.

Jenner moved slowly across to the far side of the room. The floor was pockmarked with large holes. Immediately to his right was an unlit room, an unlocked padlock dangling from the open metal latch, the door ajar. Beyond it, a wall of windows looked out over the river.

He breathed in, held the gun up, and stepped quickly back as he pushed the door forward.

Nothing.

Pointing the muzzle of the gun into the pitch-black cell, he leaned forward, then directed the beam into the tiny side room. It wasn't much more than a closet, on the floor a bowl with water, a filthy mattress, and a couple of threadbare blankets. He stepped inside. Just beyond the mattress was a large hole in the floorboards near the outer wall—no wonder the room was so cold.

Turning to leave, he was stopped by an array of photographs nailed to the door. They were all there—Andie Delore, Katherine Smith, Barbara Wexler, and Lucy Fiore, each image wreathed in dense Coptic text.

Holding the gun tighter, he stepped back into the main room. The bead of his laser sight skipped from surface to surface. To his right was a workbench, scattered with tools and unusual objects; lined up neatly on a small tray was a set of antique scalpels, and behind them a small case with what appeared to be lancets. Next to the tray were several peacock feathers and a small box of hunting arrow tips. There was a loaded homemade crossbow and some assembled arrows, and a vise of the sort used for tying trout flies.

There were actually two engines running, the air compressor and a more raucous gas-powered generator at the end of the bench. The workbench had a familiar smell, dry and powdery with a metallic tang; in the middle of the clutter, a slender soldering iron emitted fine wisps of white smoke. Next to it, fitted together like pieces of a jigsaw puzzle, were the remaining fragments of the original Coptic manuscript, now just flaked fragments of tan parchment.

*Where were they?*

Maybe Farrar was out, foraging for supplies; from the looks of it, he seemed to be getting by mostly by scavenging. But he wouldn't leave the soldering iron on like that, let alone the generator and compressor.

No, he was here.

Jenner turned to face the empty room.

Could they have left the building? He walked over to the windows and peeled back the plastic to peer down on the ground below. This wing, too, was surrounded by a rubble-strewn wasteland.

He turned back to the room, uncertain.

He shone his beam around the room. Then he heard a grunt.

He turned off the flashlight immediately and pressed against the wall in the shadows, squinting into the space, trying to find the source of the sound. There was another grunt, and a silhouette began to take shape in front of the compressor, swelling up from the floorboards.

It resolved itself into the shadow of a man, but instead of standing, he remained bent, worrying at something at his feet. Slowly, the man dragged another body out onto the floorboards, then stood straight.

Farrar turned and immediately saw Jenner.

He took a step toward him, uncertain.

Jenner said, "Don't move. I have a gun. I'll kill you if you give me an excuse."

He held his arm forward a little so that Farrar could see the pistol.

Without a word, Farrar dipped to one side and began to run at Jenner.

Above the noise of the engines, he heard Ana shout, "He's got an ax!"

He squeezed the trigger, but it wouldn't budge, and Farrar kept coming. Jenner fumbled for the safety, couldn't shift it, threw the weapon down, grabbed the crossbow from the desk, and spun around to pull the trigger.

The crossbow bolt shot into Farrar's chest, near his left shoulder. He staggered in surprise, stopped and coughed.

Jenner frantically searched the bench top, hands tearing up the surface, feeling for another bolt, but all he could see were arrows. His scrambling fingers tipped a narrow box, spilling stubby crossbow bolts across the bench. Jenner grabbed a bolt, pushed it into the groove, and started to pull the bowstring back.

Farrar was standing halfway across the room, staring at the shaft of the crossbow bolt sticking out of his chest, his breath coming in fast gulps. He coughed again, spitting blood.

The bowstring bit deep into Jenner's fingers as he pulled. He pointed the weapon down, pinning the small bar at the tip to the floor with his foot, then leaned back, putting all his weight into dragging the string back to cock the crossbow.

Farrar straightened with difficulty. He grinned as he watched Jenner struggle with the crossbow, then lifted his hand to show Jenner the hatchet. He steadied himself and stood staring at Jenner, tossing the ugly little ax effortlessly back and forth between his hands. He sprinted at Jenner, the hatchet held high.

He lunged, swinging the hatchet down, but stumbled as his foot plunged into one of the holes in the floor, the hatchet sweeping short of Jenner. Jenner brought the crossbow up, squeezed the trigger and shot a bolt into Farrar's flank, then ran past him to the other end of the room, to the girl.

He knelt by her, touched her face, felt her move.

Turning, he saw Farrar moving toward them, the crossbow bolt protruding from his chest, the second dangling limply from his side, the small ax held low.

Jenner backed up, deliberately drawing him away from Ana. Farrar veered wide around her, cutting off Jenner's route should he try to make a run for the stairway, then came straight at him, pushing him back.

His hands bleeding, Jenner hurled the useless crossbow at Farrar, missing him. Jenner grabbed an old wooden chair, lifted it, and pointed it toward Farrar.

Farrar swung at it hard, the blow of the hatchet reverberating up through Jenner's arms as the chair cracked open.

Jenner held the chair back up, lunging at Farrar, trying to push him away as he came forward. Farrar steadily hacked at Jenner. A final, violent overhead swing shattered the chair, leaving Jenner holding the back strut and one of the legs.

Jenner tossed the back away and lifted the wooden leg. Farrar edged forward, the hatchet at hip height. He was baring his teeth in a bloody smirk, and then Jenner knew why.

Farrar had backed him into the corner, deliberately cutting off his escape routes. And, even wounded, Farrar could move faster than him.

He held the chair leg up and braced himself.

Farrar took his time, moving in closer, carefully shifting his weight from foot to foot. He planted his legs squarely in front of Jenner, feet apart, then slowly raised the hatchet above his head, breathing in slow and deep as he steadied himself for the strike. His eyes locked on Jenner's, his torn mouth hanging in a sneer as he prepared for the kill.

He froze, then staggered a little. His expression changed to one of surprise, eyes unfixed and mouth open. The hatchet dropped from his hand as he stumbled forward, a dark stain spreading along his side.

He kept coming toward Jenner, gait wide-based like a toddler's, arms open, pushed from behind by Ana, who was still clinging to the long black pole on which she had impaled him.

Jenner stepped around him, grasped the pole as she collapsed, and pulled it out of Farrar, sending him slumping against the corner.

Leaning against the wall, Farrar turned to Jenner. He saw the pole, saw the girl on the ground, and understood. His head bowed slightly.

Jenner stood there, pointing the pole at Farrar's chest.

Farrar coughed, blood spattering the plastic over the window next to him. He looked at Jenner, struggling to catch his breath.

Farrar's speech was glottal and wet, but Jenner managed to understand "She would have been the best . . ."

Jenner didn't answer.

Farrar bent over, panting. He looked up at Jenner and said, "It hurts! Doctor! It hurts!" twisting his mouth back into a grin.

He half straightened, smiling wider, a small knife hidden in his palm.

"Should I lie down? If I lie down, will I bleed slower?" He spit out a gout of bloody slobber. "Help me, Doctor? Will you help me?"

Jenner didn't move.

Farrar looked at him. "It would be better if I lie down." His mouth was bleeding faster now, thick dribbles onto his shirt and neck.

Jenner said, "Lie down if you want."

The sound of a siren filtered into the room. Through the windows over the water, Jenner saw the blue light of a police boat.

He turned back to Farrar.

Farrar spat blood and murmured, "Ah. The cavalry." He nodded. "I'll greet them on my feet."

"Okay, stand if you want."

Farrar straightened and then bent double, clutching his belly with both hands.

After a couple of seconds, he straightened again, his breathing fast and shallow. He asked, "How many do you think they'll be?"

Without waiting for an answer, he sprang forward, the tip of the knife flashing as he slashed at Jenner. The blade carved into Jenner's arm, but he pushed past it, driving the pole deep into Farrar's chest, ramming it deep into his trunk, trying to force it out through the other side. He wedged Farrar against the wall, leaning on the pole with all his weight, feeling Farrar's body lift as the warm blood poured down the shaft onto his fists.

Farrar twitched on the rod, gasping, eyes glassy. He tried to speak, but managed only silence and bloody spittle. He twitched again, and was motionless.

Jenner carefully gathered Ana up into his arms and carried her to an old sofa by the windows, dragging it to turn it away from Farrar's body.

She was shivering; he took off his coat, wrapped her in it. She was thin and pale, her face filthy, crusted with mud and dried blood, her eyes swollen near-shut. He held her, stroking her matted hair, held her face to kiss it.

His hand swept down her shoulder, over her hips, to stroke her leg.

He stopped; there was a nail protruding from her skin. He pulled it out, then knelt in front of her, feeling her for injuries, pulling out two more nails. She barely flinched.

Over on the workbench he found a plastic bottle of drinking water and a rag. He wet it and wiped her face. Then her wounds, and his shoulder, and then sat with her, pulling her close, holding her against him as they waited.

They lay together for a while; eventually the room began to strobe with flickering blue-and-white shadows. Later, he remembered pulling himself to his feet, tearing down the plastic over the windows to shout to the harbor patrol.

He remembered yelling to them, Jun pointing up at him from the lead boat, the blue light the white light, the blue light the white light, lighting up the girl on the sofa by the window, the blue light the white light, and beyond that, across the water, across the river, the light of New York City, vast and brilliant and impossibly beautiful.

# ACKNOWLEDGMENTS

Thanks to my long-neglected family, who've been wildly supportive throughout; to all of my wonderful and peculiar friends, who've made my life in New York City far more exhilarating and exotic than I could ever have dreamed possible; to my esteemed colleagues, past and present, at the Office of the Chief Medical Examiner of the City of New York, the New York County District Attorney's Office, the Dade County Medical Examiner's Office, and the New York Police Department; to every magazine editor who's trusted me with an assignment, and then shown me how to make it better; and to the agents and editors who've carefully shepherded this project right from the start.